P₁

This is a story based part on the life of my father and whose name I share. It charts his journey from early teenage years and the onset of WW2 in 1939 up to his return home to the UK in 1948 after completing his national service.

Bullied and ridiculed as a teenager, he overcomes his fears and his tormentors with guidance from his father, a former bare knuckle fighter. He is taught the necessary skills to defend himself against adversity whilst moulding his body into the finest physical shape.

Still only 21 and in a foreign country, his talent and phenomenal strength is discovered in the wrestling arena's of the Far East. His determination to succeed in the ring, take him to within reach of the Wrestling Championship finals. His hopes of achieving this prestigious belt are seriously curtailed, when unimaginable occurrences blight his sporting advance, and find him fighting for his life.

His sporting success and his ability to speak the local Malay language bring him into contact with a very powerful and corrupt syndicate of men. He is offered a life changing amount of money to drive a truck, unaware that he is being lured into the murky underworld of Singapore's dark and dangerous drugs trade. He discovers that senior army officers are involved in the organisation of one of the most daring drug heists of its day, and which he is expected to play a central but unwilling role.

A 'Mystery Man' plays a pivotal part to the story and to the trafficking of drugs worth millions of dollars. What is the identity of this man? The exposure of his name and his dignified position of that time will send shockwaves throughout the establishment.

THE
UNTAMED
WHITE
SAVAGE

DEREK CALLON

THE
UNTAMED
WHITE
SAVAGE

Matador
9 Priory Business Park
Kibworth Beauchamp
Leicestershire LE8 0RX, UK
Tel: (+44) 116 279 2299
Fax: (+44) 116 279 2277
Email: books@troubador.co.uk
Web: www.troubador.co.uk/matador

ISBN 978 1848767 249

British Library Cataloguing in Publication Data.
A catalogue record for this book is available from the British Library.

Typeset in 11pt Adobe Garamond Pro by Troubador Publishing Ltd, Leicester, UK
Printed and bound in the UK by TJ International, Padstow, Cornwall

Matador is an imprint of Troubador Publishing Ltd

This book is dedicated to the most important ladies in my life and whom
I love dearly;
Marie Georgina, my mother.
Patricia, my wife.
Sarah and Helen, my daughters.
Isabella Scarlet, Jasmine Grace, Lilli Sophia and Holly Nicole, my
granddaughters and my inspiration.

To Stephen.
I hope you enjoy
the book.
Very best regards
Denly.

Quote

The fight is won or lost far away from witnesses - behind the lines, in the gym, and out there on the road, long before I dance under those lights.

Muhammad Ali

PART 1

Chapter 1

The driver of the truck partially rose from his horizontal position. Lying across the large seat in his ten ton Mack army truck, he was keeping out of sight from prying eyes. Raising his head enough to look through his huge steering wheel into the early evening, he did a quick reconnaissance of the scene around him. The dull light was beginning to change the landscape somewhat, but more importantly, everywhere around was deserted and quiet. To the outsider, the main Empire dock in Singapore was sleeping. The docks were a vital cornerstone of the Singapore economy and it was a hive of activity during daylight hours. It was almost two years to the day since the end of the Japanese occupation in September 1945, when Singapore was handed back to British rule. The truck park was 200 yards from the Customs Office in a straight line. As the driver, slowly and carefully, did a sweep of the area from his now seated position; he could see the dim light flickering as day turned to dusk. His movements were measured and controlled, not wanting to bring any attention his way.

Thirty minutes had elapsed since the driver flashed his headlights into the shadows, to indicate to his four helpers that the coast was clear. The helpers were local Singaporean workers from the dockyard who the driver had carefully selected. They had waited until the port had emptied of all personnel and were now secreted in the back of his truck. It was time to move, the driver slipped quietly from his cab and walked to the back of the vehicle, gently tapped on the large tail board, and one of the helpers popped his head out from under the tarpaulin.

'Yes, boss,' said the man. He spoke in a quiet whisper in his Malay tongue.

'Okay, we go now, follow me, be quiet and keep your heads down,' said the driver, his instruction returned in their native tongue. They moved as a tight unit with stealth and speed, to another identical truck parked 50 metres from where they were. The driver had earmarked this vehicle earlier in the day. He knew it had ample fuel on board to cover the relatively short distance required, but just as important, the truck was empty of goods. He would need every square inch of space that the truck yielded for him to load his precious and intended cargo. The driver, a regular soldier with the British army worked on the docks and was familiar with the layout and the routines which dominated its very existence. Part of the British and Commonwealth units serving in the Malayan emergency, his unit was close to the docks in Singapore where his duties were to distribute and supply the army base's with essential goods. His unit was the RASC Supply Depot 436 Transport Company. The supplies, ranging from weapons, artillery, and machinery to food and clothing were shipped in and coordinated from UK held stores overseas. His intended cargo today however, was none of these essential goods. The removal of illicit cargo from its secure dock location would be a huge and devastating blow to the Singapore government and its authorities. The driver was a very well known and respected individual, both inside and outside of the dock area, so he could not risk being seen. To use his truck would be suicidal. This was a one way journey never to be repeated, not by him anyway. He needed to introduce some means of anonymity. He did not want any finger of blame pointed at him, especially after the shit finally hit the fan.

There was no ignition key in the truck, but this presented no problem, the driver was used to 'hot wiring' these vehicles as keys often went missing. He helped the four men into the back of the identical Mack truck and then pulled himself up into the cab. Touching the right wires together brought the huge machine into life. He had done this hundreds of times before, but this time it startled him as he jolted backwards into his seat. He dare hardly rev the huge monster in case it aroused attention as its hungry diesel engine bucked under tick-over. He selected the gear and moved off, slowly and cautiously. The bonded warehouse, their intended location was another 350 yards away from the direction of the Customs Office. Slowly he moved the ponderous truck towards its destination, looking left, looking right. He saw no one as he stared into the fading light.

There was a large space in front of the two huge warehouse doors, large enough to accommodate several trucks. The driver positioned his Mack to reverse into the building. The gates would open outwards, so he had prepared his park position for this. He would soon be facing the first of many obstacles, some more dangerous than others. Would the small personnel door through which he had entered a few days previously to check the cargo, be open? If not, then the large steel doors would be impenetrable. Instinctively he looked around for movement or noise before trying the handle, then placed pressure on the lever and pushed. The door remained shut.

'Shit, shit, shit,' he said under his breath. He pressed the lever again and pushed his shoulder against the small door this time. To his surprise, the door relented. Access was gained! He knew that this had been left unlocked by one of the customs men. They had full charge over this restricted secure area. He was sure that after he left, it would be made to look like a forced entry. He went to the back of the truck and motioned for the men to get out.

'You two, open the big doors, now, and be quick.' The men worked swiftly and efficiently, viewing the activity through his wing mirror he saw the 'thumbs up' signal to reverse in. With a loud grinding of gears, the driver cautiously moved back. The large warehouse doors were closed as the truck passed inside. The driver jumped down from his cab and scoured the walls, looking for the warehouse lights which would illuminate the area where they would be working. He found a bank of light switches and switched furiously, until he found the right one. Then, reversing back to the bay where the goods intended for loading were, he finally killed the engine. He rolled the tarpaulin back enough to work and pointed at the pallets.

'This is it, guys, load it.' The four men looked at each other in disbelief, not moving from their positions. 'What is it, come on, guys, start loading this now?' said the driver.

'Boss,' said one of the men, 'no, this is too dangerous. This is big trouble for us and for you.' The driver had not anticipated any reaction from his carefully selected helpers. He had not disclosed what the cargo was they would be moving. He felt bad about it, but it was too late for sentiment, the point of no return was well and truly breached now!

'Look,' said the driver as he searched his brain for the right words to say in Malayan. 'I only want you to load the truck. I'm going to drive it out of here, not you. Now get yourselves together and start loading.'

'But boss, big big trouble with this stuff,' said the same man.

'That's why I'm paying you big big money.' The driver motioned for the men to stay where they were with a hand movement. He went to his cab and brought back four envelopes, each stuffed with small denomination used US dollar bills. He took out the contents of one and flicked the notes with his thumb. He pointed at the man who spoke. 'Here, this is for you, this represents wages for a whole year. This is for a few hours work only.' The man held his hand out but the driver pulled the envelope away. 'It's for you when the jobs done, now come on, we're losing time, let's get the truck loaded.' The four men looked at each other with wide startled eyes, searching for mutual and moral support. No words were spoken, only shoulder shrugs and nods of the head. The man who spoke earlier finally said, 'okay, boss, we do this for you, we trust you.'

The driver slapped the man on the back with relief and said quietly, 'thank fuck for that.' He explained how he wanted the pallets stacking. They had lost time because of the misunderstanding, they would be up against the clock now. The truck had to be driven out through the Customs gate at precisely 19.30. They now had only one and a half hours to meet that deadline. They could not leave any of the goods in the warehouse. Every pallet had to be loaded, and loaded by hand.

'Come on, come on, I have to be at the front gates in five minutes, now hurry it?' The driver was trying his best to get the last few pallets on board. The stacking had worked out well in the end. The main thing was that all the goods would fit into the back of the truck. As the men loaded, the driver had secured the load. All five men were soaked to the skin with their own sweat. The temperature inside the warehouse was stifling, for heat in Singapore was unrelenting, irrespective of the time of day. The task to load the truck in the time required looked impossible, but now, a huge area where the goods had been stored was empty except for the last few pallets. The men had worked tirelessly to load it in time.

'Let's get out of here,' said the driver. Before jumping into his cab, he did a quick survey of the area where they had been working. He was sure that nothing was left behind to link them to this multi million dollar theft. Droplets of liquid from the sweating bodies of the men peppered the concrete floor, the only visible evidence that anyone had left. Even this would evaporate within minutes of them leaving the scene. The driver hot wired the Mack and it burst into life again, coughing poisonous diesel fumes into the warehouse with only minutes to spare. Two men jogged behind the truck, the two men in front opened the huge metal doors. Steadily and carefully he drove the Mack to the outside of the warehouse. The doors clunked shut behind the truck, hiding the unmistakeable void which was left on the warehouse floor. The most audacious heist this century was now well underway. The driver went to the rear of the truck, pulled back a small section of the tarpaulin to allow the four men to get in. The arrangements were that he would drop the men at a safe distance outside the main gate of the docks.

'Come on, jump up,' said the driver with real urgency in his voice.

'No, boss, we will not come with you, too dangerous,' said the lead man.

'What are you going to do for fuck's sake, sleep here until morning?'

'No, boss, we can get out of here another way. Going through the main gate is too dangerous. If we get caught with you, we die.' The lead man for the second time mentioned danger in his response within the space of seconds. This heightened the tension as the driver tried to recover the situation.

'Listen, I pay you now, okay, but if you get caught getting out of here, you are on your own. You know nothing about what has happened this evening. You speak to no one about this, are you clear? You must never mention my name.' The driver put two fingers to his temple to indicate they would be shot, though of course he lied.

'Yes, boss, clear. Don't worry; we are for you, boss.' He handed an envelope to each of the men. They took the packages and left the area as quickly and as quietly as they came.

He jumped back into the cab. His adrenalin was pumping and his heart racing as he realised how critical the next phase of the operation was. He inched forward and steered the truck in the direction of the main exit, moving very cautiously and very slowly.

Calm down he told himself, calm down. Remember that this operation has been carefully planned and nothing can go wrong as long as you keep to the time schedules. There are people in place to ensure that you get away from the dockside area. Your safe passage from here has been arranged.

The dockside remained eerily quiet as dusk had turned to darkness. Not another soul or vehicle moved as the huge truck, conspicuous by its own presence and precious cargo, moved slow and laboriously forward. Low gears were engaged and necessary for the heavily laden vehicle. He moved closer and closer to the gates where customs men had been paid generously to ignore a truck which would pass by them at 19.30 prompt. The driver could now see the light illuminating the small area around the office. The customs men would also be able to see him now as their line of vision covered a long length of the exit road which he was on. If they didn't see him, they would surely hear him now. The engine noise from his huge truck was unmistakeable. The gates to the docks and to the outside world were closed as expected. This was a very secure area. He reached the point where he would make his presence known to the paid customs men. The signals to be given were clear and straightforward. The driver would give a short flash of the headlights and continue slowly towards the gates.

'Why is nothing happening?' he said to himself, gripping the huge steering wheel, 'come on, open the bloody gates?' Still nothing happened. He was starting to feel nauseous when he saw the first flicker of light and human movement. He was sure the door to the office had just been opened. A customs man appeared at the gate. He never looked in the direction of the vehicle, nor paid a cursory glance to see who was driving the truck. The guard had his back to the vehicle as he opened the large gate, pushing it back on its long slider. Everything so far was going to plan. As he passed the office window, the driver could not avoid looking inside. Another customs man was sitting at a desk with his back to the window doing nothing, appearing only to be staring into space. He was now beyond the gate, and out of the stifled confines of the dock yard area. The driver breathed a sigh of relief as he turned his truck onto the road which would take him onto one of the main roads through Singapore and towards Johor in Malaysia.

As he pulled onto Keppel Road, he thought about how smoothly things had gone up to this point. He knew the loading would be challenging, but that was behind him now. Leaving the very secure dock area unchallenged was a major obstacle already passed. His heart was still racing though as the challenges still to be overcome were just as daunting. He hoped that the four helpers would now be away from the dock area. For them to be apprehended with that amount of money on them had inevitability written all over it. The authorities would soon find out who else was involved in spite of putting the frighteners on the four men. The authorities know how to extract information from frightened young men, he thought. He knew if they were caught, they would sing like birds. He was unhappy that they had chosen to make their own way from the docks, but understood their anxiety at been caught with this illicit cargo. The four men were prepared to take their chances and he admired their spirit. The driver pondered on their response to seeing the goods to load, piled up high on pallets. He had neither anticipated nor expected their reaction. Their references to danger disturbed him somewhat, as he tried to put the comments out of his mind. He wondered who would explain the theft of this precious cargo, from under the nose of the tight customs control. This was not his problem however, that was for someone else to worry about.

'It just shows the power of money,' he said out loud.

Everyone has a price, he thought, even him.

It would only be a matter of minutes on Tuesday morning when the alarm would be raised. He would turn up for his duties as normal with his schedule for picking up army supplies and dropping them off at specified military locations dotted across Singapore. He would expect the dock area to be swarming with police, customs personnel and government officials. Serious questions would be raised and undoubtedly heads would roll as a result of the audacious heist. He stopped his mind from wandering now and thought about his next rendezvous point. At the junction where Keppel Road runs into Robinson Road, he would pull over to the side of the road and wait. The area was a dusty patch of land with very few buildings around. Thick vegetation ahead was picked up by the beam of the headlight as the driver waited and pondered for what seemed like an age.

The next phase of the journey was about to begin. As the huge truck was shifted into a neutral gear, only the loud tick-over was audible. The driver stared into the darkness, trying to focus and to look for signs of movement or life. There was none, except for hundreds of species of flying insects which were caught dancing in the headlights. He continued to glare ahead, stroking the large steering wheel nervously as he did so. He glanced at his watch, there was just enough light from the dashboard to see that it was 19.40. This was the time he would signal to someone in the dark ahead of him. He gave three short bursts of his full beam and waited. He saw no one, but somehow he knew that his signal had been received by the persons for which it was intended. In less than a minute, from nowhere, he saw four single headlights heading straight for him from the direction of Robinson Road. The headlights danced and dipped at the mercy of the contours of the road as they sped towards him. Dirt and sand spewed from the rear wheels as the four Military Police Redcap motorcyclists skidded to a halt on the dirt, directly in front of the truck.

Chapter 2

Each rider took up his pre-appointed position and manoeuvred their cycles into motorcade formation. The driver selected his low gear waiting for his signal to move. Two motor cyclists were now up front and in his view, the other two positioned themselves at the rear. He adjusted his mirrors to ensure he could see all four outriders at any one time with just a short movement of his head.

One of the lead motorcyclists held up a thumb, the driver looked at the nameless, helmeted rider and gestured back positively. Flashing beacon lights attached to the motorcycles burst into life, as the riders prepared themselves for the short journey. The two lead motorcyclists pulled away onto the open road, slowly to begin with, the driver unaware of his intended destination. He knew only that he was heading towards the Straits causeway; a short stretch of road which separates Singapore from Johor in Malaysia.

The motorcade was travelling northwards now at a steady pace after their very brief rendezvous. They had driven down Stamford Road before emerging on to Selegie Road. This stretch was travelled to its demise, before making a left turn onto Bukit Timah Road. This took the motorcade in a northerly direction, towards the causeway. This road was the most important and well known one in Singapore, its distance almost dividing the full length of the Island.

The driver felt a great sense of security travelling with the Military Police. These four men would have been paid a princely sum of money to carry out these unlawful duties, turning a blind eye to the consequences of failure. The driver continued to check his mirrors every few hundred yards.

Check back left mirror, okay, rider in place. Check back right mirror, okay, rider in place. Front riders, both in vision and in place.

All riders were present and correct. Since his exit from the docks, he had been travelling for only 15 minutes. The riders in front kept a steady pace as they made their way northwards on the arterial backbone of Singapore.

The driver allowed his mind to wander; he had been under immense tension and pressure, mainly from himself. He wondered again what kind of life changing effect the money from this heist would bring to him and to his family back in the UK. He would be a very wealthy young man, there was no disputing that. An offshore bank account had been set up for him by the trafficking syndicate, to receive a substantial amount of money once the job had been completed.

His family would be his focus now. He knew he had neglected them and that they deserved more. His quest to become one of the best sportsmen in the Far East had come at great personal cost. His selfishness had left gaping holes in his family life. He had gone month after month without contacting them. He had received letters from home, but had ignored the pleas to write back from his young wife. Up until quite recently, she didn't know if he was dead or alive. He had a son he had never seen, who up to now was a stranger in his life, and already past his second birthday. He had missed the first steps his son had taken; he would never know what the first words were he'd spoken. This was for later now though. He could put all this behind him and hoped his wife could do the same. He would now of course, be able to shower them with untold gifts and money. This would make it alright, he was sure.

The roadside buildings were becoming fewer now as the tight unit continued on its journey, away from the city and through the spine of Singapore. Buildings were replaced by thick vegetation either side, as light traffic gave way to the important motorcade as it made its way unhindered, northwards towards its end goal.

Check back left mirror, okay, rider in place. Check back right mirror, okay, rider in place. Front riders both in vision and in place.

The huge diesel truck, straining against a full cargo of goods saw the end of Bukit Timah Road as it passed seamlessly into Woodlands Road. It would be this stretch that would take them into and through to the Singapore customs check point. Once past this tricky phase, it would be relatively straight forward. The safety of the Johor Straits causeway into Malaysia, a route the driver had travelled many times, would soon be in view. One difference this time being that the cargo was not legitimate and he carried no paperwork validating its movement. The timing of the operation was faultless and running like clockwork. The time of arrival at the Singapore customs was 20.00 hours. Their arrival would not require any signal, as the lights from the motorcade would announce quite clearly their arrival.

The driver's body was becoming clammy and he was feeling nauseous again. The feeling would not leave him, knowing that he was approaching the most vital phase of the plan. Up to now everything had gone as expected, there was no reason to feel this way.

Come on man; hold it together, stay calm, he told himself.

The checkpoint was in view, the driver could see from his elevated position of the cab that he was only about 400 yards to the border. The entrance was unmistakeable as large floodlights lit up the area to daylight proportions. He checked his watch again. The motorcade slowed slightly with only 300 yards to the border. The thick vegetation on the road side was replaced now by sparser growth as the approach to the checkpoint was nearing.

You're doing fine, he told himself, two minutes and you will be through the most critical phase of the operation.

The driver, trying to remain focused, was trying to anticipate what would happen after the safe passage through Singapore was secured. He wondered about the Malaysia customs and if they would be ready to receive the multi million dollar cargo. One thing was sure, the Malaysian customs was organised and controlled by a very powerful individual. The mystery man had masterminded the whole operation, a man whose name the driver was sure of, but denied by those close to him and around him. The location where this plan had been hatched and financed was in one of the most beautiful buildings he had ever seen, and the only Palace he had ever had the opportunity to set foot in.

Any issues on the Malaysia side he knew would be simply brushed away. The Singapore checkpoint was now looming closer, only 200 yards further to go.

The motorcade slowed down, the two front riders were looking across at each other. They were shouting instructions to each other which the driver could not hear. The motorcade continued its agonisingly slow approach.

With only 100 yards from the crossing, the driver went down the gears of the huge Mack to accommodate the slow advance. The two lead riders were again shouting instructions to each other. The driver had the window down hoping to get an indication of what was being said, hoping they were sorting out their operational procedure and what to do next. The driver was not aware of the arrangements at this border crossing, only that people had been paid to allow free passage to the truck and its outriders and no questions asked. It was only 50 yards to the checkpoint and there were no other vehicles in front to impede their entry. The driver was sweating profusely, yet he felt cold. A bead of sweat ran between his shoulder blades and he shivered. The tension of this operation was a strain, his trembling hands steadied only by the huge steering wheel. The guards from the checkpoint were making their way into the path of the motorcade. He was straining his eyes to see ahead and take in as much of his surroundings as possible. He could see the barrier was down across the road, the obstacle which would determine success or failure. The truck was down to walking speed now and the two lead riders were talking to each other again with one gesturing with his hand as he spoke.

Check back left mirror, okay, rider in place...........

PART 2

Chapter 3

8 years previous.

As soon as Derek Callon sauntered into his house without an obvious care in the world, the young 13 year old schoolboy knew something was wrong. He had timed his entrance home to coincide with school leaving time. There was a strange atmosphere as he entered the room, an atmosphere which he had not detected previously. His mother and father were both in the sitting room with faces as long as pokers. His father was stood in front of the coal fire, absorbing as much heat as he could from the few bits of coal still burning in the grate. It was a grey cold day outside, with a biting wind.

'Hi, mam and dad, what's for tea?' The youngster didn't wait around for an answer; instead he made for the seclusion of his upstairs bedroom. He didn't like what he was seeing and wasn't particularly bothered about what was causing the glum faces.

'Not so fast, lad,' said his father in a manner which lacked any kind of sentiment. The young man turned in his tracks, he had heard that tone in his father's voice before and seen that look on his face, and it always ended up with him getting a good hiding. The young boy faced his father, dreading what he was going to say next. 'How was *school* today?' he said, emphasising the word school.

Surprised by the question, the teenager replied, 'it was okay, dad.' There was hesitation in his reply. He felt dread flowing through his lithe body, he knew his worst fears were about to be realised. He readied himself, knowing that a clout round the ear was imminent. He didn't know what for just yet, but he knew he was going to find out very soon. It could be a hundred things, thought the teenager. He prepared for being hit, hoping that whatever was the cause would not result in his father taking his leather belt off. Instinctively, he hunched his shoulders up in readiness, expecting a good hiding coming his way anytime soon.

'Okay was it, you lying little bugger?' his father's eyes were stood out like stoppers. He held his hands in a way which suggested a strike was coming. 'Come here,' he shouted. His mother was fidgeting in the chair holding her hand to her mouth.

'Don't hit him, Tom,' she said, knowing how agitated he was.

'Don't hit him,' he said through clenched teeth, I'll kill the little bloody liar.' The young schoolboy moved slowly towards his father. He wanted to pee; he felt the first involuntary spurt of urine escape from the end of his penis. The young boy tried hard to control his bladder. Quickly he held himself with both hands between his legs to counter the sudden urge. He realised immediately that his guard was down and there was nothing he could do about it. His father's right hand caught him at the side of his head and left his ear ringing from the contact and sending him sideways. His father didn't hit by half, it was a full swipe around the head. The young man cried with the impact and was now holding his face. More unintentional urine escaped as his concentration shifted from crutch to ear. He felt the warm liquid running down his leg and into his sock but could do nothing about it. Crying, he hoped, would prevent any further punishment.

'Let's try again shall we? Now, how was school today?' His father stooped over his son, ready with another assault if the truth did not come.

The teenager looking down towards the floor said, 'I didn't go to school, dad.'

'I know you didn't go to bloody school today,' his father snapped. He straightened up to his full height trying to give more authority to his next sentence. 'Do you want to know how I know you weren't at school today?'

'Yes, dad,' he replied with a small voice and a slight nod of his head.

'We've had the school police inspector round here today wanting to know why you weren't at school. He also wanted to know the reason why you were missing from school on 20 odd other days. Have you any idea how stupid that makes me and your mother feel?' His father grabbed him by his coat collar and lifted his feet full off the floor. He held him inches away from his face. 'Have you, lad, have you any bloody idea?' The young teenager knew well not answer back to his father as he looked into his eyes, just inches away from his own. He was told in no uncertain terms, that he would be 'knocked into next week' if he answered back. Telling lies was worse however, unforgiveable in his father's view.

He stood trembling, holding his groin and hunching his shoulders, expecting the next clout anytime soon. He knew he could only defend himself with words now.

'I don't like school, dad, they pick on me all the time.'

'Who are they?'

'The other kids, dad, they laugh at me when the teacher asks me a question. Mr Geoghan picks on me all the time. He asks me really hard questions and I never know the answer.' The young boy sobbed, not wanting to feel that right hand of his father again.

'You're never at school to learn the bloody answers,' shouted his father in disgust. 'And you expect me to believe that little cock and bull story?'

'It's true, dad, they all laugh at me. I can't do the sums, and there are words....words I can't read.' He wiped the tears away with his coat sleeve. 'Mr Geoghan writes long words on the blackboard and asks me to tell the class what it says. He never asks anyone else, it's always me. He knows I can't read it, dad, he makes me stand in front of the blackboard, spelling it out letter by letter, but I still can't read it. I always get it wrong, mixed up somehow.' He wiped more tears away using the back of his hand this time. 'I can hear them sniggering behind me as I try to read the word. The kids in the playground then make fun of me. I just don't like school, dad. Don't make me go, please!'

'And what do you do when the kids make fun of you?' said his father. Suddenly there was more compassion in his questioning.

'I don't do anything, dad, I just want to run away. The older boys pick on me too. They push and prod me in the playground, calling me names. The girls also think it's funny, they laugh at me when the older boys gang around me. I don't like it, dad, It's a horrible feeling, I just can't stand it.'

'Why the bloody hell don't you push them back?'

He looked up at his father and then across to his mother with a forlorn look across his face. 'There's loads of 'em, dad, they'd kill me, I wouldn't stand a chance.' His sobs were becoming less now as he felt the situation normalising.

'You don't have to hit them all,' said his father forcefully. 'You hit the one making all the bloody noise. Keep him quiet and you shut the lot of them up.'

His mother for once had a sympathetic look on her face as she looked up at her husband. 'What are you going to do, Tom? This isn't right. We have to stop this bullying now! Why didn't you tell us about this before?' she said, directing her question at her son.

'I don't know,' he said. 'I was afraid of telling you.'

'He's going back to school, bullied or not, make no mistake about that.' His father's face was still fierce, not at his son, but at his son's perpetrators and his predicament. He was going to make them pay for making his son's life miserable. His initial reaction was to confront the teacher, but he knew that was not a good idea. He could go to prison just thinking about what he would do to Mr Geoghan. The stark reality was that he would probably put him in hospital. Tom Callon was a tough campaigner and did not take prisoners. His eyes were watery and moist as he contemplated what to do next.

'I know what you're thinking, Tom,' said his wife. 'I don't want a son of mine learning all that fighting stuff. You promised me you wouldn't teach him those things. You promised, Tom, look where it's got you?' She held her head in her hands and was shaking it from side to side, 'no! No, Tom! Please?'

'Don't be bloody stupid, woman, he has to learn to stick up for what's right. I don't want a son of mine who can't fight his own battles. Now is as good time as any to start.' His father was punching his right fist into the open palm of his left hand. He was not going to be swayed by anyone; he had made his mind up at exactly what he wanted to do. He had always intended to teach his son the art of self defence, but more importantly, how to deal with aggression and put your opponent away!

He was a man who would not stand any nonsense. He was someone who would stand his ground and called a spade a spade. He was as tough and as hard as chiselled granite. His best days were behind him, and he knew that, but he still cut a very formidable figure. The late 1930's was a tough time to bring up a young family. Wages and work were hard to come by. Britain was still repairing itself from the aftermath of the 1st world war. This temporary peace was now threatened by a further world war. All the signals were pointing towards this end.

Tom did not drink or smoke, but some years ago, he thought nothing of walking into a pub and turning a beer glass over on the bar. This was the signal for taking on all comers for a small wager. This was bare knuckle fighting in its most archaic and primitive form. It was a tough hard life for a very proud man. Money, dignity and nourishment, were scarce in those days, to say the least, but backing down to an opponent, no matter the size or age was not an option.

They called him the 'Wild Man of Billinge,' a small town in Lancashire. It was his birthplace and where he grew up, one of ten children. The 'Wild Man' nickname came about because of his notoriety and his bare knuckle fighting prowess. In his younger days, he would run substantial distances and maintain a pace no one else could equal. He needed to keep himself in top condition for his next contest. He was a regular sight to those living in the surrounding area as he pounded the streets night after night in his quest to keep fit. He honed his boxing skills in the small gymnasium close to where he lived. A large wooden hut was cobbled together by its members and kept in reasonable condition against the hard winters. It served a purpose and took people away from the impending threat of another world war. He always sparred against heavier and taller men, unafraid of his quarry, irrespective of their reputation. Wearing his hair longer than most people in those days, he presented quite a spectacle; and was partly the reason behind his wild man image and appearance. He would run as if his life depended on it, and to some extent, it did. This fitness regime was part of his attempt to stay ahead of his game and remain focused. These contests put food on the Callon family table and helped to pay the rent and other household bills. These fights were in fact, crucial to him and his family's existence. He could not risk getting beaten or even worse, getting injured, as this would prevent him from earning his regular wages working down the pit. His philosophy was simple when it came to having the basic instincts for survival in this cruel world;

'You have to be able to look after thissen, no matter what,' he would say. It was this stubborn insistence which he now wanted to impart into his son's psyche. This was going to be a dominant part of his baptism of learning from now on. It would be just as important as reading and doing sums as far as he was concerned. He was going to make sure that his son was not going to be pushed around any more. He knew he couldn't help him academically, but he could sure as hell help him physically.

After several months of intense training and tuition at home, he noticed that his son's body shape was beginning to change markedly and that his mental toughness was already starting to come out. His young son was gaining confidence both towards him, and towards other people. He appeared taller and was starting to fill out. Though he was sure this would have happened anyway, he liked to think it was hastened through his intervention and his training techniques. Moreover, his young protégé was enjoying the programme which his father had set for him. Sparring sessions in their dank and dingy cellar were punctuated by light body building exercises. As time progressed, heavier weights were introduced in an effort to keep up to his son's appetite for training. Tom Callon had not realised it at the time, but his son was displaying strength, speed and dexterity way beyond his tender years.

In order to quench the young man's thirst for more intense training, Tom introduced his son to an ex-Olympic trained wrestler. Freddie Wilson was a soft spoken individual who disguised his skills and techniques behind his plain and ordinary exterior. In spite of this untoward façade, Freddie could immobilise an opponent within seconds and have them begging for mercy. Freddie Wilson mentored the young teenager as he introduced throws, kicks and holds into the young mans repertoire. He was instructed how to use the bodyweight of his aggressor to his own advantage in holds and throws. He was taught how to manufacture holds from improbable situations; but just as important, how to get out of them in upright positions and on the ground. The precise application of pressure points which left opponents supine and helpless was also taught. The young teenager would no longer be easy prey for his would be bullies or aggressors.

His father knew his training was beginning to pay off when he could no longer push his son away too easily during their many sparring sessions. If further proof were needed, the young man, now approaching adulthood, could catch his father off guard and leave him with a bloody nose. Not many grown men had been able to do that.

During his bare knuckle fighting days, he never came away from one of his contests with a second prize.

The young teenager's confidence grew at school from both a physical and psychological perspective. His educational standing did not improve that much. His struggle to overcome those early learning difficulties were never identified and as such never corrected, but this never aroused ridicule now. Even the teachers directed their questions to a different corner of the class. He had paid back some of his earlier debts to the erstwhile boys who once preyed on his vulnerability. Some of the boys who taunted him and made his days at school a living hell were now some of his friends. He kept them at arm's length, in the knowledge that they had provoked him in the past and poked fun at him. He knew that without his new found status, they would have continued to make life hell for him. In a strange way though, it was through their cowardly actions that had made him what he was today. It was the trigger his father needed; it was always his intention to teach his son the skills which he had learned on the streets and in the cruel world in which he had lived. His young protégé could never have thought that having this robustness, which he now had, would create so much respect from so many.

His toughness was tested to the full when an older boy, taller and heavier, decided to poke fun at him. A large circle of schoolboys and girls gathered around them in the playground; they could see that a fight was beginning to develop. He continued to back away from his aggressor, using the whole of the large circle to his advantage.

He judged his moment and allowed the bully to come forward, but not allowing him close enough to get the first punch in. It looked as though he was afraid of the bully as he was prodded at arms length and retreating backwards at the same time. The moment to move forward was instinctive and lightening fast. He struck his opponent, catching him full in the face and totally off guard. The bully staggered back, surprised at the punch, breaking the circle and landing on his backside with blood streaming down his nose. He followed him to where he sat. He landed another good punch at the side of his head. The older boy rolled over as he took his arm and pushed it up his back until he screamed. It was all over within seconds as the bully lying in a foetal position on his side, was beaten into submission. He was unwilling to get up and face his opponent. He knew that day, that he had turned a significant corner in his life, unafraid to face his aggressors, relying totally on what he had been taught.

Tom Callon knew that somewhere down the line his son would thank him one day for turning his world around. He also knew that the skills and techniques he had been taught would in some way help him. How, when and where, he wasn't sure, but it would definitely help him.

Bullying at school was long behind him now. He held his head high; confident about whatever the world was going to throw at him. His father was quick to remind him that he should always be on his guard, but at the same time, treat his skills with respect. 'You should never underestimate your opponent,' his father would say. 'Danger doesn't always lurk in large men. Danger can also come in small packages too.' He himself had come close to grief several times in his bare knuckle fighting days, not by large opponents, but by small thin and wiry characters that possessed strength way beyond their relative size. Tom's other piece of sound advice to his son was, 'It takes a good un, to beat two bad un's. Always be aware of your surroundings and be on your guard,' he would say.

His father's words were etched into his brain and it was something which he would carry with him throughout his life and never forget.

Derek Callon left school without a single academic qualification to his name, but a reputation that suggested you don't mess with him.

The understanding between Tom and his son blossomed and was to become an unbreakable bond. The slap round the ear was a turning point in their relationship. Before that incident, Tom Callon treated his son like a child, but as a man from that day forward.

'A good hiding never did anyone any harm,' he said to his wife that day. His son's predicament had upset him beyond words, knowing the circumstances that his son was been picked on by older boys, and teachers that should know better. He knew now though, that he had done a good job in preparing his son for whatever the world may throw at him, and he was very proud of the result. Tom knew also, deep down, how much his son admired and was proud of him; he could never anticipate though, that this admiration, love and respect would nearly cost him his son's life?

Chapter 4

It was just after his 18th birthday around the end of March 1944. The days were beginning to lengthen now, as spring, still in its infancy, was beginning to make its presence felt, though the weather that day had the last remnants of a hard winter, with a cold sting in its tail. Derek Callon had just finished his shift at the local foundry where he worked as a core maker. The work was dirty, hard, hours were long and the pay was crap, but it was work nonetheless. Before going home though, his journey would be interrupted by gym work and a general workout in the ring, sparring with whoever was available. He had carried on with his training and fitness regime where his father had left off and was pushing some serious weights for his age. He regarded his fitness and strength exercises as the motivational key to what lay around the corner. The war was still raging in mainland Europe and the Callon household knew that call-up papers were due any day soon. It was three and a half years since Germany had invaded Poland and there appeared to be no end in sight to the end of the war.

The letter was waiting for him on the sideboard as he entered through his front door. The letter was not unexpected, nor was it welcome, but it had arrived all the same. His mother and father had waited in silence in the front room with a kind of unknowing anticipation of their eldest son's reaction to the letter.

His father stood in front of the open fire with his hands behind his back, contemplating his thoughts and his worst fears. The last time he remembered seeing his father in that stance, he got a clip round the ear. This was different now though, and the enormity of the moment was about to break. The fire distracted him for a moment; it spit out small sparks, as the coal and wood mixture began to catch hold in the grate and burn fiercely. A fine gauge metal mesh fire guard would prevent the sparks from flying out onto the thick wool rug which was butted up to the hearth.

His mother was sat in her favourite armchair as close to the fire as she could get. She was knitting the sleeve of a cardigan from a tangled hank of wool which had been secreted out from one of the local mills. There was a freshly brewed cup of tea by her side which would go cold before she would finish it. The click clack of the wooden needles interspersed with the crackling of the fire were the only sounds in the room. She looked unperturbed; she already knew what the letter was about. Jane Callon was not one for showing her emotions anyway. There were no tears to wipe away, in spite of knowing that she may never see her son again after his training was done. After all, anyone with a son who was his age or older, was going to have, or already had, a similar letter to deal with.

Many sons, waved off from their home and who went to war, never did come back. The war had made people hard and more prepared for bad news, she thought.

His father was the most affected by the unwelcome mail, trying as much as he could to remain composed, knowing full well that his eldest son would be put in harm's way. He knew that a front line position within the army was the most obvious slot for his son to fill. His academic skills suggested that any type of office duty away from active service would be out of the question, he would never get past the first exam. The pained look on his face could not hide the fact of how much he cared for his son He had intervened and seen to it personally, teaching him how to look after himself should he ever be in a situation where actions speak louder than words. Dodging live ammunition rounds, or the threat of deadly shrapnel from a hand grenade or a bomb however, was something he couldn't do a damned thing about. His fighting skills would be useless against the kind of artillery fire he could be confronted with. From the outset, his father had expected that survival for his son would be similar and as violent as his own. He had not taken into consideration the war of course. He wished it was his name on the letter and would do anything to change the circumstances, but realised that matters were out of his hands.

He'd only glanced at the letter up to now, confirming that it was his name on the envelope.

'It's arrived then?' he said, with an air of reticence and waving the brown envelope by one corner.

'Aye, lad,' said his father, 'that bloody letter spells danger. I can smell it from here.'

'We knew it was only a matter of time, dad, now it's my turn. Nothing we can do about it.' No one returned his remark as he immediately went upstairs to his room. He wanted to read the letter without an audience or distraction. He needed to study the contents slowly and carefully word by word. This letter was going to change the course of his young life. He also recognised that the letter was about to tear his family apart and potentially, worst case scenario, add him to the statistics of the already dead soldiers in this God forsaken war!

He was going to miss his father most, he knew that. His father had been a rock and whom he respected more than anyone. He had also guided him through most of his teenage years and kept his feet firmly on the ground. He taught him never to abuse his strength or his ability over someone less able to defend themselves, that he should use his strength and knowhow only in time of need. This advice had kept him out of trouble growing up; he had often walked away from situations which he could easily have resolved by brute force.

From as early as he could remember, his relationship with his mother was not one of love. She found it almost impossible to show any kind of mother and son bonding. Her thoughts today would not be one of sadness because her son was going away to war, but because she would lose her son's boarding money. Losing his wages to the army would have a direct impact on the Callon household. His father, also a wage earner, was often on short time and rarely contributed a full week's wages to the coffers.

In addition, she would have fewer opportunities to relieve her son of his pocket money. Jane Callon played cards at every available opportunity. She never played for fun; it was always for money, serious money in her view. Her main concern now was that one of her beneficiaries was going away. This would be a double blow for her. She always seemed to win at cards anyway. He thought his mother was cheating somehow, but he could never prove it. She always knew when to close her brag hand when there was a better one on the table? It couldn't always be good luck, he thought. He suspected that the cards were marked, but even under his close scrutiny, he couldn't find any evidence of this.

The information from the call up letter was matter of fact and to the point. He was instructed to report for a medical examination in York first. This for him would be a breeze. He was one of the fittest and finely toned specimens for his age and was in great physical shape. His muscle definition was beyond compare on someone so young. On completion of the medical, his training at Fulford barracks in York would commence. He would be conscripted into the Army by the beginning of May 1944. He didn't have a choice or a say in any of these decisions, the army had seen to that.

There was however, a sense of adventure and excitement in where he was going and what he would be doing. It was the not knowing that excited him most. Anything, he thought, had to be better than working in a dirty old foundry for a pittance. The work he did wasn't considered essential to the war effort, but his duty to serve his King and Country was. The war was continuing, and his call up was just weeks before the operation Neptune/Overlord, the Allied invasion of Normandy.

Up to this point, he hadn't had the opportunity to travel much outside of his native Yorkshire. Holidays were day trip affairs, so he never experienced overnight stays, just as well, he didn't have a pair of pyjamas to his name.

There were other considerations in his life too. He had a steady girlfriend of several months. Georgina, an 18 year old girl, was introduced to him by one of his friends after a night at the pictures and had asked her to join them for a drink afterwards. Their friendship blossomed after that chance meeting and they continued to see each other at every available opportunity.

Georgina knew and accepted that their time together was limited and that it was just a question of time before his call up papers arrived. Their relationship was still quite new, but their love for each other was getting stronger by the day. War had a habit of doing this to couples. Friendships and love were never more quickly formulated than when couples found themselves together, only to be thrust apart, quite soon after meeting, by the war. The discussion about his impending call up was a daily issue, and it would be hard, telling Georgina that he was leaving home to join his fellow countrymen in the British army. They'd known this day was going to arrive, they just didn't know when. In the end he had just three weeks notice to prepare himself for a journey which would have, both amazing and disastrous consequences for him.

Chapter 5

May 1944 had come around all too quickly. He was drinking a cup of tea with his father in their kitchen, a floor below ground level in their house. Few words were exchanged between the two men. The silence spoke volumes about what they were both going through mentally. His father had prayed for an end to the war, but like many others before, it had made no difference and his prayers went unheard and unanswered. His son could only think of what might be, yes, he would be stepping out into the unknown, but that was what excited him. Fighting a war which he knew so little about held no fear for him. He knew it would be dangerous, statistics don't lie, but as yet, he had no idea where the army would be taking him. The brown tattered suitcase which he'd packed that morning was placed close to the front door. It contained the few changes of clothes he possessed. His cosmetic requirements were the essentials; a toothbrush, a comb and a razor.

Goodbyes were not something he was good at; after all, he had never had to do it before. His father kept a pace back to allow his son through the front door.

'Take care of thissen, son.' There was the slightest hint of a tear in the corner of his eye and he struggled to get the last word out of his mouth. He had never outwardly shown any emotion to his son previously and was quite embarrassed by his lack of self control. He studied his son carefully, feeling very proud of the young man stood before him and how he had matured. The ordinary clothes he wore disguised the extraordinary body that lay beneath. He had honed his physique to perfection through his rigorous training schedules which he set himself. His father's emotions were on the cusp of outwardly showing themselves. He needed to steal himself from the moment and not allow himself to follow his father's example. The last time he had cried was when his father clipped him around the ear for playing truant. His father had always promoted the 'hard man' approach and never let his softer side slip.

'Crying was for babies,' he would say!

'I'll take care, dad, don't worry, I'm well prepared, thanks to you.' Their two hands locked together with the firmest of grips. The two men stared into each others eyes for several seconds. His father could see the sparkle of anticipation and adventure in his son's eyes. By contrast, his eyes were filled with emotion and were deep pools of sadness and despair. His father knew in that moment that he was losing his best friend. 'Remember what you've learnt, son,' his father said, raising a clenched fist, 'and you won't go far wrong.' He bit his lip, trying desperately not to allow tears to well into his eyes.

It was a very simple message from his mother.

'Bye, son, take care,' she said. He had never kissed his mother in his life before, not that he could remember, so he was not going to break the habit of a lifetime now. Certainly not out in the street where someone may see him.

After a few more words of encouragement, his father turned to go inside. He went upstairs dragging his feet on the stairs and to watch his son disappear out of sight from his landing window. He went to the privacy of his own bedroom and cried unashamedly.

The bus journey into town to catch the train to York was uneventful. The bus stop was several hundred yards from where he lived. Georgina was already at the stop waiting to travel the short journey to the railway station with her boyfriend. The upper deck on the bus was blue with spent smoke, but it was better than mixing with middle aged ladies and young mums with snotty nosed kids on the deck below. He slid the window open, searching for fresh air before they took their seat for the short ride into town.

The railway station, grimy from the endless comings and goings of the steam trains, nestled in the bottom of the Aire valley.

After the briefest of goodbyes, the train pulled out of the station. They held each other until the moment the whistle blew to announce its departure. There were few words, but more tears as their hands slipped apart as the steam train began its slow journey from the platform into the unknown, for him at least. It would be several weeks before they would be together again, where plans for their future would take on a much greater importance. Low hills embraced either side of the track to begin with, interspersed with heavy industrial buildings, textile mills and tall chimneys; his adventure was underway.

His destination, York, was the furthest he had travelled from home. He felt confident in himself, in spite of his limited travel experience. He walked proudly, mingling amongst the other travellers with his chest out and shoulders back, making the most of his five foot eleven frame. His physique and a talent yet to be discovered would soon be put to the test. He had been brought up the hard way and was prepared, he thought, for anything this world was going to throw at him. His new life was about to take on a new dimension.

There were obvious signs around that he was not on his own in his journey to wherever in the world. Making the same solemn trip, were other faces which told their own story. Grim faces on young men with solitary cases held close to their sides, portraying uncertainty, with a kind of disbelief spilling from their eyes. The weather by this time, had taken a turn for the worse. It was cold, wet and a filthy miserable day. The incessant rain was falling on already soddened grey pavements and grey people, the last remnants of a winter, thankfully on its way out. He spoke to no one on his travels; his head was just full of his own thoughts and what life was to have in store for him. On arrival at York, the recruits were shepherded onto a waiting bus to take them to Fulford barracks.

Chapter 6

Sergeant Major Whitcombe was a tough old campaigner and he wanted nothing but the best from his recruits. If they did not produce results, they were subjected to his vicious tongue and harangued in front of their fellow soldiers. Parade ground drill after parade ground drills were practised until they could do the manoeuvres in their sleep. Everyone was in the same boat; no one knew each other and had no idea of each others strengths or weaknesses. They were just a rag tag of individuals from every corner of the county brought together for one common purpose; to fight in the war, joining many thousands more, already in the thick of battle. To get any kind of respect in this environment, meant that you had to earn it. Being spoken down to was the best a recruit could hope for, until he could prove otherwise. The stark reality of war was beginning to dawn on the young men. They would be the new cannon fodder for the German's or the Japanese, depending on where they would be posted.

Away from the parade ground drills, training consisted mainly of keep fit, and boxing. For some of the lads, this was sheer purgatory, for Callon though; he loved every minute of his induction. The boxing trainer, an Army corporal, spoke to the group narrating words which had been spoken many times to new recruits.

'This training is vital to your survival, lads, and could save your lives. So don't think you're doing this bloody training for my benefit. No, it's to get you lot in shape!' For some of the lads, training was going to nearly kill them anyway. Unless they were prepared in advance to apply themselves, then people were going to suffer in more ways than one; giving up was not an option in this training camp.

Fitness was the pre-requisite of the British Army and the recruits were really put through their paces. A letter to the army Major from their mother was not going to get them excused from these exercises, not even when their training was deemed satisfactory and complete.

Callon treated the boxing lessons with respect, doing just enough to satisfy the trainer. The skills he developed with his father, really showed when he got into the ring with the other recruits, but kept them partially hidden. No one really offered him much competition and nobody could get close to landing a punch on him, doing only enough to avoid been hit. Hurting someone or causing injury was not something he wanted to do. He'd nothing to prove at this stage. Trainers put similarly matched opponents together to identify any potential champions in their ranks but his unwillingness to spar competitively went unnoticed. Size was immaterial; he had the technique, speed, and strength to deal with everything put in front of him.

The trainers were diligent in their technique at showing the recruits the finer points of their trade, but in general, progress was laboured. After a few weeks into the programme, more effort was expected from the new intake.

During one of the boxing sessions, the unit was introduced to a new trainer. Dave Walsh was an army Captain and twenty seven years old. He was a seasoned boxing campaigner and had been teaching his boxing skills for several years. He knew the lads were only a few weeks into their training schedule, but he was keen to show them how boxing should be done. Captain Walsh was a thick set man, powerfully built with short cropped dark hair standing around six foot tall. He looked like he'd picked up a few second prizes in his time. The trainer's nose had been broken in the past and it was spread across his face and pointing markedly to one side. All in all, his facial looks gave him a hard man appearance. He was quite a frightening individual to look at and the trainer knew this. The Captain was intending to make his presence felt towards his new audience. Captain Walsh had watched with a degree of interest, the sparring going on between the groups of lads and was not impressed.

'What have you lot been doing for the past weeks?' he shouted. 'You look more like a bunch of bloody schoolgirls than potential boxers.' The group was sure he treated all new recruits to this kind of tongue lashing, but he was clearly expecting a better level of technique.

'Who thinks they can box then?' There was deathly quiet in the hall. The Captain pointed at one man close to him, he was lean and gangly with a very slim frame.

'Do you think you can box?'

'No, sir, not well enough,' came the reply.

'You, do you think you can box?' The trainer was playing a game now as he picked on another recruit.

'What about you,' as he pointed to someone else, 'can you box?' Another negative response came back from the floor.

'What a bunch of bloody turnips,' he scoffed shaking his head. The Captain was going to demonstrate the art of boxing to his new audience, and he wasn't going to hold back.

The group were assembled around the trainer in a circle, very attentive but unaware of what was coming next. After some discussion about himself and how many conquests he'd made, he pointed at one of the lads close by.

'You, jump in the ring with me.' There was disbelief on the young man's face.

'What's your name, son?'

'It's John, Sir, John Draper.'

'How old are you, Draper?' said the Captain, immersed in confidence and grinning from ear to ear.

'I'm 18, Sir,' he said in a low tone, displaying no commitment in his reply. Most of the lads were still finding their way; they were surprised to be singled out in this way.

The recruits were all dressed in shorts, pumps and training vest. The ring was about twelve foot square and perched a few feet above ground level, in the centre of the main training room. Nobody boxed in the ring unless it was for real. There was a look of fear, trepidation and apprehension on Draper's face as he stepped over the bottom rope and into the ring. The Captain, a seasoned and experienced fighter limbered up in his corner before calling Draper to box.

The Captain was allowing Draper to come forward, as he backed away in a very relaxed way. He let his hands drop in a way which encouraged Draper to come forward and punch. The Captain was able to duck, weave and then back away without having a glove laid on him. These tactics made Draper look rather foolish and desperate as he lunged forward trying in vain to get a punch on the Captain. The second round started like the first one ended. Then Captain Walsh started to attack, little jabs to begin with, this intensified as the Captain was beginning to tire of his meek and mild aggressor. Jabs were being delivered on his opponent with more venom. Draper's head kept going back sharply every time the trainer connected as though it was going to be knocked off his shoulders. Jab, jab, everyone a nose breaker. A combination of shots to the body caught Draper by complete surprise, left then right, bang, bang into Draper's ribs as he winced with pain. The defenceless young man went down on both knees. The Captain was now in overdrive, and his adrenalin was beginning to kick in. He screamed at his opponent.

'Get up, Draper, get up, I've hardly bloody touched you yet.' Draper looked up at the trainer with a stare of defeat on his face. He stumbled to his feet out of sheer pride, and carried on, but he was already spent.

'Come on, hit me man.' The Captain was trying his best to inject some enthusiasm into his luckless opponent. He stood in the centre of the ring with his gloves down by his side, willing the young man forward. The Captain then continued to overpower his opponent and drive forward in spite of Draper's inability to counter the punches. The lack of retaliation fuelled the trainer's attack as he continued to pound the young man. It was only a matter of time before the recruit was on the floor again, this time holding his stomach and retching. Draper's half hearted attempt to fight back was no match for Captain Walsh. The trainer just picked him off at will. Flailing arms and desperation was no match for skill and experience. He had reduced his opponent to a gibbering wreck in the space of a few minutes. Callon had witnessed this mismatch from the back of hall. He was seething at this brutal attack on one of his colleagues. He didn't know Draper that well, but he felt for him as he was helped from the ring by a friend. Draper's nose was dripping blood, staunched only by the back of his glove. He was still holding his stomach and ribs where the Captain had pounded them unnecessarily. He thought back to the time when he was a schoolboy in the playground, and when he was picked on by bullies. He saw this man as no better than they were. The trainer had a huge advantage over these young men, he thought, and he was taking this to levels which were uncalled for.

A short session of explanation followed from the trainer; trying his best to illustrate the mistakes his previous opponent had made.

'There was not enough commitment or determination in that man', he shouted. 'I want someone to come into this ring and bloody well hurt me.' This statement pricked his ears as he stood passive at the back of the group.

I could hurt you, he thought. You've shown me nothing yet which frightens me. Bide your time Callon, and let's see how this develops.

'What have you lot been doing these past weeks,' he yelled again at the group. He pointed at another young man. 'Have you been knitting since you arrived here?' This brought a smile onto a few faces, not knowing what to expect next. The recruit responded,

'No, no, Sir.'

'No, Sir, what?'

'No, we haven't been knitting, Sir.' Another short burst of laughter erupted as the trainer continued.

'If this is the standard I can expect from you lot, then I'm going to flatten a few fucking noses this afternoon.' This was said in a tone which the trainer meant and which he was going to carry out. Callon stirred and raised his head to get a clearer view. He had an idea what was coming.

Don't hurt anyone else, Captain, just because you know you can. Pick me; I'm not afraid of you or your bullyboy tactics!

He scoured the group, turning 360 degrees to make sure everyone within the circle heard him make his point.

'I need to see some aggression,' as he continued to rant on, trying his best to make his point. 'I want to see some determination and fight, not some bloody sissy in a playground. War's about fighting, lads, you'll do well to remember that.' The Captain turned again before making his next statement. 'You, lads will be thanking me in a few months time, when some bloody German is trying to shove a bayonet up your arse.' Another trickle of muted laughter went round the hall. The trainer had decided he had made his point now and wanted to move on. He looked around and picked another unsuspecting youth from the group.

'What's your name?' said the Captain abruptly. The man chosen this time and standing a few rows back in the group looked startled. He was a far more formidable opponent, standing six foot two, and one of the tallest men in the group. He was well developed, but looked a full stone too heavy.

'It's Martin Thompson, Sir,' he said, with an air of concern.

Size counts for nothing, thought the Captain, being bigger probably meant being slower. 'And how old are you, Thompson?' said the trainer threateningly.

'I'm also 18, Sir.'

'Okay, let's get started.'

Captain Dave Walsh anticipated that the outcome would be the same as before and would punch his opponent into submission. He had decided earlier that his approach to Thompson would be more aggressive and would instil a degree of fear to make him react. The trainer jumped into the ring and called Thompson to box. The Captain had not even broken sweat at this stage. He started his attack as he intended and was able to pick off Thompson at will. The trainer's opponent was strong and looked like he could box; he applied himself well, listening to his instructor, but he was too slow in his execution. The Captain continued to talk his way through the round explaining his techniques. Thompson was avoiding as much as possible being hit, but flinching with each attack of the trainer, and trying to counter back when he could. He was trying desperately to avoid going down on the canvas, knowing what humiliation this would bring. The Captain couldn't push him around like he could Draper, but the big guy eventually succumbed to the onslaught. More body shots this time and jabs to the head were raining in fast. The Captain shouted abuse at the big man as he lowered his guard for him to come forward. A flurry of body shots then a couple more jabs to the head from the trainer saw Thompson scrambling on his knees.

'Get up! Show me some bloody courage.' Thomson had had enough, he was not going to get up and face more punishment. He was down on the canvas on all fours with his head bowed. He looked resigned and all in. Thompson had not even lasted one three minute round. The Captain was not going to change Thompson's mind, as far he was concerned it was over.

The hall was eerily quiet, no one knowing what to expect next. All the noise was coming from the Captain who was stood in the centre of the ring, trying to encourage his opponent to his feet. The group refused to be drawn into any kind of contest. No one was willing the big man to get up and fight on, on the basis that their voices or comments would draw the attention of the trainer and thus bring them into the ring next. The group thought the lesson was over when the Captain shouted out.

'Okay, who's next? I want a volunteer this time; I want somebody to challenge me?'

The hair on the back of Callon's neck stood up as he pondered the trainer's question.

Put your hand up, you can beat the shit out of this bully. Show him what you're made of. What are you waiting for?

The room went silent as the Captain continued staring at the group from his elevated position in the ring.

'Come on you fucking wankers, one of you, challenge me!' Everyone in the group looked at each other, not offering themselves up to get beaten.

This is your chance, show the Captain who's a wanker! Let's see how good you think you are! Show this bully some fucking manners of his own.

He raised his right hand slowly and deliberately. No one had seen him make his gesture. It took Captain Walsh and the group a few moments to register the raised hand as he turned slowly amongst the group. The hush which had descended on the hall suddenly developed a different kind of atmosphere. This acceptance to the challenge took the Captain by surprise. He finally had his willing opponent. Since Captain Walsh had been a trainer, hardly anyone had ever taken on a challenge before. Those that did ended up like Draper and Thompson, only worse. In most cases, the Captain had always ended up dragging the most unwilling opponent into the ring for his final lesson of the day.

He had stood towards the back of the group whilst all this previous one-way sparring had been taking place and had studied the Captain's style closely. His weaknesses and strengths were already identified and logged into his mind. He felt his heart rate surge from a near normal rate to somewhere off the scale in an instant. This sudden rush of adrenalin incorporated with anticipation was something he had experienced before. His father could trigger this in him, in an instant. He loved to feel this sudden explosion of energy which coursed through his body. The circle split to allow the captain's challenger to the front of the ring. There was a palpable relief from the rest of the group, he had just saved one of their arse's being kicked from pillar to post and he knew that. He needed to know himself if he was any good against a man who was already well advanced in his sport. Getting a few knocks didn't bother him; he'd had plenty of those in his relatively short lifetime. Getting hit was part of the game; you just had to avoid it as much as possible. He felt in great shape and was confident he could handle himself. He'd seen nothing in the trainer which rung any alarm bells, but he realised his first two opponents had not challenged or tested the trainer's mettle. He was soon going to find out if he was any good or not.

'What's your name, soldier?'

The word soldier caught him off guard, it was the first time he'd been referred to as this since his training started.

'My name is, Callon.' He dispensed with the, Sir. He hated what had just happened to Draper and Thompson and had lost his respect for pleasantries and the Captain's rank.

The trainer shot back.

'You mean, Callon, *Sir*.' The Captain emphasised the word Sir, saying it very deliberately so there was no misunderstandings in his delivery.

'No, it's Callon, Captain. Derek Callon.' He stood his ground knowing he was going to suffer the verbal wrath of the trainer. Trying to get his opponent rattled was part of his ploy. Something his father had taught him.

Captain Walsh studied his opponent and considered a charge of insubordination. He was looking him up and down without trying to be in the least discreet. It was only after this brief and cursory inspection that he realised how well proportioned Callon was. He was a different shape and build to anyone else in the room, including himself.

The Captain allowed the 'Sir' episode to pass. He knew he would be able to extract that word from him whilst in the ring. He would beat Callon until he called out, 'SIR' to the group at the top of his voice.

'How old are you, Callon?' asked the trainer dismissively.

'I'm 18, Captain,' again, his response bordered on contempt.

The Captain's patience was now thinning.

'I'm going to teach you some fucking manners. You've accepted the challenge to box me and I'm going to make you regret you were born.' There were several gasps from the group as they continued to listen to the verbal jousting between the two men.

Not unless my observations are totally wrong!!

'We box for real, are you clear about that, soldier?' The Captain was seething as he delivered his next warning close up into his face. 'I'm going to hurt you, just so you know my intentions. You've been warned, you've seen nothing yet of my capability.'

'Okay, let's get started,' the reply from him was curt and to the point. The Captain was beside himself at the arrogance of this young upstart.

'I hope you know what you're doing?' said one of his colleagues in a low whisper.

'Me too,' he said in reply.

'Good luck mate, take care, I think he means what he says.' He winked at his helper and did some warming up in the corner. He shadow boxed making slow jabs and body shots into thin air, not wanting the Captain to witness his real speed of hand. He was not going to take the trainer for granted, he knew he had to be careful and would be very cagey. His father's words were resonating in his ears; take nothing for granted, but more importantly, make sure you get the first punch in, and make it count! He turned round in his corner to face the Captain and decided on his strategy, it would be aggression, the likes of which his colleagues had not yet witnessed. He thought momentarily about his father and what he would have done in these circumstances; he would certainly have taken up the challenge. The trainer was staring at him from his corner, and was punching his clenched gloves together. He wanted desperately for Callon to look at him; he wanted his opponent to be afraid when they locked eyes. He wanted to gain some territorial advantage before any punches were exchanged, but he was unfazed by any of the trainer's ploys. He'd never been hit by a stare before, so this didn't worry him one iota. It would be the intent behind the punches which would count in the end and not the glare from his stare. The two men eventually exchanged eye contact as they came together in the centre of the ring.

'Get ready for a good hiding, soldier,' said the trainer in a low whisper and close up.

'I'm ready when you are, Captain,' said Callon in a tone everyone could hear.

'It's, Sir to you, and I'm going to make you shout it from the bloody rooftops.'

Before meeting the group, the Captain had enquired from the other trainers if there was anybody to look out for. The trainers hadn't flagged up anyone; he had escaped any kind of scrutiny and clearly appeared under their radar. Negative thoughts were suddenly entering the trainer's head; had he missed something which was so obvious. He'd made his own cursory observations around the room as the young men sparred together. There was no one standing out; maybe this kid is just going to throw the kitchen sink; thinking he can apply pub brawling tactics. If this is the case, it would all be over in less than a minute, thought the Captain. No one had appeared this cocky before a contest though, no one, and he was suddenly feeling uneasy about the man stood opposite. In all of his work as a boxing trainer, he'd never missed talent or application by a student; but maybe he'd missed something this time?

Steve Ormondroyd was his closest colleague in the camp. They'd been thrust together more by chance, sharing bunks next to each other. Steve was aware that there was something different about his colleague, but he didn't know what it was. His approach to training in general, was very different to the rest of the group. Steve admired the courage of his new friend, but taking on a trainer some nine years his senior with all his boxing experience and acumen, was seen as nothing more than a great act of bravado.

'There's something special about him,' said Steve to Thompson, who was now back with the rest of the group, albeit with his pride somewhat dented. 'When I sparred with him, I never laid a glove on him. He had answers for every attacking move I could muster, but he didn't tell me he'd boxed before. I'm not sure he can cause the trainer any real problems?'

'You're right, Steve,' said Thompson, standing tall within the group. 'I also sparred against him, I never laid a glove on him; never got close to him, but then I never got close to the Captain either.'

'We're soon going to find out if this bravado is in fact, an act of stupidity,' said Steve, scratching the back of his head.

'I hope he doesn't become mince meat for the trainer.' Draper had cleaned up and had now joined the small group at the corner where Callon was preparing. 'The Captain's as mad as hell, just look at his bloody face; I wouldn't want to be in Callon's shoes just now.'

There was an air of expectation around the training hall; the guys in the squad could speak out loud with confidence now. The focus was not on them. Volunteering to box a training instructor was not something you'd do unless you could handle the situation; or you were a complete fool of course. To make matters worse, there was no referee; the trainer would be the judge and the adjudicator when the bout got underway.

Three by three minute rounds were agreed with one minute in-between. This was the real deal, he thought; this was really going to put his father's training to a severe test. The Captain was searching the face of his opponent looking for some kind of fear or weakness, but there was none, he gave nothing away. There was however, the slightest hint of apprehension in the trainer's eyes; Callon was able to spot this ever so slight betrayal on his face.

He had an advantage over the trainer, he'd just seen him box. He'd watched and observed his every move and ploy, but the trainer knew nothing about him or his style. His physique was not an indication that he could box, thought the trainer. He wasn't going to be a match for him, no way, not with his superior experience. With this in mind, the trainer approached the contest with an air of expectation and a degree of casualness.

A bell and timekeeper was installed to oversee the three rounds. The Captain had already decided his strategy. From the start, he was going to attack, force his opponent back onto the ropes and then into the corner, hit him with left and rights. Attack the head; left, right, left, then down to the body, left, right, taking the wind out of him. He wanted the young soldier begging for mercy, but most of all, he wanted him to shout out 'Sir' from the top of his voice. It could all be over in the first round, he thought, and was going to teach this 'son of a bitch' a lesson in good manners! The Captain was shadow boxing in his corner now, practising his already set routine. Callon continued to give nothing away about his technique he simply had his arms draped across the top ropes and studied the trainer intently. The Captain was perspiring a little through his exertions; he was ready now though. He waved Callon to the centre of the ring and asked the timekeeper to get prepared. The boxers backed away from each other momentarily, the bell sounded; then the two men approached each other, touched gloves and started to box.

The Captain was able to view his opponent in a boxing pose for the first time, surprised to see his stance and his gloves held in the classic defensive position.

'This man has boxed before,' said the Captain under his breath. 'Why didn't I spot him previously?'

As the trainer went aggressively forward, his attempt to make Callon go backwards was paying off, but he wasn't agile and quick enough to get him tied up on the ropes. He was able to defend the jabs without being hit.

You will need to be much quicker than that, he thought if you're going to land one of those jabs on me.

The Captain was talking with every contact, trying to unnerve his opponent.

'You're going down, son,' said Captain Walsh in a condescending tone. He dismissed the Captains dialogue and concentrated only on the boxing. Talking made for distractions, and he wanted none of that.

The trainer was anticipating more of what had just been presented to him, and was quite lax in his attack. He was not expecting the first counter attack. He defended one of the trainer's text book jabs and countered him in a flash by planting a peach of a punch on his left temple with a right hook. He backed off and retreated immediately to a safe distance out of arm's reach. This created much amusement and excitement amongst the onlookers. He was up on his toes, just as his father had taught him, dancing, both gloves held high, jinking and ducking. Shouts and jibes were coming from the floor as the two opponents stepped forward again to meet each other. This had all the makings of being a 'real' boxing match. No one previously had been able to land anything on the trainer, so this was a great start to the bout. The trainer must have thought it was a lucky shot as he composed himself. He never anticipated that punch and was surprised at the speed and power of its execution. It took the Captain by surprise, he never saw it coming. The trainer held his guard, his gloved hands covering his face as he came forward. He cursed himself having fallen for that soft shot. He approached again, this time a little more prepared, more aggression, more determination and more power. Though that punch had hurt him, nonetheless, he was sticking to his strategy to jab away first before executing his lethal body shots.

He had recognised in these early exchanges that he was a match for the trainer and felt confident of his own ability. He felt good and in control as he jinked and dodged the trainer's thrusts. He was now moving forward a little after a few more of his head shots landed. He was on his toes darting in, then darting out, offering little jabs of his own. The idea was to keep moving. It was more difficult to hit a moving target. He also thought about his fathers words. 'There's always someone out there better than you. You just need to identify that person when you come across him.'

He continued to be cautious, not taking any chances and certainly not taking anything for granted. He realised however, that the man facing him across the ring was not that better person.

The trainer was fast realising at this early stage of the bout that his opponent, this young upstart, was not going to be a push over. After a few more exchanges Callon was landing some meaty shots. The trainer was now beginning to lose his composure, his breathing a little more laboured, his incessant talking, kept now to profanities only. His first two opponents were weak and lacked strength and savvy. He could not push this man around as he wanted to. This just added to the derision from the group. There would be no tutoring from the trainer now. Suddenly the talking stopped. He needed all his strength and stamina to stay in this fight. He was concentrating real hard, giving his full attention, trying to avoid being hit. The punches which landed were stinging where they connected and were beginning to take their toll. He had only found himself in this position in competition once before, never with a recruit though. The trainer's pride and integrity were being openly displayed in the ring and was already wishing he'd not asked for a volunteer to fight him. The trainer was still trying to work out how this eighteen year old could have such a wise old boxing head on such young shoulders after only two weeks of training. How could he possess such skill and guile?

The bell was rung to end round one and the two men retreated to their respective corners. The trainer sat down whilst his adversary stood. The trainer took on gulps of water and splashed the bottle contents over his head to refresh himself. There were already pinkish marks on the trainer's head and body where shots had impacted. The Captain's initial strategy was being questioned. He was not allowed to come forward as he had wanted. Callon was able to pick him off at will, with piston like thrusts of his fists the moment the smallest gap appeared in his defence.

The hall had come to life with a renewed vigour; there was an expectation in the room. The underdog was making a fight of it and up to now was gaining the upper hand. The group knew the trainer was under pressure and the shouts got louder. No one was shouting their support for him.

The bell rang for the start of the next round. The trainer continued to come forward as Callon decided to back away. As he did, he picked the trainer off, just as he'd been taught. Bang, bang, a couple more body shots into the ribs at lightening speed, back away. He could hear the wind expelling from the trainer's body as he landed more punches. Callon was caught a few times in some of the exchanges, but the blows were mere glances and lacked any power or threat.

The trainer was beginning to lose his control. Callon knew that once this started, all the natural skills, the training and basic instincts go out of the window. The best the trainer could hope for was just a lucky punch. He was dancing, up on his toes, moving in, tat, tat to the head, then body, then out again, varying his line of attack with lightening speed and intent. Keep dancing, keep moving, he told himself. More head shots, bang, bang, and then back off. Grunts from the Captain were getting louder as more shots landed. The trainer's hopes of teaching his pupil a lesson were getting more and more remote with every punch. He was very thankful for his father's tuition as he countered every move the trainer made. Surprised at his own strength, he was able to push the trainer around bodily, as he now forged forward.

By the end of the second round, the trainer was beside himself, seething with anger at being beaten by a young recruit. Sweating profusely, he was going to throw everything at this young pretender in those last three minutes. The trainer had hardly laid a glove on his opponent yet.

'Knock him out!' rang out shouts from the floor.

There was a renewed confidence coming from the onlookers and now they wanted to be heard. Whoops of laughter and encouragement went all round the ring.

'Finish him off, Callon, do it for me,' He recognised the voice of Draper as he prepared himself for the final round.

He moved towards the centre of the ring to touch gloves with the Captain as a mark of recognition to the last round. As they approached, the trainer hoping to catch him off-guard launched a desperate right hook. Fortunately, he had his wits about him and managed to sway away from this potential knockout punch but was caught a glancing blow to his cheek. He staggered backwards, more because he was off balance and slightly unprepared, but he wasn't hurt. There was a gasp from the floor as they thought their man was going down on the canvas. The trainer, by his actions, confirmed that the Marquis of Queensbury rules were off the table and that it was winning at any cost.

Okay, Captain, if this is how you want to play. So be it!

The trainer launched himself again, folding his arms around his opponent in a bear hug. They both went down clumsily. The surge from the trainer caught them both off balance.

'You clever bastard,' said the Captain breathlessly, as he remained on the floor momentarily. Callon was up on his feet in an instant and ready to box. The trainer's effort to stand up was more laboured as he rested for a few seconds on both knees. Another desperate lunge from the trainer ensued, but this time he threw his arms around his opponent's neck and screwed his head into Callon's face. He was trying his best to draw blood; this he thought, would at least be small comfort. He withdrew from the trainer easily, but he still hung on, desperate now to stop himself from being hit. The best he could hope for was to stifle his opponents lightening movements. He was lunging again with arms that had no strength. The trainer needed to keep his attacker close by, he was hanging on for dear life, trying to stop himself from being hit.

With no referee to intervene and call, 'break,' he had to wrestle free from the trainer's clutches, and he was strong enough to do this. The trainer was now very tired; perspiration was dripping from his body. It was time to call a close on these proceedings, he thought. He launched a devastating combination of body and head shots with unrelenting force, speed and effect. This brought gasps of amazement from the group watching and deep groans from the Captain as he tried valiantly to avoid the onslaught. A couple more shots were landed to the head, splitting open a wide cut above the trainer's eye. Blood immediately started to run into his eye, blurring his vision, but the Captain still came forward as if spurred on by the sight of his own blood. Within thirty seconds however, the trainer was on the canvas, flat out, breathing very heavily and dazed. Speed, surprise, strength and execution were something the trainer had not bargained for.

He stayed on the canvas with his head tilted backwards, breathing heavily and making no attempt to get up. The lads started to count him out, one, two, three…. until they reached ten. A couple of recruits tended to the trainer and inspected the gash over his eye, but provided him little comfort. He was still dazed and wondering what had just hit him, he was helped onto his backside, with support.

He looked up to the roof space of the training hall and thought how well his father had prepared him for days like this. You taught me well, Dad, I just proved today how well!

The lads in the group were ecstatic, cheering and jumping up and down as they came into the ring. Everyone wanted to pat him on the back in praise of his achievement. They wanted to congratulate him, particularly Draper and Thompson who'd been subjected to the trainer's brutality.

'That was great fun watching you bring that bully down a peg or two,' said Thompson, 'we all thought you were going to get a good hiding.'

'I think the Captain had the same idea.'

'We can't thank you enough,' said Thompson. Both he and Draper were nodding their heads in agreement.

'I enjoyed it,' he said taking his gloves off, 'and you don't need to thank me. Maybe the Captain will think twice next time before he asks for volunteers to fight him.' He paused momentarily, 'and maybe, Captain Dave Walsh has just had his payback day?'

Without further hesitation, he strolled into the centre of the ring and held his hand out to the Captain; he was still groggy but sat upright on the canvas. With as much humility as he could muster, he spoke loud enough for everyone in the hall to hear.

'Let me help you, Sir,' he said, wanting to emphasise that his respect of the Captain's rank, but not the man, had been fully restored.

Captain Walsh looked up towards his victor with heavy eyes but managed the faintest smile before accepting the offer. The two men embraced momentarily before Captain Walsh was led from the hall shaking his head.

He never saw that trainer back in the camp after that brief encounter; and he never boxed again after that day.

Draper and Thompson had already forgotten their beatings at the hands of the Captain. They would remain firm friends and colleagues with Callon until cruel fate would intervene, and cast its unforgiving web.

The military training continued at Fulford for several more weeks. Drills and weapon training were interspersed with the physical training, bringing the men up to the required fitness level. He continued in his own way on weight training. In fact, the trainers at York introduced some of his weight and fitness regime now. Weight training and physical exercise had been a part of his life from his early teenage years and up to him joining the Army. He was in fine physical shape and it seemed that army life in the beginning at least, had been invented for his purpose only. Up until now, everything he was asked to do was playing to his strengths. His training pre army was now mirrored in his new life. This aspect of his was to stand him apart from the rest of the group.

He could push phenomenal weights for his age and was able to concentrate his training and focus on what he loved most. The army training procedures were beginning to develop his physique, putting extra definition and bulk to his already muscular frame. At five foot eleven inches tall and weighing close to 200 pound, he possessed physical strength way beyond his weight and height. He considered that this was his God given gift; inherited from his father. They both discovered and loved the competitiveness of competing against one another, stretching their own personal boundaries. His daily routines involved pushing more weight to become even stronger than he already was; and to run faster and longer than ever before. He was able to perform strength exercises which made even the army trainers pay attention. Training sessions and techniques attracted the scrutiny of army personnel from outside their camp. During routines, small audiences would gather to see him perform some of his remarkable feats of strength and stamina. Press ups and pull ups by the hundred were no problem. Single arm press ups came without difficulty. Bench pressing more than double his body weight was commonplace. His problem was keeping this raw strength and energy under control and channelling his abilities in the right direction. He did not want to turn into the 'Wild Man of Fulford Barracks.'

Draper and Thompson were now increasingly enjoying their physical training, having persuaded Callon to take them under his wing and include them in his fitness regime. Their brief venture into the boxing ring had lit an inner fire within their bellies and they wanted to copy the level of fitness training that Callon was achieving. They had both approached him, but it was Draper who spoke first; his lean gangly frame looking forlorn and undernourished in his training kit.

'We wondered perhaps, could we train with you today?'

He viewed the request with some hesitation, looking over the two men in front of him.

'What's wrong with the regular army training, lads? I do this extra work because I enjoy it, not because I need to.'

'That's the difference.' said Draper, 'we need to do it, and we both realise that. We both want to do what you're doing.' There was a slight pause, 'at least we want to try.'

He hesitated, never having trained anyone other than himself before. 'I'll warn you, I don't play at training, you can train with me only if you are serious about it. The minute you lose interest, then you're gone. Are you clear on that?'

'We're deadly serious, both of us,' said Thompson, 'we don't want to find ourselves in that situation again. What happened with the boxing trainer was a real wake up call.'

Callon decided to put his strategy to the test.

'I'm doing a five mile run tonight....it's something I do most evenings. I guess it's a good place to start, are you up for that?' Both men nodded their heads in approval and grinned at each other.

'Count me in too,' said Steve. 'I want to be a part of this elite group,' having listened to the conversation from only yards away. He had always backed his ability as a man who could handle himself, but witnessing the destruction of the Captain by his colleague made him realise very quickly that he was a long way from where he needed to be. It was better, he thought, to be with Callon than against him.

He was now becoming a minor celebrity, especially around the camp. This notoriety had spread to the streets of York and unfortunately made him a legitimate target in the eyes of some people; people who thought they could take him on. He never went seeking out trouble; however, it somehow seemed to follow him around. These altercations often coincided with frequent trips to the pub. If he was intimidated, then he would not back down; it was not in his nature. He remembered thinking how much his temperament was like his own father's. The big difference was his father went out of his way to fight. This was his way of earning extra money and putting food on the table. Being challenged without provocation though was something he would not let pass.

After the initial training was over at York, the recruits were allowed home for a few days. The stress of the intense training they had endured suddenly seemed to evaporate, accompanied by a great sense of achievement. Everyone was on a high as they made their respective journey's home, albeit briefly. The recruits had arrived at Fulford barracks as a bunch of misfits, as individuals, caring only for themselves. Suddenly they were a tightly integrated unit with organised discipline and a very special kind of camaraderie. This however, was only the first rung on the ladder as far as training and discipline were concerned, from now on, it was going to get a lot more intense, harder and more dangerous.

The unit moved down to Burford in Oxfordshire for further training. For Callon, some other important decisions had to be made. After training was completed in Oxford, his unit could be posted anywhere overseas, wherever there was conflict. Things were moving at a pace now; and he had to make decisions which would be life changing. He was leaving Georgina at home, his long standing girlfriend; visiting each other would be out of the question during his training period, except perhaps, for very short periods when he could probably get home. Further training was going to push boundaries. He knew that she could not visit him in the south of England, this was virtually impossible. This speculation only accelerated their discussions of getting married, for though very young, they were in love, which is what mattered most. The uncertainty of not knowing what their futures would hold was a major factor in this thought process and cemented their ultimate decision. They knew if they were going to do anything positive, they had better do it soon as time was running out.

His unit, 436 Royal Army Service Corps (RASC) was rumoured to be going overseas. Most able bodied men who had been conscripted ended up somewhere overseas, so why should 436 RASC company be any different? Where and when was speculating, and the other burning question that went unanswered was for how long would this posting be for? Another question never uttered, but constantly in the back of Georgina's mind was, would he ever come back home at all?

In early August of 1944, they were married, having taken advantage of a small window of opportunity. He would be home for a few days only; those few days would constitute their honeymoon period. They were both still only 18 years old.

Chapter 7

Operation Market Garden. September 17th 1944.

Life in Oxfordshire was much more frenetic but more focused as Callon and his unit were put through their paces yet again, with more emphasis on weapons training. The whole unit achieved a combat level of fitness and sufficient weapon training to take it to the next stage. Inevitably though, thoughts and minds became more associated with war and weighing up their prospects of staying alive. This war had already taken many young lives. Everyone within the unit either knew someone or was related to individuals who went to war, never to return.

Steve, Draper and Thompson continued to maintain the daily keep fit regime Callon set for them. Significant bodily improvements could be seen as they replaced fat, or lack of it in Draper's case, with muscle. All three were proud of their progress and their personal motivation to get really fit and stay fit. Running several miles every day also saw their stamina levels increase. Callon would always set challenging runs, mixing up his speeds and distances to improve their personal goals.

Callon was already an experienced driver; and the army put these driving skills to good use. He had previously driven heavy vehicles back in his home town. His tasks for now involved moving large pieces of artillery and other equipment from camp to camp or to different strategic locations where they were most needed, and ferrying troops around the country. He noticed a definite increase of activity, tension and intensity during the first two weeks of September 1944. The movement of troops and equipment was increasing. Something was about to happen, but neither he nor anyone else had any idea what it was.

Thousands of paratroopers, some from US bases and throughout Britain were despatched around the various airfields in Oxfordshire and Gloucestershire. It transpired that these paratroopers would be dropped some 100 miles behind enemy lines in mainland Europe. The date set for this daring act was 17th September 1944. The Operation, codenamed 'Market Garden,' was about to be unveiled.

He was just six weeks into his marriage and apart from the briefest of honeymoons, had not been back to see his wife. He was unaware at this stage, just how his mental and physical strength would be put to the most stringent of tests.

The main objective for this brave body of paratroopers was to secure bridges across the rivers in Holland, which would allow the allied forces to advance more rapidly northwards, turning right into the lowlands of Germany and skirting around the Siegfried line. This line was a defence system stretching some 630 kilometres with more than 18,000 bunkers, tunnels and tank traps. It went from Kleve on the border with the Netherlands along the western border of the old German empire as far as the town of Weil am Rhein on the border to Switzerland. If the planning and execution went to plan, then this would bring about the end of the war by Christmas 1944.

This huge military offensive involved massive movements of troops and equipment including jeeps and guns. The troop numbers were made up from the US 82nd and 101st Airborne and the British 1st Parachute division. An operation of this type and scale had never before been attempted. In all, some 2,500 gliders would transport 12,000 men and equipment, whilst 24,000 troops would be deployed by troop carrier planes.

The Douglas C-47 aircraft was used and often referred to as the Skytrain, Dakota, or Gooney Bird. The Dakota was not a large plane, with only 28 fully kitted troops on board at any one time.

Huge numbers of these aircraft were deployed for this daring offensive. Prior to the launch of 'Market Garden,' long lines of Dakota C47's were readied on runways with their loads of men and machines armed to the teeth.

As well as transporting troops and cargo, the DC-3 also served as a glider tug in support of operation Market Garden. The Dakota was instrumental and vital in getting the troops to their chosen parachute drop zone. The surprise effect of deploying large number of men and equipment was diminished as it was clear that an operation this size could not be carried out in a single day. It would take three days before all equipment and men were in place.

The success of 'Operation Market Garden,' relied on three critical assertions.

Firstly, the German defences were believed to be undermanned by less-trained soldiers defending the Eindhoven-Arnhem corridor.

Secondly, the narrow route to Arnhem was backed up on the ground by 30 (XXX) Corps' with 20,000 vehicles. This large body of men and machines had already started the offensive towards Eindhoven on this stretch of highway. This road was considered good enough to handle this volume of traffic. It soon became apparent, however, that it couldn't, and this created many obstacles and hold ups and slowed the offensive down.

The road was a two lane highway with ditches either side, totally unsuitable for the heavy artillery vehicles.

The third assumption relied on re-supplying and re-enforcing the airborne units with further airdrops. This strategy was very weather dependant, and it was to turn seriously for the worse during the operation.

The allies were also soon to discover that they had underestimated the strength and doggedness of the German troops. Important intelligence was either ignored or arrived too late that Germany's 'crack' Panzer division was returning to Holland and would be refitting close to the town of Arnhem.

The 30 Corps advance met stiff resistance in Arnhem and along the narrow road known as the corridor from Eindhoven. This doggedness delayed the Allied progress up the narrow corridor; it was renamed 'Hell's Highway' as Allied casualty numbers grew.

Problems were further compounded by the poor weather conditions. Re-enforcements for the airborne divisions were delayed because of the weather conditions, thereby minimizing the effectiveness of the re-supply efforts.

During this phase of intense fighting on the ground in mainland Europe, Callon and his unit were involved in the re-supply tasks. It was this unit's duty to ensure that supplies were despatched through open cargo hatches on the Dakotas whilst in flight. This happened at low altitude and at low speeds approaching stall conditions for the aircraft. Other re-supply planes were used from different airfields including Short Sterlings MK 1V's of 620 Squadron RAF. These planes suffered huge losses during this stage, particularly on the 21st September 1944 when seven out of ten Sterlings failed to return from their respective duties.

He flew on four of the re-supply sorties and wondered before each one whether this would be his last. He was not a religious man, but he thanked God before every sortie and afterwards for his safe return. He was also very aware as to how close he would flirt with death. Some of the friends he had trained with were not so lucky. They had also flirted with death and lost. Friends whom he had shook hands and joked with hours previously were never to be seen again. Knowing this made it more difficult for some to fly their next operation. He on the other hand, never flinched from his duties and his responsibilities. He knew that the success of getting supplies on the ground in Holland meant helping those men who were fighting for everyone's freedom and in the knowledge it could bring an early end to the conflict.

The incessant drone and vibration of the aircraft as it reached its pre-determined altitude was both deafening and frightening. The wind chill factor from opening the doors before a drop and the thought that supplies could fall into enemy hands was unimaginable. His fingers would freeze within seconds of the doors opening, making the despatching of supplies from the plane that more difficult. The wind rush would take his breath away, leaving him gasping for air with lungs filled with ice. The force of the wind ripped at his clothes like a flag left out in a hurricane. The only life-line between falling from the plane and staying on board whilst the doors were open was a thin woven strap attached to his belt at the back. This allowed for free movement whilst sending the important supplies to men below fighting on the ground. He was also to witness during the re-supply missions, Allied planes flying close by on similar sorties, hit by flak, and catching fire. These events only ever provided nightmares and statistics, never survivors!

The four friends, Callon, Steve, Draper and Thompson usually met up in the Naafi when they returned safely from another supply drop behind enemy lines. Success was measured in their safe return, nothing else. It was greeted with relief each time they returned, waiting patiently until each man had been counted back. They exchanged stories of horror at what they had experienced and seen. All four men were mentally drained, wondering if the next tracer bullet would have their name on it.

'I'm organising a run today,' said Callon, 'do I assume you're all up for it?'

'I need to get out of here for a while,' said Steve. He was usually the hardest to encourage, but on this occasion, he was the first to respond. Steve had had a narrow escape, and had been in fear of his life when his plane had been hit by flak. The aircraft had lost power and height, but had managed to land safely back at the base, thanks to the skill and courage of his pilot.

'Yes, let's do it,' said Steve, his head still filled with the horror of what he had just endured. 'We're off duty tonight lads, so why don't we get back here afterwards and have a few beers together?'

He recognised the lads needed to strip some of the images away from the dark recesses of their minds. Their time so far in Oxford had been quite harrowing.

Draper and Thompson looked at each other before Draper spoke out,

'I'm in; I need to clear my head.'

It would be the worst decision of his young life!

They agreed to meet back in 10 minutes.

As usual, Callon led the way, varying his early pace only moderately. Their route was a flat six mile circular course which he had found earlier in the week bringing supplies back to the camp. The four runners were soon negotiating their way down the narrow lanes of the Oxfordshire countryside and taking in their surroundings. He and Steve had managed to pull away slightly and open a gap of twenty yards. Steve was beginning to blow hard, but continued to match his colleague stride for stride. As the two men rounded a left hand bend, they noticed in the distance a small van travelling towards them. Since setting off, this was the first vehicle they had encountered. Steve dropped behind in single file to allow comfortable passage for the van to get by unhindered. It was not until the van got closer that they realised the driver was travelling too fast, taking into consideration the road width and conditions. It wasn't raining, but it was slippery on the wet tarmac road. The road was wide enough to allow two vehicles to pass, but with caution. The van reached the bend at the same time as Draper and Thompson were rounding it and coming into view. The van took the corner at speed, trying to cut the angle and give width to the two runners, and not anticipating another car coming towards it. The van driver swerved to miss the oncoming car, and smashed into Draper and Thompson at high speed. Both he and Steve heard the bone crunching smash and hurried back to where the two men lay. They had been thrown back some 30 yards and were both bleeding from serious head injuries. Both men had broken legs judging by the way their limbs were lying. Steve had run off to get help. Callon took Thompson's pulse. He laid still, blood flowing onto the tarmac from an open head wound; his legs were twitching uncontrollably, but otherwise his torso was unmoving. He was frantically trying to resuscitate him with small gentle hand smacks to the face. He knew instinctively that any other attempt at life saving was futile. Nevertheless, in desperation, he continued to speak to his injured friend.

'Come on, stay with me, Thompson, don't leave now, come on, we're getting help for you, you're going to be okay,' he lied. The large circle of blood on the tarmac road behind Thompson's head grew ever larger and now reached into the grass verge, life was draining away. He looked to see if he could stem the flow of blood, but recognised his injuries were too severe. Knowing he could do no more for Thompson, he moved to tend to Draper, a further 10 yards away, and hoped for a different outcome. Draper's eyes were fluttering behind lids which were almost, but not quite closed. He tried the same feeble resuscitation as with Thompson,

'Can you hear me, Draper, Draper, can you hear me?' He wanted to hold his hand, but the arm was twisted beyond its normal limits and knew hence that it was broken. He took the other hand instinctively, 'If you can hear me, Draper, squeeze my hand?' The command went unheard. He felt his pulse but it was too faint to sustain life. Draper appeared to fight his injuries, he wanted to live, in spite of his critical condition, Draper's eyelids drew back into his head displaying the pure whiteness of his eyes as if death was somehow reversing its decision, then changed to eyes which were dark empty and unseeing. He could see his own reflection in the dark empty pools as they stared back at him without life.

By the time the ambulance arrived, both men were dead. He had watched and witnessed both men take their last breath. Draper's death disturbed him most. He knew his friend was dead and attempted to close his eyes as he lay motionless on the cold road. As hard as he tried, he couldn't bring his eyelids together. The death stare was his last act of defiance, even though life had deserted his body.

It was ironic that both men had survived the aerial bombardment of enemy fire, risking life and limb in slow lumbering aircraft dropping supplies to the needy troops on the ground in a foreign land. They had all stared death in the face on several occasions, but it seemed unfair to be snuffed out by a selfless act of stupidity on otherwise peaceful English country lanes. It was he who had taken his friends down this path to their death and it would be he who shouldered the blame for this senseless loss of life.

It was becoming clear that Operation Market Garden was not going to meet its objectives. Stubborn resistance by the Germans on the Arnhem Bridge prevented it from being taken. The 1st British Airborne Division was cut off and suffered heavy losses before receiving permission to withdraw.

On 25th September after eight days of bloody fighting, around 2,000 British troops managed to slip across the Rhine to safety. Tragically, some 7,000 dead or missing were left in the area of Arnhem.

The drive towards Arnhem however was halted. The two American Airborne Divisions remained in place to prevent any further advances by the Germans. The 82nd Airborne lost over 1400 men, killed or missing and the 101st Airborne lost over 2100 men.

82nd Airborne finally withdrew on the 11th Nov with an additional 1600 lost followed by the 101st retreat on 25th Nov with almost 2000 further casualties.

Failure to take the bridge at Arnhem was a pivotal moment in the 2nd World War.

German fortitude overcame Operation Market Garden's objectives. This meant the Rhine would not be crossed and the Siegfried line would not be outflanked before the onset of winter. As a result, this failure would prevent the war from ending in 1944. Operation Market Garden ended with the loss of many lives over ten days of relentless fighting. This plan, the brainchild of Field Marshall Bernard

Montgomery, was flawed from the outset. It did not have the desired effect for which it was intended. A famous film, aptly named, 'A Bridge Too Far' was based on the failure of this mission.

Back home in his beloved Yorkshire, he re-lived his experiences in his mind and in his dreams of the dangers he faced whilst working on the re-supply of troops in Holland and Germany. He struggled to sleep in those first few days back home. He had been involved in many near misses. He had witnessed first hand, planes flying the same sorties as him, blown out of the sky, flak passing his plane by inches. With the cargo doors of the aircraft open for dropping supplies, he had seen the gunner's ground positions below. He had watched the lethal fire display heading upwards towards the open skies, skies which were buzzing with aircraft, providing a lifeline to the unseen troops on the ground. He had prayed that none would strike the aircraft he was flying in. He considered himself fortunate that he was in the right plane at the right time. Some of his friends and colleagues were not so lucky. He had come through it unscathed physically. However, the mental scars remained. These would take a long time to heal. During his darker moments he would question the futility of what he had seen and done He felt he had come through a better person however, he was thankful to be still alive, his prayers had been answered.

'Here but by the Grace of God,' he said to himself, remembering his two fallen colleagues and friends, Draper and Thompson.

The weather was just beginning to show its intent for the onset of winter. It was November 1944. Dark mornings and evenings were his less favourite time of year; he was not worried though, because he was going overseas with his unit. Nothing could come close to his previous experiences; anything had to be better than what he had just gone through. This would be his last visit home for some time. Before he left, though, he had planted the seeds of life within his young wife of a few months. Georgina would give birth to a boy in July 1945.

PART 3

Chapter 8

Singapore 12 months later. 5 September 1945.

On September 5th, 1945, RASC 436 transport company first set foot on the shores of Singapore. They were part of the first Allied troops to arrive at Singapore docks to take control back from the Japanese after their occupation. British war ships and ground troops alike were arriving in their thousands. The Allied troops were welcomed by cheering crowds in a carnival type atmosphere by young Malayans.

Winston Churchill called the fall of Singapore, 'the worst disaster and capitulation in British history.' Singapore fell on 15th February 1942 to the Military forces of the Empire of Japan after defeating the combined, Australian, British, Indian and Malayan garrison in the battle of Singapore. Now however, Singapore was back under British rule.

The Japanese occupation of Singapore lasted from 1942 until August 1945.

On 6th and 9th of August 1945, US B29 bombers dropped atomic bombs on Hiroshima and Nagasaki. This bombing ended the Japanese occupation of South East Asia. On 15th August 1945, Emperor Horohita of Japan announced its unconditional surrender and Singapore was now placed back under British Military Administration.

The Japanese surrendered to General MacArthur on board the Missouri Battleship in Tokyo Bay at 9am on 2nd September 1945, officially ending WWII. 10 days later on 12th September 1945 at 11.10 am, another Japanese surrender ceremony was held at the Municipal Buildings, Singapore. General Seishiro Itagaki was present during the signing. The surrender was accepted by Lord Louis Mountbatten, the Supreme Allied Commander. This signing officially ended the Japanese occupation of South East Asia. This surrender represented 680,000 Japanese soldiers involved in the South East Asia occupation.

The surrender ceremony and signing was witnessed by 400 dignitaries made up of commanders and officers from the navy, army and air force as well as senior officers from the Supreme Headquarters. Some of the released prisoners of war were also present. In addition, leaders of the Malayan communities, including The Sultan of Johore, Sir Ibrahim, was also present. Callon was unaware at the time, but this gentleman and his high office status, would have a very profound effect on him and would change the course of his life. His influence would also be responsible for his extending stay in Singapore, but for all the wrong reasons.

The Surrender Ceremony finally ended, with the raising of the Union Jack flag and playing the national anthems of all the Allied nations. The flag which General Percival used was the same one when he surrendered to the Japanese. It had been kept concealed by the prisoners in Changi Jail throughout the occupation.

By 12th September some 100,000 Allied troops were on this small strip of land situated directly below Malaysia and attached only by the most tenuous of crossings, known as the Straits Causeway.

Shortly after arriving in Singapore, he had received a letter from his home in the UK and brought news he had been eagerly awaiting. The letter contained photographs of his wife and new born son. It had taken time for the letter to arrive. His son was already two months old and probably looked different from the images he was now studying. He viewed the photographs intently, trying to decide who he resembled most, but the pictures were too grainy to say for sure. The important thing was that the small child in the photographs was healthy. The birth had gone without any complications. Mother and baby were now home with his parents after staying in hospital for a week.

The reality of his new responsibilities was difficult to comprehend, with such distances separating him and his family. He wanted to feel different, he wanted to feel like a father, but regrettably, the images awoke no paternal instincts in him. He convinced himself that these instincts would eventually come when he saw his son in the flesh. All this negativity that he was now experiencing would simply be erased from his thoughts when he returned home. His son would take his father's name, Thomas, decided before he left England. They both somehow knew it would be a boy. No girl's name had been chosen beforehand.

He recognised his own father-son relationship as rock solid and one which he would not trade for anything. However, his time away from home and duties of army life had somehow dulled his senses and he failed to be moved by his new status. It was almost twelve months since he had stepped across his front doorstep, and this time away had taken its toll. He continued to ask himself, who was he, what was he doing and why?

The congratulations and best wishes from the rest of his other colleagues in his barracks belied his true feelings. There was no head wetting ceremony. This would have to wait, he thought, as he showed the photographs of his new son round his unit. There was too much work on the ground to think about celebrations just yet. His feelings would change, he just didn't know when. The 436 Unit were getting acquainted with their new home and each man had been tasked with getting Singapore up from its knees and back onto its feet. The job was daunting, but it was doable.

Chapter 9

Witnessing the surrender signing ceremony by the Japanese on 12th September 1945 at the Municipal building was an historic moment. Callon and his small group of friends were very close to all the proceedings taking place as Lord Louis Mountbatten, standing on the steps of the Municipal Hall delivered his victory speech as the Union Jack was hoisted. He was only one of a few who had a camera that day and was determined to photograph this event unfolding. The Japanese surrender party with heads bowed, flanked either side by Allied Military officers as they left the short surrender ceremony was captured on film as they descended the steps of the Municipal buildings. Mountbatten was resplendent, dressed in his full white naval attire and was accompanied by the Deputy Supreme Commander Wheeler. The car taking them to the ceremony was driven by a released prisoner of war through the streets to cheers and flag waving from the huge gathering of locals and allied servicemen.

The allied forces were in place to assist Singapore and start the process of getting things back to normal. The civilian population had suffered greatly during this time of Japanese occupation. The local people had to bow to the Japanese soldiers during this period or face beatings. Some people were even taken away, never to be seen again.

It was not until the Allies arrived in early September, that the brutality of the Japanese and the condition of the prisoners of war held in Changi jail was discovered. A War Crimes Commission was formed in light of this to investigate the atrocities committed by the Japanese. Altogether, 135 were tried and convicted.

The return of the British did not result in a speedy improvement in living conditions in Singapore. There was widespread hunger, poverty and malnutrition during the early part of the post war problems.

Special soup kitchens were eventually opened, offering meals at subsidised rates.

As Callon walked the streets of Singapore in the days after the surrender signing, there was still chaos all around. He noticed the cramped conditions in which people were living. Greedy landlords had divided and further subdivided rooms to squeeze in more tenants. In places some 2500 people would be crammed into an area measuring the size of two football fields. Overcrowding generally happened in the most dilapidated of buildings. Committees were set up making recommendations to re-house people and families and abolish the terrible slums and their attendant evils of crime and disease.

Ownerless dogs roamed the streets lean and hungry, marking their territory, but having somehow survived during the food shortages.

The early days in Singapore were frenetic and there appeared to be very little organisation. Callon was working on the docks trying to make sense of what had happened during the Japanese occupation. Taking care of unloading ships and distributing the needs of thousands of allied servicemen was no easy task. To feed clothe and provide all the other general store requirements for this number of personnel was a huge undertaking.

The main roads were mostly crammed with allied vehicles of one sort or another. Most of the unloading of cargo from the ships was done by the local population under supervision, recruited specifically for this task. There was no shortage of willing hands, most ready to do anything for a few dollars per week. Large cargo ships were unloaded daily using hand and heavy lifting equipment. Long lines of circular rollers in cradles were coupled together to form a horizontal moving platform from the edge of the dock to the holding areas. Cases and boxes could be moved and pushed physically along by the rollers at speed. There would be many hands required along its length to make sure that goods didn't fall off the tracks.

Much of his work allowed him to navigate the Island's road network in its entirety. Singapore was not that big after all. Work with the locals for the unloading and storing of goods which were non perishable was also going well. The locals were hard workers and always willing to do that extra task. In spite of their malnourished bodies, they were strong and resilient in everything they did. When he was required off docks to take goods to another part of Singapore, he travelled with the aid of local helpers in his ten ton Mack truck. He was keen to pick up and learn the local Malayan language, and the local men he travelled with knew just enough English for this to become possible. His journey to become a part of the local culture was already starting. After several months, he was able to make short sentences and converse with his Malayan helpers. His sleep pattern was disturbed and his head constantly filled with his desire to learn. His command of this language would be a help to him, he thought, it may even offer reprieve from some of the dock duty from time to time. For now though, he continued to practise his word skills with his travelling companions. He approached the learning in the same way he approached his physical training. It was repetitive, until he could speak words without thinking.

The army base was a combination of large huts and tents spread over uneven scrubland and sandy ground. The wood based barracks were raised on breeze blocks of varying height to counter the unevenness of the ground. Raising the huts above ground also prevented them from flooding. Whilst Singapore was a hot and sticky part of the world, torrential rainfall was common, especially in the monsoon season. The rain never lasted for long, but when it came, it came with a vengeance. Within minutes, a dusty dirty sand track could be transformed into a river. The camp was a jigsaw of small mini gulley's and valleys. Previous downpours had compacted and moulded the sandy terrain into this weird formation, providing its own routing for the rain to follow. The camp had a large central area which was flattened and smoothed, used exclusively for parade ground drills and military training. This patch of ground was inviolable and considered sacred to the highest degree!

Callon would use the outer confines of the parade ground to train. His daily routine before an early start on the docks would be to run the equivalent of three to four miles. It was better to run in the early morning, it was cooler for one thing and he avoided the strenuous rays of the ever burning sun. It was during his training exercises that he was also able to think more clearly. Coming to terms with his new found fatherhood was still something he was working on. His thoughts were never far from the photo images his wife had sent. He was keen to see new images, to see if this would spark some kind of paternal attachment. For now though, he could only deal with the images he had.

After completing his morning run, he would commence his strength and weight exercises. His motivation to do this whilst his colleagues slept was admired. He had maintained his strength and physical fitness throughout his army days and was proud of his ability to stay toned and ready for anything that was going to come his way. Coming to terms with his own conscience however, was something he could not be proud of.

The temperature in Singapore varied only slightly between 25 to 28 degrees centigrade the whole year round. Most of the army lads during duty hours and working days wore only shorts and footwear.

The first months in Singapore passed without incident. Most of the time was work related as Singapore started to regain its own social character. Cinemas and amusement parks were starting to come back to life after falling silent during the Japanese occupation. There were several cinema halls within Singapore, each trying to attract not only the locals, but the Allied forces as well. The military had money to spend and the amusement park proprietors wanted some of these rich pickings. Areas such as Tanjong Pagar Road adjacent to the docks had started to bustle with a way of life which originated almost a century before. The thousands of Indians and Chinese workers who relied on the docks for work had left an indelible mark on the landscape. This mosaic of colourful street life with shops and brothels was beginning the slow return to the local community, where it belonged.

At the end of a very long hot sticky week, working in and around the dock area, Callon, Steve and two other friends, Don and Mike decided to visit one of the amusement parks and sample the atmosphere these arena's were creating. Other colleagues had shared their experiences of visiting these parks and the small group were keen to sample this for themselves.

Don Markham and Mike Radley both worked on the docks with Callon. They were a couple of likely lads from opposite ends of England. Don was from Newcastle and Mike was from London. Although he was not a 'true' cockney, he portrayed himself as such. Both were involved with the unloading of the ships as they brought important goods and provisions onshore. Don and Mike had had problems with some heavy lifting gear close to where the huge ships docked and needed help from the local men to assist in putting the problem right. The first Callon heard were raised voices as the two

Englishmen held a local Singaporean worker up against a wall threatening him with violence. Four other local men were agitated and looked to join in the argument and support their colleague. The local men had no idea what was happening because neither side understood what was being said. Callon intervened as the situation was about to get out of control. Without hesitation, he thrust himself into the middle of the fracas and asked the local men to back off, speaking instructions in their native tongue. Don and Mike stood watching the chain of events with open mouths as he brought the altercation to rest. It was soon under control when each side recognised what they needed to do. This short introduction to Don and Mike was the start of a friendship which would last the duration of their stay in Singapore.

The allied forces had found the amusement parks their preffered choice of evening entertainment. They were also popular, because it provided female entertainment in the form of dancing. It was local dancing, but any chance to see or hold a woman close up, was considered worth it. The amusement parks were huge facilities, providing both family and adult entertainment. Great World, Happy World and New World, were all emerging entities and competing against each other, trying to bring variety to its paying customers with sport and film as well as dancing. Singapore was beginning to enjoy itself after the occupation. People had work now, and money, and they wanted to spend it. A large black cloud had descended on Singapore during this time of occupation, but now the sun was beginning to shine in more ways than one on this small slip of land.

'Are you out of your mind, Callon? I'm not going to let you do this,' bellowed Steve. Don and Mike were also trying frantically to talk him out of his stupid actions. Steve was pulling his arm in a gesture to get his friend out of the arena. 'He'll screw your bloody head off, now come on let's get back to camp. These guys are professionals and they'll hurt you. They do this all the time. It's cheap entertainment and you're going to be the one providing it.'

He stood his ground, adamant that his actions were not stupid.

'I'm going to have a go at this,' he said, 'trust me; I wouldn't do it if I thought I couldn't handle myself.'

'Have you done this before?' said Steve.

'Yes,' he said in reply to the group, which surprised every one of them. 'It's a long story. I haven't done it under competition rules, but I know this sport.'

'It's not a sport,' said Steve. 'This is barbaric. Did you see those guys; they were tearing lumps off each other. Come on, Callon; let's get out of here before it's too bloody late.'

Steve's mind went back all those months when his friend volunteered himself to fight the boxing trainer, but he knew this was different. It required a different kind of skill.

'How long is it since you wrestled?' asked Mike, doubting that he could actually wrestle at all?

'It's been a while, but it's never left me, I can still remember the holds and the throws. Don't worry, I've had some training, I'm in great physical shape. I'll be fine.'

'How long ago, tell me, how long is it since you last wrestled?' Steve was trying frantically to talk his friend down.

'I don't remember exactly, about two years back I suppose, just before I joined the army. What you should know is that my tutor in those days, was one of the best in the country.'

Steve shook his head and looked straight at him before replying. 'I hope you know what you're doing, buddy; I don't want to carry you back to the camp on a bloody stretcher.'

'You won't be doing that, I assure you,' he said, with a glint in his eye. He saw this as a means to earn some extra money.

Bloody hell, he thought to himself, just like my father did all those years ago.

The Great World Arena was situated on Kim Seng Road in the heart of the city. This venue for wrestling was to become more than that for Callon. This amusement park, built in the 1920's had a wide variety of other entertainment. It was well known for its *Bangsawan or Malay opera* performances as well as several cinema and dance halls. It also had one of few night clubs in Singapore, 'The Flamingo.'

With the demise of the Japanese stranglehold, these amusement centres were beginning to come back to life after falling silent for the past three years.

He and his three friends had arrived at the Great World venue with the intention of dancing. Their enthusiasm soon evaporated when they realised they had to pay the ladies to dance. As the group exited the dance hall, their attention was attracted by wild cheering and clapping coming from another corner of the amusement park. Their curiosity got the better of them as they wandered further into the park and followed the noise.

'Come on you three, let's see what all this excitement's about.' Callon was leading the group across a grassed area to a huge hall where the noise was emanating from. He had a good idea what was creating all this mayhem, but he wanted his friends to see it too. He wanted to work out how good the sportsmen on show actually were. He had a burning ambition within him, which he had spoken to no one about. As they approached the entrance to the hall, the shouting and clapping became louder and more intense.

'What the hell's going on here?' asked Don, wanting to find the cause of this frenzied activity. Within seconds, the group would learn that a live wrestling bout was underway. They paid their few dollar entrance fees, and went inside. A haze of blue cigarette smoke welcomed the group as they adjusted their vision to their new surroundings. The smoke climbed slowly and swirled up against an unlit ceiling. Beyond this haze of smoke, their eyes were attracted to the ring which was positioned central to the hall and emblazoned with light. The huge bank of lights illuminating this spectacle, were suspended high, directly above the ring on long chains. Several thousand people were enjoying the wrestling with a great deal of animated enthusiasm. There were people standing on their chairs and gesturing at the two men battling their wits against each other. Both men were European looking, but it transpired that one was American and the other was an Australian.

The American was using a combination of throws and holds to try to weaken his opponent. At this stage, the Australian wrestler was having little success. He was smaller and giving away a good stone in weight advantage to his opponent. Callon was mesmerised as he watched every move and hold with great interest.

Brief surges of activity saw both men produce acrobatic throws and kicks with punishing consequences for the recipient. Movement and turn of speed was electrifying as the wrestlers used the ropes as momentum to gain power and speed against their opponent. As the bell was sounded to indicate the end of the round, both wrestlers received warm applause from the knowledgeable crowd. This was entertainment, the likes of which, he or his friends had ever witnessed previously.

The crowd appeared to favour the Australian, and he wondered if it was because he was the underdog, disadvantaged because of the weight disparity.

This renewed support for the smaller wrestler was beginning to make a difference. The tide was turning and the American wrestler was tiring rapidly and wanted to bring a swift end to the proceedings. He hurled himself into the ropes and rebounded towards the centre of the ring, to collide fully with the Australian. He had prepared himself to shoulder charge and take his opponent out completely for a knock out. He had not anticipated the agility and speed of thought of his opponent though. A millisecond before colliding with his full weight, the Australian dropped onto his haunches, then sprung up immediately afterwards. The American unable to adjust his position, was catapulted high into the air and landed awkwardly on his back, trapping his arm in the process. The American was unable to get back onto his feet and was counted out.

The whole thing happened so quickly, the speed and the excitement of the contest captivating. Callon could not believe the frenzy which the audience had whipped up. From the corner of his eye, he observed his three friends; they were also animated over the proceedings, hardly believing the physicality of the sport and to some extent its brutality.

Another bout followed and the frenzied pandemonium continued. This contest was over when one of the wrestlers had his opponent beaten by two consecutive submissions. The victor of this contest was a large stocky man with huge hands and a considerable waistline. He stepped into the centre of the ring to jeers and shouts as he waved his arms aloft. The crowd didn't like this man. He was a dirty fighter and would do anything to beat his opponent. He was clearly not the spectator's favourite. The booing continued when the triumphant wrestler went back to the centre of the ring to gesticulate to the crowd disgusted at his treatment from the floor of spectators. He started waving and shouting loudly at the people close to the ringside to come in to the ring and have a go for themselves. There was a short discussion between the referee and the wrestler.

The referee took hold of the microphone from one corner and

announced to the crowd that Jonny Eagle, an American, would take on all-comers. This was an offer to anyone in the audience who fancied their chances to wrestle against him. Callon stood up instinctively and thought about the challenge. He had seen two contests now, and felt he could make something of this. He'd witnessed nothing which he thought he couldn't handle.

I could do this, he thought, what are you waiting for!

He waved both his hands high above his head and accepted the challenge from the American, much to the annoyance of his friends. Loud whoops of support went up all around the arena as the spectators realised they had an extra wrestling match. He was surrounded by his colleagues eager to talk him out of his stupid, split second, decision.

'This is one mean bastard, Callon, he will hurt you, don't do this, what have you got to prove?' Steve was concerned that his stupidity would leave him with a broken limb at best or a broken neck at worst. He knew Callon's strength and fitness was without question, but to compete at this level was crazy. He was ushered away quickly by one of the wrestling marshals, recognising that his mates could quickly make him change his mind. His friends' shouts and protest went unheard and ignored, even though they felt he was putting himself in danger. Newcomers attempting to wrestle, very often, were one of the highlights of the evening, so getting this man away from his friends, was a priority for the Singapore wrestling promoters.

The changing room was large and busy with wrestlers and their respective entourage. Hooks on walls cluttered with clothing, discarded shoes lying on the floor were waiting to be retrieved by their rightful owner. Brightly coloured dressing gowns, full length on men he did not know, but whose names were spelled out in appliqué on their backs. A strong smell of oils and balms to be massaged into aching and sore limbs, wafted through the room. The showers were communal, personal privacy was protected by a wall which was only four feet high. There were two changing rooms, one for the wrestler whose name appeared on the contest sheet first and was the favourite. The changing room which he stood in was for the challenger. The intention was that any two wrestlers fighting together would not see each other before the contest started. He was shepherded to one side of the room by one of the stewards and introduced to a smartly dressed Asian gentleman in an immaculately turned out dinner jacket. His name was Kazar and he was the wrestling promoter.

He shook his hand warmly and spoke to Kazar in Malayan. The promoter was impressed and greeted him by the friendliest of hand shakes and welcomes. Kazar reverted to English hoping to similarly impress his new acquaintance. His English was excellent, unlike most Singapore-Chinese, he hardly had an accent. Kazar was a sophisticated gentleman and oozed charisma. He was different to the Singaporean people he had met previously. He also recognised that Singapore was not just a one class society; Kazar was living proof of that fact. In the background, another contest was underway, and the thunderous noise from the competition floor was heaping itself into the changing rooms. Callon felt that he could touch the atmosphere as he soaked up the cheering and jeering.

Kazar studied the young man standing in front of him with huge interest. He now had his shirt off and Kazar could see for himself the superbly toned physique of this fine specimen. Kazar knew instinctively that a 'diamond,' had just walked into his life. He stood and smiled broadly, his teeth appearing whiter against the contrast of his coffee coloured complexion.

'What's your name, kid?'

'My name is Callon, and I'm not a kid.' Kazar smiled a broad grin again and liked the attitude of his new find. In that fleeting moment, a friendship was forged which would have both amazing and devastating consequences for him. Kazar asked him in a calm and reassuring manner.

'Have you wrestled before, kid? Oh sorry, look, I don't know where that kid thing came from?'

'Yes,' he answered confidently and letting the kid reference go, 'but it was about two years ago. I was taught as a schoolboy to wrestle in my home town, back in the UK.' Before he could continue, Kazar shot back with some alarm.

'As a schoolboy?' he said, 'but this is not schoolboy stuff, this is for real and against grown men. Do you think you are up to the challenge?'

'I wouldn't be here if I thought otherwise. I trained after I left school until I got my army call up papers. My trainer was one of the best.' He hesitated for a second then continued. 'I still remember the moves and the holds.' He hoped that this statement was going to convince Kazar of his wrestling credentials.

'The man who challenged you out there, do you know anything about him?' asked the promoter.

'I've just seen him wrestle, that's all I know, and his name, I know that now, It's Jonny, Jonny Eagle!'

'He's a wily old campaigner,' said Kazar, 'and he's with the American navy. He hurts people, especially if he is put under pressure. I don't expect you will be able to do that on this occasion.' Kazar raised an eyebrow waiting for a reply.

'Let's see,' he said positively.

'Look, I want you to be careful out there. The spectators love to see this type of contest, but we don't want anyone getting hurt, this isn't our intention, but sometimes it happens. Jonny's a very strong man and he tries to fight using his rules sometimes. Because you're a newcomer, no one's expecting a lot of wrestling technique. Stay close to the ropes as much as possible, if he gets hold of you, you have some protection at least.' Kazar was trying to protect what could be his new protégé. 'Try to keep him at arm's length as much as possible. I know this will be difficult. He's no respect for his opponents, no matter how experienced or inexperienced they are.' Kazar looked into the young man's eyes and saw no fear, but needed to emphasise his next words. 'Remember, kid, he fights dirty.'

He compared his situation to the boxing bouts he had experienced in the UK during his initial training. Of course, he had come a long way since then. This was different, he was fighting in front of a crowd who had paid good money to be entertained and secondly, it's more difficult to stay out of trouble wrestling. You can ride a punch, but you cannot ride someone squeezing the life out of you or twisting your arm where it doesn't want to go.

He looked at Kazar, unfazed by his advice and said rather cockily,

'Do you know what we do with Jonny's back in the UK?'

'No,' surprised by the question.

'We cover our dicks with them.'

Kazar laughed out loud and slapped him on the back. He had a good feeling about this young man.

The steward, who introduced him to Kazar minutes earlier, arrived back with a pair of wrestling trunks and boots.

'Try these on, they should fit. Then take some time practising holds and throws with one of these guys.' He pointed to a coloured wrestler. 'Hey, Hassan, show this guy a few holds and moves will you, he's about to face, Jonny Eagle?' Hassan was a large man, completely bald and fierce looking with tattoos up either arm. 'You've about twenty minutes before you wrestle.' said the Steward. 'Go easy on Hassan though, he bruises easily.' The steward chuckled at his own joke expecting that he would not be taking this seriously. How wrong he was.

That steward may have to eat his own words, thought Callon.

Kazar was still in the changing room, he and several other wrestlers were watching Callon with interest. The wrestling trunks only served to accentuate his physique. He had a very narrow waist extending to a V shape to his shoulders with exceptional pronounced body and arm muscle. Legs were long and powerful with great definition on his thighs and calf. His hair was full, dark, and combed back straight. He had smouldering dark eyes. He was exceptionally good looking, thought Kazar. If this kid could wrestle, he would have the full package here. He was still only 19, so his prospects in this exciting sport were incalculable.

He cut a formidable figure as he sauntered across to Hassan the Indian wrestler who would test his basic skills. There was no time to do anything else; he only had minutes to prepare. He was not afraid of the man he was about to face. Overweight and unfit, he thought. In terms of outright strength, he would back himself against anyone who he had seen in the ring so far.

Whilst driving around Singapore, he had spotted the wrestling placards and posters pasted on walls, windows and posts, advertising the contests. It had occurred to him then, that he fancied having a go if ever the opportunity arose. He could not believe it when Jonny Eagle, foul mouthed and shouting profanities, asked for all-comers to wrestle him. His thoughts returned to his training days with Freddie Wilson as a 16 year old, he showed a great deal of class, strength and dexterity then. He was much bigger and heavier now, of course. Wilson had insisted that stamina was as important as style. Regular training runs were an important part of the whole package. A successful wrestler needed stamina to assist his strength in getting holds on his opponent, and just as important, getting out of holds. Usually getting out of holds required greater strength, because, the advantage of the hold was always in the hands of the aggressor. He was in excellent shape however, and had both strength and stamina. He would be a handful for Jonny Eagle that was for sure.

You can do this, I know you can, he said. Think about your strategy and take him by surprise, remember he will not be expecting anything from you. Volunteers who do this sort of thing are never expected to win...made a fool of, yes, but they never win...do they?

'Why didn't we stop him?' asked Steve, looking round at Don and Mike. He was biting his nails and expecting the worse. 'The American wrestler Jonny Eagle will break him in two. I have a bad feeling about this.'

'Have confidence, Steve.' Don was trying to look on the positive side. 'Callon will be no pushover, he trains every day and he seems to know what he's doing; after all, he's strong and has some experience at least.'

'He doesn't train for wrestling, though. Yes, he's fit and he's strong, but did you see how those guys laid into each other? I thought they were going to tear each other apart.' Mike jumped into the conversation but needed to shout above the noise of the arena.

'It's too late for all this; we can't do anything about it now. Let's get ready to give him some great support when he walks out.' Mike was trying his best to remain calm and composed. In desperation, he shouted to his friends, 'hopefully the referee will protect him anyway.'

There was a tremendous atmosphere in the hall and a palpable anticipation. The spectators were a mix of Allied servicemen and a large smattering of the local population. It was only occasionally that the halls asked all-comers to wrestle, but volunteers usually had had too much to drink and provided more comedy than fight. These volunteers presented no issues or problems for the wrestler concerned and were soon overwhelmed by superior holds, speed of execution and their superior strength and skill. Callon was as sober as a judge when he put his hands in the air. His decision to take the challenge was not affected by any alcohol induced state of mind. He would be a different proposition to any other volunteer these spectators had seen previously.

The hall was brought to silence by the wrestling announcer. He introduced Callon as a newcomer and a wrestling unknown, a volunteer weighing in, just less than 200 pounds, and representing the British Army. He had not expected or anticipated that last remark, he was there for himself, he thought. No, he would do this for his new son, this would give him the strength and determination he needed. He wanted to have this connection more than anything. It would be the catalyst he required to bond and take his responsibilities seriously. He was then escorted from the safety of his changing room to the ring in the centre of the hall to great applause. He'd never experienced anything quite like this before as the scene around him erupted. He felt his pulse rise up to the noise around him and was surprised at the level of support afforded to him. He had borrowed a dressing gown from the changing room; it didn't have a name on the back and it was for someone shorter in stature. For the time being, he was wrestling as an unknown, but he was sure he could become someone, if only he could pull this short contest off. He stood in the corner looking a little overawed by the reception. He waved to his friends who were now only a few rows back from the ringside. They'd been given permission to move closer to the action. The steward who had escorted him away from his friends, were taken aback when he returned and offered the alternative seating arrangements.

'These seats are the best in the house,' said the steward to Callon's three friends. 'You'll have a good view of your colleague from here. He's practicing out back. He looks in good shape.'

'We want him back in good shape too,' said Steve.

'Don't worry about your friend,' said the steward, 'referee keep eye on him. Should be over in first round anyway, always same with Jonny Eagle.'

'Will the referee protect him?' said Steve looking worried.

'Yes, but you can never tell, Jonny is a very tough man and he fights rough too. He has no problem to hurt opponent, even if he's new.'

'That's all we needed to hear,' said Mike.

His tuition with the Indian wrestler Hassan had gone well. They practised on a surface similar to the main ring in terms of its feel under foot and flexibility. This ring was without ropes though, but good enough for the purpose it served. It was used for wrestlers to warm up on and practise throws and holds. The Indian had great strength and good overall wrestling acumen, but he surprisingly, matched him. He practised a few holds and throws and was pleased with his execution. He was rusty, but that was to be expected. What was important, he had maintained the technique, this had not deserted him. He recognised that he was a complete novice and was not going to beat his opponent in skill terms, but he was a quick learner. He felt good, he felt strong, and he felt the adrenalin rush. This would only add to his overall performance.

The atmosphere in the hall was building nicely when the announcer barked for order and introduced Jonny Eagle. Jonny was almost a stone heavier than he was, but a much stouter individual. The announcer mentioned that the US navy wrestler Jonny Eagle had not been beaten in his last six contests. Callon viewed his opponent as he entered the ring. He was much older, he guessed about 30, but was slightly smaller in height. His frame was solid with large tree trunk thighs and thick upper arms. His belly button was the one redeeming feature; it distinguished where his chest started and where his waist began. Booing erupted from all around the hall and spectators were up shouting their disapproval of Jonny Eagle. He certainly had the support of everyone, but did he have the knowhow to out manoeuvre this hulk of a man?

He was not sure if he could beat the man facing him. Jonny was scowling, shouting obscenities at him and edging closer to his corner, trying to intimidate him. The referee intervened and Jonny put his huge frame into reverse but continued his tirade whilst never releasing his stare. Jonny was not expecting this contest to last more than a round, a couple at the most, they never did. He quickly went through his own positives. He was strong, he was younger, he was probably quicker, he was fitter for sure and the added plus, there was a referee.

The referee had spoken to him briefly before he left the confines and safety of his changing room. He said he would keep his eye on him bearing in mind his inexperience. He would not accept any foul play from Jonny. If he thought he was in trouble or pain, he would step in and stop the contest immediately.

He did a quick review of his chances against his recognised and experienced opponent. The minuses were fewer, he had no experience of wrestling at this level; his skill was unknown and untried in this atmosphere. Youth, strength, fitness and some wrestling technique were in his favour though, and he would display this with unabated aggression. He wasn't going to make a fool of himself, that he was certain of. He would go away from this contest giving his all. Giving his all for his son!

He thought about his father as well and his face came immediately to his mind. He looked up into the lights before focusing his eyes on Jonny, and wondered what his father would have done in these circumstances. In that instant, he decided what his strategy would be.

Jonny was whipping the crowd up from his corner, raising his fists aloft and shaking them at the spectators. He was not looking for support; he wanted to be the unpopular bad guy that nobody liked. He wanted the crowd to hate him. It would make his success against his 'nobody opponent' all the sweeter.

Only three rounds of five minutes each would be allowed. From past experience, this was more than enough for the wrestler to get a submission. It was not a scheduled contest, only one submission would be allowed and not the customary two. The other scenario of course was a knock out, but he quickly dismissed this from his thoughts.

Just before the bell rang for the start of the first round, he looked around the hall soaking up the applause offered to him and he liked the feeling. The adrenalin rush was still with him and he felt an invincible cover around himself like a protective coating. It was like a warrior would feel going into battle with a suit of armour, fitted for his personal protection. He had to be vigilant, and not show his Achilles heel, unsure if he even had one? Then he remembered his father's words;

'There will always be someone out there better than you; you just have to recognise that person when he appears.' Kazar the promoter was ringside in the front row and raised his hand to acknowledge him as the bell rang.

The two men facing each other across the ring prepared their approach. He watched his opponent intently; he didn't want any sudden surprises. Jonny would be the one surprised, he thought, because he would not anticipate what he had in mind. Both men closed the gap with arms raised and hands outstretched with fingers splayed. Their hands would come into contact and lock. This would immediately let each other know the other's strength potential. This did not happen though; a split second before any contact, Callon dropped his right hand and dipped his shoulder thrusting it into Jonny's body with his full weight, ripping into his solar plexus. The gasp from Jonny could be heard all around the hall as the wind from his stomach was exhausted into the smoky atmosphere. He had left this very vulnerable area of his body exposed. This area protects a network of nerve tissues and fibres at the front of the stomach. Jonny was hurt and winded. He went back towards the ropes, and using them as a cushion landed on his knees in the middle of the ring.

The referee started to count animatedly, not expecting this scenario.

As the seconds ran down, he reflected remembering his father's great advice, 'Make sure you hit your opponent before he hits you. This way you gain the momentum and the initiative.'

Jonny Eagle had not expected the downright absurdity of his opponent and the element of surprise. He had decided that he was going to meet fire with fire. Attack from the start and remain aggressive and give the spectators what they want to see and more besides.

Jonny raised one knee off the floor and was trying desperately to get oxygen into his aching lungs. The referee was viewing him with concern as he continued his count. The round was barely seconds old!

He raised his other knee slowly from the floor as he crouched on his toes in a foetal position with his hands outstretched on the floor. He stood upright, using all his strength just before the count of ten from the referee.

Callon seized his moment and prevented his opponent gaining back any of the initiative. He grabbed Jonny's free arm, and whipped it behind his back into an arm lock. Jonny's strength was not sufficient to prevent the hold, stretching his pectorals and shoulder joint beyond their intended limits immobilizing the arm. In the same movement he took Jonny's feet from under him with a strong sweep of his leg. Falling backwards onto his shoulder, Jonny took the full weight of his body. Still gasping for breath, he rolled onto his stomach and turned a full 360 degrees. He remained on the canvas for a count of eight. The spectators joined in with the counting as if it were a children's game.

He spotted Kazar the promoter, stood with his hands apart above his head with his mouth partly open, disbelieving what he was seeing. The contest was less than a minute old, and Jonny Eagle had been on the canvas for two counts already.

Jonny used the ropes to pull himself up onto his feet. He held the ropes to allow himself precious seconds of recovery time. The jeers from the crowd were getting louder and only provided more encouragement for Callon. Jonny looped his damaged arm around the top rope and rubbed it vigorously with his free hand. He then held his flat hand out like a policeman on traffic duty wanting the oncoming vehicles to stop. Callon was dancing on his toes as his opponent bought more time. Jonny was still a dangerous individual and was looking for instant revenge. He knew that Jonny Eagle was waiting for the smallest opportunity to retaliate and hurt him.

Jonny was talking loudly to himself as he played for time holding the ropes.

'No bloody novice is going to out wrestle me,' he said, with pure hatred in his eyes. He rubbed his aching gut, but he was beginning to recover as he gulped air. Jonny needed to get hold of his unknown quarry and let him feel the power of his strength. Up to now, he had hardly had a chance to lay a finger on him.

Steve, Don and Mike were amazed at the audacity of their young friend and were standing waving arms and shouting wildly with the rest of the spectators.

'What did I tell you guys, he can take care of himself,' said Don.

'It's still too early, but I sure feel better about his chances now.' Steve was on his feet shouting his encouragement.

Jonny was cradling his arm as though in a sling. He was feigning injury as he went down on one knee to another count by the referee. He needed Callon to be closer. His next move would be decisive and instant. Jonny sprung at him from his crouched position and they both headed towards the ropes. Jonny with all his strength and know how, was able to turn his opponent and apply a headlock as they used the ropes to arrive in the centre of the ring. Jonny was now talking and dragging him around the ring and shouting obscenities.

'I'm going to bloody well throttle you,' he said, as he tightened his vice like grip and rubbed Callon's face with his free hand. The headlock was starting to cut off his air supply, this was illegal, but this was how Jonny Eagle played the game. He was turning his opponent away from the referee to avoid him seeing the distress. He didn't want to release his grip; he wanted his opponent to weaken; cutting his air supply for some time would achieve this. Callon was weighing up his options, he knew he had to do something quickly, his head was about to burst.

'You're not so funny now, boyo,' shouted Jonny through clenched teeth.

He knew Jonny would have to readjust his hold at any moment as he moved frantically to get free. He could feel the grip slackening as he wriggled his body from side to side, then up and down.

He instinctively felt the readjustment and threw himself onto the canvas bringing Jonny down at the same time. He exploded from his hold as Jonny's elbow hit the floor. The American was astounded by the speed and execution of his opponent's move only to find himself on the floor and on his backside. Callon's timing was slightly off and he missed applying a few classic holds, but he knew this would come with a little more experience and some tutoring.

Jonny knew he would have to get dirty, really dirty now. He had had enough of this no name character, taking the piss, literally. He back heeled Callon whilst he was attempting a half Nelson, catching him fair and square in the crutch with his boot. He saw stars momentarily, winded and realising his mistake in not protecting his most delicate of regions.

The bell rang for the end of the first round.

Jonny Eagle refused to go to his corner and was mouthing off. Callon grabbed him by the throat at arms length and pushed him backwards before the referee intervened. The young wrestler had decided he wasn't going to be pushed around.

He added his voice to the throng. 'Try that again if you dare?'

'And what are you going to do about it, Sonny?'

'I'll break your fucking leg, that's what.' The two men came together again, the referee trying his best to keep them apart.

'Let's see how good you are in the next round? You'll wish you'd stayed at home, soldier.'

Jonny hadn't been expecting such aggression from someone with so little wrestling experience. Normally, his opponent cowered in his corner after the first round not wanting to take further part, but he realised he had a different kind of opposition today.

The Indian wrestler, Hassan, who helped him prepare for this short contest was acting as Callon's second. He flicked water into his face before sitting him down. The water stung on contact, but refreshed him all the same. His ears were ringing due to the exertion from Jonny's grip, he felt as though he had left them behind when he exited that headlock. He took water from the bottle and gulped an amount down before spitting some into a bucket. The water was bloodstained; the headlock had serrated the inside of his cheek against his teeth as he fought frantically to free himself.

'You're doing okay,' said the Indian, 'but be aware, he'll take any advantage he can, and by whatever means. This man's still very dangerous. You're too inexperienced to deal with his trickery yet.'

The bell for the second round rang and both wrestlers came together. Callon had to regain the initiative; he too could play dirty if necessary. Finesse would come later, for now though, he was only interested in stopping his opponent and being ultra aggressive. He grabbed the outstretched arm Jonny was trying to protect and yanked it in its sockets, then, pressed it up his back as far as it would go and rammed him into the ropes at full stretch, tripping him as he rebounded onto his back. He retreated to think about his next move. Because of his inexperience, he wasn't instinctively thinking about his next attack in advance and what he was going to do.

Jonny got to his feet.

'Going to break my leg are you, *boy*,' he said dismissively making a disparaging reference to his young opponent.

He was caught flat footed and was not able to sidestep as Jonny used the rope to accelerate his approach towards him and apply a bear hug. Once again, Callon took the move down on the canvas and was able to break the hold. Jonny was restricted by this tactic unable to press home his superior advantage over his opponent. In a turn of extraordinary speed with both men down, Jonny seized the opportunity to apply a neck scissor movement and managed to get a leg either side of his head. He was able to cross his legs to apply the hold and exert huge pressure. He immediately felt the compression of his throat and started to stand up using his considerable strength, while still in hold. Jonny was lifted five foot from the floor which brought him into a sitting position balanced precariously on Callon's shoulders. The crowd were going berserk and could not believe the strength of this young man. In order to escape from this crippling hold, he simply fell forward with Jonny's legs strapped around his neck. Jonny immediately let go as he fell awkwardly on his shoulder, neck and head with his opponent on top of him. He immediately jumped on Jonny's back and in the same movement applied a Japanese strangle-hold. He grabbed his wrists, crossing them under his chin, after rolling him on his front. Jonny was now gurgling and out of the game and concussed. He pulled to exert more pressure with his knee in the centre of his back. He wanted his quarry weak and he wanted Jonny stood up now. Keeping the Japanese strangle hold, he hauled him bodily into an upright position and ran at the ropes letting go just before contact. Jonny catapulted over the ropes and landed on his back at the feet of Kazar sat in the ringside seats. Jonny was counted out by the referee. It was apparent that he had sustained a serious injury. He was stretchered back to the dressing room and transferred to hospital for treatment. It would be many weeks before Jonny Eagle would be goading an audience and asking for volunteers to fight him, and it would only be days before Callon had a name on the back of his own silk dressing gown.

'That was some performance out there tonight, kid. You impressed a lot of people, but tell me, where did you learn to wrestle like that?' Kazar was speaking to Callon back in his office at the Great World arena.

'I told you, back in my home town in the UK. My father made sure that I had all the best tuition when it came to looking after me. This was not done for competition though, more for survival.'

'Well, let me tell you, your father did a great job in achieving that. The guy you dumped out of the ring tonight is one of my top wrestlers. You made mincemeat out of him. He won't wrestle again for some months. He's at the hospital; I think his arm's broken.'

'He's lucky it wasn't his leg. That man upset me tonight; you were right, he plays dirty, but he got what was coming to him.'

'Your destruction and demolition job on Jonny Eagle leaves me with a little dilemma.' Kazar was wondering how to approach the next part of the discussion without frightening the young man away. Never in his whole life had he seen such dominance and power in a young man. Kazar pulled out a wad of US dollar bills and slid five 20 dollar notes across to his side of the table; he watched his eyes light up as he stared at the notes for a few seconds. 'For you, kid, take it.'

Without any hesitation, the bills were shoved into his pocket. 'This is only the start, there's a lot more where that came from.'

He sat upright in the leather chair across from Kazar to listen intently to what he had to say next.

'I want you to consider this. I'd like you to join my team of all-in wrestlers.' He paused, leaning back into his quilted leather swivel chair before continuing. Kazar was looking for any outward signals Callon may be giving away. There weren't any of course, he was an ice cool customer, and he waited for the wrestling promoter to continue. 'I'll pay you 200 dollars a week, plus 200 more every time you win.' Callon tried to remain calm as he digested what was being said. He took a moment to look at his surroundings, a fancy office with expensive décor and furniture. Water coloured scenes of a primitive Singapore from days gone by. This amount of money was unimaginable and many times more than his paltry army wages.

'Okay,' said Kazar, not waiting any longer for a reply, 'I'll make it 250 dollars a week plus 250 if you win. How does that sound?'

He had not hesitated purposely; he just wanted to savour what had just been said to him. This was an offer no man in his right mind could refuse, thought Callon.

'I like your offer, but I'm in the army, I'm a soldier, I don't see how this would work.'

'Who's your CO?' asked Kazar.

'Major Reece,' replied Callon. Kazar picked up his pen and scribbled the name on a leather bound pad.

'Which base are you on and where do you carry out your duties?'

'My company unit is on the Orchard Road site, but I spend most of my day working on the docks moving supplies around the place.'

Kazar's ears pricked up. 'Which docks do you work on?' There were several in Singapore, but Kazar was only interested in one, he felt his pulse racing, hardly able to contain himself.

'The Empire Dock mainly, but I have access to all of them.'

'You speak to your CO and I will speak to my contact. There should be no problem in getting you released from some of your duties.' Kazar was already planning his next move. 'Listen, kid, we need to get you doing some training. You're already very strong and very fit and well versed in wrestling terms, but we need to improve your technique and make you slicker in your execution of moves, throws and holds. We also need to get you measured up for some proper kit. Do we have a deal?' asked Kazar, in a very positive tone.

'Provided I can get time off to train and wrestle, we have a deal.' They shook hands as Kazar's face lit up. He beamed, displaying his brilliant white teeth and thinking he had just cut a deal which would make him a great amount of money, both inside and outside of the wrestling ring.

'A name, we need a name for you?' Kazar looked at his surname written on the leather pad and studied it for a moment. Before looking at the young man sat opposite, he said, 'that's it, 'that's it; I've got it,' banging his desk in triumph at coming up with a name so quickly!

Chapter 10

The telephone rang in the Colonel's office; it was mid afternoon in Singapore. He had just returned from Malaysia on an unofficial visit to see Sultan Ibrahim Iskander Al Masyhur ibni Abu Bakar, better known as the Sultan of Johor. Johor is the southernmost region of Malaysia and attached to Singapore by a long sliver of road known as the causeway. The causeway and the stretch of water it crosses are known as the Johor Straits and the only thing that divides the two countries. A five minute drive is all it takes to pass from the border of Singapore to the Johor border. The Colonel had met the Sultan several months back during the signing of the Japanese surrender ceremony and they had become close friends due to a passionate mutual interest. The Sultan, one of the richest men in the world, and a man who wanted to become much richer than he already was. The Colonel just wanted to get rich. They both had a plan as to how they could achieve these ambitions.

'Yes,' barked the Colonel down the phone in his pristine British military accent. Without wasting any time and getting directly to the point he asked abruptly,

'Who is it?'

'Kazar here, Colonel, I've some good news for you, Sir. Following on from our discussion regarding a suitable candidate for the job, I think I have found just the right man.'

'Goooood,' said the Colonel, indicating his pleasure at Kazar and finding someone suitable so soon since their last meeting. 'Do I need to know who it is?' There was a slight pause before Kazar spoke.

'One of your men, Sir.'

'Whaaat?' replied the Colonel, again elongating his words, to express his displeasure this time. 'I thought we agreed it should be a local man, what about the damn language consideration, have you gone out of your bloody mind, man?'

'Sir, he speaks Malayan, not fluently, but probably has enough command of the language already to do what we need. Remember, this job could be many months away yet, so his language skills will be even better by then. In the meantime, we can observe him and watch him at close quarters. This young man introduced himself to me in my native tongue. He spoke to me in Malayan, Colonel.' Kazar's excitement was lost on the Colonel. 'It's better to be prepared well in advance, would you not agree, Sir?'

'If this is an officer, then you really are; stark raving mad, Kazar.' The Colonel could not contain his anger any longer. 'There are already too many officers involved in this operation for my liking anyway.'

'Sir, please, no, he's not an officer, he's a soldier,' blurted Kazar, trying to contain his enthusiasm. 'He's a regular soldier, Sir, but he is an extraordinary young man. More importantly, he has the temperament for this job. He strikes me as not being fazed or frightened by anyone.' Kazar continued to tell the Colonel of how this 'unknown nobody,' entered his wrestling world and how he overcame great odds to throw one of his best wrestling performers out of the ring, breaking his arm in the process.

'What, he speaks Malayan too? He sounds like bloody Superman to me!' Give me the name of this 'unknown nobody' and I'll check him out?'

'Sir, one more thing,' Kazar waited just enough to play his ace card.

'This soldier, Callon, he works on the Empire Docks already and has access to all the other dock locations too. He doesn't have authorised access to the bonded warehouses, but he knows where they all are.'

The Colonel leant back on his chair after putting the telephone down and contemplated Kazar's words. He thought about how this could work. What were the chances of finding such a person who had all the necessary requirements, including the language skills to pull this plan off! The Colonel would take good time to study the name of the soldier he had just written down on his pad. He needed to know everything there was to know about this man, including where he takes a shit.

He picked up the telephone again and dialled.

The junior officer knocked on Major Reece's office door and entered after he had shouted, 'come.' The huge man behind the desk looked up at the young officer as he spoke and offered his salute.

'Sir, Private Callon's here to see you'. He had requested a meeting with the Major through this same junior officer.

'Send him in.' He heard the booming instruction and prepared himself. He was a little apprehensive about asking for 'special privileges.' He would need to ask for time out to train and to hone his wrestling skills as well. Fight nights were usually on Friday or Saturday, so he would need special dispensation from duty at weekends too. It felt like a lot to ask for, after all, he was not doing this just because he enjoyed the experience. It was because of the money. Two hundred and fifty dollars per week plus the same again if he won was the only motivation he needed. This would launch him into the stratosphere in monetary terms. He had already decided that like his father, he was not interested in second prizes. He wanted the full cash bonus as well as his performance fee. What he didn't know, was that the Major had been expecting him. He entered the office and saluted.

'At ease soldier, what is it you want to see me about?' The Major cut immediately to the point, he was not interested in any idle chit chat. 'Tell me, soldier, what's on your mind?'

He explained to the Major that he wanted to join a downtown all-in amateur wrestling team and would require time off from his normal day and weekend duties.

'Give me one good reason why I should grant you this time off, soldier.' The Major wanted to make this as difficult and as painful as he could. He did not want to give the impression that release to wrestle and train was a foregone conclusion. Callon had not anticipated to be asked to give good reasons for his request and did not have a pre-prepared answer ready.

'Sir,' he hesitated, looking for words, anything, he just wanted something to say. Finally he spluttered and said,

'I would be representing the British Army, Sir, the RASC Unit.' He had remembered the announcers few words when he was introduced at the Great World arena as a potential newcomer.

The Major liked his reply, he thought it was commendable. If he was any good of course, it would be good for the morale of the camp and its men. The reality, however was, he would have accepted any reasoning. It was in his interest to allow the man stood across from him special privileges. The Major then asked, 'And what do we get from you in return?'

He was dumfounded by this question, was he looking for free tickets, or something more, he thought?

'Sir,' he asked quizzically, 'what do you mean?' he had his head slightly tilted to one side.

The Major shot back.

'If I grant you this request, I want you to promise your loyalty to me.' The Major paused and studied the young soldier, knowing full well that loyalty would play a much larger part in this arrangement as the weeks and months progressed. 'And your loyalty to this unit also. You keep your nose clean, soldier; I want none of this wrestling stuff to spill over into this camp. Do I make myself understood?'

He was expecting to concede much more than that.

'Yes, Sir, you have my word on that.'

'Speak to my corporal outside and he'll make the arrangements to work around your schedule. One other thing soldier, your work on the docks continues, whatever else happens with your sporting commitments, your official work as a result of this all-in wrestling caper must not suffer, is that clear?'

'Yes, Sir and thank you, Sir, you won't regret your decision.' He saluted, turned and opened the door before coming face to face with the corporal. His new schedule had already been typed out and prepared.

Chapter 11

Callon trained every morning for the next week, working with the regular wrestlers which Kazar had under his wing. Training every day was not unusual for him, but he had a specific purpose to train for now. The afternoons were business as usual down at the docks, overseeing goods arrivals and organising the distribution to the various allied camps which were dotted around Singapore. The training was something which came easy to him. His fitness level, pound for pound was unequalled in the training camp. He was also making great progress with the technical side of wrestling too. His ability to perform the moves, throws, kicks and holds were quickly being accomplished and refined. He remembered the moves and throws which Freddie Wilson had taught him some years previously, how grateful he was at this moment for that tuition. His father's own dedication to ensure his son's safe passage through life was paying off in ways which he could never have dreamed of. As a family, they did not have a lot of money, but what his father had taught him and provided for him was beginning to look priceless. Never did he think for one moment that he would be able to make money doing something he loved so much. It was not until half way through the first week that he realised he could make a living out of this gift, which by pure chance had come his way. His strength, fitness and skills would become his road to better things, he knew that. His own father had done something similar, but for little reward only. His father risked his life and the life of others, taking on all comers in bare knuckle fights in pubs or on street corners. For what, for a pittance, he thought. There were no referees to step in and protect the man getting the beating when his father was plying his trade. Callon relished his new status and he was going to wrestle in his first scheduled bout the coming weekend. He had only a week to prepare for this, but Kazar knew his newly found treasure would have no difficulty in dispensing with his opponent.

Kazar had asked Callon back to his office where he had sat almost a week ago, with his proposition.

'How are you settling into your new life, kid?'

'Things are good, Kaz; I'm ready for my first contest.' Kazar had insisted that he call him Kaz in future. He had also been following his new find very closely, but he needed to know a little more. He also needed to get some further background on his star in the making. He had also introduced him to a personal trainer, a local man. He had little or no command of the English language. With strict instructions from the promoter, he told him that he should speak Malayan to this new wrestler at all times. Kazar needed his new protégé to have good communication skills also in the local language. This was not for wrestling though; this was for a plan on an unimaginable scale.

'I want to show you something, kid.' Kazar stood up from his desk and walked to a narrow wardrobe in the corner of his office. He opened the door and pulled out a full length silk dressing gown, still on its hanger. He held the black dressing gown up high so that his young wrestler could see the full effect. The light caught the sateen finish as it shimmered in the subdued light of Kazar's office.

'What do you think, do you like it?'

'It looks great, is this for me?' Without speaking another word, the promoter turned the dressing gown around and emblazoned in big gold appliqué lettering was 'KID CALLON.' This would be his official wrestling name.

Several months had passed since Callon started his army wrestling career and he was flying high, getting great reviews about his wrestling style and conquests. He had demolished everything and everyone put in front of him up to now. No one had been able to live up to his skill and theatrical performances. He was certainly beginning to make a name for himself. His audience and fan base was growing by the week. Kazar's gut feeling about this young man's potential had far exceeded what he had thought he was capable of. He had gambled in that first meeting, when he first saw Callon as a wrestling novice at The Great World when all comers were asked to fight an experienced wrestler. He realised then that he had an extraordinary sportsman in his presence.

Kazar had immediately put him on top money, and up to now, his gamble was paying off handsomely. He was being challenged each successive week by a wrestler with greater experience. Kazar, even at this early stage in Kid Callon's career, was thinking about the Light Heavy weight Championship of the Far East.

If he continued to progress in this way over the next year, then there was a distinct possibility that this prestigious title and wrestling belt could be his.

A lot of work had been put into his programme already, irrespective if he fought or not, he would do his strength and stamina training every day. He had also perfected many of his hold and kick routines; some of which he had forgotten since his early days of wrestling for fun. Kazar was careful not to push his young star too quickly too soon, but Kid Callon was beginning to earn a reputation which was making other, more senior wrestlers, take notice of.

His technique and approach to wrestling was different and more exciting to watch than anyone else on the circuit. His delivery was one of speed and now included better and very precise execution of holds. His speed at getting out of holds was also acrobatic. He could flip over both front and backwards to escape his captors grip. This left his opponents mesmerised and was often the beginning of their demise. The kid was clearly the fittest man and one of the strongest on the circuit.

One of his other attributes to winning his contests was his aggression. This was raw and was sometimes his downfall. Not in the ring, because this is where it served him best, it was outside. Conflict was happening more and more frequent, as he socialised with his friends in the bars and clubs. These joints were becoming popular again in Singapore and Callon attracted trouble like a magnet. He never went looking for trouble, he didn't need to. It would usually find him. He was becoming a celebrity and this annoyed some people. His reaction to anyone fronting up to him in a conflict was adverse and would usually end up in a brawl. He wanted to distance himself from this, but time and again, there was always one person wanting to have a pop at him.

The bar and clubs clientele were a mixture of Allied service men and the local population. Work situations in Singapore were improving as this once occupied state was slowly returning to a degree of normality. Normality would in fact be years away, but things were moving in a positive direction. Since the surrender of the Japanese, there was more work available, which meant people had more money for leisure activities. For those that could afford it, they grabbed every opportunity they could for their family's pleasure. They had been starved of this commodity for so long during the occupation and were now taking advantage of their freedom. The locals enjoyed been around the Allied forces, and of course, there were women. Wherever alcohol and women were present and the ratio of man to woman was ten to one, then there was always trouble.

Wrestling had awoken in him a tolerance which operated on a short fuse now. He could turn aggressive and be violent at the drop of a hat. This was his escape mechanism in the ring and ultimately the reason behind his new found success. He could control this to some degree when wrestling. If things got out of hand, then the referee would step in anyway and cool things down. Outside of this roped territory however, rules become secondary and could of course be broken. He was very aware of his shortcomings and realised that he was falling into the hands of the perpetrators. Reacting to a slur or a comment and answering back with his fist was not always the correct solution.

Kazar was aware of what was happening outside of Callon's wrestling duties, becoming concerned at his sometimes violent reaction and conduct. His underlings would report anything untoward back to him. He did not want to risk his star performer getting into any business which would bring him in contact with the police; more importantly, something which would take him off the wrestling circuit. He needed his man to be squeaky clean. Some of the bar brawls which Callon and his friends had been involved in had caused damage to furniture and fittings, including mirrors, glasses, and drinks. The cost of damages was always taken care of by Kazar's people but unknown to him.

Kazar could not risk any proportion of blame to land at the feet of his wrestler, not for a few hundred dollars anyway. There was far more at stake than that. Kazar was a very astute man who had tendrils which reached out and stroked many people. People with power and influence and people who would stop at nothing to get what they wanted.

Kazar from his side had spoken to him at length and very forcefully. To risk any kind of injury at this stage in his progress could put his attempt at the Far East Championship at severe risk. He could not afford to get injured or damage a hand or worse. Not at the expense of a few idle words spoken under the influence of drink. Callon needed to channel this pent up aggression and save it for the ring. He was now a high earner after winning all of his bouts so far. He himself did not want to jeopardise or compromise this, and promised to keep himself out of trouble.

Callon had seen his name on posters in small print, advertising upcoming wrestling bouts. He had seen his name increase in size with each success and he liked it immensely. He also started to notice that it was his name printed first, before his challenger. The pendulum had swung so quickly in his direction. It was a train running which he didn't want to stop. Upcoming wrestling contests were now one of the most popular attractions in Singapore and Johor. Posters were stuck on posts and in bars across Singapore advertising these events. In addition, small photographs of himself against his name in wrestling pose were also starting to appear on the posters. Whilst he was not top billing just yet, he could see the print size of his name increasing with every contest where he was successful. His reputation around the army base and in downtown Singapore was also growing as his successes started to add up. Callon was now referred to as 'Kid' wherever he went. It was from his very first meeting that Kazar had referred to him as Kid. The Kid had just turned 20 years of age now and his fighting name was a complete contradiction in terms. The Kid was a man, doing a man's job and beating every man put in front of him. He himself was amazed at how quickly his journey to reach this stage had been. Wrestling every weekend was of course a major contributor to his success, but he had to keep on winning and keep fit to ensure nothing interrupted this run.

Chapter 12

12 months later. June 1947.

Up to now, Kid Callon had fought in each of the three Singapore wrestling locations. Great World was where he made his wrestling debut and where Kazar had his office. The other two locations were the New World and Happy World. These alternative wrestling venues did nothing to change the outcome of his wrestling contests. Callon's wrestling matches were just as successful. Of the many contests he had wrestled in so far, three quarters of his opponents had been beaten by a technical knock out. They had been dispensed out of the ring, either on their heads or on their backsides. Injuries to his opponents were never too serious, but enough for his next challenger to think about. The other contests were won on submissions. Winning by submission for him was somewhat of a disappointment, his speciality was to get his opponent out of the ring by whatever means. The main objective of course was to ensure that they could not get back in. They either didn't want to, or couldn't. This was becoming his 'trade mark.' His spectators and followers were coming to expect this as he progressed through his opponents. They wanted to see the end of his contests with his man on the deck, outside the ring.

From the start of any contest now, his spectators would be chanting, 'out, out, out.'

The contests which ended with a submission were tougher opponents. Whilst he beat them convincingly, they were more determined not to become another one of his statistics. Even with his strength advantage, sometimes it was not possible to achieve his goal of ejecting them out of the ring.

'You're late, Kid, where have you been?' Kazar had been waiting 20 minutes for Callon in his office at the Great World Amusement park. Before he could answer, Kazar spoke again in a raised voice which Callon had not heard previously.

'You know how important this coming weekend is to both of us.'

'Yes, sure, and I will be ready, don't worry.'

'Not if you turn up to training looking like that.' It was Sunday morning after another huge win the previous night at the Happy World Arena. He had fought in this venue, but in contrast to its name, this was his least favourite arena. He could not however explain or give reasons for this. He had been out celebrating with his army colleagues afterwards. The contest had ended like his previous contests with a win. His opponent had ended up outside of the ring unable to get back in. Hassan had suffered a broken bone in his hand, damaged as he caught the corner stanchion of the ring. He felt bad about the injury; he had been wrestling Hassan, whom he considered a friend. Hassan had proved a formidable opponent but could not compete with his speed, dexterity and aggression. Hassan had helped him during that first evening in the Great World Arena. He had given him tips and ideas for some of the moves he would make during that extraordinary night. This counted for nothing now of course, Hassan was his next opponent and he had to dispense of him to progress to the next level. Callon could not afford to let his feelings get in the way of his success. He had to go!

'I want to see you in the ring this morning working on your holds. You won last night, but some of your moves were sloppy.' Kazar lied, but he needed to keep Kid Callon focused. 'We can't afford to waste precious time, next time you're late for my training session, it will cost you, Kid. I will fine you.' Kazar hesitated; he had never had to issue an ultimatum to any of his wrestlers before. 'Are you clear about my instructions?'

He stood with his mouth open. 'You wouldn't do that.'

'Oh yes I would, now go and get ready to train, I have brought men in today, especially to work with you. We need to get you fight ready. Wrestling on consecutive days is a huge undertaking, believe me, and as of now, you are not ready. No further discussion, get kitted up!'

He left Kazar's office without another word and headed for the changing rooms. He was determined to put the men brought in to train him through hell. He would show Kazar who was ready to wrestle or not!

Kazar knew that this upcoming weekend would be a huge test for Kid Callon and he was not prepared to allow complacency to take control. His opponents would also be challengers for the Light Heavyweight Championship of the Far East. Kid Callon was faced with a double header. He would fight on Friday the 13th June at Johor Bahru and again on Saturday the 14th June at the Great World in downtown Singapore. The Great World Arena was by far his favourite wrestling venue. Whenever he fought there, it was to a full house and huge support. Kazar was certainly getting his initial investment back and more besides. Provided Callon could win these contests, he would be amongst the top four wrestlers throughout the Far East and would put the Light Heavyweight Wrestling Championship within his grasp. What he didn't realise at this point; he would top billing in both wrestling contests. His name, spelt out in bold letters on placard sized posters would be displayed throughout Singapore and Johor, Malaysia. His opponent in Johor would be a six foot ten inch giant of a man named Banta Singh from India. Banta Singh was from a dynasty of wrestling brothers. Banta was the eldest of three brothers and the most experienced. They were all fighting on the same circuit. He had only heard of this giant of a man, and had never seen him wrestle, so he only had his reputation to go on. Singh's height advantage troubled him somewhat; he was almost a foot taller. He also had a formidable wrestling record, but unlike Callon had been beaten once before, but that was earlier in his career. Nevertheless, this small chink in Banta Singh's armour was all that Callon needed. If he had been beaten before, then he could be beaten again.

The Johor Bahru Amusement Centre in Malaysia was a huge complex and similar to the ones in Singapore and equally well supported. This venue also hosted dances as well as several cinema halls. Its biggest attraction though was wrestling. It attracted all the big wrestling names. They did not come any bigger than Banta Singh. Johor Bahru was only a 30 minute journey from central Singapore to the hall.

This contest would be ten five minute rounds, so he needed to focus all his efforts on this forthcoming weekend. His second contest to be held on the next day at the Great World was also scheduled for ten five minute rounds. He needed a quick resolution to his contest in Johor particularly. He could not risk this going the distance; otherwise his energy reserves for his second fight against Son of Anaconda on Saturday night would be too draining. Never once did he contemplate losing either of these bouts. His mind was now centred on the coming weekend. The short discussion between himself and Kazar had refocused him and he knew he needed to be in the best shape of his life.

Chapter 13

Callon was not a superstitious man, but the date somehow seemed to prey on his thoughts. Friday 13th June 1947 had a strange feel; his sixth sense told him that this would be no ordinary day. The day was almost over now, he thought, and was thankful that nothing untoward had happened to spoil or interfere with the challenges which he still faced. It was 22.00 hours already and his wrestling contest had gone to plan. He put the negative thoughts to the back of his mind as he prepared to leave the Johor Bahru Arena in Malaysia. Kazar was waiting for him as he exited the changing rooms in this huge hall.

'There's someone I want you to meet,' said Kazar. Callon had seen the gentleman he was about to shake hands with in the audience during his successful defeat of the giant wrestler, Banta Singh. He had also seen him at several of his more recent contests in Singapore. He had seen Kazar speaking to him at the Great World arena, but he wondered why he wanted him to be introduced now. The man was surrounded by a posse of hangers-on paying great attention and detail to his every word. He was exceptionally well dressed in superbly tailored, local attire. His entourage wore a mixture of local and European dress, but all were Malaysian in appearance. The man was very charismatic and charming and spoke excellent English with hardly a hint of accent. He must be someone very important, thought Callon, but he was not offered his name. The handshake was very firm and brisk. It was a handshake that business deals would be made on. No contracts necessary after shaking the hand of this gentleman, he thought.

'I enjoyed your contest tonight,' said the mystery man. 'I thought you handled the tall Indian perfectly, after all, it looked like a mismatch in the beginning, what, with his height and weight advantage and all.'

'Thank you, Sir,' said Callon, unsure how to address such a

distinguished looking gentleman. 'I was pleased with my performance.'

He had totally out wrestled the Indian. Within five rounds he had secured his second submission over the giant. He had wrestled him mostly on the canvas, not allowing his opponents height advantage to dominate the bout. The Indian was strong, but he lacked the kind of agility and movement which Callon was able to exhibit on the canvas. The contest was well supported, with several thousand spectators, all wanting to see a little bit of blood letting. They were also a very vocal and passionate crowd. A couple of the earlier contests involved local young men who were learning to ply their trade, hoping one day to compete at a higher level. He after all, was less than two years into this sport and was held in the highest of esteem by his fellow wrestlers.

The Indian had proved to be clumsy and inhibited by his height. Callon had studied his opponent for some minutes only and watched him step into the ring and stoop awkwardly to bend down. He had once again chosen the correct tactics. It was his intention to get his man on the ground as soon as possible. The big man had a potential back problem and he sought to capitalise on this weakness. He did not hesitate to push his fingers and bony knuckles hard into the vertebrae of the Indian at every opportunity. He could feel the Indian squirming and arching himself backwards as he applied great force into these very vulnerable regions. This was all accomplished out of the sight of the referee. He was not able to remove the giant from the ring, but came very close on a couple of occasions. Some of his fans had travelled across the Causeway from Singapore to support his contest and had urged him to eject his man into the ringside seats. Defeating the Indian made his attempt of the Light Heavyweight Championship of the Far East very real. His reputation was growing with each contest. His skill level within the wrestling fraternity was now at a standard which every wrestler was trying to bench mark. He was introduced as Kid Callon, the RASC thriller-king of the British Army with a strap line which would stay with him in all of his future contests.

'The Untamed White Savage, always hectic and exciting,' said the man with the microphone. From now on, he would be top billing in all of his contests and up to now, undefeated.

'Will you teach me some of your basic moves and holds?' said the mystery man. 'Nothing too complicated you understand.' He was completely taken aback by this most unusual request. This was not what he had expected the man to say; after all he was not a young man. 'I will pay you well for your teaching.'

'Yes, of course I'll show you, but payment won't be…,' the mystery man put his hand up to stop him finishing his sentence. He continued, 'when do you want to start?' thinking it would be next week at the earliest.

'Straight away!' said the man without hesitating for a second. 'There is no time like the present; if that is okay with you of course.' He paused momentarily, looking for a sign of approval.

'Tonight?'

'Yes, why not? I have several residences close by, we could figure something out I'm sure.' Kazar was ushered to come closer. He turned his shoulder to Callon as he asked Kazar to arrange to bring him to a specific address. It was a place that he had never heard of before. He made a mental note of the name which had been mentioned and thought he would find out its location later on. Kazar was to arrange for himself and Kid Callon to be there that evening. It was already late, but he was curious to know what this was all about. He was also curious to know what he would be paid. He had already picked up his appearance fee and his bonus for a win, so he was keen to add to his purse.

Kazar and Callon travelled together in a luxuriously equipped, long black limousine car provided by the man. The car was driven by a chauffeur dressed in a smart black suit, immaculately pressed white shirt and black tie. The outfit was finished off with a traditional flat peaked cap. The man was very British in his dress for the job, with a much tanned complexion. A small grey moustache suggested that the driver was not a young man at least, but heavy and thick set in his build. He also looked as though he could handle himself as he inspected him from his rear seated position in the car. He had thick hairy wrists and fat fingers, wrapped around the steering wheel and biceps which left little space in his jacket sleeves. The driver never spoke during the whole journey. Callon wanted to know about the mystery man from Kazar.

'Who is this man?' he asked.

Kazar was not going to answer any direct questions. He just kept saying that any information about this man, was on a 'need to know' basis and for now, he didn't need to know.

'Why all the secrecy, obviously he is someone very important?'

Kazar refused to be drawn by his wrestler's insistence. 'Just show him some simple moves, Kid, but do not hurt him. Treat him with great respect and he will reward you well for your services.' Callon was suddenly beginning to feel very uneasy about the whole thing. Something was troubling him, but he was unsure of just what it was. He was sure there was more to this than a few wrestling holds. He was not afraid, he could take care of himself; he did this every day. It was the not knowing, that triggered his feeling of uneasiness. It was still Friday 13th, he thought; there were still two hours left in the day, but what could possibly go wrong...?

The sheer opulence of the building and his surroundings were the first thing he noticed. Who lives in a place like this, he thought? Both men were ushered into a room close to the huge entrance hall. As they sauntered into this large room, it contained a table, laden with food that catered for everyone's taste. Whole fish displayed, cooked and presented like a piece of decorated art. Lobsters and Cray fish, looking resplendent, still wearing their armour plated shells took centre stage in the middle of the display. The finest caviar in small glass dishes interspersed with other delicacies; one could only speculate as to their origin.

Callon was sure there was food enough to feed 50 people, but only five people in total were present in the room. Whilst he ran a cursory eye down the table of food, Kazar was speaking in low tones to the other three people. The mystery man was not one of them. The room itself was superbly decorated by frescos and paintings and from a time which Callon could not begin to know. Chairs adorned with gold leaf, with rich velour fabrics and small tables for guests to sit at, whilst taking their food. The food would be helped on its way by the finest pink champagne, the bottles in a large deep silver dish, chilling down to just the correct serving temperature.

A door opened to the left and in walked the mystery man. Everyone turned to face him. He felt sure that the people in the room bowed their heads ever so slightly to acknowledge the man's entrance. He was wearing shorts and a white loosely buttoned shirt with plimsolls, but without socks. The casual clothes somehow looked wrong on him and out of place, especially after seeing him in his local dress. He had very tanned arms against the white shirt and long thin brown legs protruding through extremely baggy shorts. The wrestling lesson was about to begin.

He had spent a half hour with the mystery man in another room off to one side where the food laden table was situated. Through the door there was a fully equipped gymnasium and a large area in the middle with rubberised matting. This provided a near perfect surface for him to demonstrate with his mystery partner some of the more basic wrestling moves and holds. During gaps in the training, he would ask him about his work on the docks. He would then throw in the occasional sentence in his native Malayan tongue, only for Callon to reply back in Malayan. His command of the language was improving daily, as were his wrestling performances. He felt as though he was being interviewed for a job which he knew nothing about.

'Okay, that's enough for today, Kid.' The lesson had been sedate and leisurely compared to his usual workouts. He had not even broken sweat, but the man had shown a willing desire to learn the skills and was surprisingly strong for his years.

'Let's take a shower, then I have a relaxing massage organised for you. It will give you a good appetite.'

Alarm bells were suddenly ringing in his head, he could not think about the amazing table of wondrous delicacies. He felt for sure someone was going to shaft him from behind, or try at least. The last person who had tried something like this on him had ended up in hospital. He had been drinking with his mates Steve, Mike and Don and a few other friends in a bar close to the barracks just off Orchard Road. He was singled out by an unruly Scotsman, who was worse for wear, having consumed almost a bottle of Scotch to himself. He was carrying the remains of what was left in the whisky bottle and offering a swig to him. He knew that the missing contents of the bottle were in the stomach of the Scot by his loud and obnoxious behaviour. Not content with putting his arm around him in a gesture which indicated friendship, he grabbed Callon by the crotch and told him he fancied him. He took immediate evasive action, grabbing the bottle from the Scot in one slick move. He pinned him to the floor with the bottle across his throat. One arm was pinned behind the Scot and the other under Callon's knee, rendering him completely defenceless. This all happened so fast, the Scotsman did not know which day it was. A small stream of blood trickled slowly down the forehead of the man and into his eyes. He had caught his head on a chair as he was manhandled to the floor. He drew his face close to the Scot, keeping pressure on his neck.

'If you ever try that again with me, my friend, I will shove that bottle up your arse, bottom first. Do you understand, Jock?' He gave a nod of the head, his eyes still wide and wild as he suddenly realised he had picked on the wrong man. The small group of friends extracted themselves from the bar. A few tables were upended and several drinks spilt, but otherwise, the fracas was contained in those few moments. The Scot would wake up with a sore head and a few stitches in the open gash and nothing more. If he could remember, he would also think twice about touting his sexuality in open public places, especially to someone like Callon. The scar above his eye would be a lifetime reminder of making a bad decision every time he looked in a mirror.

After showering separately from the mystery man, he was approached by another man in the changing area. He had not seen him before and wondered where he had been waiting. He asked him to follow him, speaking in his Malayan tongue. The young wrestler wrapped his towel around his waist and followed. They entered a small but very dimly lit room with a massage table in the middle covered in towels. There was a small hard pillow at one end. The man pointed to the table and asked him to lie down on his stomach. He felt very nervous, but did as the man told him. The door opened and the man left. He laid there contemplating what was going to happen next. He felt very vulnerable at this point trying to predict what the hell was going on. A soft hand touched his shoulder and made him jump. He raised himself up on one elbow and was shocked to see a very beautiful young woman with straight shoulder length black hair standing before him. Even in the dimmed light, he could see warmth in her eyes; she had the most demure smile. She had entered the room as silently as a fragrance touches the senses. This exchange of bodies happened as the man he had not seen before left the room. She was dressed in a white silk see-through blouse, as light as butterfly wings. Through the subdued light, he could see the outline of her small breasts and her large erect nipples. He resisted his temptation to reach out and touch them and removed his stare. This had been the closest he had been to a woman since saying goodbye to his wife many months back. She was barefoot, making no sound as she moved her position around the table. Her mid-thigh length shorts could not disguise her exquisitely shaped legs and calves.

He felt the immediate stirring beneath the towel as he tried to reposition himself without making obvious movements.

'Hello, my name is Suzi, is it okay to massage you…you like, yes?' Her voice was young and sweet and her English was heavily accented with the Malayan dialect.

Suzi moved across the room as his eyes followed her, trying to take in her grace and her beauty.

'Yes,….yyes, I would like a massage, yes, very much.'

She picked up a glass bottle with a crystal stopper containing aromatic oils. She had anticipated his answer.

'What your name, Sir?'

'Call me, Kid.' He stopped himself from staring at her. He was now perched on both elbows with his back fully arched and his crutch pressing hard into the leather covered table.

She repeated his name, 'Ki.' she couldn't pronounce the 'd.'

'Yes, that's near enough,' he said.

She touched his head gently, suggesting he lay flat on the bed and relax. She placed his hands above his head so they draped over the top of the table. Every movement she made was in slow motion and without sound. She reached underneath him to release the towel. He assisted her by raising his hips and taking his weight with his outspread elbows; she then parted his legs by holding each ankle ever so gently. He laid there under the subdued lights, stark naked feeling strong and hard and at peace.

Bloody hell, he thought, I'm getting paid for this!

Suzi inspected the fine specimen of a man laid bare before her. She had never seen a man with such a splendid physique and muscle definition. She wanted to press her body against his, but for now she resisted. Her subject matter was perfect in every way, she thought, as she moved her eyes up and down his finely shaped body. His face was young and fresh with good bone structure. His hair brushed back from his handsome face yielding a strong nose and brow. She knew exactly what she had to do. Her instructions were to stimulate the body before her and to make him want her. Within minutes she would have her subject writhing in ecstasy before her, wanting to take her on the bed where he lay.

He could hear the crystal stopper being removed from the bottle. He also heard the soft background music playing, soothing his senses. His mind had been distracted since Suzi entered the room. He had not heard the music until that moment. Kid Callon was more concerned about controlling his arousal and emotions. He reminded himself that he had a wife and son back home in England, but his concentration was interrupted by the sensuous strokes and touch of Suzi as she worked her soothing hands across his back and lower body.

Her hands were small yet strong as she massaged his shoulders and neck, pressing her thumbs into tight shoulders and breaking the tension held within them. From the nape of his neck and with open splayed fingers, she moved her position to massage his head with strong strokes, pushing her fingers and nails into his scalp, bringing goose bumps to his strong arms. Suzi was now working her way down his torso with long controlled sweeps of her hands, slowly kneading the defined muscle areas across his back. Her hands were soft and warm as he purred when she touched more sensitive areas. She moved down his body, always keeping contact with one of her hands. She massaged the middle of his back slowly, pressing her fingers hard into his vertebrae before moving across to his side and then returning to his middle back. Long swirling movements of her hands now moved down to his buttocks with heightened sensuality. Her fingers were probing areas which she had no right to explore. He was trying to control his natural instincts, thinking about his life pre war and how different things were now, but everything that Suzi did with her long swirling hand strokes brought him back to the moment. He was aroused now and Suzi could sense this as she teased him by allowing her fingers to drift into his private areas before pulling away at the very last moment. The sweep of her soft velvety strokes, softened by the fragrant oil, brought quiet moaning sounds of ecstasy from his mouth in harmony with the massage strokes. Suzi's long finger nails cut into his soft flesh as she purposely squeezed sensitive tissue to make her presence and her own feelings obvious. Suzi opened his legs further as she widened her arc of contact. She moved to the top of his leg, a small hand down the inside of his thigh, moving slowly and rhythmically to the soft music. She was teasing him again, allowing the back of her hand to touch his sac ever so slightly with each downward stroke of her hand. He was now arching his crutch away from the table as though to give easier access to those soft silk like hands and to the whole of his manhood, but she resisted the temptation. The aromatic oil was intensifying the sensation of touch as her hand moved ever closer to his hardness, only to retract her movement at the last moment. As a final move of sexual defiance, she allowed her body to press against his. He could feel her hard nipples against his skin through her blouse as she pressed herself forcefully to him. He could not control his emotions further. She had aroused his sexual sensation to a point where he thought he would explode.

He looked down at the 500 dollars which was wrapped in a money sleeve. The notes were new and unused and didn't require counting. The mystery man had been more than generous, he thought. This was the easiest money he had ever made in his life.

The champagne was a delightful tasting extravaganza. He had never sampled pink champagne previously, let alone the regular variety. This was the drink for the rich and famous to enjoy, and not for mere mortals such as himself, he thought. He only drank one glass; there was still work to do on Saturday evening. He could not risk his run at the championship at this late stage, not even for the sake of a few more mouthfuls of pure nectar. The mystery man continued to ask probing questions to Callon about his activities on the docks as they picked at the food on offer. Kazar stayed with Callon throughout the evening as did the man without a name. The three other men kept a discreet distance from the discussion, within earshot to hear what was being said, but without being obtrusive. He had no idea who the men were, he concluded that their names were also on a need to know basis. The discussion changed, he felt that the mystery man had heard what he wanted to hear. He was still wondering why working on the docks was so interesting, so important to the man before him. The Empire Dock held no mystique to him; that was sure. Why all those bloody questions, he thought to himself. To him, this was just a place to work.

To the mystery man, it was a treasure trove of untold fortune.

'Can you come back and show me some more moves, Kid?' asked the man with a hint of expectation in his voice.

'Yes, of course, just let me know when it's convenient to you.' He could see the dollar bills in his mind's eye, being flipped at the edges; crisp, new dollar notes. But he was also thinking about something else. He also wondered if he would be treated to another massage. His thoughts were full of what he had just experienced; he needed to see Suzi again and he needed to feel her soft hands on him again. He could still smell her sweet fragrance on his body. She had released an emotion in him whereby he could beat any opponent; she had made him feel invincible. As he thought about Suzi and how she had fulfilled him, he was totally unprepared for the next question.

'How would you like to earn some serious money, Kid?' This statement hit him like a bolt out of the blue. He felt like he had been shot in the chest at close range with both barrels of a twelve bore shotgun.

'Serious money,' he said, trying to feel composed and swallowing hard, not knowing what else to say. His legs were suddenly feeling unstable, unable to support his body weight. His brain was awash with confusion and incoherence as he tried to comprehend what had just been said to him.

'Yes, more money than you could imagine, Kid.' The mystery man stared at him, his eyes trying to burn into his thoughts. He needed a little time to absorb what the man had just said, but there was no time.

These are only words, man, pull yourself together!

Without any further hesitation, he replied,

'Yeah, for sure, who wouldn't,' his response was not intuitive; but he could only hope that he was saying the right things and that his words were understood. 'What do you call serious money...... and what would you want me to do?' He was now looking around the room. Kazar and the group all had eyes on him, looking pleased that his reply had been positive at this stage.

'How does a quarter of a million dollars sound, transferred to your account anywhere in the world?' The mystery man refrained from continuing, he first wanted to see the reaction from his new wrestling tutor. He wanted him to register in his mind the figure of money he had just blurted out to him. He noticed his eyes open to their maximum, his pupils dilate before returning to their normal size. The mystery man knew he had the Kid's attention. He continued in a monotone but clear voice. He did not want any misunderstandings at this stage. He needed the young man stood before him to comprehend fully what was required from him and exactly what was being said.

'I would want to you to drive a truck for me.' The man positioned himself close up directly in front of him. He was dominating the space between the two men by his closeness, as though trying to influence the answer. There were no distractions from anyone else in the room. The silence was deafening. He was looking directly into Callon's eyes, staring, not moving his own eyes away. He realised he needed to give a clear and decisive answer.

'Drive a truck, is that it? It seems an awful lot of money just to drive a truck?' He was suddenly feeling unwell. He could feel his stomach turning over. He could feel his bowels wanting to explode. He suddenly needed all his attention to concentrate on not shitting himself. Never in his whole life had he felt like this. Someone had just waved a truck load of money in front of him, yet all he wanted to do was unload vomit and excrement from their respective orifices. He broke the eye contact, walked to the table and poured himself a glass of water from a crystal decanter. He hoped nobody could see his hands tremble as he pressed the glass hard to his lips. He also hoped he appeared calm to the other people in the room. His head and body were in complete turmoil and doing uncontrollable somersaults. He regulated his breathing without bringing attention to himself. He was starting to come down now from somewhere he had never been before and within a few moments, had regained his composure.

'Will you do it, will you drive the truck?' His eyes told him he needed an answer and quickly.

'Sure, yes, I'll do it, but I need some more information first? Drive the truck, where to?'

'Listen, Kid, I just needed to know if you would drive for us first, okay. Obviously, with that amount of money on the table, there are risks involved, but the risks are both manageable and controllable. I do not have any other information for you at this stage. There are still things to sort out, we don't have everything in place yet; it could take several more weeks, maybe months, before we are ready to move. This project has been on the agenda over a year already. We just have to be patient and wait for the right moment.' The mystery man held out his hand for him to shake.

Fuck, does this gesture mean we have struck a deal or is this just a simple goodbye? There has to be so much more about this driving malarkey than he has told me so far and what about the bloody risks?

'Let's meet again next week for some further wrestling lessons,' said the mystery man, still holding his hand, as if to press home his point of reference to the agreement. The man looked down at the hands clasped together before looking at him. Little did he know, but that handshake had just committed him to a role which he knew absolutely nothing about.

With his free hand, the mystery man tapped his nose on the side with his index finger to indicate total secrecy. He knew better than to ignore this little gesture. His life could depend on this he felt. He had no idea what he was getting himself into, but it was exciting, and it would be risky, the man just confirmed that. He wondered what the penalty might be for failure, but soon disconnected with that thought. Success had a far better ring to it. A quarter of a million dollar ring!

'I may also have some further information for you when I see you next.' The man was now looking backwards and forwards between Callon and Kazar.

'That sounds good, obviously I'm keen to know more about what we have just discussed,' he said, now feeling much better. 'Just liaise with Kazar; I am sure he will make all the necessary arrangements.'

This amount of money brings with it danger, thought Callon, not just risks, but at this stage, he felt it better not to ask more questions. Suddenly, there was something other than wrestling in his life. A quarter of a million dollars...

'Bugger me,' he whispered under his breath. 'I could be a very rich man?'

One of the gang of three moved away from the party just prior to Callon and Kazar leaving the room where they had eaten. He approached the door which opened inwards, without reason, Callon's eyes followed him. He almost froze on the spot. Through the gap in the partly open door, he saw for a split second only, a man wearing a British Army uniform pass by. Worse still, it was an Army Officer in uniform, he was convinced. It was unmistakeable, he thought. He had only seen the profile of this man for a split second, but it was enough.

'That was a British officer,' he muttered under his breath, 'the uniform colour was British,' he could recognise that from a hundred paces blindfold. He did not know the rank, the look was so fleeting, but it was an officer he was sure.

'What the fuck is a British officer doing here?' he said softly to himself. He thought for a moment, then realised that no one else had seen this unintended indiscretion. The officer had not realised he had been seen either, but unknown to Callon, he knew that he was there and that he had committed himself to drive the truck. To drive the truck from where to where was unknown to him at this stage. What concerned him most, was, what would be on the truck? Before he could get answers to these questions, he and Kazar were escorted to the car that would take them back to Singapore.

He had plenty to think about as they slid down the long drive towards the main road, which would take them to the customs border and back into Singapore. He failed to notice the guards waving the car through the heavily protected gates at the bottom.

'You did a good job tonight, Suzi; do you think he likes you?' Suzi was now enjoying the pink champagne and some of the delicacies on offer from the food table. Her evening's work for the moment was done. She was now dressed in a very elegant and feminine local dress. She looked just like a princess, thought the mystery man. He also thought she was very beautiful. He wanted her, but knew he couldn't have her.

'Yes, I think he likes me, and I like him too. He is a very handsome and strong young man. I have never met such a person like him before.' Suzi was making her point very clear and very direct to the man who paid her wages. There were traits of jealousy crossing the face of the man she was addressing. He squirmed at her words and wondered if he could make her feel the same way. He now wanted to know more.

'Will he come back, do you think?' The man was searching for questions which he already knew the answers to. He needed to hear what Suzi was thinking though.

'I think that will depend on you. I hope he comes back, I like him very much.'

Her reply stung him.

'What happened?' His tone now was short and abrupt.

'I offered him everything, just like you said I should,' Suzi looked away from his stare before finishing her sentence.

The man was looking for specific answers to his questions now as his eyes burned into the back of her head.

'And did he take everything?'

'What do you think?' said Suzi, still looking away.

She stood and walked towards the door, for her, there was nothing more to say. She hoped that nothing bad would happen to the young man who had just walked into her life. She also hoped nothing serious would happen to her either, after all, she was only following instructions. They had only been together for minutes in reality, but she felt something strong, stir within her. She had never had feelings like this before, his strong hands and arms could protect her she thought, wrapped around her, taking her, and her breath away.

She thought about her reply, she had intended to hurt him.

'He has promised me so much and given me nothing,' she said softly to herself. 'I cannot and will not wait for him forever. He has used me in ways which no one would imagine. I have no more tears to cry for this man. Maybe Ki could be my escape from the clutches of this man to freedom?'

She needed to see 'Ki,' again, and already made plans and worked a strategy how she would accomplish this.

A thought crossed Suzi's mind as she retired to her quarters, maybe she would be a princess one day?

Chapter 14

'The Kid is an ideal candidate,' said the mystery man to his special guest. 'He has a good aptitude and I like him a lot.' He said this in spite of Suzi's response to him, trying to cover up his own feelings towards her. 'He has a very level head on his shoulders and he's smart. I have studied this man at a distance for some months now, as you have, Colonel. Apart from a few scrapes here and there in the bars with fellow servicemen, he is clean. Speaking to him tonight has reaffirmed my belief in this man. He knows his way around Singapore too and all the dock areas, plus he speaks the local language quite okay now. There is not another man on this land who fulfils all our objectives. It surprises me how quickly this man has learnt our very difficult language.' The man paused for a moment, reflecting about Suzi and her answers back to him. 'I think this is our man… no, wait a moment, I am convinced this man will do the business for us.' He paused again, 'what about our consignment Colonel, has it arrived at port yet?'

The Colonel was standing in the room where Callon and the others had feasted earlier. He had kept himself out of the way as the first open discussion on selecting a driver was held. The position of driver was crucial to the success of the operation, so it was vitally important to choose the right man. It had to be someone who could cope under pressure, have integrity, strength of character, but most of all; he must be able to speak Malayan. Kid Callon had all these attributes; months had passed before any one person fit all the requirements. The Colonel was helping himself to some of the fine food on offer and would not reply to the man before eating a small hard biscuit filled with the finest Russian caviar.

'No, it hasn't arrived yet, so we have a little more time to plan our operation.' The Colonel wiped the side of his mouth with a starched white cotton serviette. He had poured himself a generous helping of pink champagne and was now tilting his head back enjoying what was left in the bottom of the finest crystal flute.

'This is just the beginning of a very long road,' said the Colonel, holding back the desire to belch out loud from the effects of the champagne. 'You should not let the Kid get too close either, we need to keep him at a safe distance, tell him only what he needs to hear. I will see to it from my side that he gets all the necessary freedom to continue his wrestling. At the same time I will ensure the Kid's authority on the docks is maintained. We also need him to have access to the goods held in the bonded warehouses. We need to do this without bringing any attention to ourselves and we don't want any personal hang ups which could jeopardise anything. Let's just make sure the Kid stays out of trouble as well, from what I understand his tolerance level is very low. We cannot afford to see him in trouble at this late stage.'

The Colonel was back at the table taking more food and champagne. 'This is much better than army rations,' he said. 'I could get used to this lifestyle.'

The day was already over, it was 30 minutes past midnight, but a lot of important things had been openly discussed. They also had one of the most important pieces of the forthcoming plan in place. They had their driver, thought the Colonel. This was a huge fillip to the operation's main players. They needed someone of Callon's calibre, if this plan was to stand any chance of success.

'This lifestyle could be yours, Colonel, but first we have to make sure our plan is watertight. There are untold rewards if we accomplish all of our missions.' The mystery man stood with his eyes fixed on the Colonel.

'Let's stay in touch. As soon as I hear anything further about the consignment, I will let you know.' The Colonel had finished his food and was making his way out of the exquisite palace doors. Before leaving, the Colonel turned abruptly 180 degrees and said to the man, 'make sure that your side of the operation is ready to go when I get the green light. Timing is everything. These goods cannot be allowed to stay on the ground too long. They make everyone nervous, including me.'

Chapter 15

He awoke from a sleep so disturbed by a million thoughts that he felt he had not slept at all. He sat up from his bed in the barracks, it was Saturday 14th June and another massive night lay ahead. He was an early riser on most mornings, but his 07.00 hour wake-up call seemed to come around far too quickly. He felt completely drained from the previous night's contest and almost farcical request from a man whose identity he was still to discover and show him some wrestling moves. He should not complain though, as he inspected and counted again the dollars he held in his hand.

'Not bad for a night's work,' he said, as he prepared himself for the day ahead. He was earning some serious money now, but he remembered he still had an important job to complete and did not want to lose sight of that. He had accomplished a David and Goliath style win over his giant opponent Banta Singh last night. The six foot ten inch man was deemed to look ordinary as he out wrestled him by applying brain above brawn against him. Brawn was important of course, but Singh had completely underestimated his opponent, thinking his height advantage would frighten most wrestlers to submission. Not Callon though, his attitude was steadfast, ferocious and furious. The bigger they come the harder they fall, he thought. Everyone has an Achilles heel, he found it immediately with the tall Indian and he exploited it to great effect. Vulnerability is with everyone, including himself, he thought.

His thoughts now were on the evening's contest. He had the unenviable job of trying to dispose of his next opponent, The Son of Anaconda. No mean feat, as this wrestler was also undefeated. At least it would be in his favourite wrestling location, the Great World. His supporters would be out in full voice to ensure he remained on the right course for the Light Heavyweight Championship of the Far East. A win today would take him to the last four in the competition. It would be anyone's title then. Training today would be less intense and would be more loosening up than anything else. He would include some weight training with a few exercises only. He trained every day, so this was not different in that respect. Jogging relaxed his mind, but today it was filled with the discussions of the last evening. He kept trying to convince himself that he had not been dreaming and that the offer of 250,000 dollars to drive a truck was not a figment of his imagination. He thought about the mystery man and tried to understand who he could be. Kazar was giving nothing away. Who could live in such splendour and afford such luxuries; the house, the cars, and his entourage, this man is not just very influential, he is also very rich, he thought. These images would not leave his head as he tried valiantly to focus on the most important contest of his life so far. Why had Kazar left it so late and so near a vital contest to introduce him to this man? He must have known how an offer involving huge sums of money would effect his concentration and destroy his focus. He was a no one, back in his home town in Yorkshire; he had a job, yes, but he had no money, house, or status. Of course, the offer to make large sums of money was a huge attraction to someone with this background. He was beginning to think he was being used and that his wrestling skills were no more than a front to something which he knew nothing about. What about that officer, who is he? That was also turning in his mind as he had tried to relax and sleep last night. What could an officer possibly be doing at that man's residence? He decided at that moment that his first priority was towards his wrestling. He had won all of his contests fair and square; the championship should be his main focus now. His own raw talent, skill, fitness and enormous strength should see him through this chapter in his progress, despite all the detritus swimming around in his head. He would try to put the discussions of last night to the back of his mind. He could not adulterate his thoughts any further; otherwise he would lose everything he had fought for so far.

'But what about the girl?' he heard himself speaking out loud. He could not forget about her. 'Is she part of the deal?' he asked himself. 'Has Suzi been put there to make his decision to return to Johor that much easier?' If that was the case, then it had worked. He would return; he knew that no one could resist the kind of temptation that Suzi presented. It had been so long since he had felt the soft touch and warmth of a woman. He was not ready to wait that long again.

The wrestling arena at the Great World was eerily quiet and deserted when he strolled to the ring side. It would be a couple of hours before the contest got under-way. He was top billing, so depending on the length of the previous contests, it could be several more hours before he stepped into the ring. His contest was the last on the card. He wanted to prepare himself by immersing his whole self in the wrestling atmosphere that would consume this hall in the forthcoming hours. He needed to be around the ring and needed to feel the canvas. He wanted to test the give in the ropes as he leant his full body weight against them, testing their resistance. He wanted to be in the hall when the atmosphere was building. All these things were important as part of his wrestling contest build up. He needed to know more about what was around him than his opponent. Son of Anaconda was described as similar in style to his own. He had won most of his previous contests by submission. He on the other hand had won mostly by knock out. This statistic counted for nothing now of course. What mattered was, how could he beat The Son of Anaconda and how could he get into his opponents head. He needed to be quicker, smarter, and stronger, but most of all, he needed to be better.

Hassan, who he had beaten quite convincingly earlier in his career, had become a great friend of his. Their chance meeting all those months back when he as a novice wrestler, albeit with some pedigree, was helped by him. He was the person who would refresh his wrestling moves and holds when he took on Jonny Eagle as a newcomer and beat him. Callon was now one of the top billing wrestlers on the circuit and he looked to Hassan once again for some guidance.

Hassan had wrestled Son of Anaconda a couple of months back and he wanted to know what he could tell him about this wrestler. Hassan had been beaten by his opponent that day, but Hassan had taken the first submission. It also took Son of Anaconda the full ten rounds to get his man's shoulders on the canvas for the second time. Both men had been physically spent in the end, but it proved Anaconda could go the distance. His stamina was not something Callon could take advantage of. It had been his initial thought to wear his man down first and then go for the submissions later in the bout. Hassan was able to impart some interesting information and it helped him build up data on his opponent. Only a couple of wrestlers had taken a submission fall from Son of Anaconda, these happened in some of his earlier contests. No one in the last eight wrestling bouts had taken a submission from Callon, so Hassan's news was good to hear.

The nervousness was showing very clearly on his face. He had not been this nervous ever, about anything. He had faced opponents of all shapes and sizes and taken the contest in his stride. He was not sure why he felt such apprehension. He had come through his last evening's contest unscathed. There was always a risk of picking up injuries fighting on consecutive nights. Apart from a couple of bruises here and there, he was in great physical shape. His training build up had been undisturbed except for a poor night's sleep last night, but he had reserves which he could dip into. This was a crucial contest for sure. A win here and he sails into the last four of the competition.

He stood at the very back of the hall watching the lower ranked fights. He would be stepping into the ring within the next hour as he pondered his strategy. He was ready to wrestle, standing alone with just his thoughts, his long black silk dressing gown shimmering in the dull light but looking splendid. He never got ready this soon, he thought, but this contest felt different. He had done a little warming up and would do some more nearer his start time. A couple of small local boys were making their way towards him as he stood waiting patiently for his bout to start. Their parents were eagerly watching the tentative steps of their children. They had spotted their wrestling hero and were holding small autograph books to their chests.

'Hiya, Kid,' said the tallest one with a heavy but sweet accent, 'can we have your autograph please.' He bent down and asked their names, avoiding their request. They had seen him fight a couple of times before at the Great World, but they had never been able to get this close to their favourite wrestler. Wrestling was a good spectator sport for the young children. Staying up late to watch their favourite sportsman was quite common in these parts.

'How old are you two boys?' he asked.

Only the tallest of the small boys spoke. 'I am seven and my cousin is nearly seven.' His eyes were wide and shone brightly as he spoke, looking up to his wrestling hero. The two boys continued to hold their autograph books out to him with one hand and a pencil in the other.

'Can you write in our books please, Kid?'

Again he ignored the request but was suddenly feeling vulnerable and very anxious. He could see the children's parents looking and pointing at where they were standing.

He motioned to move away from the two boys, he was agitated and desperate to get back into the dressing room. He avoided looking at the autograph books further.

'Look, boys, see me after the fight, I have to go now.' He patted the boys gently on the head and turned quickly and looked at the parents before disappearing down towards the changing rooms. The disbelief in their eyes was palpable as he left the boys standing alone with their autograph books held at arms length unsigned.

Tears welled in his eyes as he hurried down the slope to the safety of solitude, where no one would see him desperately holding back his emotions. He wanted to be away from the stares or the ridicule. Two small boys no older than seven years of age had just exposed his Achilles heel. It didn't take a twenty stone strong man or a six foot ten inch giant to expose this, no, it took two small boys. He promised himself that this would never happen to him again. He would learn to write after this.

He looked around the ring for inspiration. Kazar was trying to lift the morale of his man. He had never seen him like this before. Kid Callon had never needed any encouragement previously. He needed to be held back, yes, but never to be spurred on.

'Come on, this is your big night, remember where we go from here.' Kazar could see that the sparkle usually present in his wrestler's eyes was missing. 'What's wrong with you, Kid, are you sick?'

'No, I'm not sick, just leave me, Kaz, I will be fine, I have a lot on my mind just now.'

'A lot on your mind, I need you to have a clear mind tonight. This is the big one; remember where we go from here?' The last twenty four hours had been such a roller coaster for him, he had not realised how unnerving the events in Johor had had on him. The lure of huge amounts of money from a mystery man he did not know. For a job he knew nothing about. The British officer, whose rank and name he did not know.

'Okay, Kaz, yes, I have a load on my mind, and I can thank you for that. What in hell's name were you thinking, piling this shit on me at such a crucial stage in my wrestling schedule; don't you think I've enough to think about?'

'I did think about it, but the timing was not something I could do anything about. People in higher places were insistent that they speak to you now.'

'Oh yes, and fuck how I feel about it, or how it would effect me.'

'Look, Kid, I'm sorry, but you have to get these negative thoughts out of your head. Think positive, think about the huge pay day coming your way, but think about Anaconda...he will have nothing on his mind except you at this moment, and he will be out to destroy you.'

Kazar slapped his wrestler on the shoulder and moved away with his head slightly bowed. He knew his wrestler would have an enormous fight on his hands tonight. This was a make or break contest, a loss tonight could really throw all their plans into mayhem.

For his part, he continued to question himself about the bizarre events of Friday 13th. 'What in heavens name was a British officer doing at that man's home?' As hard as he tried, he could not put the logic together. 'Suzi, who is she?' he asked quietly. 'Is she part of whatever was happening? Is she involved with the bigger picture, or is she an unwilling pawn in this bed of intrigue?' He was totally confused about the whole scenario, not least because he had a wife and a son back home in England, a son who he had not seen yet, other than grainy images on a photograph. This was all he had to show that he was a father, and it disturbed him. To cap it all, two small boys aged seven, made him fall to his knees and into submission. A feat not accomplished by any wrestler in the Far East thus far.

He saw his first glimpse of Son of Anaconda. Outwardly there appeared to be nothing which he could take any advantage from. There was no height or weight advantage to be gained from either side. From a wrestling perspective, the two men were very evenly matched. This was going to be a severe test of strength and ability for both of them.

Both wrestlers were introduced as serious contenders for the Light Heavy Weight Championship of the Far East.

Callon's head was still fuzzy with detail and fact, something which he could do without. Never had he gone into a contest feeling quite like this.

'Where is the adrenalin buzz, what the fuck is happening to me?' he asked himself above the noise of the huge arena. He was pumping his arms and legs trying to instil some urgency into his preparation

It was too late for sentiment now though, one of the most important contests in his wrestling career was about to begin. He tried to regain his focus, but immediately, images and thoughts from yesterday came swimming back to waterlog his brain. He remembered hearing his name called, but the rest of the words were lost in the sea of confusion, he could not recall another word spoken during the announcements. Hassan, his second could see the vagueness in his wrestler's eyes and was trying to instil some enthusiasm to him, slapping his face and shoulders as the bell rang for the start of the contest to get under way.

The round started scrappy with no one taking control or advantage, but Callon wrestled with his usual hectic and brutal style to intimidate his opponent. He felt he lacked his usual finesse and aggression. His holds were being broken too easily by his opponent. He was trying to encourage himself to pull himself together. He needed to get some kind of advantage over his opponent. He gritted his teeth together to try and will himself into frenetic action; this was his style after all. His exertions and strength were being matched by the Son of Anaconda. Holds and throws were neat and zippy in their execution, but he was unable to finish them off with a submission. He was surprised at his opponent's strength, or was it that he was unable to exert his full power on him? This would not be a contest for the faint hearted, blood would be spilt in this bout for sure but he just hoped it would not be his. He was trying to shrug off his low esteem. It was affecting his performance. His strength for once appeared to be deserting him. The end of the first round was completed by a loud interruption of the bell. Hassan was towelling Kid Callon down and talking to him constantly in his corner, trying to bring his focus back. He knew he was not performing to his usual high standards. Kazar recognised this too, and he left his ringside seat to encourage and then berate his wrestler. It was the first time his promoter had felt under pressure when his star performer was wrestling. He felt helpless, knowing that this contest could put a whole new perspective on their future plans. Before the start of the next round, Kazar frantically scanned the arena and left Kid Callon and Hassan to await the bell.

The two combatants came together for the start of the second round. He went low to get his man off balance, but he missed his hold at speed and subsequently his grip. Anaconda immediately took control of the move. This was messy from Callon, he now found himself on the floor facing a fierce attack which would severely put him at risk of a submission. He managed to wriggle free. His movements were quick and aggressive in an attempt to confuse his opponent. Anaconda however, was in the ascendency and was able to get the shoulders of Callon on the canvas twice for counts of two. The subsequent energy required to free him self from these attacks were tiring. He was literally a second away from conceding the first advantage to his opponent. He was still not out of danger as he continued to be on the defensive. His head was forced back to its fullest extension by the heel of Anaconda's hand as they both worked on the ground for better positions. His right arm was being twisted now and his wrist forced back. He was still on the ground and his movements were being restricted because of this. He needed to get back on his feet, somehow, otherwise the arm would be immobilised completely and he would be in grave danger of losing the round and possibly the contest. He could not risk either of these options. He grimaced in pain as his arm was again been forced into positions which it should not go. He was somehow able to twist his body round on the floor and relieve momentarily the strain. Anaconda was clearly targeting his right arm and trying desperately to weaken it. He knew Callon had great strength, so immobilising one of his greatest assets would be to his gross benefit. Up until now, Anaconda was bossing the round and not allowing Callon to get settled in any way. He was talking to him in close hold now,

'You are on your way out, Kid; you have met your fucking match.'

'Fuck you,' said Callon, it was the only reply he could muster, but even that lacked authority. He could only consider what he would do next to relieve his pain. He found himself in unchartered territory and felt he was letting his chances of the title slip by, but could do nothing about it. He was able to negate Anaconda's holds, but found himself again facing another uphill challenging hold. The strain to get out of one hold then another was stripping his energy and he was weakening. This was still only the second round. He managed to move himself towards the ropes eventually, after his opponent tried valiantly to stop him. The referee intervened and called for a break. Callon remained on the canvas trying to get air into his lungs and try to remain steady for the next attack.

As he rose to his feet slowly rubbing his shoulder, Anaconda delivered a flying scissor kick, full in the chest with great accuracy. This flung him backwards into the ropes and he finished up on the floor, on his back. Anaconda was gaining ground now and seizing his moment. He fell on Callon with his whole body weight, dropping onto his head and his right shoulder. Anaconda delivered the killer blow by holding his opponent's shoulders down on the canvas for a count of three. The bell was rung furiously to indicate the submission and the end of the round. He could do nothing about this attack. He was weakened and dazed by the speed and force of the move. He remained on the canvas for some moments, motionless. The referee checked to see if he could continue, he was looking into his eyes to see if there was evidence of concussion.

'You only have one minute, Kid,' said the referee as Hassan, his second came into the ring to help him to his corner. He was still groggy and dazed when he sat down.

The Son of Anaconda had struck the first devastating blow. He had taken the first submission from Kid Callon and hurt him in the process. No one, except a couple of opponents in his earlier contests, had been able to do that.

To lose tonight would be devastating. It would take him a further six months at least to get back to this level of wrestling, but could take much longer to gain his self respect. The crowd in the Great World Arena were subdued into silence and were not expecting this outcome so early in the contest. Kazar was at the ringside again trying to urge the crowd to get behind their man. Some of the spectators, recognising his dilemma, stood up trying to urge Kid Callon on; stamping their feet in encouragement. He knew he needed to get his head in gear, but he saw no way back. He could not erase the negative thoughts which were furring his mind and his thoughts. He was sat with his head bowed in the corner when a gentle hand touched his calf. He looked down to see who was trying to attract his attention. Suzi stood there, looking up at him, lovingly and with eyes which melted his soul. Her long black hair was glossy and strong resting on her shoulders. She tilted her head upwards towards his gaze. He bent down to touch her face, but she raised her hand and they touched fleetingly.

'What are you doing here? I had no idea you were out there,' he said, in a voice just loud enough to be heard over the noise in the arena. 'I am here for you, Ki; I needed to see you again.' She blew a discreet kiss in his direction. Kazar had known Suzi was in the arena and urged her to go to his corner.

'Just let him know you are here, Suzi,' half pleading with her. Kazar had organised for her to be at the contest, she had been able to get a message to him before he left the mystery man's residence last evening. Kazar could see his protégé was in mortal danger of losing this contest and felt that Suzi could be the last toss of the dice. Kazar did not have a contingency plan. They had never contemplated Kid Callon losing.

The bell rang for the start of the third round.

He felt energised somehow by Suzi's presence. He approached Anaconda in the centre of the ring. Anaconda deliberately went to grab his right hand knowing he had weakened it somewhat, but in a flash produced a solid forearm smash and sent his opponent careering backwards into the ropes. Anaconda catapulted himself off and sent his full weight into Callon's body, flooring him. He went down to a count of eight, slightly dazed but unhurt. He used the time on the count to work out his next strategy. In spite of him being on the canvas, he felt his confidence returning. This wrestling match was not over, not by a long way. He was still on the back foot, but felt the adrenalin from that last hit, return to his body. He was reacting to his opponent's aggression; he had not been doing that previously. As he raised himself to his feet feigning grogginess, he anticipated Anaconda's next move. He attempted the flying scissor kick again, but at the last moment he was able to sway away without contact being made. Anaconda fell awkwardly, not expecting to kick fresh air. He was arching his back on the floor as Callon fell on him, leaving the point of his elbow into his ribs. Anaconda was now hurt and turning over and over. He could now see his chance; he dragged him into the centre of the ring, away from the safety of the ropes. He needed to keep Anaconda hurt. As he stood up, he immediately fell on him again, this time catching his mouth and nose with his forearm. Anaconda expressed air from his lungs on contact with the canvas spraying blood from his mouth into the air like a whale in its death throes. Anaconda was hurt badly now and concussed slightly. He picked his man up by the crutch and throat above his head and applied an aeroplane spin, disorientating his man before throwing him to the canvas onto his back. He fell on him for a third time, holding his shoulders on the canvas for an easy count of three. Anaconda gave no resistance to the submission and he knew he had his opponent where he wanted him. Kid Callon was back. He found himself in the zone and there was no return for Anaconda. The crowd knew at this stage in the contest, that The Son of Anaconda was history and could not live with the Kid on this re-energised form.

The famous long bar at the Raffles hotel was buzzing with excitement and its clientele. The waiters and bar staff, looking resplendent in their smart tailored attire, were on hand to serve the group of revellers.

'Singapore Slings for everyone here please,' said Kid Callon to the bemused looking bartender. He was ordering celebratory drinks for Kazar and his loyal band of supporters and friends. Steve, Don, Mike and several of his other army friends were lapping up the eloquence and grace that the hotel transmitted to its guests. His friends knew that their meagre army wages would not run to this kind of luxury, so they took advantage of the moment. His colleagues from the Army base were supporting him in good numbers, and this support was growing as his success increased. They had seen him emerge from nowhere to a serious contender for the Far East Asia title. He fished a wad of dollars from his pocket and placed them on the bar before saying to his friends,

'Nobody leaves until we've spent this money.' Several hundred dollars would buy many Singapore Slings, he thought. He had placed his winning purse behind the bar to celebrate. Also there was Suzi; she had been instrumental in the amazing turn around of the contest's fortunes at the Great World Arena and his subsequent success. He was so grateful for that short exchange of words and simple gesture of touching hands. This had provided the spark he needed to ignite the fire in his belly and rid his mind from all the negativity which had been there.

Kid Callon had secured his passage to the last four in his attempt at the Light Heavyweight Wrestling Championship of the Far East. He had been on these shores almost two years and was now one of the top sports celebrities in the region. He was still only 21 years of age, but mature way beyond his years. His win had been most convincing and conclusive in the end, finally despatching his opponent out of the ring for a knockout in his inimitable style. This was now becoming his trademark. The Son of Anaconda had found himself on his backside on the wrong side of the ropes unable to return in the ten seconds allowed. Blood had flowed from a head wound, earlier inflicted as he raced him towards one of the corner stanchions face first. This had restricted his vision and his ability to defend himself, however, the contest result was predictable by this time. Kid Callon's support at the Great World was tremendous, with the hall erupting into chaos as The Son of Anaconda was counted out on the floor of the arena concussed and confused.

Kazar was feeling ecstatic that his little ploy had paid off; getting Suzi to go to his corner after the first submission was a masterstroke. He was now feeling the effects of the alcohol as he organised for himself and Suzi to leave. Kazar could only ever drink a couple of glasses of alcohol before it started to affect him.

'I will make sure she gets home, don't worry, Kid.' They walked outside together where Kaz's car was parked. He held the door for Suzi to get in. Kazar went to sit behind his driver; It was a far cry from the mystery man's chauffeur driven limousine, but he was grateful that Suzi would be escorted back home to Johor.

'Listen.' said Kazar, slurring his words and craning his neck to make eye contact with his wrestler. 'I will be in touch this week to arrange another wrestling lesson in Johor, are you okay with that?' Callon smiled at Suzi before answering.

'Yes, you know my answer, Kaz; just make it as soon as possible.' He bent down into the car and attempted to kiss Suzi gently on the cheek. She held her hand up, resisting the approach.

'No, Ki, we must not do this. It is too dangerous for me.' She looked across at Kazar as she spoke; he was nodding in agreement with her last remark.

'Too dangerous,' he said, 'too dangerous, why?' He looked at Suzi then across to Kazar, 'what does she mean?'

'She is correct, Kid; we have customs here, don't take chances out in the street. Walls have ears; and our mutual friend has eyes in places you wouldn't believe.'

He shrugged his shoulders, but held Suzi's hand anyway. 'Thank you for being here. You've no idea what it meant for me tonight. I want to see you again… soon.'

'Me too, Ki, goodnight.'

He watched the car pull away into the night and wondered if she really knew how important her being there had been. He was drained from his back to back contests and headed off to the barracks with his friends to get some well earned rest. He felt good inside about his weekend so far. He felt on top of the world and he could sleep soundly; knowing that a few more contests could change his life.

It was late as he entered the barracks with his friends, not trying to be quiet in their triumphal return. A muffled voice from the far end of the room, whose identity was unknown to him shouted out.

'Kid, is that you?'

'Yes,' came back the reply.

'There's a telegram for you in the mail house, I think it's important.'

'Okay, thanks. A telegram for me, I wonder who that could be from?' He was talking to himself as he undressed. It was too late to do anything about it now, he thought. He would pick it up in the morning after his training. Nothing interfered with his training regime. Nothing! And nothing was going to spoil his triumphant weekend by trying to get hold of the mail sooner than he needed to. The alcohol had made him tired and he longed to lie down, but those few words spoken to him out of the gloom, kept replaying in his brain.

A telegram, he thought, I have never received a telegram before in my life. Is something wrong? Who the fuck could it be from? He sensed that it could only be problems as he sat on the side of his bed. He had no idea that the telegram would in some way almost cost him his life.

Within seconds of his head hitting the pillow, he was sound asleep.

Chapter 16

As he walked from the mail room and skirted around the parade ground in the centre of the army camp, he was clutching a small scrap of paper. This had been handed to him by a fellow soldier whose job it was to man the mail room this particular day and carry out the respective postal duties. Smythe was someone he knew only casually, but was not regarded as one of his friends. He somehow felt his day was not going to get any better. The camp had been his home for the past year and nine months, and up to this point he had led a life not expected in these parts, but all this was just about to change.

It was just after 10am on Sunday 15th June 1947 and the sun had already commenced its day some hours earlier. Its rays were already beginning to penetrate and burn his skin through the thin cotton army shirt and khaki shorts he was wearing. It was a perfect sunny day, but blisteringly hot with just a few wispy white clouds scattered against the most brilliant blue sky. The sun was occasionally hiding its ferocity behind this white floating flotilla, allowing only a little respite for those unfortunate enough to be out in its full glare.

The army camp was quiet compared to other days of the week. His duties at the docks were very relaxed due to his wrestling activities and he was not due to be there this day after his weekend exploits in the ring.

The heat seemed more oppressive than normal; however, a feeling of nausea was beginning to overwhelm him. His mind was playing games with his emotions which for now; was unrelenting and unforgiving. He steadied himself momentarily and studied his surroundings; wondering what on earth he was doing here. A ramshackle array of tents and barracks resting mainly on the perimeter fences, with a large area for training and parades in the middle. His posting here after his initial training in York and Burford in Oxfordshire was a pleasant surprise. There were much worse places to carry out his national service, he thought, but he now had to reconsider what he needed to do next. He was proud to be one of the first units to arrive in Singapore after the surrender by the Japanese in September 1945 but this feeling was now wearing very thin.

He looked down at the scrap of paper he had just been handed, it was a telegram from home. Home felt like a million miles from where he was just now and he felt alone, helpless and angry.

'Why had Smythe given him that telegram?' he asked himself out loud. 'Why? Just because it had my fucking name on it,' he thought. 'No one has the right to hand me this kind of news.' He'd detected an air of smugness when Smythe handed him the telegram. He had a smirk on his face when he said,

'I hope it's not bad news, Kid.' Smythe had already read the telegram he was sure, the flap of the envelope holding it was unstuck and creased, so he had known it was bad news. He wanted to go back there and wipe the smile from that smug bastard's face.

His mind strayed to his home back in England as he continued his walk away from the mail hut. Almost three years previously, he had been waved off from his Yorkshire dwelling to go and do his bit for King and Country. The house was not his, it belonged to his parents, and they shared the living quarters, which was not ideal. It was nothing special, but it was all he had for the time being. A stone terrace house next to a main road and built on four levels. He considered this house his temporary living accommodation only, just until he could get on his feet. It was not home to him, it was however, home to his wife and two year old son. A wife he was just getting to know, before the British army put paid to them being together. He just wanted to be home now though, but there were complications in his life here in Singapore. Some of which were his and some which had unexpectedly developed through his wrestling activities. Nevertheless, these complications could have a significant impact on his life. He wondered how long it might be before he could walk back into his shared home and see his young son for the first time. Little did he know then that his son would be almost four years of age before he would see him for the first time?

His thoughts were muddled and he was in a state of agitation. He had a mixture of emotions swirling around in his head. Angry and confused, he couldn't think straight. In addition, he could not take in the few lines which the telegram had spit out to him.

'Telegrams never bring good news,' he was cursing under his breath, 'and this telegram is no different.' He stopped in his tracks. He wanted to read the telegram again. He had only gone 20 paces, but he needed to be away from that place, that place where he wanted to do some serious damage to Smythe. Maybe he had made a mistake, perhaps the few lines he had read a few moments back were just made up somehow in his mind. Maybe he had not taken in the words of the telegram properly. After all the written word was not his strong point. His schooling had been a hit and miss affair to say the least with countless days lost to playing truant. Fishing, stealing apples from orchards and general fooling around was much more fun than school.

Without realising it, he had crushed the telegram into a small ball in his fist. This had been his initial reaction on reading the message. Destroy the information; crush the words, as if to make the problem go away. He had awoken early from his rather spartan surroundings with the thought of the telegram on his mind. He had done some limbering up exercises first, before doing his daily rigorous workout which involved weight training and stamina building exercises. He repeated this regime every day for two hours solid. After warming down and cooling off with a tepid shower, he then shaved ready to take on the day. The thought of the telegram had disturbed him and was never far from his thoughts as he went about his daily routine.

His colleague from his barracks had said it sounded urgent, but he was not expecting this kind of news. He felt the first tinges of bitterness towards where he was and what he was doing. It took a few seconds for him to straighten the paper out as he swayed on his feet. He dared again to read the message. Word by word he was slowly taking in the magnitude of the telegram. The words remained the same as before. As hard as he tried, he could not unscramble them and make them into something which was far more pleasant and nice to read. How could such a small piece of paper with so few words bring such gut wrenching news into his life? The telegram was printed in a heavy type face and read as follows:

MESSAGE FOR DEREK CALLON STOP DAD SERIOUSLY ILL WITH MENINGITIS STOP NOT SURE IF HE WILL PULL THROUGH STOP YOU SHOULD TRY TO GET HOME URGENTLY STOP MAM STOP

He was suddenly aware once again of how fierce the sun's rays were. He tried in vain to compose himself as he moved away from the mail hut. His eyes were looking skyward as if he was seeking divine intervention which would come and take his problems away. The message had set a time bomb within him ticking. The ticking would get ever louder. He wanted it to stop, but nothing except a minor miracle could prevent this from happening now. Someone was going to pay for bringing such bad news to him, someone was going to pay big time. Kid Callon was ready to explode!

His father was his inspiration and the source of both his inner and outer strength. The thought of losing him to this deadly disease was not on his agenda.

'How could this be happening to me,' he said out loud. 'How could this be happening to our family again?' Four years previously his elder sister Eunice had succumbed to the same illness. She was only sixteen when she died. It had brought such pain and sorrow to their lives. Still he could not comprehend her passing. It had a profound effect on him. In many ways, it was seeing his father cry which left him with memories of utter remorse, memories which he simply could not erase from his mind.

The thought of never seeing his father again alive brought dread to him. The sheer anguish that the telegram had brought to his door filled him with rage. He was in no mood to speak to anyone just now though, but knew he had to speak to someone. Getting off this godforsaken army camp and onto a plane home was now his number one priority. He thought about how long it had taken him to get to this sweaty outcrop of land close to the Equator, but now was the time to put this process in reverse. He needed to see his father, but quickly.

His immediate plans in Singapore would have to be put on hold, he thought. He recognised that by going home, it could have severe consequences for his professional sporting career, and there were other considerations too; considerations which would change his life forever. Would he ever get back, would the army be prepared to give him a free passage home and back? Whatever the outcome, it was more important to see his dying father. The message had read, not sure if he will pull through,

'What the fuck does this mean, is he still alive?' he said through gritted teeth. The telegram after all had come to him with some delay. For some reason, the message was already three days old when he'd received it. 'I need to get home to see my father,' telling himself the urgency of his situation. 'I only need a few minutes with him,' he uttered. 'I only need to say goodbye or say thanks for being the best dad in the world.' He needed to look into his eyes before they closed on this world forever. He kept telling himself and repeating it over and over to himself,

'Don't die, dad, don't die, dad, please don't die.' There were so many questions he still needed to ask his father. He had witnessed close up how quickly this illness had taken his sister's life. A healthy bubbly girl, with her whole life in front of her one minute, then struck down the next with fever, severe headaches, nausea and vomiting, and falling in and out of consciousness. She was rushed into hospital, but succumbed to the illness the following day. The thing that hurt worst of all was that no one in the family got to say goodbye. It all happened so suddenly and so quickly. Sadly she died alone in a hospital bed.

Oh fuck, I need to get home quickly, he thought to himself!

As he walked back in the direction of his barracks, he felt the mist which had been fogging his mind, beginning to clear. His thoughts were starting to crystallise and sharpen and he realised what he needed to do. The initial thought of 'making someone pay' for his unfortunate bad news, was now receding. He would speak immediately to his Commanding Officer, Major Reece, ask for compassionate leave and be on a plane home within the next 24 hours. Nothing would stop him from getting on a plane home to see his seriously ill father. Major Reece would see to that. If nothing else the Major was a man with compassion and who cared about his soldiers.

This would be a piece of cake he said to himself. He had a telegram from home which told its own sad story.

'They'll not prevent me from travelling home, will they?' he murmured with a little hesitation. He would need to show a little bit of emotion, but not that much, He certainly didn't want to display any kind of weakness on his part. He would want Major Reece to be considerate with his request; perhaps he'd just display a hint of anxiety.

There would be no tears though, no bloody way! He needed to show just enough emotion to get Major Reece to agree to send him home. The Major was in charge of about 120 soldiers and lower ranking officers and led his company through their training and operations. He also oversaw the administration and welfare of his command.

One less soldier here was not going to make a jot of difference, he thought. The war was over for God's sake!

He had diverted his course instinctively across the parade ground almost without thinking, as this shortened the route to the Major's office. This piece of land was off limits to the likes of an ordinary soldier or anyone else for that matter. To cross this precious piece of land or place a footprint on its surface, you had to be doing parade drill practice or marching. Kid Callon was doing neither of these things. His mind was preoccupied with what he was going to say to Major Reece to worry about small matters like that. He was now in sight of the Major's office door. There was someone in his peripheral vision now though, but he paid no heed to it. He only had one thought in his mind as he continued forward. A fleeting thought passed through his mind at this point, would he ever get the chance to ask the Major that vital question to go home? The person in his peripheral vision was looming ever closer.

His pace gathered to reach the confines of Major Reece's office; he still felt irritated and wanted to retch. The unthinkable then happened. Callon was about to put his foot on the first step to the Major's office, when, twenty five yards to his left, out of the corner of his eye he caught a glimpse of the one person he didn't want to see. It was his new Captain. Captain Black was approaching him at speed from a right angle and had spotted his minor indiscretion; he had not only stepped on the parade ground, but walked across it. The Captain was shouting 'CALLON' in an intimidating way and at a decibel level that anyone within 100 yards would hear.

Captain Black had arrived at the camp just a few weeks previous and his first introductions to the captain suggested that they were not going to get on one bit, or have any kind of sensible relationship. Captain Black had taken an instant dislike to him. On their first meeting, he had been introduced to the new Captain as the camp's rising young star. The Captain was very dismissive of him and his reputation in the world of sport. As he lined up with the rest of the lads in his barracks for inspection by their respective bunks, Captain Black rounded on him. He positioned himself directly in front of Callon. The Captain was slightly taller, standing at around Six foot one and appeared a little slimmer. His hair was dark brown but visible only from the side of his head. His peak cap appeared glued in position and was pushed forward; almost covering his eyes. The Captain raised his chin to look directly into the steel cool eyes of Callon before he spoke.

'We have means of dealing with people like you, lad, especially if you get out of hand.' Captain Black's face was inches away from his. The Captain allowed the peak of his cap to touch his head as he shouted his noxious remarks. The Captain then proceeded to walk to the side of his bed which had been immaculately manicured for this first inspection. Standing still for a few seconds by the bed, he then started to pull the sheets off and tipped the thin mattress onto the floor. He then opened the locker belonging to Callon which was positioned directly to the right, next to the head of his bed. He started to empty its contents one by one onto the floor. Photographs of his wife and young son were torn from behind the locker door and thrown to the floor with a nonchalant flick of a wrist, as though they were spent cigarette butts.

Whilst this was continuing, he stood unmoving except for his fist which he clenched tight and closed his eyes. His breathing had become heavier, more laboured and more rapid. He could not see what was happening, as he had his back to the Captain, but he knew his personal belongings were being openly discarded for all to see onto the wooden floorboards. Something inside him was telling him not to react, this was a senior officer. He tried to control his breathing, taking a lungful of oxygen at a time through his nose and expelling it through his slightly open mouth. He could still feel the anger welling up inside him. If the circumstances were different, he would have dealt with this in his own way. He only knew one way to deal with incursions like this, and it was not diplomacy or the spoken word. It was action, brute force. Not pleasant for the receiver, but it had to be done. The circumstances for now however, dictated that events should be different.

Stay as calm as possible, he said to himself.

Steve was stood to attention in front of his own bed directly opposite him. Some five feet separated them as they made eye contact. He was his closest friend and someone he could trust. Steven

Ormondroyd was a fellow Yorkshire man and he knew better than to let things get out of hand over something like this. He recognised the fragility of the situation, knowing his friend could end up in serious trouble if he reacted to the Captain's behaviour. Seeing the danger signs emerging over his friends face, he stared with huge wide eyes across to him. Steve knew it was better to be an ally of Callon than to be against him, the Captain was oblivious to this fact of course.

His friendship with Steve was galvanised shortly after arriving in Singapore, towards the middle of September 1945. The two men and a smattering of other friends decided that they had worked long and hard. They went downtown for a quiet night out together, visiting the bars and getting acquainted with the city. The outcome was different to what was intended and led to a 'wild west' style brawl. The spirit of the men was high and perhaps a little more animated than was expected for this part of the world. Company 436 RASC had had no permanent base for months now and were thankful to be settling in to a place which offered more than their previous locations. The regulars of the drinking establishment took great exception to their presence and the behaviour that members of the Company were dishing out. A fight erupted with Steve and another allied serviceman. He had allowed a stray hand to linger on one of the girls a little longer than he should have. The girl in question was providing light pleasure and entertainment to one of the paying servicemen.

The bar was filled with a rich cross-section of military personnel from different countries as well and interspersed with local males and their women of the night. Most servicemen were dressed in uniform, proud of their respective rank and unit. The 436 company were regarded as the lowest of the low in military terms. They were at any rate, the lowest denominating factor in terms of who should, and who should not be occupying this bar. It had all started with a push and a shove. Steve took great exception to being called a 'stupid bastard' by one of the allied naval crew. The 436 Company numbers were not sufficient to be creating problems against a potential mob, if things got out of hand. Steve was no slouch though; he stood six foot two and weighed the best part of 16 stone. He was not going to be pushed around by someone four inches shorter and some 30 pounds lighter. Steve however, had not anticipated the next move from the naval serviceman. He was caught off guard from a punch which grazed his cheekbone. The speed and strength of his adversary took him completely by surprise. As Steve went down he took a few chairs and a table with him. Drinks were spilt and glasses were smashed in a wide arc across the floor. Before he could regain his balance and composure, he was jumped on by another two attackers from the same group. They had managed to turn him over and had him flat on his back. He was now being punched and kicked in the face and body. Steve was making it as difficult as possible for his attackers as he wriggled and fought back the best he could. He was trying to get to his feet, but was continually been knocked back. Callon instinctively threw himself into the melee. He did not summon help from his other colleagues; there was no time for that. He simply waded into the pack, throwing men away from Steve and throwing punches at as many of the attackers as possible. It looked like all hell had been let loose now, as further drinks and tables were upended. A circle formed around the fight area as if in a school playground. Chaos was now prevailing as bodies not wanting to get involved, blended with bodies who did want to chance their arm. He was mindful of his poor position as he fought to regain a better vantage point. He was aware his back was not covered, and therefore vulnerable to a bottle, a fist, or a chair at the back of his head. Having secured a more favourable stance, he and Steve, who was now back on his feet, were able to resist the onslaught more purposefully. By this time, there were another half a dozen of their company trying to push and shove their way to the edges of the action. Company 436, were outnumbered, but having Callon on their side taking men out with each thrust, shortened the odds considerably. His strength and speed of aggression was unequalled as he continued to slow the opposition down. There was a momentary lull in proceedings as each group found itself now on opposite sides of the circle. Shouts and small skirmishes were still continuing, but it was more threatening words rather than any action. Divided only by a few feet now, the naval group had had enough. Both he and Steve had their backs to a wall, urging their attackers to come forward. No one did, they just stared at the two men and backed away, slowly and gradually, not taking their eyes away from them for a moment. Callon began to clear the broken glass by swinging his foot across the floor from around himself, to give a better purchase on the wooden boards. He never once allowed his stare to leave the group. He was not going to be taken by surprise. He and Steve were readying themselves for the next onslaught, as they moved from side to side in a synchronised fashion. It never came, the fight was over.

There were a couple of navy guys spark out on the floor. They were moaning and needed attention.

'Pick your friends up and take them home,' said Callon, without once relaxing his glare. 'Take them now.' One of the men on the floor was bleeding from his nose and mouth quite badly and had a gap where teeth once filled. He was going to need some urgent dental attention for sure. The other sailor was laid on his back unmoving with a head wound. Four men came forward very cautiously and propped the unconscious bodies onto their backsides, before helping them to their feet. Within a couple of minutes, both injured men were conscious and speaking. They had no idea where they were, but they were speaking.

'No real harm done,' he said to Steve over his shoulder. The injured men were helped bodily out of the bar to a safer environment. Both were very groggy, and would not be partaking in any further festivities or violence that night. Some of the sailors towards the back of the group were looking back as they passed the doorway exit. They wanted to make sure they were not been followed. The look on their faces as they left the establishment suggested that they were happy to get out of there with nothing more than a few sore heads.

The 436 Company had just witnessed the amazing power, strength and speed of their colleague. He had intervened at the risk of his own safety, knowing full well that he was grossly outnumbered.

'There was no time for dawdling,' he told his friend, Steve, 'you needed immediate assistance.' It was a selfless act and one that would stand him apart from the rest of the group. In the months following, his friends witnessed much more of Callon's skill, strength and speed. There was more to their colleague than meets the eye, but this group knew that and held him in awe of his successes this far. They had been a tight unit since coming together in York for their initial training, all those months back. Apart from a few bruises and some sore knuckles here and there, a bloody nose and a bust lip on Steve, 436 Company were unscathed as they made their way back to their barracks and relative safety.

Steve could see that Captain Black was antagonising his friend and he knew what was about to happen. Callon had a temper and a fury from hell if he was intimidated unjustly. The Captain was sailing very close to the wind, thought Steve. He never sought violence but under certain circumstances, he operated on a very short fuse. The fireworks were about to begin any minute if something or someone did not intervene. Steve locked eyes with him and shook his head almost without moving it, enough only for Callon to register the signal, but for no one else to see it. This most discernible movement was enough to take the heat out of the moment.

'Clean this fucking mess up, soldier,' shouted the Captain.

'You're a disgrace to this unit.' He stood without moving or answering just sufficient enough before a charge of insubordination could be handed out. The whole barracks heaved an invisible sigh of relief when he answered in a booming voice after seconds of absolute silence.

'Yes, Sir,' The Captain came back to face him, staring at him intensely with piercing eyes. The delay in his reply to the Captain was nothing short of contempt, he thought. Callon stood looking forward without making eye contact.

'You step out of line once soldier and I will have you. I will fucking have you!'

Callon stopped in his tracks on hearing Captain Black bellow his name. He was now only 15 paces away and gaining on him fast. He turned 90 degrees to face the Captain. When he was within five strides of where he stood, he saluted,

Please go away, Captain Black, he thought, I really do not need to hear this.

'Sir,' he said without any kind of conviction. He was not in any mood for much more discussion than the regulation requirement and certainly not in a mood to take any instructions. He had the greatest of respect for rank and position, but not when it was being abused. He needed to see his CO and secure his place on that plane for home. He would sort out his unfinished business in Singapore on his return. For him it was a case of life or death, his father was dying for fuck's sake! As Captain Black rounded on him, he positioned himself inches away from his face. The stance was instantly recognisable by Callon, he had been here before. He knew what was coming, unfortunately for the Captain, he didn't know, what was coming to him. The Captain was screaming his name, trying to intimidate his target; his eyeballs were red and bulging from their sockets.

'CAAALLLLON, who do you think you are, and where do you think you are going?'

You shouldn't have done that Captain, I'm in no mood for playing silly buggers!

The Captain shoved his face into Callon's. Their noses were touching, but he did not back away, he held his position and ground and kept his neck, ram rod stiff.

Just keep pushing Captain, keep pushing if you dare. I am losing my fucking patience.

The Captain was trying to force his head backwards by his actions, as if to give greater credence to his authority, but he continued to stand his ground.

Stop now, Captain, if you know what's good for you. Stop now. Stay calm, Callon, stay calm, don't react.

He could smell the Captain's cheap cologne, and wanted the Captain to back off, but he continued ranting and raving like someone gone mad. His spittle was spraying into his face and his breath was like shite.

You are asking for one bloody good hiding, Captain. Stop now!

He turned his head to avoid both the spray and the breath. This brought about a further tirade from the Captain.

'Look at me when I am speaking to you, you worthless piece of shit,' he yelled. The Captain was now turning purple and the veins in his neck were about to burst.

Okay, you have asked for this. I cannot take any more of your bloody crap!

At this point, he stepped back, away from the Captain; he needed space because he was going to shut this bastard up. He was too close for him to be able to inflict the pain and the injury he felt he deserved. At this moment, he remembered thinking nothing about his desperate situation to get home, only to attack his aggressor and hurt him. Hurt him bad! He knew he could do this; it's what he trained every day for.

And fuck the consequences, he thought.

In one swift movement, he hit the Captain full face with the flat of his hand. His cap flew off his head and rolled on its rim in a small circle before coming to rest. A rage and a phenomenal strength surge, was now coursing through his body. The Captain went down, pole-axed by the force of the punch. He grabbed him by his crutch and his shirt collar, taking a handful of chest and genital hair at the same time. He lifted the Captain bodily above his head, straining every sinew with his actions. The Captain was screaming like a baby as he launched him upward in one movement. He proceeded to throw him to the ground onto his back. He fell into a crumpled heap, writhing with pain. This move was one of his specialities, but not normally executed at the edge of a parade ground. It was usually performed in front of a baying crowd of wild supporters in a wrestling arena. He could only carry out this manoeuvre in the ring when his opponent was supine, dazed and groggy. Because Captain Black was fully clothed, it was easier to get a good firm hand hold.

As Captain Black lay on his back groaning and holding his crutch area, he fell on him with his knee into his chest. He knew he would do some damage; he heard the crack of his ribs. Injuries like this can often cause a punctured lung. For good measure, he smacked him full in the face again, with the flat of his hand. He did not want to risk damaging his hand or fingers. His hands, kept him in a lifestyle which was envied by everyone on the camp and he was not going to jeopardise that. Breaking a few bones in his hand against a mouthful of teeth, whose owner he now despised was not his idea of fun. Blood sprayed from the Captains nose and mouth and peppered his shirt. He knew he had done some serious damage, but regarded his actions unavoidable and necessary. The Captain's nose was broken; it seemed to be pointing a good way off centre. One of his teeth was missing from his front top set and no doubt a few other loose teeth as well. Job done! He stood up from the attack and studied the Captain momentarily. He was breathing quite deeply. He was laid on his back on the ground, his chest rising in two stages as though painful in its execution, then falling in one, as he exhaled. He left him where he lay. Apart from the visible signs of him breathing, he was both unmoving and unconscious.

He looked around as he walked away; he did a 360 degree rotation of the scene with his fists clenched, as though expecting others to come at him and attack. In this mood, he would take the whole regiment on. The red mist he had managed to dissipate earlier on reading the telegram had returned with a vengeance. He noticed that this indiscretion of his had caught the attention of at least a half dozen service personnel who were doing their own thing, on this seemingly nondescript kind of day. His actions had caused each of them to stop momentarily in their tracks. His actions were completed in a few seconds and carried out with such speed and precision. No one approached or interfered with what was happening. No one wanted to get involved; they were already aware of his reputation and knew better than to stick their nose into his affairs. One of the soldiers closest to Captain Black then went to his assistance, once he saw he was walking away from the scene.

He knew he was in deep shit. He had just assaulted an officer; not just an assault, this was grievous bodily harm.

He deserved it, he thought, the Captain had it coming. There was no need for all that ranting and fucking raving!

It would be a few weeks before Captain Black and he would set eyes on each other again, and it would be several days before Captain Black was out of hospital. This was not the end of this little tête-à-tête however, as Callon would find out to his cost. Catching a plane home was now very far from his thoughts. Going to see Major Reece was not an option any more either. It would be the Major asking to see him, but for actions and reasons which he could not explain. Callon had only one option left open to him.

Chapter 17

He entered the guard house as though preparing a mass surprise break out, throwing the door open and nearly taking its hinges off. He was confronted by two military policemen wearing red berets pulled to one side. (Red Caps). Both guards had been taken by surprise at this rather theatrical entrance. They were wearing shorts and neither had a shirt on. One of the guards had an armband wrapped around his bicep to indicate his rank and his MP status. The guard without the armband came towards him, whilst the second one backed off slightly. Both guards looked at each other and shrugged their shoulders wondering what the hell was going on.

The guard closest to him spoke. 'What do you want, soldier, this guardhouse is out of bounds!' Both guards recognised the man before them, but kept with military protocol.

'You'd better lock me up,' he blurted. Shocked, there was complete silence from the two guards. The guard with the armband shrugged as he tried to make sense of the situation.

'Nobody ever volunteers to be locked up, so tell me, what's going on?' Callon reckoned that giving himself up was the best and the safest option. This would create fewer problems for him and the camp as things settled down. How wrong he was in making this split second assumption!

'You will find out soon enough,' he told them.

'That's not good enough soldier; tell me, what you've done?' The guard without the armband was scratching his head in wonderment. There was a defined reluctance not to do anything with him from the guard's perspective. They needed a good reason or an official instruction to take a soldier out of service. The officer in charge, he with the armband, took him to one side and asked him to explain what was going on. Callon explained what had just happened, stating that he was provoked by the Captain. Without further ceremony or hesitation, he was then bundled into a cell.

The guardhouse was not the most secure of buildings; from the outside, it looked just like a regular army barracks but with fewer windows. Keeping someone locked up in these huts was more of a cosmetic exercise than anything else. He knew he had just forfeited not only his freedom but much more than that in reality. He had allowed his anger and his frustration to get the better of him, merely to teach that son of a bitch Captain a lesson. With one swift movement of utter stupidity, he had jeopardised his whole future. His chances to go home to see his sick father were now impossible. He had sacrificed his chances to compete further in a sport which was heading towards its climax. An outcome which could be life changing. There was also the darker side, stretching way beyond the boundaries of sport, a side which he knew little about, but a side which could potentially bring him riches beyond his wildest dreams. The girl too, whilst he knew he could never have her, she also inspired him. She inspired him for reasons which he hated himself for. His life before this incident was complicated, but it was about to get a lot more complex from now on. He was going to serve time now, he was sure of that. What would his future hold as he found himself confined to the guardhouse, probably facing a court martial? He wondered how long his incarceration would be. He would soon find out, he was sure of that.

What he didn't know was that he would have to go through hell and back and fight for his life.

He took stock of his dull surroundings, berating himself for ending up in this mess. He was furious at his actions, as he inspected his new home in close detail. He leant back on the door which had just been closed and locked behind him. He felt violated at this moment, in spite of his own violent attack on an officer. Still hyper from what had just taken place, he felt like a caged tiger. There was no window; he had expected a view at least. The cell was extremely hot, sticky, lit only by one low wattage light bulb. The bulb was swaying ever so slightly of its own accord and attracting the attention of several flying insects. These, no doubt, would be feeding themselves at the first opportunity from his blood. He could feel the warmth from the bulb despite the heat in the room. He looked towards it and wondered when he would see daylight again.

What have you done you stupid bastard. He was disgusted with himself. You are the most respected sportsman in Singapore, he thought to himself, and now look at the mess you're in.

The bed was a very basic wood frame with a thin mattress on top of thin wooden slats, with a small thin pillow, a towel and a blanket. The room filled him with dread, the bare wooden walls gave no comfort and he despaired at his actions. Only in the room a matter of minutes, he was already bored with his surroundings. One cursory glance around the room took it all in, captured completely all there was to see. He started to count the boards which made up his room and thought better of it. Now was not the time to do this, he was sure there would be plenty of opportunity later.

Apart from a wooden fold up chair and a small table measuring two foot square, the only other accessory in the room was a metal bucket. He had no use for it at the moment, but mentally was 'shitting himself' at the consequences of his actions.

He thought about his weekend and triumphs on Friday and Saturday night in Johor and the Great World arena in Singapore. It was a tremendous strain on his body to wrestle back to back contests, but it had been worth it, he had won both contests convincingly in the end. This weekend had been his most successful since arriving in Singapore. Having reached the last four contestants in his quest for the Light Heavyweight Wrestling Championship of the Far East, he would soon learn his fight dates and who his competitors would be. He thought about the sheer joy his winning had brought to his loyal fan club and that of his wrestling promoter Kazar. He was top billing in Singapore and in neighbouring Johor. Now he was incarcerated in a dingy cell facing consequences he could only begin to imagine.

I need to get a message to Kazar, he thought. This is my only hope to get out of this mess. He'll know what to do, who to speak to. Kazar has friends in high places, yes, Kaz is my only hope now.

'What the fuck is going to happen now?' he said to himself in a soft whisper. From his seemingly hopeless position, he wondered if he had completely blown his chances. Maybe there was a small chance or some minor miracle in the making, which would allow him to continue wrestling before going home briefly to see his sick father.

Don't be bloody stupid, Callon, get real, there is no easy way out of this mess. You have fucked up big time.

He was where he was; in the shit, and he was not dreaming, he was consumed by his own stupidity. His celebratory Singapore Sling drinks last night at the Raffles hotel were a reminder of how far he had come in such a short time. The most prestigious hotel in the whole of the Far East, if not the world, and he was now reduced to this, standing in a cell room measuring eight feet by ten feet. He knew he would have to wait some time before he could sample the unique bitter sweet flavours of Singapore's most famous drink again. He wanted to take back his actions, but it was too late for that. He did not want to hurt Captain Black in this way.

In the dark recesses of his mind he did. He wanted to see him hurt badly. The bastard had plagued him since the moment they set eyes upon one another. He deserved everything that came to him. Why was he so dismissive of his wrestling success? He wanted to beat his fucking head in. Now, right now! Yes, he thought, he'd do it all over again. It was the Captain's fault he was in this mess.

He composed himself, trying not to think too much about what could or might have been. He considered his situation again, unable to change a damn thing. He looked around his cell, unable to comprehend his pitiful surroundings. In places he could see daylight, where the combination of heat and moisture had taken its toll on these flimsy wooden walls over the years. The guardhouse was a very basic structure which lacked any feeling of promise, built of horizontal wooden tongued and grooved boards supported by vertical pillars every six foot or so. A single horizontal beam ran around the whole cell providing the strength and the stability of the structure. Former inmates had used this as a shelf. A dirty old toothbrush and an old photo frame without a picture were left at the side where the bed was. He wondered where the poor bastard was today who last occupied this cell. He did not suppose that this same poor bastard would be thinking about him. The cell was finished off with a flimsy corrugated roof. Escape was as easy as you like, a good shoulder charge at the door would do the trick but where would he escape to? When all said and done, the people already under guard here were in the real scheme of things, petty offenders. Callon's offence was now head and shoulders more serious than this camp had seen before. He had just battered an officer into the ground.

He was considering whether to lie down on the bed to take in the seriousness of his situation, but immediately dispelled this thought. His voluntary incarceration and the sudden exhilaration of energy to put Captain Black out on his arse had already started to wear off, his adrenalin rush was now over and he felt jaded. He was still wearing his army issue boots and socks, khaki shorts and shirt, but feeling uncomfortable and clammy. His ears suddenly pricked up when he heard the commotion coming from outside his cell. The walls of the cells provided little or no sound protection. At least two, possibly three other guards from within the camp, barged into the guardhouse shouting at the men on duty.

'Arrest, Callon, arrest, Callon!'

'He's just assaulted, Captain Black,' said another voice.

'He's been taken to hospital,' he heard one of the junior officers say, 'he's in a bad way and having difficulty breathing.'

Callon recognised the next voice. The head of the guards cut in with his verbal offering.

'Holy shit, we had no idea he was hurt that bad. It's okay though, it's okay,' as he tried to bring order to the proceedings. 'We already have our man, he gave himself up 15 minutes ago; he's in cell number seven down at the end.'

The discussion inside the guard house became much quieter and he was straining to hear what was going on. He pressed his ear to the door, feeling very uneasy about the atmosphere outside of his cell. There were things happening, he could hear them, but the voices were muffled. He felt irritated and very restless; he wanted to lie down on the bed, but not a sensible option just yet. He moved from behind the door to the farthest point in his cell and walked back to the door again. He stopped occasionally, straining to hear what was been said, but he could hear nothing.

This is not the time to lie down, he told himself.

His instincts told him that he should occupy the furthest point away from the door. The urge to lie down on his bed and rest was becoming greater, but he resisted in spite of feeling very tired.

Come on, Callon, you need to stay alert. Don't be caught off guard.

'Do not lie down,' he told himself, denying his natural instincts, 'no, not yet anyway.' The lack of noise and activity was almost deafening, but something did not feel right. He was suddenly feeling very hot and very thirsty, his tongue and mouth parched as he tried to add moisture to the back of his throat.

'I hate whispers, they involve conspiracy,' he told himself. His instincts told him that this is exactly what was happening, conspiracy, and it involved him.

He decided to call out to the guards and make his presence heard.

'Guards, can I have some water please?' He spoke loud enough for anyone in the guard house to hear. He needed to make contact with the guards, he needed to know what they were planning or saying. He received no response, only silence.

'Hello,' paused for a moment, then added, 'can I have some water please?' There was something going down for sure. His call went unheeded again. He tried in vain to find a crack in the wood panelling which would reveal a little more than was been offered now. He wanted to see what was happening if he could. More bodies arrived in the guardhouse. He could hear the rustling of clothing and the increased activity of leather boots on wood. He could hear the whispers again, the conspiracy continued. The whispers were inaudible, but they threatened him. This was a conspiracy, he knew something was happening, but he did not know what. He approached the back of the door very gingerly, but there was no sound or activity coming from beyond.

'Hello, anyone, can I have some water please?' Another inmate realising his plight spoke out.

'You can have my water pal, but the buggers won't let me out of my cell.'

'It's okay, friend,' he said, as he spoke back to his unknown comrade and into thin air. He received no reply back from the guards, not even a confirmation of his request. He shouted a little louder this time.

'Come on, guards, someone, please, at least answer me?' he was now becoming edgy. He continued to listen intently for any kind of response or movement. Nothing stirred outside; he could only hear his own shallow breathing. A trickle of sweat ran from the back of his neck between his shoulder blades, he shuddered slightly. His shirt and pants had wet patches all over from his perspiration. They were suddenly becoming very sticky and uncomfortable. He moved back to the space at the side of the bed with his back to the wall. Just then, all hell let loose.

The door imploded with the lock and hinges flying everywhere as two guards rushed in. Fortunately for him, they were both slightly off balance through the exertion of breaking the door down. They were followed in by four more military policemen.

Without having any time to think other than to defend himself, he instinctively moved forward, a half stride, to counter their attack and provide some room for manoeuvre. More room would give him more scope, but space was very limited, everywhere was so cramped. Within a second, the whole cell was full of bodies and they were all trying to get a piece of him. He managed to get several blows and kicks in to the first two guards. This quick thinking had provided a welcome barrier as they went down in front of the invading pack. The guards behind now had to hurdle and trample the two front guards to get to him, adding further to their injuries. The small table and fold-up chair were in pieces on the floor. He was moving around like a madman in the space which was available to him. It was fist and feet now, he was in survival mode. Any let up in his ferocity towards this bunch was going to be his downfall. He did not want them to hold him down or get him on the floor, if they did, then he would be fucked, well and truly fucked.

His father's advice rushed through his head as he continued to confront and deny his attackers with his single man defence. He had told him many years ago,

'It takes a good un' to beat two bad uns,' and here he was fending off six good men, strong and true. There were only four now though. He had connected better than anticipated with the first two guards and they were out for the count. They were not going to play any further part in his intended beating. Blood, spit and hair was flying all over the place and the guards left standing were shouting instructions at each other.

'Hold his bloody arms, then get him on the floor,' there was urgency in the guards voices. Never before had they encountered one man taking so much of a beating and being so difficult to stop. Further shouts from the guards as they pushed him backwards towards the cell wall. 'Stop this bastard from moving! Hold his arms for God's sake?'

He was fully against the back wall now and was trapped in the corner, the most vulnerable position for anyone being attacked. He had nowhere to go and was running out of options and ideas as to how he could defend himself. Several body blows one after the other began to take effect and he was now beginning to tire and to feel the full force of his attackers. He remembered hearing the metal bucket. It was being kicked around as it had somehow found its way unintentionally into the middle of this mass of bodies. Arms and legs were flying everywhere, as they frantically fought each other. He wished he'd taken a shit in the bucket now. His attackers would be gagging by now. The bucket had now taken on a mind of its own and was spinning around somewhere on the floor.

Yes, a good shit in the bucket would have slowed this lot down!

Above the noise emanating from his cell, came a different kind of eruption. The whole guardhouse was now coming to life. The rest of the inmates were shouting their disapproval at what was taking place. They were banging anything and everything they could get their hands on against their flimsy wooden cell to make their objection and create a noise. They knew someone was getting a good beating. It made no difference though, the onslaught inside Callon's cell continued. The guards' ferocity was unabated in spite of the external verbal pressure from the inmates. The guards were avoiding hitting his face as much as possible. Most of the attack was to his body and arms, or they were kicking his legs.

'Stay away from his bloody face,' said one of the attackers. They knew they could not hide facial injuries and wounds. As he became weakened he shouted hard and blasphemed against his attackers, thinking this would in some way add to his defence.

'You bastards, you fucking cowards,' he was beginning to fight on instinct alone now. He was now stood up and held with both arms behind his back. He was also prevented from using his legs. One of the other guards was on his knees and pressing his body tight against his legs to prevent him from kicking out. He tried to tense his body muscles to prevent further damage to his ribs and stomach, but he could not sustain this. The body blows were raining in now from all angles. He had no means to defend himself, and after what seemed like an eternity, he passed out.

He woke up, or regained consciousness, it was too difficult for him to tell. He was lying on his back on a bed, with every part of his body hurting, some parts more than others. He was not covered up. In spite of the blistering heat and the high levels of humidity which Singapore always provides, he felt cold. He fumbled feebly with hands swollen and sore for a blanket. His search was in vain. He wanted to cough, but it was too painful. He had few recollections of what had happened to him. He remembered giving himself up to the guards, but he couldn't remember anything after that. Something was different about where he was. The room had the same familiar construction as the barracks, but he was not there, he was sure about that. There was a light on somewhere, it was too bright though, he wanted to shout out for help, but no noise came from his lips. He wanted to shout for help because he thought he was dying. It was too painful and he was too weak to call out. His tongue was dry and his mouth parched; he needed water. Day or night, the room offered no clue, his pain was excruciating and every muscle and bone in his body was telling his brain to shut down. He realised he was in a very bad way, but he did not know why? He was scanning the room with his eyes only, making one sweep after another, trying to make sense of where he was. He was scanning without moving his head, but his scope of vision was very limited. The pain was becoming unbearable, he needed help, and he needed water now. Where was everybody? Was he paralysed and why did everywhere hurt so much? Why couldn't he answer his questions? He wanted to close his eyes, he wanted the pain to go away. Was he in a hospital, had he been in an accident? He did not recognise his symptoms, was he in shock!

The nightmares which followed this period were as real as they were frightening.

His outside world was black as thunder. He was running as fast as he could, taking huge strides towards safety. He could see clearly the outlines of the beasts as he peered over his shoulder. His whole body was wracked with pain but he needed to keep running. He could see the jagged white teeth against his blackness and their snarling jaws, dripping with slaver. They wanted blood, they wanted his blood. There were at least a dozen beasts pursuing him as obstacles were put in his path from a source he could not identify. The obstacles were slowing him down preventing him reaching safety. Safety was twenty strides away but the beasts were almost upon him now. His pain heightened as he forced himself to run faster. He could feel the hot breath from the beasts bearing down on him. Another ten strides and he would be safe but the crazed animals were now tearing at his clothes. He jumped from the cliff edge with arms outstretched and horror across his face. He was falling fast now, he was going to hit the rocks at the bottom of the cliff and smash his body. He started to slow down as the rocks loomed ever closer. It was a miracle he survived the fall and the clutches of the beasts. He was shouting out in terror as he opened his eyes; he was dripping with sweat. His world was still black as thunder.

He sensed there was someone in the room. He felt a presence like some kind of sixth sense; then someone was touching his face in a comforting way. His skin felt clammy and damp. He also had a blanket pulled over him now. Someone had been to his bedside. Why didn't they wake him? He wondered if they were feeling for a pulse, or if they were checking his temperature, what were they doing, checking if he was still alive? When he focused his eyes, there was no one there. He didn't hear anyone come or go. He still couldn't remember what had happened to him. He knew he was severely injured, but what had caused it? He was passing in and out of consciousness. Why does his body hurt so much, what could possibly have caused this? His whole body was in spasm now; every part of his body was shaking and convulsing uncontrollably. Was he dreaming and why wouldn't his pain go away. He did not know what day it was or how long he had been in this comatose state. He felt himself drifting away again. The pain was too much to bear.

Was he dying? he asked himself, he wasn't sure. Did he wish he was dead? YES!

After waking again sometime later, not knowing if it was day or night, he realised that he was still in a guard cell. It was different to his first cell. His memory was beginning to come back in parts, and he was able to understand what had happened. He started to piece small sections of the jigsaw together. The cell had the same solitary light bulb illuminating the room as before. Even though the light bulb suggested it was daytime inside his cell, he somehow felt it was night. His convulsions and muscle spasms had abated. It was so still and peaceful, yet the pain in his body was screaming at him. No windows still, but the room was a little bigger than before and it was a different shape. There was life around him. He could hear very faint voices, footsteps on the wooden floor boards and the closing of a door some distance away. He would occasionally hear a chair being dragged into position over bare floorboards before hearing muted voices again. Both movement and memory were returning to his aching brain and body. He remembered the guards barging in to his room. He remembered fighting as if his life depended on it. He tried to move his fingers first, slowly, one hand and then the other. He was trying to make a fist, then releasing, make a fist, release. There were cuts across the knuckles of his right hand as he managed to raise it and inspect it. No broken bones, he thought. He could move his head slightly, and he noticed on a small table by his bedside, a metal cup filled with water. He had no idea who had put it there, or for how long it had been there? He needed to reach this cup somehow, he felt so dehydrated, his tongue was beginning to swell and his lips were cracked. Make a fist, release, make a fist, release. Now he tried to move his arms together; this was more painful. Reaching for the cup of water was futile, his pain was so overwhelming.

'What have those bastards done to me?' he asked.

They had beaten him until he had passed out and then carried on beating him afterwards. In spite of the excruciating pain searing through his body, he managed the faintest of smiles, remembering that it had taken at least six men to do this to him. He also knew that most of his attackers would be nursing some serious cuts and bruises as well. Some would be possibly nursing broken bones, and certainly missing teeth. His attack on the guards did not restrict him to just head and body shots. The Marquis of Queensbury rules were definitely off the table during his battle. It was a question of hitting them with everything and anything, wherever he could connect with fist or boot, it did not matter. Both his arms hurt like hell and he was convinced they were broken. He tried with one hand to inspect the other arm, feeling for swelling or something that would tell him what the problem was. Nothing was broken; it was simply the pummelling his body had taken. His wrists had almost been screwed off as the guards tried to apprehend him. He had no strength in them whatsoever and they were swollen and weak from being twisted and bent beyond their normal limits. He tried to reach the cup of water, but the pain in his hand and arms was intense. His thirst however was greater. He reached over with his right hand again and had to retreat his action because of the pain and the physical exertion. He waited for a few moments more regaining his determination, and tried again. This time he got closer to the cup, but the pain was so acute and he had to retreat his action again. One more surge he thought, and the water was his. His lips were cracked and craving the liquid which the cup contained. He waited a couple of minutes, he was thinking about how good the water would taste. If only he could get the cup to his mouth, he was parched beyond words. He needed to drink, he needed to drink now. This exertion was beginning to make him drowsy; he thought he was still going to die. Why else would he be left like this with no one to attend to his injuries, his crushing thirst was now burning into his mind. He leaned over again and reached for the cup, fighting the ravages of pain in his attempt. He managed to reach the cup; he held it between his thumb and his fore finger. As he started to lift the cup, precious drops were spilling. His hands were shaking with the exertion and pain coursing his body. More of the water spilled over on to the floor. He managed to rest the cup on his chest, dipped his fingers in the water and brought them to his cracked lips and mouth, sucking at his fingers to get every drop possible. He did this a few more times. He could not move his head off the pillow, so managed to position the cup over his mouth and tilt it slowly. He could not afford to spill any more of this precious liquid. He felt his life depended on drinking this water. As the cup tilted, the anticipation of feeling the water surge into his mouth was almost unbearable. At last the flow reached the back of his throat.

'Nothing will ever taste as good as this,' he said softly. He remembered the Singapore Sling he had tasted however many days back, but nothing compared to this feeling of relief. He had no idea how long he had been like this. He felt the strength which this small amount of liquid gave him. More of the water was spilling, some around his mouth and onto his chin. He used his fingers to try and scoop and push the liquid into his mouth; he could not afford to spill a drop more. He got the cup back on his chest and passed out.

The nightmares returned with a vengeance as his broken body was continuing to react to his injuries.

It was black as thunder as he manoeuvred the light aircraft through the raging storm. He was piloting the small craft and trying to land the plane but he knew it was going to crash. The plane was shaking and bumping against the turbulence. The fuel gauge was sounding and flashing against the blackness all around. The other instruments were not working and he was losing height. He wanted to parachute out, but something was stopping him getting out of his seat. The sides of the blackness were closing in, he was concerned the tips of the wings would touch the black sides and catapult the plane to earth smashing his already aching and swollen body. There were mountains ahead which he could see through the darkness as the sides of the blackness came ever closer. He needed to turn the aircraft; he was approaching a bend in the darkness. It would be touch and go that he would make it. He turned the corner, but there was a mountain face directly ahead of him, he needed to gain height, but his fuel had gone. He slowed down and the plane gained height to land safely on the mountain top. He was screaming at the top of his voice when he opened his eyes, he was dripping with sweat. It was still black as thunder.

He continued to drift in and out of consciousness; time was of no consequence or use to him just now. He hoped that when he awoke next time, the pain ravaging his body would have gone. He heard the door of the cell open. Heavy footsteps came towards him. He wanted to drift away again, but he was disturbed by a gentle hand on his shoulder.

'Kid, are you awake?' said a guard. This guard was not one of the gang of six who used him as a human punch bag, he was sure he would have remembered, intuitively. The guard's tone was pleasant and conciliatory, only concerned about his patient's wellbeing. He must have known about the unfair advantage of his attackers.

'I've brought you water and something to eat,' he said.

'Can you help me?' his voice barely audible. Without hesitation, the guard bent down and with his right hand lifted his head from the pillow and with his left lifted the tin cup of water to his lips. He took a few sips, but then he needed to get his head back on the pillow, the pain was unbearable.

'Thank you,' he said, in a very weak voice.

'Do you want something to eat?' said the guard. He had heard him scream out and was concerned about his condition. It had been several days since he had taken solid food.

'I can't eat anything, I feel terrible,' he said. The guard gave him another drink. Callon savoured every last drop of the water, not wanting to drink it in one go, he let the water just slip down his throat in small gulps.

'I need to see a doctor,' he said, his voice trembling with the exertion of speaking. The guard stood to his full height and looked down at him. He was shaking his head when he replied,

'No doctor, Kid, you are refused any medical attention. Do you realise what you have just done?' He was imagining the worst outcome for his actions.

'No,' he replied, in a soft voice and shaking his head ever so slightly at the same time. 'Singlehandedly, you have just put one officer and three guards in hospital, all with concussion and all with broken bones of some kind or another,' said the guard.

'Are any of them seriously hurt?' he asked, in a slightly stronger tone, but still finding it exhausting to speak.

'Do you care?' said the guard.

'No,' came back his reply, he rested his head to one side and passed out again.

He awoke some time later, again, not sure if it was day or night, the light bulb still on, disguising and confusing the reality of the time of day. He shouted feebly for some help and more water, but no one came. Was he hallucinating? Everywhere on his body still hurt or ached. He turned his head slightly to the right he was looking for a chink of light between the ill fitting boards of his cell. This would tell him if it was daylight or not, but he saw nothing but blackness. He then passed out again.

When the guard came in again some time later, he had only been conscious for a few minutes. He knew he had to start getting mobile. He was still very thirsty. The guard had always left him wanting more and he was beginning to feel the pangs of hunger. Being hungry was a good sign as he could begin to regain his strength. The guard helped him to eat and drink a little. Unexpectedly, the guard opened his hand and showed him two white tablets.

'Take these, it will help your pain, but keep your fucking mouth shut, Kid, remember you have been denied all medical attention.' The guard helped him take the pain killers and then left without saying another word. The guard repeated this act of humanity several times and was instrumental in getting him back on his feet and freeing him from some of the pain at least. The guard always referred to him as 'Kid.' He did not know the name of his guard, but regarded him as his guardian angel in a uniform. The next time the guard entered the cell, he spoke to him.

'I've seen you wrestle in the Great World arena downtown,' he said, with more than a hint of pride in his voice. 'The whole camp is talking about your wins last week.'

He thought about the guard's words. 'Last week, how long have I been here?' There was surprise in his voice as he tried to get up from the bed. He gave up almost immediately; the pain was still too intense.

'This is your fourth day, Kid. You have been out of it for most of the time. We've kept a close eye on you though, but you have been someplace else these past days. You've been shouting out in your sleep and fighting demons. You had us all worried at one stage. We thought you wouldn't pull through.' The guard held a cigarette out to him, but a slight shake of the head determined that outcome.

'Tell me, where did you learn to do all that wrestling stuff, Kid? Everyone in the camp is saying you're the best anyone has seen in these parts?'

'It's a long story; my father saw it as part of my personal survival.' He paused and reflected momentarily about his desperate situation before continuing. 'It didn't do me much good though did it,' he added.

'You didn't see the state of the guards. No one could believe one man could inflict so much damage on six strapping guardsmen. As I said, some of the guards finished up in hospital, and none of them are back in service yet.'

The faintest of smiles swept his face as he studied the guard and his facial expressions. He was a good man and without his help, he would have suffered much more.

'If there's anything you need, Kid, just let me know. I have to be careful though. You've hurt a lot of people here, and they wouldn't take kindly to me handing you out favours.'

The guard was about to leave and lock up when he asked,

'There is one thing. I need to get hold of my wrestling promoter. They call him Kazar; his office is at the Great World Arena.' The guard made a note in a small diary.

'Leave it with me; I will see what I can do.' He let his hand linger on his shoulder as he left, just long enough for him to know that he cared about him and that he wanted him to get better, then just as he was about to leave his cell, the guard returned to his side and said in a low voice,

I understand now why they call you, The Untamed White Savage, Kid!'

Before he could answer, the guard had locked the door to his cell and gone.

That little discussion helped him as he lay on his bed, still in pain. He felt better knowing a little more about what happened. He was concerned that he had lost four days and hoped that Kaz would make enquiries as to his wellbeing. Kazar could help him if anyone could, he knew people who could make a difference to his situation. He wanted to ask the guard what was going to happen next, but he felt he was not yet ready to face that answer. Deep down he knew he had pushed his luck beyond acceptable boundaries. He could not see a good way out from his predicament. He had abused his privileges and he was going to pay. At least he had a friend on the inside; this could be helpful to him, how or why would have to be determined later. The guard could be his lifeline in a tortuous journey to get back to full fitness and he needed to start this process as soon as possible.

He was now trying to stand upright. Up to this point, he had been flexing his arms, fingers and hands whilst laying flat on the bed. He was also able to bend his legs slightly, trying to pull them up to his chest. He wondered if they were strong enough to carry his full body weight. The bed was becoming uncomfortable so he had to make a determined effort to get himself mobile. He was able to move reasonably freely, albeit in a prone position. This was progress in his mind. Pain was more manageable, but still his body ached. He did not know of course how much the painkilling tablets were helping him. He managed to turn over on to his front and attempt a push up, but he abandoned it immediately. Prior to his beating, he could bench press twice his own body weight and do press ups by the dozen.......with one arm! Pain in his ribs and chest suggested that he should leave that for another day. He attempted to get out of bed; he had movement in his legs and was able to swing them across the bed on to the floor. With one hand on the bed, he started to manoeuvre himself into an upright position. His legs felt very weak, but this was understandable, he had been flat on his back for five days now. He could stand for a short period, but was unable to take more than a few steps yet. Another major concern for him was passing blood in his urine. He knew that his kidneys had taken a fair old beating. His back was also very weak and very painful, those guards did not leave a muscle or a bone untouched. Bit by bit he started to regain movement, slowly but surely he could do a little bit more. In spite of his body being wracked with pain, he somehow knew he was in recovery. Miraculously, he had not sustained any broken bones, so it was just a matter of time before he could start to get back to normal, whatever normal was?

Through the wafer thin walls, he had heard his friend's frantic efforts to visit him. They had heard about the beating that the guards had meted out to him and were furious. He could hear their frustrations in their attempts to gain access to their friend. The guards were under strict instructions and were refusing any contact of any kind from anybody. He felt that the raised voices from his friends against the guards were for his attention and that he knew people were concerned about his well being. On one occasion he had shouted back reassuringly that he was okay. Steve had confirmed his short reply and said that the camp was rooting for his safe return back to soldiering. Steve was been ushered forcefully out of the guard house as he returned his message. He wondered about Kazar, had the guard made contact with him? He must be frantic, knowing about the wrestling schedule and being unable to visit him. Maybe all opportunity to wrestle had now been sacrificed due to his stupid actions. He had no idea what was happening, but he needed to know something very soon.

Time now was passing really slowly. He still had had no contact from anyone outside except his jailers. In the beginning he had lost days, but now every hour was dragged out. His daily intake of pain relief tablets was abandoned for now. He needed to know what the damage was to his still very painful body. The painkillers were masking any pain he still had, so he needed to know what hurt and where, and to what extent. This way he could start to take corrective actions to help mend the injuries. He was now able to move around the cell more freely as previous shuffling steps had progressed to short strides, but he still walked with a limp. This was progress. His food intake was also increasing. His guard friend was sneaking in extra rations of high protein food despite being on a bread and water diet as decided by his captors.

Reflecting on his precarious predicament, he wondered what was going to happen to him next. Now with a clearer mind he considered what the options might be. A good beating from the guards would not be considered sufficient punishment for his actions, irrespective of how much he hurt. How long would he be held in this so called detention cell? He would not be walking away from here with a slap on the wrist, of that he was sure!

How was his father? In spite of five days in recovery, he had not given a great deal of thought to him and he felt sad about that. Tears welled in his eyes as he pictured his father laid in a hospital bed unconscious. Was he alone? Would he die without any of his family by his side? He hoped he would be okay, but how would he find out now? It was the telegram and its grim reading which had sparked this situation. His father's condition bothered him immensely, and he experienced some further agitation again. His sisters shocking and sudden demise from this same illness was all too painful for him to bear. For all he knew, his father could be dead by now. He put his head into his hands, sobbing loudly, and prayed that he wasn't!

As he studied his body in the confines of the cell, he realised how severely beaten he had been. The bruising was now beginning to come out and reveal itself, he was literally black and blue all over. His face however, showed none of the terrible thrashing his body had endured. There was a little puffiness around his eyes, but suggested nothing compared to his bodily injuries. The guards had done a good job in preventing any outward presence of injury, they had hardly touched his face, but he had taken a battering to the back of his head and neck. Fortunately he had a very high pain threshold, though this had not prevented him from going into spasm shortly after his beating. Maybe a less fit man could have succumbed to those injuries. He was now standing, albeit with some laboured and slow movement It was now time to move on. The guards had beaten him to within an inch of his life! He considered himself lucky to be alive.

The next day, he was told to expect a visit from the CO in the afternoon and was given permission to clean up. He had now been in detention for almost a week. His personal hygiene required some urgent attention, bearing in mind the importance of his pending visitor. He also needed to shave, since his incarceration and beating he had the makings of a full beard. He was directed under supervision to the shower room. This seemed to bother the guard more than it did him. It was going to take a whole lot more than a swinging dick to embarrass him, and he was certainly not ready to slit his wrists.

He allowed the water from the shower to cascade over his head. It was the most wonderful sensation to feel clean again. The water pressure from the shower head across his shoulders still caused some pain, but it was worth every moment. The shower gently massaged his aching body as he soaped himself with his open hands all over. The pain which had gripped his body seemed to be ebbing away as the water washed over him. He watched as the water disappeared down the drain, taking with it, some of his pent-up feelings. He was hoping it would also take his pain, but that wasn't going to happen. The shower reinvigorated him unbelievably and brought new life to his aching and swollen body. Clean clothes had been brought from his barracks, and he felt at least half human again.

Chapter 18

The CO arrived at the guard house and sat behind a very basic trestle table on the right side facing him. The Major was with another officer who he had not met before. There was something familiar about him; perhaps he'd seen him somewhere before, but where? For that moment, his thoughts were distracted, trying to put a place or a time where he'd seen him previously? The connection was not with Major Reece or on this base. It was from somewhere else, he was certain of that. Trying to place the officer was side-tracking his thoughts and his reason for being summoned to this meeting. It would come back to him; for now though, he had to concentrate on the important proceedings facing him.

The trestle table had to be repositioned to accommodate the Major who was a very large specimen of a man. An assortment of papers lay in front of each of the officers. Escorted from his cell to the front of the table, still limping and in some discomfort, he positioned himself to face the officers. Ordered to stand to attention by a Redcap guard directly behind the Major, it was still a huge effort and saluting even harder. The Major was shuffling the papers and appeared to be reading some points from them whilst liaising in whispered tones with the officer to his right. More conspiracy he thought. Neither of the officers had even looked up at this point as the two men passed more documents to the Redcap guard standing behind them. The officer, who looked familiar, seemed to inspect him in detail. He could see the officer in his peripheral vision but resisted the temptation to look down. The officer continued his inspection, looking intensely at his face. He felt as though he was trying to make eye contact, but ignored the visual scrutiny, continuing to look forward over the top of their heads.

He was again distracted by his own thoughts.

'Who the fuck is this man?' he thought. His uniform suggested Lieutenant Colonel. But why was such a senior officer presiding over a charge of assaulting an officer? Perhaps the charges against him were more serious than he had thought?

'Was Captain Black going to be okay?' he thought. For all he knew, he could be dead! He had not held back in his attack on the Captain, but surely not enough to kill him?

As the two officers continued their inaudible discussion, Callon lowered his eyes when he felt it safe to do so. He was distracted this time by a cigarette resting on an ashtray. It belonged to Major Reece, and it had been some minutes since the cigarette had been touched. The length of the already spent ash was ready to fall. It would only be seconds before the ash dropped away, he thought. The cigarette was allowed to continue to discharge its smoky trail into the atmosphere. The air was still and very humid as the smoke from the cigarette rose very slowly and lethargically above their heads. It mingled and swirled ever so gently with the already spent smoke, lurking in the roof space of the guardhouse. His eyes were following the homogenous blend of grey white mist when Major Reece finally looked up. He lifted one eyebrow as he watched Callon standing uncomfortably before him. The Major returned his gaze to the papers in front of him and signed the top sheet passing it to the guard behind him who appeared to be directing the proceedings. He coughed slightly whilst standing to attention as though in protest of the Major's unhealthy smoking habit. The smoke had caught the back of his throat, but his feeble attempt went unnoticed and without comment.

Major Reece was a strapping Six foot four inch man mountain who clearly worked at his physique. He was also well tanned from time spent overseas in tropical climates. His peaked cap was upturned on the table to his right hand side. The Major had a few beads of sweat on his brow, and wiped them away with a perfectly ironed white hanky, pulled from his breast pocket. He was dressed smartly but casually in a khaki short sleeve shirt with epaulettes. The shirt was unbuttoned at the top and was already beginning to show early signs of perspiration under the arms. The guardhouse was stiflingly hot and extremely humid. The Major's trousers were immaculately pressed and creased. His boots were sticking out from under the table on his side. He could see part of his own reflection in the shine. Someone had spent a great deal of elbow grease getting them to polish up this much. He guessed it was not the work of the CO himself. He sported a rather bushy moustache peppered with hints of grey. His hair, thick, dark and wiry, had less grey. His hair was cut short and quaffed to one side with a parting that could have been drawn by a ruler. The Colonel was shorter by at least four inches, estimated from his sitting position. The unsmiling thin lips and his sunken grey eyes gave nothing away. He too was feeling the heat, but seemed to cope with it better than the Major. His frame was much thinner with sharp features, the drawn face lacked any pallor and only accentuated his long nose and pointed chin. Thin fingers on scrawny arms suggested he never over-indulged on the food front. His hair was fine and combed straight back showing obvious signs of hair loss on his receding temples.

Major Reece looked up at Callon again, with his piercing blue eyes. At the same time the Major went to pick up the cigarette. With the faintest of touches, the ash fell away. Major Reece took a long drag on the cigarette and snuffed out the butt.
Before speaking, he blew the smoke upwards away from himself and his fellow officer.

'You are in deep trouble, soldier. We have an officer in hospital with broken ribs, a punctured lung, broken teeth and severe facial damage. What have you got to say for yourself?'

He explained to Major Reece how he felt he had been provoked and intimidated by Captain Black. He also spoke about their first encounter and the remarks which Captain Black had made. As he spoke, he alternated his eye contact between the Major and the Colonel looking for some kind of sympathy towards his cause. He mentioned that all this anger towards him was without any kind of provocation. He was on his way to the Major's office, he said, when for a small misdemeanour on his part, Captain Black rounded on him. His mind was occupied and disturbed by the serious news which had just been delivered to him about his father. He handed Major Reece the screwed up piece of paper and he read it studiously. The telegram had somehow survived. He had found it in his pocket almost a week after his beating. The Major already knew about the telegram anyway; he was in a position to examine and intercept mail if he felt it was necessary or deemed sensitive, or if an individual was under surveillance.

Unknown to him, he was already under strict surveillance, the Major and the Colonel had a good reason for taking this measure. He was going to become an important part of their forward-thinking strategy, a strategy which would make all of them very rich men. Little did he know at this stage though, it would be him taking all the risks.

'I was seconds away from your office to ask for compassionate leave, Sir,' he said in a voice which reeked sympathy. 'You see, I need to get home to see my very sick father. I'm not even sure if he's still alive. I've no means of finding out his condition, sir.' There was a repositioning of the Major's posture in his chair as he shot back a sharp reply.

'You are going nowhere, soldier.' The Major's face was stern as he delivered his next words. 'On the contrary, your conduct is such that you will face a court martial. Pending your date for the court martial proceedings, you will be confined to detention in these cells. Do you understand, soldier?'

'Yes, Sir.' There was an air of dejection in his voice, he felt sick to his stomach, but had expected much worse anyway.

There was a slight pause as Major Reece took one of the typewritten sheets of paper from his desk.

'Your action and your complete disregard to authority and your insubordination are such that this will not, and cannot be tolerated. I'll have you thrown out of the army if your behaviour does not improve, soldier; now get out of my sight!' The Major lied about him being thrown out of the army, but he wanted the man who stood before him to know exactly who was in charge.

'Guard, take this man away now.' He saluted the two men and turned 180 degrees with difficulty towards the direction of his cell. He'd only taken a couple of steps when the Colonel spoke audibly for the first time in his presence.

'Soldier, why are you limping; and what's the cause of the bruising and swelling on your forearms?'

He turned round to face the Colonel rather awkwardly and stood to attention intuitively.

'Sir, I slipped in the shower.'

Major Reece and the Colonel studied his response with a degree of incredulity then dismissed him without saying another word. The Colonel's facial features softened, as he detected the slightest almost discernible smile cross his face. Had the Colonel and the Major expected him to tell the truth about the guards beating him, after all, they must have known what had happened? They must have known six guards had been sent in to attack him. Why did the Major not mention the injuries to the guards, were the guards carrying out the Major's instructions or the Captain's? Why did he wait almost a week to see me? Why did he wait until he was mobile again? He rather hoped his response would gain him some extra points somewhere down the line. But there were still a great deal of questions he couldn't answer. The most burning question in his mind just now was, 'from where did he know the Colonel?' It was drilling a hole in his brain'

The Colonel and the Major left the guardhouse went outside and walked some distance away, far enough to ensure no one would overhear their conversation. The Colonel spoke first.

'I like this soldier, Major and I'm convinced he's our man for the job. He possesses all the right credentials in my view. He is tough, resilient and not fazed by authority. He showed no sign of nerves and stayed calm throughout the cross-examining. What also pleased me; is that he recognised his guilt and accepted the good hiding given to him, never once did he mention his attackers or involve anyone else. These are the qualities we need, Major.' The Colonel paused as Major Reece took on board what was said before continuing. 'He has the right temperament too.' He was confirming what the mystery man had said to him during their last meeting in Johor. The Colonel continued. 'His life outside this camp grants him privileges and I don't want these privileges to be totally taken away. This soldier works on the docks, he has access to all the areas, including the bonded warehouse facilities and he has been security cleared. This is a perfect fit and a perfect cover for our plan. He is as clean as a whistle, well, apart from this incident. I want this man back at work as quickly as possible and I want this man back wrestling.' The Colonel stood making eye contact with the Major, looking for a nod of approval.

Major Reece straightened up and wiped his brow with the already soiled hanky from his breast pocket. He looked skyward as if looking for a possible gap in the relentless sunshine beating down.

'Callon is a young man, Sir; if this goes wrong we are all in serious trouble. Forget about rank and reputations, these go down the pan and so will we. Can we trust him to carry out this…?' Before the Major could finish his sentence, the Colonel retorted back with his voice half raised but controlled.

'This is an order, Major. Do you think I don't realise the consequences? Showing my face today has compromised me and my rank and could have untold implications for me should this exercise turn sour. Yes, he is a young man, but he is also very mature in many ways. Unless you can come up with a better alternative, then this is how we proceed, is that clear?'

'Yes, Sir,' Major Reece replied. 'Leave it to me, I will organise it in such a way that he receives leniency for his sentence. One more thing we need to consider, Colonel. What about Callon's father? As you know, he has meningitis and is seriously ill back in the UK. How do we overcome this, given his father was the trigger for this unfortunate episode in the first place?'

'Contact his family for an update, get in touch somehow, but keep any bad news out of any discussions you have with him,' said the Colonel. 'Whatever happens, this young man does not leave Singapore.' There was great emphasis placed on that last sentence by the Colonel. 'Remember, even if the news from the UK is bad, we use his Court Martial as a means to keep him here. Our plan is too important and too close to worry about the welfare of some soldier's father.'

'What about Captain Black, Sir? He comes out of hospital tomorrow.'

The Colonel was enraged just to hear his name.

'I want that son of a bitch out of here. I don't care how you do it, but I don't want to see that man's face around here ever again.' There was real contempt on the face of the Colonel. 'Black had no right to order that beating, I do not accept that the guards were set upon by Callon and were simply there to escort him to your office.' He pointed his finger at the Major, trying to emphasise his point. 'They were there to carry out the instructions of, Black. It was he who ordered the beating of that soldier. I have spoken to several of the guards involved; perhaps you should do something similar. That young soldier had no chance against such a determined force. You do realise that Callon could have died from his injuries, don't you, Major?'

'Sir, Captain Black almost died too.'

The Colonel returned his reply instantly.

'I don't give a shit about, Black. From what I have heard so far, he bloody well deserved it.'

The Major had never seen such hatred on the Colonel's face; and was taken aback by the tone of his voice.

'Captain Black could easily have scuppered our plans,' said the Colonel dismissively.

The Major realised in that moment that the plans were far more important than anything to the Colonel. If someone got in the way of this operation, then they would be dispensed with, by whatever means.

Captain Black had unwittingly put a huge spoke in the Colonel's wheels and he had to go. After all, they were both to earn substantial sums of money from their audacious operation.

The Major saluted the Colonel and watched him walk away towards his waiting car.

A recently discovered photograph of my father as a thirteen-year-old boy.

All the pictures contained herein are from 3 photograph albums brought back to the UK by my father of his time spent in Singapore from September 1945 up until 1948 after completing his national service.

1) The surrender of 680,000 Japanese soldiers in South East Asia took place in the Council Chambers at the Municipal Buildings in Singapore on 12th September 1945. The picture shows a military parade of Allied servicemen prior to the surrender ceremony in front of the building.

2) The 7 strong Japanese party are escorted to the Municipal Buildings for the short surrender ceremony.

3) Lord Louis Mountbatten, Supreme Allied Commander (Southeast Asia) briefly addresses the allied forces and onlookers before the start of the surrender signing. Deputy Supreme Allied Commander (Southeast Asia) Lieutenant R. A. Wheeler US is directly to the left of Lord Mountbatten and partly hidden by the lectern.

4) Lord Louis Mountbatten, Supreme Allied Commander (Southeast Asia) accepted the Japanese surrender by General Itagaki Seishiro in the Council Chambers. Lord Mountbatten is far left centre in white with the Japanese surrender party opposite.

5) The Japanese led by General Itagaki Seishiro left the Municipal Building after the short surrender ceremony with heads bowed.

6) Lord Louis Mountbatten acknowledging the joyous crowds of Singapore people after the surrender signing.

7) Singapore street life in late 1945, returning to normality after the Japanese occupation.

8) One of the first photographs taken of my father soon after he arrived in Singapore. He was still only 19 years of age.

9) A view of the army barracks where RASC 436 Transport Company were stationed.

10) Some colleagues from the RASC 436 Company. My father is on the back left of the back row.

*11) An effortless lift on one of his
colleagues on the army camp.*

*12) Japanese soldiers were
put to work at the docks
unloading the ships soon
after the 12th September
1945 surrender.*

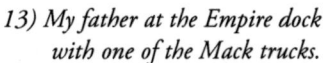

*13) My father at the Empire dock
with one of the Mack trucks.*

14) Mack trucks lined up at the docks awaiting their heavy daily routines.

15) In reflective mood on board one of the ships for unloading.

16) My father showing some of his early wrestling techniques with one of his friends at the docks.

17) The Great World Amusement arena in 1946, my father's favourite wrestling venue.

18) The Happy World Amusement arena, one of three in Singapore in the 1940's, the other was The New World arena.

19) An early wrestling pose of my father soon after being signed up by his wrestling promoter.

20) A little relaxation away from the wrestling and the docks at the Singapore swimming club.

21) At the beach close to the swimming club with his three friends. Not sure if the danger from sharks is from the sea or the land? My father is the one seated.

22) The world famous Raffles Hotel in 1946, one of my father's favourite 'after wrestling' venues.

23) The Union Jack Club in Singapore, another of my father's regular haunts.

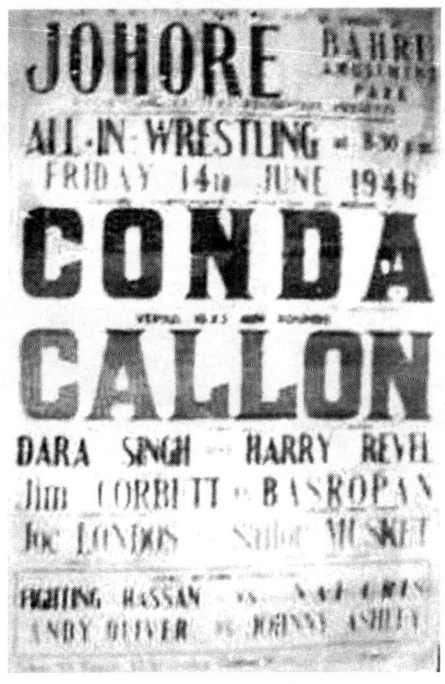

24) A placard announcing one of my father's wrestling contests at the Johor Bahru Amusement park in Malaysia on Friday 14th June 1946. Already top billing.

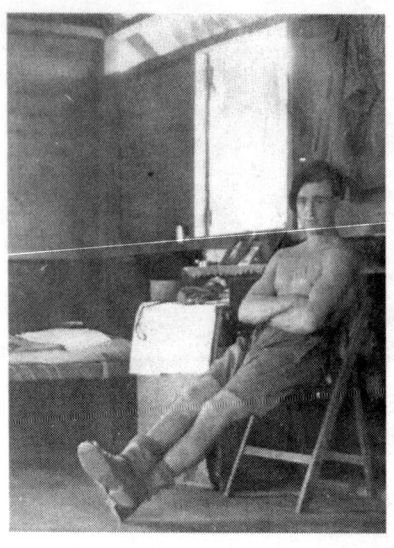

25) *Looking somewhat forlorn in the guardhouse. My father was moved some days after his beating and his meeting with his CO to a larger room to assist in his recovery.*

26) *Some training in the guardhouse in my father's quest to get back to full fitness.*

27) *Almost back to full strength and fitness but still in detention.*

28) *Two of the guardhouse personnel.*

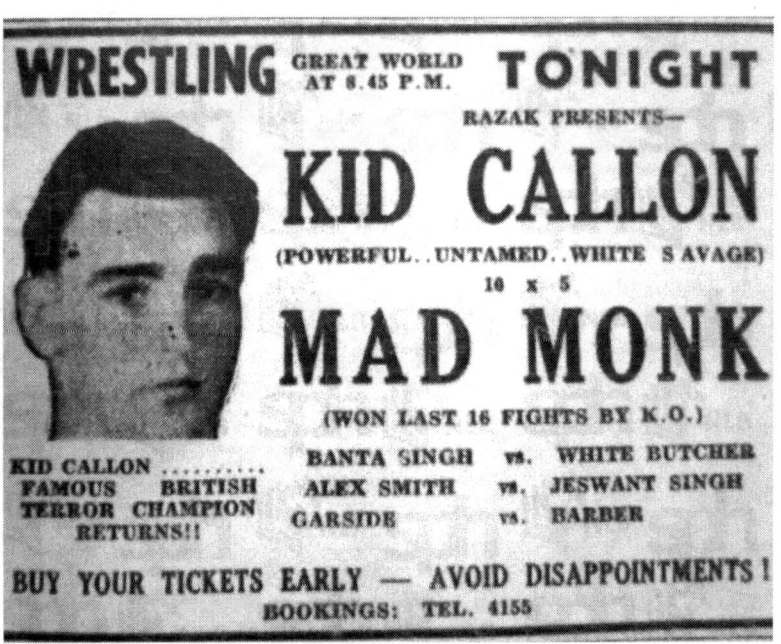

29) *Another contest scheduled in 1947 showing a photograph of my father top billing and the strap line 'Untamed White Savage' from where this book takes its title.*

*30) My father photographed
with some of his young fans.*

*31) One of my favourite
photographs of my father
wearing his bush hat.*

Chapter 19

'This has to be a two way thing, Major Reece, you help me and I help you.' Kazar emphasised his point to the Major with great strength of character and was determined to get what he had come for. He had arrived at the Major's office to negotiate on behalf of his young wrestler Kid Callon. It had been almost ten days since he had assaulted Captain Black. More important to Kazar at this moment though, his star wrestler was coming to terms with his own beating at the hands of the six guards. He was still in recovery, but he was improving with each passing day. That was the most important thing.

'What do you expect me to do, Mr Kazar? The soldier will have to serve his sentence; he assaulted Captain Black, a serving army officer. This is no small matter. The court has been lenient to Callon anyway. A mere 30 days in detention for this kind of brutal attack is unheard of. If this occurred in Civvy Street, he would be serving a minimum of two years in a secure jail, probably sharing a cell with a number of undesirables.'

'Major, come on, please, we both know why he has been treated leniently. You need this man as much as I do. From where I'm sitting, this young man has the potential to go all the way to the top of the wrestling ladder. In all my days in this sport, I have never seen such strength and skill from someone so young. He has the potential to win the Light Heavyweight Championship of the Far East. If we stop him from wrestling now, then his chances of winning this title are gone.'

'And whose fault is that, Mr Kazar?'

'Let's not start apportioning blame, Major. I have a proposal to put to you. We can both have a win-win situation here, but you have to be a little flexible in your approach to the Kid. We both have plans for this special young man.' Kazar composed himself for the final twist of the knife. 'I just want to say this; your plan can only go ahead if I get the chance to continue with my wrestling plans too.'

'Explain your proposal, Mr Kazar.' The Major was all ears.

Chapter 20

He was able to move around much more freely now and he had started his road back to full fitness in earnest. Much of the discomfort and the pain from his severe beating was easing and he was starting to feel energised. The beating had certainly taken its toll on his body but it was nothing he couldn't handle. It had been 11 days since his meeting of minds with the guards. He was not taking painkillers any more, so he knew exactly where his main problems were on his body. There was still bruising around his arms and abdomen, but these were now more superficial than anything else.

The sentence from the Court Martial was surprising. A month in the guard house was the best he could have hoped for. His sentence took into consideration intimidation by an officer, and hence was granted leniency. The Major had gone to extraordinary lengths during the court hearing to speak in defence of his actions by mentioning his excellent conduct up to this point and his reputation on the wrestling circuit. Another vital piece of his defence was that he worked on the docks, and that his specialist local language skills were essential to the port's management and organisation.

'It is important that all these factors are taken into consideration when making judgement and that this soldier is not out of service for too long,' said his commanding officer.

What had surprised Callon was that his beating by the guards and their subsequent injuries were never mentioned during the court hearing. This did nothing other than confirm that his beating was both unlawful and unrecorded.

Kazar had called to see his young wrestler as visiting rights were now restored. The situation created by Callon's court martial sentence was a problem, but not something which was insurmountable. The top four contestants left in the competition would wrestle each other for the title. The victor would be the one who won most of his contests. Kazar had told him that he could delay the start of this competition, but it would begin within a day of his intended release from this enforced incarceration. The title would he held over three week ends commencing Friday 18th July 1947.

This created its own problems as it would mean he would have to be ready to wrestle immediately after his release without any prepared competition. This would put him at a clear disadvantage versus his opponents. He somehow had to work round this dilemma. It was not just the competition wrestling, it was the whole process of staying fit, maintaining his stamina and his strength exercises.

'This just about seals my fate, Kaz, how am I expected to prepare for this contest wasting away in this dump?' He was looking for some sympathy now, forgetting that it was his own stupidity which had landed him in this mess. 'There's no way I can continue in this competition, is there nothing you can do? Can you extend the start date and give me at least a week to prepare?'

'The dates are set, Kid, no way can we change these now. The posters will be going to press once we establish who fights who and when.'

'Is this the best you can do?'

'No, Kid, it's not. I've organised a contingency plan and I can get you out of here to wrestle in a couple of bouts during the build up to the real competition.

He was staggered by his promoter's reply.

'How on Gods earth are you planning to do that?'

'Let's just say I have made a deal. It's not without its risks, but I think we can pull it off. During the time leading up to the competition, I also need to get you across the water to Johor. My man over there wants to see you again. He also wants more wrestling tuition. You made a good job of the last lesson. He likes you a lot.'

He was suddenly reminded of his first meeting with the mystery man. He had thought often about his words and the offer to earn two hundred and fifty thousand dollars. Whilst convalescing, he thought what he could do with this kind of money. It would certainly be life changing. He thought about the kind of house he would buy. This sort of money would give him limitless possibilities. He could even buy a new house for his mother and father as well. He was still concerned over what he would be expected to do though. He remembered he had agreed to drive a truck, something he had done every working day since he arrived in Singapore. Okay, his incarceration had prevented him from doing it lately, but, what is so difficult about driving a truck? He also remembered shaking hands with the mystery man. Perhaps that was a stupid thing to do. Had it committed him to driving the truck? No, he would always be able to say no when he knew more of the details. He had no idea where he would drive the truck to and from, but more importantly, what the cargo would be? He was sure he would be able to reverse his decision when he knew all the details. Deep down however, he knew that backing down was not an option. There were certain forces in play which suggested it would not be in his best interest to walk away from this operation, not if he valued his life.

The mystery man had shown me his hand after speaking to me, and I took it. The man got what he wanted, a driver; there was no way he could go back on this. This was a matter of principle and integrity; a handshake was a commitment which could not be broken, a gentleman's agreement.

'What about, Suzi, Kaz?' I was supposed to be in Johor last week?'

'We've had to readjust all our plans. You've caused my friends undue concern. It was not part of the scheme to have you banged up for a month. We've had to pull a lot of strings.'

'That's not what I asked. What about the girl?'

'If I can get you out of here, then I'll make sure she is there for you; don't worry yourself about that.'

'Kaz, please don't play tricks with my emotions. I need to see Suzi, no games, remember.'

'I said she will be there, relax, I will sort it. Now I need to find the best way of getting you out of here without arousing any suspicion. Remember, it wasn't me who got you into this mess.'

'Can't wait for your next trick, Kaz, getting me out of here to wrestle when the whole of Singapore knows I'm locked up. It'll be a stroke of genius on your part.' Kaz stood and left the confines of the cell. The guard was about to lock the door when he heard his return footfall on the wooden floor. 'I almost forgot,' Kaz said gleefully, 'I need to take some measurements.'

'You're not thinking of taking me out of here in a box?'

'No, don't worry. My master plan will work, now get some rest. You also need to consider your training. You'll be wrestling very soon. The guards will help you get established with whatever you need.'

He sat with his mouth open, staring at the doorway where his wrestling promoter had exited.

What the hell is this guy going to do? Yes, I know Kazar has friends in high places, but what he has just said sounded preposterous.

Chapter 21

The door of his cell opened without a knock or cordial greeting, his recent actions towards the Captain and his subsequent incarceration had seen to that. He leapt up from his bed in double quick time and stared in surprise at his visitor. The Major had had to duck slightly to enter his room. He saluted instinctively, albeit a little delayed.

'Sir,' he said.

'At ease, Callon, I'll keep this brief.' Major Reece was carrying a letter in his left hand. 'Here, read this.' The Major thrust a small airmail letter across to him with a hint of disgust on his face. His tone and demeanour were both unforgiving. He could only think that this was bad news about his father, the news he had been dreading. He did not want to read the letter. He held it reluctantly in his hand. He wanted to crush the words like before. It was bad news from home that got him into this mess in the first place. He felt the familiar dread of bad news consume him as his brain refused to comprehend the situation, he heard himself saying.

'Please, God; don't let this letter be bad news about my Father. Oh shit! It must be bad news, why else would the Major personally hand me a letter?'

'Read it, Callon, read the bloody letter.' The Major stood waiting for a reaction.

He turned the envelope over and was not surprised it had been opened. He guessed that this is what happens to your private mail when you are serving a court martial sentence. There was something not quite right about this though, and it took him a moment to understand what was happening.

'Sir, this letter, it's addressed to you. I don't understand?'

'Read it, Callon, it's from your wife in England, you should be damned ashamed of yourself!' Major Reece was shaking his head as Callon unfolded the letter and began to take in the words one by one. His fear and his anger returned, but it was fear and anger for different reasons;

June 1947

Dear Major Reece,

I really need your help. I am writing this letter in desperation, to find the whereabouts of my husband Derek Callon (436 RASC Unit). It is more than a year since we have heard from him. I have no idea if something has happened to him or where he is.

I have been writing to my husband on a regular basis since he was shipped abroad, but I continue to get no reply. I am not even sure he is receiving my letters. Please help me to find out his whereabouts.

His Mother sent a telegram a short while back. His father has been very ill, but thankfully he is much better now. I have a very young son here with me and we are concerned something dreadful has happened to him Thank you for your help in this matter and look forward to receiving your news.

Yours sincerely.

M G Callon (Mrs)

He put his head into his hands and sat on the edge of his bed, now distraught at his own misgivings and selfishness. He had only cared about himself and what he was doing. He had a wife and child who had become secondary in his life. Up until his incarceration, he had lived the life of a prince; eating the best food and drinking fine wines. He had plenty of money, money he squandered on himself and his friends, not for his family back home, giving little or no consideration to them, his personal disgust was overwhelming. He questioned himself about what he was doing and what he had done. Was he doing this for his self esteem or for his family? The answer was staring him in the face; it was for him and him alone. Then there was Suzi; he could have rejected her advances, but again, he chose the easy option. It was not her fault that there was this physical attraction to each other. She would be totally unaware of his marital status, how could she know? He had never told her and she had never asked. He didn't love her, not in that way; she was just another part of his huge jigsaw puzzle which was suddenly losing some of its key pieces.

'You know what you have to do, Callon,' the Major said with contempt in his voice. 'You write home immediately, I will arrange the guards to organise writing material for you.'

He was still in shock, this was the last thing he had anticipated and it threw his mind into a spin. He needed to face up to his shortcomings, and do it now. It was going to hurt his pride more than anything else as he blurted out to his CO.

'Can you help me, Major?' as he finally plucked up the courage to face his demons.

'What kind of help are you looking for, Callon. You can fix this by writing home to your bloody family!' said with no pity for the soldier staring wide eyed at the open letter.

'I can't fix it, Sir,'

'And why the hell not, soldier?'

He was looking for the right words to explain to the Major. 'Sir,' he paused, 'I...I can't write very well.'

The Major stood open mouthed for a few seconds, his attitude and expressions softened. 'But you can read, and you can speak the local language too?'

'Yes, I can read, but I have difficulty with some words. The teachers gave up on me at school and I knew I'd live to regret this one day, Sir. I was absent from school a lot, sure, I learned a lot of things, but it was mainly about life in general and how to take care of myself. When I got into difficulties, I could always fight my way out of trouble. This was my only defence sir.' He clasped his fist defiantly, so the Major had no difficulty in understanding his meaning.

'And the language, how did you learn that?'

'Just from listening and speaking, Sir. Repeating words and phrases over and over again, out loud, until I could repeat them in my sleep.'

'It takes a lot of guts to own up to something like this, soldier. Does your wife know you cannot write?'

'No, Sir. We were married shortly before I left for this overseas posting. I just about managed to sign the wedding registry. I get very nervous especially if I think someone else is watching.'

'Would you like to learn now; you have some time to spare?'

'Yes, Sir, I would like that very much.'

'Leave it with me, Callon, and by the way, I was pleased to read your father was getting better.'

'Thank you, Sir. I've been waiting for this information. It's the best news I could have hoped for.' He felt a weight had been lifted from his shoulders. He knew he was a very fortunate individual, taking into consideration what might have been; he could have lost everything that was within his grasp, including his family. If Kaz could get his wrestling schedule back on track, then he was not going to screw up the opportunities which now lay in front of him.

In the meantime, the Major was already making arrangements to have help brought in immediately. He would make sure that a letter was in the post that evening addressed to the UK by special delivery.

For the moment, he was allowed to roam within the confines of the cell block, but only as far as the door to the outside world. Most of the guards were quite sympathetic to his situation as they knew he was not going to run away. What he didn't know was that the Major had stipulated his detention should be of a relaxed nature. All the guards had been told of this special privilege, and for some, this didn't sit well, therefore the Major had the six guards involved in his beating transferred to other duties, not risking any kind of retribution towards this soldier. He had to be protected and helped back to full fitness. With the freedom to roam the guard cell at will, he made good use of this.

His sentence was counted from the day he handed himself in. Since then of course, his Court Martial had determined the rest of his detention. He would not get any time off for good behaviour, but he never expected that anyway. However, being confined to barracks was going to cause him some fitness problems. He wondered about what Kazar had told him. He would soon be testing the practical, based around the theory which Kazar had spoken about. For now though, he could not begin to imagine how his promoter was going to extricate him from his surroundings. He had to work on the knowledge this was to be his home for the next few weeks and that he needed to make the most of it. There was an open area within the cell block for communal breaks and general relaxation and he had plans for this space.

The end of June was fast approaching and his first competition fight for the Light Heavyweight Championship was scheduled for just over two weeks time.

The guards relented finally, relinquishing the free space and creating an area for him to train and exercise. It was in the guardhouse area that he commenced his personal quest to get back his strength and fitness. Gentle exercises to begin with, as the body tissue was still mending and still sore in places, so he had to be careful not to undo what time had successfully achieved so far, but it would only be a matter of time before he was back to peak strength.

Most of the guards and the other inmates were keen to assist him in his quest to get match fit again. The guardhouse was turned into a mini gymnasium with the guards and inmates prepared to join in with the rigorous fitness regime which he set himself. They erected a heavy duty steel bar from the ceiling of the guard block which one of the guards had borrowed from the vehicle maintenance section. They did punishing pull up routines, then, press ups in quick rapid succession. They tested themselves against each other, then against the clock. He set himself targets, he would double whatever the best guard or the top inmates could do, though no-one in the group could do one arm press ups so he was up against himself in this routine. He was now completing his training with the same ease and regularity as before his beating. The group would just stand and watch in amazement as he would do twenty press ups with one arm, then twenty with the other. He would repeat this repetition four or five times in succession. Taking into account that it had been just two weeks since his beating, he was making a miraculous recovery. He could also sense that the guards and the inmates were also enjoying the training routine. The procedures also tested them, and were much better than having to sit around all day merely watching the clock go round. He had brought a sense of purpose and pride to the guardhouse.

He had arranged with the guards to have his weight-training equipment transferred from his own barracks to the guardhouse. Once again, the routines were taken up by the guards and inmates. They were beginning to enjoy the competition, one against another. In a strange way, this enforced detention was in fact allowing more time to tone his body than would otherwise be the case. The time he would normally spend at the docks or distributing the necessary stores and equipment, was now filled with training. It appeared to him that he was been granted special dispensation to do whatever he wanted within the confines of the cell block. He found himself leading all the training drills, bossing the guards when they were doing something wrong in respect to weight-training. The guards realised that they were benefitting from a young man who had been doing this kind of thing since he was an early teenager. They only needed to look at his physique to realise that he knew what he was talking about and what he was doing.

He knew it was easy to lose interest in this kind of training. He could not afford this to happen, especially with the guards. He needed their interest to remain focused so that he could pursue his own goals. He developed weight training routines which involved bench-pressing an inmate. He would lie on his back with his arms stretched out above his head with his hands flat. Two guards would lift one of the internees onto his outstretched hands so his head was over his right shoulder and his legs were out to his left shoulder. The trick was for the man he was holding to remain stiff bodied once the weight distribution was evenly spread. He would then lower the man to his chest and then push him back until his arms locked. Down gently, then push, down gently then push. It was ideal for keeping the interest focused and quite often would attract officers and off duty guards to witness these amazing feats of strength. In addition, he would show the guards some of the wrestling moves and practice his techniques on them. A large roll of carpet had been found from an old office on the camp and brought to the guardhouse for them to practice on. It wasn't ideal, but it was better than training on bare floorboards.

After several days of this routine, he was beginning to feel good with himself again, but he lacked the exercises which would provide the stamina required for a potential ten round wrestling bout. His bouts never lasted ten rounds, he could generally see off his opponents after four or five rounds or maximum six. It was generally fatigue and his pure physical strength grinding them down which would sap the energy of his aggressor. His championship fights would be more difficult though, so he had to be prepared to go the distance if necessary. He could only build stamina by running and sprinting and somehow he had to include this into his daily rota. Up to now, he was not permitted outside the guard room.

Food was also vital to his progress. He had to get the right energy level back to be able to maintain his self-imposed fitness regime.

The words of his wrestling coach Freddie Wilson resonated around his head.

'If you don't put it in, you can't take it out,' was a remembered saying. If he was not thinking about training, he would be thinking about eating. If he was doing neither of these things, then he would be planning his strategy to overcome his opponent. During meal times, all inmates were sent back to their respective cells to eat. This too worked in his favour. The meal rations for the inmates were brought into the guardhouse by a local Singaporean. He was able to speak privately to the local and organise extra rations. It would cost a few dollars a day, but money well spent. It meant that he could sustain his fitness regime. When the duty of bringing food changed to another local man, it made no difference, the information flow continued and he was always getting the extra calories and helpings he needed. Some days it would only be an extra piece of bread, but every little helps when you are trying to maintain strength and bulk.

Wrestling had enabled him to mix with rich and powerful people. It had also paid him quite handsomely and now was the time to spread a little of his wrestling earnings in the direction of the guards. He realised he needed to be careful though, he did not want to land in trouble again by bribing a guard. At this stage, he had no idea how receptive his captors would be. He accepted his daily ration of cigarettes even though he did not smoke. Cigarettes were seen as one the best bargaining tools to promote favours, so he used this to gauge their reaction to accepting a little extra pocket money. He needed to keep the guards on his side, but he also needed to test his stamina. This could not be done within the confines of the guardhouse. He needed to get outside and only the guards could arrange this. He remembered what Kazar had said to him, the guards would help him with whatever he needed.

The back of the guardhouse was out of sight from most onlookers. The security risk he presented to the guards or the camp in general was zero. He could walk away from his jailers at any time, but this would be futile. He had nowhere to go, so he hatched his plan.

Callon approached the head of the guards and asked to use a small plot of ground immediately behind the guardhouse, explaining he needed to do some running. Whilst his strength exercises were now on track, his stamina was yet untested.

During periods of low activity in the camp, he was allowed to train on this barren piece of land, accomplished with the guards' permission and consent, but it cost him his cigarette ration and a few Singapore dollars for each of the guards on duty, a small price to pay for keeping himself in fighting condition. Granted, the guards would have allowed him this request without the offer of incentives, but they took advantage of anything they could lay their hands on extra.

What intrigued him was the ease at which his captors agreed to allow his training to continue unhindered. He had already taken a huge step forward, being allowed outside his cell. He wondered if what Kazar had spoken about some days back would in fact be possible. The only thing now lacking in his build up to the Light Heavyweight Championship of the Far East was actual wrestling competition.

This would be challenged in the forthcoming days, but just how Kazar would accomplish this seemingly impossible feat would remain a mystery for the moment. The wrestling venues were a magnet for the army camp, especially since one of their own was doing so well. The camp also knew their wrestling star was residing in the guardhouse. So how could he compete in the arenas he had wrestled in previously? A few cigarettes or a few dollars from Kazar to the guards would not be sufficient to make this happen; a minor miracle, yes.

The perimeter fence was some six or seven metres from the guard house. He was able to create a small circular route giving him sufficient space to exercise. He needed to build his leg muscles back up. He had lost a lot of strength from them during his inactivity periods in the guardhouse. The ground was sandy but firm underfoot and quite uneven in parts. His continuous running across the same ground created a small furrow, so he now had a good enough running surface to develop his stamina. He would run clockwise for some distance and then reverse his direction. The overall ground area was quite small in reality and did not allow him to run in an upright or straight position, but he was thankful for the opportunity anyway. Repetitions were his thing, and he soon discovered how much his stamina had been depleted. Running repetitions for several hours were not uncommon; his stamina level was still some way off where it should be, but this would improve day by day.

Chapter 22

Kazar sat on the end of the bed looking through some papers he had brought to show his wrestler. He wanted some privacy, away from the guards and the other inmates to discuss the next phase of the wrestling plan with him. His friends from his barracks had just left; they were regular callers now that visiting rights had been normalised.

'What do you think of this, Kid?' He handed him a printed poster. It contained all the wrestling bouts for tomorrow, Saturday 5th July in Johor Bahru Arena.

'Why are you showing me this, is it supposed to make me feel better?'

'Well it should, you're wrestling at this venue tomorrow night.' Kazar had a grin on his face from ear to ear.

'What the hell are you talking about?' He went through the programme again looking for his name.' Where does it say I'm fighting, my name isn't on this programme?' He held the flyer for Kaz to take it back.

'Your name is there, you just don't recognise it. You will be wrestling under another name.' He scratched his head looking for a clearer explanation.

'Who the hell am I supposed to be then? Show me!' Kaz pointed to one of the lower order and earlier bouts. The contest was between Jim Johansson (The Viking) and the Masked Marauder, a new name on the wrestling circuit.

'You are the "Masked Marauder," Kid, wearing a full face mask for your contest. It's the only way we can keep your identity undisclosed, and keep you wrestling. You just have to make sure you keep your identity hidden. Under no circumstances must you let Johansson expose who you are. You do *not* allow him to remove your mask, at any cost.' Kazar adjusted his position on the bunk. 'Wrestling in Johor will also help preserve your identity; there will be fewer people there from this camp.'

He knew of Johansson, not that he had wrestled him before, but he knew of his reputation. He was a tough campaigner but lacked finesse and the stylish approach which he brought to the arena. Johansson was strong though, catching him off guard, he could do some serious damage. Johansson would clearly want to expose his opponent's true identity. He on the other hand wondered if he would be disadvantaged by the mask. Not only would it be very uncomfortable, but it could restrict his peripheral or line of vision.

'Okay, now I understand. A great idea if I may say so.' He was grateful for the wrestling duel; he needed this bout more than anything.

'Thank you, Kid, but this puts a big responsibility on you. If this goes wrong, then we could lose everything from a wrestling championship perspective. Wrestling with a full face mask on won't be an easy affair, and we've no time to prepare. The masks will not be ready until the evening of the contest. I've arranged for several to be made, so hopefully we can find a comfortable fitting one for you?

Suddenly he was concerned about the bizarre arrangements. The restrictions that the mask would bring would be impossible to gauge at this stage, so he just hoped the feeling of constraint by the mask would be considerably outweighed by his hidden identity. He needed to keep his wrestling skill level up though. He would wrestle Johansson in such a way that he would use this as a practice session only. Beating Johansson was important, but it was more important conceal his identity and to use this opportunity to its full advantage.

'And how do I get out of here on Saturday, Kaz? Have you worked that one out yet?'

'It's all taken care of. I'll pick you up from here under the cover of darkness. Other than the guards, no one else will see or hear you leave. No one else will know that you've left the camp.' Kazar studied his wrestlers gaze; he could see the mental confusion as he tried valiantly to comprehend the seemingly impossible.

'What, I just walk out of here, no questions asked?'

'No questions asked,' said Kazar smugly.

Why was everyone jumping through hoops to assist my progress? He had after all, seriously injured an officer. Yes, it would be good for the reputation of the Army if he could pull this championship title off, but he knew it was much deeper than that. For the guards to turn a blind eye to his exit from the cells, someone much higher must have given permission for his release, albeit only for a few hours. So Kazar really did have contacts in high places.

'You will be expected to give a few wrestling lessons afterwards, Are you okay with that?' Kazar was already on his feet, as far as he was concerned, he was ready to leave, his job for the day over.

'My other alternatives are not great, Kaz. Coming back here fills me with dread. So the longer I can avoid the return here, then the better it is for me.' There was a slight hesitation from him. 'I presume I still get paid?'

'Let me check it out. We've had to bend a lot of rules to get you out of here at some cost.'

'Who the fuck is, *we*, Kaz, answer me?' he paused for a moment. 'You're not telling me our mystery friend is involved in my short vacation from the guardhouse?' He began to feel a sense of rage waiting for a reply.

'How else do you think this works? I don't have the money or the wherewithal to arrange this for you on my own. All you need to worry about just now is that it's being sorted.' Kaz stared hard at him trying to get his point across as forcefully as he could.

'Why is he so fucking influential around here? Who is he? For God's sake, I need to know some answers, Kaz. What does he want from me?' His voice was now forced but muted, allowing for the proximity of other inmates.

'Calm down, Kid, walls have ears and I don't want to have to change my programme. Think about what's happening here.'

'That's just it; I *don't* know what's happening.'

'Let's discuss it tomorrow evening, after your bout with Johansson. I am sure things will become a little clearer then.' Kazar was annoyed at his young wrestler's attitude. 'Just remember this; it wasn't me or anyone else that put you in here. You have a chance at a very prestigious title here. Be happy about it!'

'What time are you picking me up?' he asked dismissively.

'You need to be ready to move by 18.30. It will be dark by then. We'll be taking the tradesmen's exit on the way out of the guardhouse.'

'Make sure I get paid, Kaz. I also want to see the girl. If our friend can organise this much, then arranging for the girl to be there should be a pushover?'

The Johor Bahru Arena was starting to fill up in anticipation of the wrestling bouts due to begin within the next 15 minutes. It was always good to see a new name on the wrestling circuit, but this was laced with further intrigue, for the new name would be faceless. The crowd would be looking to Johansson to unmask the Marauder. They would want to know who this man was and to see his face.

'It's too bloody tight. I can't breath and I can't see well enough. This is not going to work, Kaz.' He'd been trying several versions of masks since arriving at the venue. Kazar had taken the measurements from his head, but the man who made them had not allowed enough tolerance in the fit. The fabric was also very strong, inflexible and quite harsh to touch. It needed to be of course, after all, the wrestling focus would be on this item of wear. 'We've only one more mask to try.' Kazar was working frantically to try and get the mask to fit comfortably. He slipped the final mask into place, but the problem was still the same. It was also too tight.

'Let me try the first one again, It's not ideal, but it probably felt better than this last lot.' He was shaking his head at the thought of going out into the ring wearing this frightening head gear. The mask was fully covering the head and fitted under the chin. It was fastened at the back of the head by a shoelace, through a series of holes.

'It's still tight,' he said, but accepted it was as good as it was going to get.

'It has to be tight, Kid, remember, he must not expose your face, or we are all in deep shit.' Kazar was very sure to raise that essential point again. 'We can't allow him any finger space!'

'Does Johansson know he is wrestling me?' asked Callon.

'No, of course not, nobody knows, he just thinks he's wrestling the Masked Marauder, a man in a mask. Don't show any of your old tricks, otherwise, he'll know it's you and so will half the audience.'

The mask was black with two eye cut out's, a cut out for the nose and mouth also. The fabric was heavily stitched around the cut out's to provide extra strength to the mask. When he looked at himself in the mirror, he felt different. His vision was slightly impaired, but staring him back in his face was this grotesque masked man. It was enough to frighten any opponent and send them scampering for safety. It was the sense of people not knowing who he was that pleased him. He could be anybody he wanted to be, providing he didn't get unmasked. It was a great idea to hide the face, he thought, but there was no hiding his physique. No wrestler on the circuit had the definition of Kid Callon and he wondered if people would suspect that it was him. He had no external birth marks or tattoos which could identify him as such. For now though, he would be the 'Masked Marauder.' His role in the ring would be very different to the one everybody recognised. The Masked Marauder would be the bad guy, the guy the audience would hate and would want unmasking. The spectators would be shouting for his blood. Maybe he would give them that, he thought, but it would take more than Johansson to relieve him of his mask. He had decided at that moment just how he was going to approach this wrestling bout.

The adrenalin rush was back, he suddenly felt supercharged. He wanted to wrestle, he wanted to wrestle dirty. He wanted the crowd to hate him.

He had arrived at Johor Bahru under cloak and dagger circumstances. Back at the guardhouse, the guards simply turned their backs when Kazar strolled in there to pick him up. They exited through the back of the guardhouse and across the small running track which he had developed, bundled into the back of Kazar's car and covered by a blanket. The guard on the gate simply waved him through onto Orchard Road. Someone clearly has influence, he thought. On reaching Johor Bahru Arena, he was whisked into his own personal dressing room still with a blanket over his head. It was also important that the other wrestlers on the circuit did not know the Masked Marauder's identity. Only a handful of people very close to Kazar knew his real name. He hoped it would remain this way.

The long walk to the ring was like Daniel walking into the lions den. By divine intervention, the lions had left Daniel unharmed, demonstrating to King Darius his innocence and his faith and the power of his God. The Masked Marauder was looking for the same kind of divine intervention when he too enters the wrestling ring. It was something he had never experienced before, but was relishing the challenge.

The commentator introduced the Masked Marauder and asked the crowd if they wanted to see this new talent on the wrestling circuit unmasked. The crowd were going ballistic at the very sight and appearance of him. This was a new experience for them, and they wanted to witness the chance that his face would be displayed for all to see. There were people shaking their fists and booing loudly to vent their anger at the very sight of this fearsome wrestler. He felt protected and he also felt superior because he knew more than they did. He would play their game, he would be mean, he would be nasty, he would be dirty, but most of all, he would win. He could play this any way he wanted, but he would not play fair. He was a name nobody knew, hiding behind his grotesque mask. As Johansson entered the ring, he enjoyed the cheering and the warm applause afforded to him. Johansson was a big man and would take some stopping, but the Masked Marauder was one of the best wrestlers on the circuit.

As the Marauder went to his corner, he was instantly provoking the crowd, threatening them with his gestures, asking people to come into the ring, to take him on, if they dare. It was more theatre than wrestling at this stage.

There was only one thing on Johansson's mind as the two men came together for the first round. Johansson wanted to wrestle in close contact. He wanted a chance to remove the mask early. This would be Johansson's downfall, because his concentration was not with the man in front of him, but with the mask around the man. The Marauder kept his distance, not wanting any early advantage going to Johansson. Body checks and forearm slams were connecting as the booing around the arena intensified. It was not the intention for the Marauder to get on top in any way. Even up close Johansson was no match for the slick wrestling technique of the Marauder. He was enjoying his new role, plus it gave him an opportunity to experiment on different approaches and holds. This was ideal build up for the Light Heavyweight Championship and he felt good about his preparations.

The second round started like the first with the Marauder dominating. Midway through the round Johansson caught the Marauder in a head lock and was able to undo the shoelace fastening on his mask. The Marauder needed to be careful now, because slackening the mask also impaired his vision. The mask twisted and completely blocked his vision in one eye. As he was adjusting the mask, he was hit by an unsuspecting scissor kick high up on the chest which sent him reeling backwards into the ropes, almost falling through them. The crowd sensed the chance to see the face of the masked man. The Marauder went down for a count of seven adjusting his mask as he got to his feet. The mask was a hindrance now, it was moving across his face interfering with his vision. His peripheral vision was never good with the mask on, but because of its slackness, it was acting more like blinkers on a horse. He could only see directly ahead. He needed to see out the rest of this round whereby he could repair the damage in his corner. Johansson seized his opportunity and grappled the Marauder to the canvas. His sole attention was on the mask, he now had his fingers in the bottom part of the mask which was under the chin and he was pulling for all his worth. The spectators were shouting, 'off, off,' over and over again. The Marauder only had his physical strength to defend himself now. This mythical figure, created overnight, would be plunged, all too soon, back down to the ranks of the all too human. He had to resist these attempts to unmask him, otherwise his reputation and his façade would be stripped in an instant.

The Marauder's concentration was now intense as he fought with all his strength not to be exposed and unmasked. The loss of the mask is the ultimate defeat, he thought. Unmasking him meant he could not continue anyway, his credibility and his reputation would be blown. There was more to it than that, of course. Why was a man serving a court martial sentence for attacking and seriously injuring an officer, be allowed out to wrestle?

The Marauder grabbed Johansson's wrist and squeezed as hard as he could. He knew he was hurting him as he felt the fingers loosen slightly under his chin. Johansson was still holding onto the mask as he tussled with The Marauder's grip. The Marauder had thirty seconds to the bell and to last out the round. Squeezing as though his life depended on it now, he started to twist the arm. Once again he felt Johansson's grip slacken. He now only had two fingers under the chin of the mask. With his free arm, he swung it into his face knocking him backwards, but he somehow still held on.

With twenty seconds to go, the Marauder was now holding the mask onto his face with one hand. The shoelace fastening was becoming looser because of the tension applied by his opponent. With one arm practically out of action defending the mask, he shoved his face into Johansson's very forcefully. The Marauder was on the verge of disqualification for that move, but he now had to play dirty, for this wasted precious seconds, but moreover, preserved his identity. With his free hand again, he shoved Johansson's face backwards with the heel of his hand, but grabbing the flesh on his face as his eye sockets grew ever larger as his nails gripped his cheeks. The Marauder needed to do anything which allowed him to escape his desperate opponents clutches.

Ten seconds left and he was still restricted, the Marauder was on the ground but not in control. His movements were slow and laboured. He seized the opportunity to put his free elbow under Johansson's chin, trying to force him away. The referee was looking intently at the move trying to work out if it was legal or not. The bell rang, but Johansson held on, he was not letting go of his grip. The referee was slapping him on the back to break the move up, but he still held on. The referee now had Johansson in a headlock trying to get him off. It was now farcical with all three men rolling around on the floor. The crowd continued to shout, 'off,' over and over again. The bell rang continuously as this melee rumbled on. The Marauder's second came into the ring and slapped Johansson hard at the back of the head with very little back lift, but enough to make him loosen his grip. Johansson was momentarily stunned. Calm was temporarily restored as the two men returned to their respective corners.

It took seven rounds for the Masked Marauder to eventually dispose of his man. He walked from the ring with a posse of protectors surrounding him. People were clawing at him as he went back to his personal dressing room, they wanted more, they wanted his mask. The excitement that this contest had generated was beyond Kazar's wildest dreams and would be a format he would build upon for the next season. This contest was a low key bout to give Kid Callon some wrestling opportunities before his championship fights got underway; it was considered a rip roaring success for everyone concerned. Johansson would question that perhaps, as he was forcibly ejected from the ring nursing a severely swollen arm and a sore back as he landed awkwardly outside the ring.

The mystery man seemed to appear from nowhere as he and Kazar were helping themselves to a table laden with food, fit for a king. They were both starving after another successful night at the wrestling arena in

Johor Bahru. He turned around from the table not expecting to see anyone, for neither man had heard anyone enter the room. He must have overheard their brief discussion as he tried to extract information from Kazar about who he was.

'Good to see you again, Kid, how are you?' The man held his outstretched hand to greet him. He held it with the same warmth that the mystery man bestowed upon him.

'I'm good, thank you...sorry; I didn't catch your name last time we met?' The man ignored the question and turned towards the food. He could only wonder why he was so protective and secretive over his identity.

'Please, come, take more food?' He was aware that he would be teaching the man who stood before him more wrestling moves sometime soon. He would take his fill later, after his tuition was complete. 'You had another successful night, Kid? Johor is becoming a lucky place for you.'

'Were you there?' he asked, needing to know.

'Yes, I saw your performance. No one would have guessed that the man behind the mask was you. Apart from the way the contest ended, your style was completely different.' He moved to shake Kazar's hand, almost as an afterthought. The two men just nodded to show their mutual appreciation. 'Taking into consideration your unintended break from the sport, I thought you did remarkably well.' The man continued, 'let me tell you what I like about you, Kid, it's your attitude, you put your heart and soul into everything you do. You're honest and sincere in victory. Those are qualities I admire in someone so young.' He realised he was being verbally massaged by the man's kind words. Kazar was nodding his head in total agreement to the mystery man's comments. 'Your sincerity in victory tonight however, was less evident. I thought you played the role of villain quite well.'

He was unconcerned about any further small talk and caught the two men off guard with his next line of questions. He wanted some answers of his own.

'What do you want from me? What do you want me to do?' His voice was not raised, but it had the sufficient strength in its delivery to sting the two men. 'I have been court martialled, banged up, yet I'm being treated with great care and courtesy. Whatever I ask for I get, so I want to know what the hell is going on?'

'We had this discussion the first time we met. I want you to drive a truck. This has not changed.' The man's response was calm and composed.

'And I get quarter of a million dollars for doing just that?'

He hunched his shoulders before replying.

'Yes, that's it, that's what we agreed.'

He had to admire the coolness of the man and wondered if anything would melt this icy exterior he portrayed.

'Where do I drive the truck to and from, oh, and I want to know what the cargo is? Otherwise I'm out of here.' He could feel his adrenalin building, but for different reasons now. He was panicky and he was beginning to feel anger towards the mystery man. He needed to give an outward impression of being in control, but his insides were doing cartwheels. 'What the fuck is going on here, why won't somebody tell me?' he asked again.

'Have you forgotten? We made a deal. We shook hands, remember?' His attitude was of calm and reassuring, but the underlying message was menacing. 'I can tell you this much, you will drive the truck from a port in Singapore across the Johor causeway into Malaysia.'

'Is this an instruction or a request?'

He once again ignored the question.

'And you will have complete protection from my associates.' Alarm bells began to ring in his head and perspiration started to pepper his brow.

'Protection from whom? protection from, what?' He turned away from the two men before they answered. He was rubbing his sweaty temple in consternation from that one word, *protection*. He wondered what he had got himself into, feeling he had been lured into a trap, and none of it was his doing. He still didn't know what the intended cargo was.

'What's on the truck?' He looked across at Kazar's expressionless face. 'Someone tell me, what's on the fucking truck?' his voice lifting significantly on that last sentence.

'Look, let's take a little time out and come back to this. You were going to teach me some more wrestling moves. Come, follow me, this way.' The man turned to the door which led to the gym.

He was most definitely not in the mood for more silly games, but he reluctantly followed him. He felt he was drawn to him by some kind of invisible magnetic field.

'She's waiting for you.' He nodded his head in the direction of the door and hated himself for allowing this meeting to take place, he wanted to keep Suzi for himself but knew, for now; he had no other option but to let him go to her.

Amongst all the distractions, he had almost forgotten about Suzi. His mind was full of the discussions he had just had. He had shown him some further wrestling moves, remembering what Kazar had said to him on their first meeting.

'Don't hurt him, treat him with respect.' He had plenty of time during the tuition class to hurt him. He wanted to screw his arm off unless he told him what was going on and what the cargo was, but each time he baulked away from applying the pressure which would have him begging for mercy. It was clear from the exchanges of dialogue he had had, that he would be told about the truck and its contents when they were good and ready, and not before.

Suzi looked stunning, dressed in casual high quality western clothes. He looked at her, studying her face and petite features, wanting to absorb her every detail. The smell of her hair and her lightly perfumed skin tormented him, knowing that he could not allow himself to get too close or too serious.

She led him to the same small room with the massage table in the centre; its subdued lighting and room temperature at perfection. She locked the door with the internal key. He undressed and laid himself bare on the bed for Suzi to work her hands and fingers into his flesh and take his pent up anger and tension away from him. He could not help thinking that this was for real. He felt Suzi must be a part of a much larger plot. He resisted taking the pleasure which Suzi's fingers and hands brought to him. He needed to know for his own self esteem what Suzi's role in this plan was.

He lifted himself onto his elbows and looked up at Suzi from the massage table before asking.

'Who is this man, Suzi? He worries me!' Before giving her a chance to answer, he followed with a further question. 'Do you know what's going on here or have any idea what they are planning?' She was standing in front of him now, the long hair coming forward over her shoulders as she looked down at him. With her arms spread on the edge of the massage table, she answered carefully.

'You are asking too many questions, Ki, I don't know what it is he wants you to do.'

'Are you here because you want to be here, or has he told you to be here?' He wanted answers to this question particularly. He needed to know exactly how she felt.

'I want to be with you; I really like you. I like you very much, Ki.' Her eyes did not betray her as she answered.

'Why won't you tell me who he is, what's his name, Suzi?' His eyes were pleading for answers.

'He lives and works from here, that's all I know.' She was lying; he knew that for sure and she was protecting him. The mystery man must mean more to Suzi than he could ever imagine.

'Where is here, Suzi? Where are we?'

'You don't know where we are? she asked quizzically, 'no?' she repeated.

'No, I have no idea,' he said, searching for answers.

'This is the Palace of the Sultan of Johor!'

Suzi motioned for him to turn over. She pushed his head gently backwards onto the table and massaged his upper body. He was trying his best to take in the information Suzi had just imparted to him.

'Fuck, is this man the Sultan of Johor?' he asked himself quietly.

Chapter 23

'Wake up Kid. You're getting a visitor later this morning, its 07.30, come on, rise and shine.' The guard had unlocked the cell door to let in the Singaporean peon with his Sunday morning breakfast.

'Who is it?' he asked, still rubbing the sleep from his eyes. It had been late when he was spirited back into the guardhouse and returned to his cell bed.

'I am not allowed to say who it is, Kid, let's just say you know him quite well.' The guard disappeared with a mischievous grin before he could be interrogated any further as to his visitor's identity.

He momentarily thought about his current situation and where he spent last evening being wined and dined; he had been drinking the finest Champagne from very expensive crystal flutes and eating the best cuisine that Malaysia could offer, in one of the finest Palaces in the whole of Asia. The wake up call had been a complete reality check; he was clearly back to earth with a bang.

His breakfast offering was served up on a tin plate with a few slices of dry toast. All this would be washed down with lukewarm tea from a tin mug. There were no extra rations this morning. He would have to wait until lunch time for that.

He ate his breakfast at the small square table as he pondered the events in the ring last evening. He was very thankful for the wrestling contest. He felt that it had put him back to where he was before he took that terrible beating at the hands of six guards. It had taken him seven rounds to beat 'The Viking' Johansson, but he kept the bout going for a couple of rounds more than he needed to, just to get the feel of the canvas and the ropes back. The mask idea was a great one and he enjoyed the mystique which it created. He would get the opportunity to wrestle with it again next week. The weeks following would be the start of the championship title. He needed to keep focused and out of trouble. He would train daily as normal, but push himself further each day to lift more weight, to run more miles and not allow anything to interfere with his preparation.

Kazar had given him the names of the other three opponents he would face and they were each very different, but nevertheless formidable contestants;

Red Rivers, an American with a Sioux Indian ancestry. A very worthy opponent scaling just less than six foot with an excellent range of holds and throws.

Jack 'Boulder' Harris. As the name suggested, a big man and just able to meet the weight restriction for light heavyweight. Shorter than Callon with a large barrel chest and waistline to match. His body shape underestimating his agility for such a big man.

Miraj Kamrul. His nickname, the Destroyer. Born in India, this ape-like man was a short but fearless wrestler; as hairy as an Orang-Utan with long rangy arms and enormous strength.

Kazar had told him that there was only one man to fear. It was Miraj Kamrul, the ape-man. He stood only five foot tall, but was as wide as he was tall. He had the physical strength of a horse. In all of his contests he had not lost one submission. Most of his bouts had ended through submission. He was a human boa constrictor; he squeezed the life out of his opponents. No contest he had been in so far went further than three rounds. Neither he nor Kazar had worked out a formula to beat this man yet. They knew he would have an Achilles heel, but finding it was the problem. Luckily for Callon though, Miraj Kamrul would be his last contest. He would have the opportunity to watch two of the men wrestle, but his particular interest was the Destroyer; he would need to build as much intelligence as he could to prepare for this match.

As he lay on his bunk, thinking about his day ahead, he wondered who his visitor could possibly be. Receiving advanced notice of a pending visitor, especially on a Sunday morning was not the norm. It wouldn't be one of his friends; he never needed advanced warning about one of them.

He went through his normal morning routine. He felt slightly sore from his previous night's work, but all in all, he was feeling quite good about himself and his preparation. It was hard to believe that a month ago, he was fighting for his life, a total physical wreck, unable to stand, walk or talk. Throughout his regular morning work out, he wondered if his visitor would spoil his day. He had a strange feeling that somehow he would.

It was 10.30am and he was showered and ready for the rest of the day. Around this time he would normally practise his foreign language lessons. He was almost fluent now, only occasionally coming up against new words or ones which he could not remember. He treated his language skills similar to his training techniques. He believed in repetition. It was his recipe for learning and for keeping fit. An active body leads to an active mind.

He had plenty to think about now, he was just a few weeks away from his dream championship, something he could not have even thought possible. He was not going to let this opportunity slip through his fingers, no way. Nothing gets in the way of this chance; he told himself, a chance to really make a name for himself. He'd left the UK an unknown, a no-one. Within nine months of reaching the shores of Singapore, he was one of the biggest sporting attractions in the Far East. His rise to top billing, in a sport he loved, was beyond his wildest dreams. He had almost screwed his chances, he knew that. But by some quirk of fate and a fistful of dollars, he was allowed to continue his quest for the championship title. Kazar had done a great job in delaying the competition and organising his release from detention to wrestle. He could hardly believe his luck, but he was also very aware that there could well be a price to pay for this. The privileges afforded him were part of a much bigger plan, a plan which would involve him and put him in serious harm's way if things did go wrong. He thought vividly about his late evening discussion with the mystery man and Kazar. This troubled him somewhat, his handshake several weeks back with the mystery man meant he could not go back on his word. He was dealing with very powerful and influential people. This was not apparent until yesterday evening when Suzi had told him where they were. He had no idea he was in the palace of one of the richest men in the world!

His thoughts were disturbed by a key being inserted into his cell door. After a little fumbling, the guard opened the door just enough to allow his head through the gap and announced his visitor was here.

'He'll see you here in your cell, Kid.' The guard turned away to bring the visitor to him. He stood up and awaited the person with a degree of anxiety and concern. The door opened and there stood Captain Black. He immediately stood to attention and saluted, not wanting to be discourteous to the rank.

'Sir.' He stood waiting for a response. Captain Black was the last person on his list of possible visiting candidates, he thought. The Captain walked forward a couple of paces and closed the door behind him.

'At ease, soldier,' the Captain had a look of contempt across his face. 'You've got friends in high places, Callon.' The Captain's teeth clenched when he spoke his surname. He realised this was not a 'nice to see you' kind of visit.

'I wanted to see you before I leave.'

'You're leaving, sir, I didn't know?'

'How could you know, but then nothing surprises me about you any more. It's because of you that I am leaving, I wanted to remain here to make your life a fucking misery, Callon, but it's not to be.' He shifted on his feet before continuing. 'I called to see you last night, but unfortunately you were otherwise engaged. Tell me, you little shit, how did you pull that one off?' The Captain winced as he put extra effort into his verbal attack. He was still hurting physically from his parade ground pounding.

He stood impassively. He was not going to add further injury to the Captain's condition. He could see from his eyes and facial expressions that he was a very troubled individual. He wondered if it was his mental state which was most affected by what happened. He knew from his own experiences that physical scars can heal and mend. He guessed it was the former from their initial exchanges. He did a quick scan of the Captain to make sure he was not carrying anything which he could use as a weapon. Captain Black had the look of a wounded animal written all over his face and he was taking no chances, this was a man out for revenge.

'I want you to know this, when all this soldiering is over, Callon, you had better watch your back. Don't think for one minute that this is over. I know where you live, I know you have family. I will be watching you, remember that.'

'Are you threatening me, Captain?' He stepped one pace towards him, he felt the hair on the back of his neck standing up. The Captain didn't move or flinch.

'Hit the bastard, hit him hard, take his bloody head off; what are you waiting for. How dare he come in here and threaten you. His actions nearly killed you, are you going to let him get away with that. Take another step forward, get in his face, and see if he moves. Make him hit you first though; it will be his word against yours. He has no authority over you now, he is leaving, remember. He has come here for revenge. Go on, get in his face, if he moves even a muscle, take him down.*

He moved forward another stride. He was within striking distance of the Captain. He repeated the question again.

'Are you threatening me, Captain, if so, we have a whole new set of circumstances here?' His voice was spoken in a low whisper but with the intent it was meant to give.

'Now you remember this, SIR,' there was great emphasis on the word sir, 'I can take you down now, right here right now; and you should remember that.' He squared his shoulders and clenched his fists as if ready to prepare himself for what might come next.

Hit him, you know you want to. Don't touch his face though. Play the same game that he played; you would only need to squeeze this bastard and he would be squealing all the way back to the hospital.

'You're not here to say goodbye Captain, you're here for one thing and one thing only, retribution.' He stood as tall as his frame would allow. 'I will defend myself; I am entitled to do that, Captain.' He pushed his face forward towards the Captain before continuing, 'You do not frighten me one bit. There are no witness's, Captain.' His face was now only inches away from the Captain's. He thought about how the roles had suddenly been reversed. 'I could put you back in hospital with a shake of my dick. So now, if you've finished, Captain, I bid you farewell, now fuck off!'

'You are a cheap load of shit, Callon.' The Captain stood back a pace nervously, not wanting to show any physical threat towards him. The Captain's hands were clamped down by his side unmoving and not wanting to give any indication of movement or intended violence. He could already see that his attempt to put any frighteners on this soldier were futile. The Captain turned round, opened the door and left without looking back. He walked away from the cell with the satisfaction of at least having had the last word. Just as he turned to leave the guardhouse, the Captain heard a shout.

'Fuck you, Captain.' It was meant for everyone in the guard house to hear. The Captain hesitated for a second before stepping over the threshold and taking the safest option to leave.

'I don't want a repeat of what happened four weeks back,' said Callon. The Captain in charge of the guards was reassuring him that what happened to him, would never happen again; not on his shift anyway.

'That man is not right in the head, he gives me the impression of someone very disturbed.' He wanted to make his point clear. He wanted it documenting that he and his family back home in England had been threatened by the Captain. He was not afraid of his threats personally, but to threaten his family, that was a different thing altogether. He also wanted to protect his build up to the Far East Championships. He wanted no distractions, fighting off another six guardsmen was not on his agenda. He had come too far to compromise his position and his chances now. He had learned his lesson the hard way.

Chapter 24

'That's better, Kaz. This feels much more practical.'

The texture and the feel made it much more comfortable to wear. The Masked Marauder was trying out his new accessory. The ill fitting mask he wrestled in last week had nearly scuppered any chances of his Championship challenge and threatened to reveal his true identity. That would have been a disaster for everyone involved. Kaz had called to the guardhouse where his newly created wrestling phenomenon was trying on his new mask for an initial fitting.

'It should be better, Kid, for this is the finest leather available. It's not just strong it's flexible as well and shouldn't move around too much on your face.'

'I like it, let's go with this.' The shape was similar to the one he had wrestled in last week, but sleeker. The improved fabric had the shine of an army boot toe cap ready for parade inspection. The helmet construction gave greater security and fewer areas where an opponent could poke a finger to grip when trying to rip the mask off. He had also allowed a few days growth of stubble to develop; this would act further as a base to prevent movement of the mask during the bout.

'Let me show you the poster for tonight's contest.' Kaz had waited for the right moment to show him the flyer. The Masked Marauder was billed much higher up the wrestling pecking order. He would be fighting just below the top billing contests. Kaz had been surprised at how successful this clever introduction had been and the interest it had created. The enthusiasm had spilled over from Johor Bahru last week into Singapore and a full house was expected at the New World Arena. He had wrestled here a couple of times and he enjoyed the venue. The ring was slightly bigger which favoured the wrestling style of Kid Callon. Tonight however, he would be stepping into the ring as The

Masked Marauder, and his style and approach would be very different. In an extra effort to disguise his star performer further, Kaz had also organised a tight fitting black leotard to match his black helmet mask. The look was frightening and menacing. It was important for his world championship opponents to know that Kid Callon had not wrestled since his incarceration. What he was doing was not illegal, but it would give his opponents the impression that he was not match ready.

The Masked Marauder's opponent was a very popular wrestler on the circuit called Salvador. The contest was a perfect pairing. It was billed simply as the Good against the Bad.

Salvador was born in Britain, but his father was of Spanish descent with an Irish mother. He had a soft Belfast accent, but this soft spoken Irishman was to belie his tough exterior. He was similar in height to Callon, but heavier by a stone. Like most wrestlers on the circuit, no one had the physical build of Kid Callon. The leotard would be a whole new experience for him.

'What time are you picking me up, Kaz?' He could not wait to get out of this place now. He was beginning to weary of his situation. He knew he had only a few more days of his sentence to serve, then, he would be a free man. Detention had worked in his favour in many respects. He had been able to concentrate fully on his training, with no interference from any outside influences. His health was as good as ever now. Apart from a couple of champagne drinks from last week in Johor, he had also remained alcohol free. His stamina level had improved markedly as a direct result of this.

'I will try for 18.00 hours, be ready to move as soon as I get here.' Kazar left feeling quite good about his day's work so far. His office was in the Great World Arena, but he would not be taking this road back there, he would be taking a different road from the army camp which housed his star performer.

Chapter 25

'Welcome gentlemen, and thank you for attending this meeting at such short notice. I wanted to have this informal get together. Let's call it a meeting of minds, shall we?'

There were nods of approval from the other five people present. It was the first time the Colonel and Major Reece had been seen together in the same company as the two customs men from Singapore and Malaysia. Kazar was also at the meeting, having just made the deadline for the start. His crossing from Singapore into Malaysia was never straight forward. The main person missing from this meeting was still finishing his 30 day sentence in an army guardhouse.

The mystery man continued as he pushed back on his plush leather chair inside his palace office. 'We each have a pivotal role to play in the success of our planned operation and I want to hear from each of you in turn if you have any concerns. I also need to know about your respective duties and how these arrangements are progressing.' The man was calm and confident in his delivery, spoken in rather eloquent English prose. He continued first however, with his own self gratification. 'I have now secured our driver. As you all know, this has been the most difficult position to fill, but I'm convinced we have the right man to carry out our plans. You have all seen this young man, albeit not all of you have been introduced to him. This is an important and pivotal recruitment and he will be one of our most crucial and key players.' Only mineral water was served for this meeting, the mystery man wanted no cloudy versions or indecisions which could be influenced by alcohol. Mistakes were costly and this operation could not afford any mistakes.

'Perhaps you could start, Colonel, do you have anything you would like to say?'

'Yes,' came the reply, 'do we now have all the people in place we need from your side, and have they been briefed on their roles?' The mystery man lit a cigarette before giving his response. The other members of the meeting looked around at each other before the mystery man spoke.

'I have taken every precaution I can think of to ensure the safe arrival of the cargo here in Johor. It is still not without risk of course, but I have left no stone unturned to ensure that all eventualities have been carefully considered. These eventualities have come at great cost of course, but that is my problem, Colonel.'

'The main issue will be getting over the causeway from Singapore,' said the Colonel. 'As I see it, there are a lot of variables and many people to consider. It took me twenty minutes to get through customs today, and I was in a bloody car. What chance has a ten ton Mack truck with a full cargo of goods got?' It was the first time that negative issues had been raised about any aspect of the plan. The Colonel looked at Major Reece and asked him, 'what was your crossing of the causeway like?'

'It took me a similar time to you, Colonel. It's not like there's one set of customs to negotiate, there is one on the Singapore side and then one other on the Malaysian side.' The Major was stating the obvious, but these crossing points were crucial to the operation's success.

'Don't worry about the Malaysian customs. This will be taken care of by me, personally. If necessary, I will be on the bridge at the agreed time of the crossing.' The man who spoke was one of the gang of three who Callon had seen during his first visit to the palace after his successful contest in the Johor Bahru Arena. Callon was never introduced to the men, it was considered too soon to play this card. This was after all the first meeting involving the key players. It was deemed unnecessary to include Callon at this meeting. The gentleman was the Head of Customs for the Malaysian government. He effectively controlled everything which came into and left Malaysia.

'What about the Singapore customs, Richard?' the Colonel asked inquisitively, 'will your side of the causeway be just as trouble free?' Richard was a senior customs officer for the Singapore Customs Department. Richard was not his real name. Many Singaporean business people adopted a British sounding name and used it in every day business for making life simpler.

Richard spoke slowly; his English was not as good as the other members of the group.

His diction was also hard to translate, but there was no alternative to speaking English of course. The Colonel and the Major's presence determined this.

'All arrangement from my side prepared,' said Richard. 'I also be on bridge crossing at time truck arrive. This way we make sure no problem.' His tone was almost sing song in its delivery and most annoying to the Englishmen present.

'What if something goes wrong, do you have contingencies in place? You have an army of people on that crossing; how many of them are in the know as far as this operation is concerned?' Richard shuffled uncomfortably in his chair with some vagueness showing in his stare.

'Only three people know. These men are my senior custom officials, so they take authority over everything that move on crossing. Nothing to worry about, Colonel, everything is taken care of.' His reply was more affirmative this time, but the Colonel stared at him, watching his expressions, unconvinced that his answer was believable.

'Will all these men who know about the consignment be on duty?'

'Yes, sure, I make all plans myself.'

'Is everyone comfortable with the border arrangements then?' The Colonel looked around the table expecting some kind of reaction, but none came.

'What about paperwork?' said Richard, exasperating the Colonel?

He responded very sharply. 'There will be no paperwork you bloody idiot. Kazar, tell him in Malayan what the arrangements are for Christ's sake.' The Colonel slapped his hand on the table, sighed and carried on, directing his question back at Richard. 'What is it you think we are bringing through customs, tins of bloody boot polish?' The Colonel looked away in disgust. He felt Richard was a weak link in the chain. He would speak to the mystery man after this meeting was over and vent his concerns.

'Let's move on, gentlemen,' said the Colonel, 'I want to tell you about the cargo. It's not in the bonded warehouse just yet. It will be moved into the Empire or Kings Dock, the location still to be confirmed. Both sites have provision for it and both sites have a bonded warehouse section. The best estimate I can give just now for its arrival, is the beginning of August, possibly the first or second.' The Colonel was looking at a small calendar and counting days. 'The Singapore government do not want it lying around too long creating interest. There are a lot of people working on those docks. The local guys know what this stuff is, word soon gets out and they don't want any prying eyes. This is valuable cargo, once it's in place; we need to move it quickly.' Kazar half raised his hand to speak.

'Gentlemen, timing could not be better as far as our designated driver, Callon is concerned. He will be wrestling in his final competition on the 3rd of August, so we could move any day after this date.' He turned to the mystery man and said, 'This could be quite a pay day for, Kid Callon.'

'What about the Redcaps Major?' asked the Colonel, have you made any progress about the close protection you promised? Remember we would need four motorcycles minimum to escort the cargo from the docks to the Malaysian border. This escort has to go the full distance.'

'I'm still working on this, Colonel I've spoken to two of my military police and will be speaking to a third this evening. I just need one more then. I have to be extremely careful you understand. Choosing the right men is also crucial, but we are going to pay them well, so this should not be a problem, Sir.'

'They don't know anything about the cargo do they, Major?' The Colonel did not want to share this information with anyone, the more people that knew about this the less chances of success.

'No, Colonel, but they know it is not a legitimate operation.' The Major drank water from the crystal tumbler in front of him before continuing. 'I've told them that it's a special operation between Singapore and Malaysia. The cash payment I've offered to each of them is however an indication that everything is not kosher. They have also been sworn to secrecy, Colonel, as part of the payment terms.'

'Of course, Major, it has to be this way.' The Colonel paused a moment,

'What about, Callon, does he have any inkling who is involved in this?' The Colonel was anxious not to have his own name mixed up in this affair. He was the brains behind this whole operation and he would distance himself from any involvement whatsoever. The mystery man answered on behalf of the Major.

'Only Kazar and I have spoken to him about this plan. Up to now he knows absolutely nothing about the cargo and its contents. He knows to drive the truck from a port in Singapore across the causeway into Malaysia. He is aware of my Head of Customs and Richard. The Kid is a little edgy, that's understandable, but he will drive the truck. A quarter of a million dollars is a huge incentive for this young man.' The mystery man stood up from the table. The three other men followed suit before the Colonel asked for a word in private.

A bottle of champagne was brought to the table by an immaculately dressed house servant. The main discussion of the plan was now over. The man and the Colonel sat opposite each other and the Colonel voiced his concern about Richard, the Singapore Head of Customs.

'He worries me, I am not sure he understands the risks and the complexity of this plan. He appears vague when we ask him a question. What's your view of him?'

'I know this man very well, for many years he has been on my payroll, unofficially of course. He will not let us down. His spoken English is not so good, but he understands very well what is expected of him. He too will receive a handsome payment for his part.' He took a good sip of his champagne and savoured its effect on the back of his tongue. It was not only his favourite drink, it was his only drink. Apart from the occasional glass of water, the mystery man drank nothing else. It had to be the finest champagne of course, and it had to be pink!

'Don't worry, Colonel, we will make it happen. Just make sure the Major organises the military escort. This is also very important to the success of the plan.'

The two men shook hands and the Colonel left the Palace bound for Singapore. He was still not convinced about Richard, his instinct was to replace this man. But it was too late now and he knew it.

Chapter 26

The atmosphere had been building throughout the evening in the New World Arena. The anticipation of the spectators seeing The Masked Marauder was palpable. They wanted to see the face of the man behind the mask. This was their only desire, and the crowd didn't care how this would be achieved.

Some of the early bouts had finished before their allotted ten rounds with a couple of quick knockouts in the early sessions. He had arrived early at the venue as it was easier to hide his identity with fewer onlookers around. He still needed to be sneaked into the dressing room, it was necessary that no one but Kazar would see him, or worse, speak to him. It was also vital, except for a couple of Military Redcaps guarding him, that no one saw him leave the army base. The military police had been paid well to keep their mouth's shut. There should be no leak of his whereabouts or his clandestine existence, albeit only for a few hours. He had had his mask on for some minutes already. He could immediately feel the transformation of his whole being as he pulled it on. It had the hidden power to turn his calm and protective exterior into an individual he himself did not recognise. He was now menacing, mean and moody and he would wrestle his opponent Salvador in exactly this way. His approach to this contest would be the same as before. His obscenities and gestures to the spectators would become automatic in order to generate whistles and catcalls. He would be mysterious, but he would also be hated at the same time. His special escort of six men would surround him as he made his entrance to the ring. The spectators would be trying to touch and tear at the Masked Marauder to taunt him and fill their expectations in the hope that this behaviour would somehow assist his opponent in revealing his true identity. There would be no limit to the power of their imaginations in unmasking this hideous looking creature as the arena reached boiling point, in this swirling sound of noise and erupting mayhem.

Little would the spectators know that beneath this grotesque leather helmet protection was a young handsome prince-like figure, preparing for the biggest contest of his entire life? Fighting under his usual name of Kid Callon, he had cultivated his reputation to such an extent that it had reached idolatry status. These same spectators would want his blood to be spilt, but more importantly, they would want him to be unmasked; creating the highest drama.

The Masked Marauder was about to make his entrance into the New World Arena. This would be storytelling of a different kind, although the basic plot would be the same, the battle between hero and villain.

He could already predict the outcome of this contest. He would not be holding back his throws, kicks and holds. He would wrestle this contest as the crowd expected him to wrestle it; dirty, ruthless and dangerous. He would use this opportunity to wrestle as his preparation to the upcoming contests. He would not be giving the crowd what they had come here to witness, his face! He would defend this as if his life would depend on it. Salvador, he thought, was going to wish he had stayed away from this confrontation. The adrenalin rush was with him, and there was a strength surge within his body which suggested indestructibility. This was his last opportunity to really test himself against a worthy opponent, before embarking on a trophy which was within touching distance. Salvador was already in the ring, to huge applause. The spectators made themselves heard, and were already in fine voice shouting support for their man.

Salvador would have no difficulty translating what it was the crowd was shouting for. The Marauder's magnificent jet black silk robe, manufactured purposely for this event, was wrapped around him, hanging majestically to the floor, keeping his body at the correct temperature since practising his warm up routine. His robe was removed as the Masked Marauder was introduced to the public. His slow advance to the ring side was hostile and violent. His circle of bodyguards protected him from anything physical. Soft objects were thrown as he retaliated with clenched fists and shouting back obscenities at the baying crowd.

He was now in the ring to loud whistles and boos. Kazar had

organised a black leather cape as an extra dimension to his already frightening appearance. Salvador turned his back on the Masked Marauder, he had no intention of being intimidated by the mask. He began to flex his legs in his corner whilst holding the top ropes. The Masked Marauder went across to his opponent and placed a forearm smash across his shoulders. He went down on his backside, more by surprise than by injury. A cacophony of sound erupted in the arena as the referee tried to bring order to the proceedings and separate the two men. The stage and the theatre were set up for a great contest. The Masked Marauder received a verbal warning from the judges for his actions, but it would have no impact on the final outcome.

Chapter 27

Salvador had put up a good wrestling contest, but he was no match for the superiority of his opponent. The Masked Marauder was clinical in his execution of moves, kicks and throws. He had allowed a few moments of drama to Salvador, as he tried in vain to overcome the defence of the mask. Salvador had his fingers under the chin part on a couple of occasions, but it was controlled by the Marauder as his vice like grip wrapped around Salvador's wrist. He had applied steady pressure, to the point of crushing if he had not released his grip. The spectators were crestfallen at him not revealing his identity. Salvador had succumbed to the skills of the unknown wrestler after seven entertaining and breathtaking rounds. It had ended as The Marauder had intended. Salvador was tipped out of the ring after a frenetic flurry of holds, counter holds and kicks, thus providing excellent preparation to his build up campaign. More importantly, he had come through the contest without injury to himself.

He was reflecting on his time spent in the guardhouse. It was Tuesday 15th July 1947 and his release was imminent. He thought about how he had entered this facility at the peak of his wrestling career, a career which happened as much by chance as choice. Within a few hours of bursting through the guardhouse doors, he had been reduced to an almost vegetative state. He had regained his fitness within a few weeks and wrestling again at the top level by the end of his detention. He felt no animosity towards his attackers, they were acting under orders. Like Captain Black though, they too had been reassigned duties which would eventually take them from Singapore.

The Captain in command of the Guards just needed to organise a few papers to make his prisoners release official. After a few moments of idle discussion with several Redcaps present, the Captain announced, 'Okay, Kid, you're free to go.' He offered a hand shake which he immediately accepted. He thanked him and the rest of the guards for their help in getting him back to full fitness. There was back slapping all round. He had been an exemplary prisoner, but more importantly, he had introduced a keep fit regime in the guardhouse which would be used going forward by both the guards themselves and the internees. It was unhealthy to see army personnel waste away in their cells for days. The guards were fitter and healthier as a result of his guidance and tuition. None of them would make the wrestling circuit, but in his view, a healthy body created a healthy mind.

'Good luck with the Far East Championship, Kid.' The guard winked at him as he declared his intention. He owed this guard a great deal, more than he could justify at that moment. It was he who had provided him with the pain relief when pain was at its height. He had been on the edge of life itself, falling in and out of consciousness, not knowing if it was night or day. Not knowing if his dark nightmares were real or just fantasy. He nodded his appreciation to the guard, further words between the two men were not necessary.

He had been treated very well, apart from those first days when he was refused any medical assistance. He recognised he had been granted special privileges in an effort to follow his dream. There were still questions for which he needed answers but he knew these would come in the forthcoming days and weeks. There were pieces of his jig saw still missing. Who was the officer who he fleetingly caught sight of at the Sultan's palace? And then there was the mystery man? Could it possibly be the Sultan of Johor? He was clearly a very powerful individual and very influential. But the mystery about him still remained nonetheless, like that which he and Kazar had created behind the mask. The identity of the Masked Marauder would also remain a mystery with the people of Singapore and Johor forever. He had fought his last contest with his hidden identity preserved. The Masked Marauder had played a very important role in his life. Without this touch of genius from Kazar, and no doubt some serious amounts of money, the championship would be a lost cause. For now though, the mask and its trapping's were laid to rest.

'I hope you'll support me in my bid for the Far East

Championship,' he said, now in possession of all his belongings and ready to leave the guardhouse.

'We'll be following your progress with great enthusiasm, don't worry about that. Perhaps if you win, we could assume part ownership of the title anyway? Remember who your friends are, Kid?'

'If I get to the final, I'll get tickets, don't worry. I think I'll need all the help I can get.' He was now almost through the door, legally a free man.

'Just get the tickets, Kid. We'll be there for you.'

As he left the guardhouse heading for his barracks, he had a warm feeling of respect for his captors. They too had great respect for him and what he had achieved, with huge odds stacked against him.

He had written home with the help of one of the guards. He had previously taught English in a grammar school before being conscripted into the Army. Hours had been spent teaching him to write. Left to his own devices, he would still struggle to put a letter together but he had made some impact on his overall ability. He was still at the start gate in reality, but his confidence in this department was increasing. He would need much more time to conquer this particular demon though.

His total concentration was now on the Championship. His letter home had explained his extraordinary rise to fame. He chose not to mention his recent incarceration, he would do that when he arrives home, he thought. Though he had made all the correct noises in terms of his wife and son, he felt his selfishness taking over again. It was this selfishness which had brought him this far. His motivation would now be driven by his family, by his son. He was repentant, but this could not cloud his overall enthusiasm and his burning ambition to achieve his goals. He still had a big mountain to climb and this could not be done by sentiment alone. It would take all his energy and strength to overcome these contests. He also needed to stay fit. He could not even contemplate an injury, for there would be no telling what this would do to his chances. For now though, he would focus his mind on the championship and this alone. His mind was set; no distractions from now on.

He was fooling himself of course; distractions were at every corner of his being! The girl, Suzi, she was a distraction but he desperately wanted to see her again. He wanted her at the ringside, remembering that she could make a difference to his performance. She'd helped him last time of course, if it wasn't for her, he would be just another wrestler on this godforsaken slip of land. Then the truck he is going to drive, what will he be carrying? And then there is the unknown officer and the mystery man? Answers to all these questions were still outstanding and they were distractions! Distractions he could do without.

Chapter 28

The Colonel stood behind his office desk trying to get some cool air from an electric fan positioned in one corner. It was 15.00 hours, and the humidity outside was reaching saturation point. He had been pacing from one side of the room to the other whilst discussing with Major Reece the plan to move the illicit cargo of drugs from a secure location in Singapore to Johor in Malaysia. Both were anxious about their respective roles and the subsequent chances of success. There were still a few things from their side which required some attention. If things did go wrong, they needed to extract themselves from any involvement in the arrangements. Under no circumstances would they risk their impeccable reputations by being implicated in this audacious plan. They would minimise their risk as much as possible.

'When are you going to speak to Callon about the fine detail of the plan, Major?' The Colonel was anxious to get this part of their operation out in the open, to Callon at least.

'I intend to speak to him soon, Colonel, but I need to wait some days, he only left the guardhouse yesterday.'

'Do you envisage any issues, after all, he's had plenty of time to think about his role.' The Colonel pulled the chair out from under his desk and decided to sit down.

'There should be no issues, except...'

'Except what, Major?'

'Well, for a start, he has no knowledge of my involvement. This could frighten the pants off him. On the other hand, it could provide the reassurance, if he needs it that is, that he's not alone in this.'

'That's a good point, Major, but he must know nothing of my involvement.'

'That's clear, Colonel, don't worry about that side of things. The other important point is, if he wants to wrestle, he has to drive the truck as well, and he wants this wrestling championship more than anything.' The Major took a packet of cigarettes from the breast pocket of his army shirt and offered one to the Colonel, but he declined with a shake of his head. The Major continued, 'Kazar is still a little worried about his wrestler's reaction when he finds out what the cargo will be.'

'Just keep any explanation to his questions to a minimum, the less he knows the better,' said the Colonel. 'What else Major?'

'Callon will need to select his team of locals to help load his truck. I need to discuss this with him. We can't afford to delay this part any longer. These men need to be hand picked and carefully selected. We cannot afford any loose talk from their side. His command of the local language should help him in this respect, plus the money he will wave in front of their eyes should ensure their loyalty. That reminds me, Colonel, I need to organise some dollars for their payment.'

'It's good that he's fully immersed back into his wrestling routine. This focus means he can keep his upcoming contests at the front of his mind and off the plan. I don't want this man sat around worrying about his role. He needs to approach this job like he approaches his wrestling contests.'

'What about the red caps, Major, have you sorted them out yet?'

'Three of them, yes, I still need to secure the last one though. This should be completed by the weekend. I'm being extra cautious, Colonel, making sure we have the men we can trust. These men also need to be the best of the best.'

'These men know nothing about the cargo, Major, and only one will know the address in Johor, is that correct?'

'Just as we discussed, Colonel, yes, that's what we agreed.'

'This group of men should be in a state of readiness at all times, Major, as we approach the date for the operation to start.'

Deep down, both the Colonel and the Major were most concerned about the smooth exit from the dock area and the crossing through the causeway at the Singapore side. This was out of their hands, they had to rely on what they now regarded was a weak player. They both felt the Singapore Head of Customs, who was to negotiate this section for the operation, was at best a liability and at worst a complete disaster. This was the most difficult and riskiest part of the operation. The dock area had fewer people involved, so this was less problematic, plus it would be completed after a normal days work. The only people on the dockside at that time would be the customs men. The Singapore causeway section though, would be heavily manned, as this part of the journey was patrolled and guarded 24 hours a day, seven days a week. Nothing gets past their strict scrutiny. Massaging their egos with a few thousand dollars is what it would take. This would always blur their vision and dull their concentration, but there would be many guards on this causeway unaware of any trafficking arrangements and this was a risk. Richard, the Singapore customs head had informed that three men only would know about the illicit consignment. Timing was the key now, not just the date, but also the time of day to pass through this narrow, patrolled road channel. This was an operation worth many millions of dollars and many people were now involved in the different aspects of its execution. The two men wondered if everyone outside of their control knew their place and where they should be at the crucial moment of the plan!

Chapter 29

He parked his ten ton Mack in its usual parking space on the dockside, his work for this day now behind him. Friday was a weekend day in Singapore, so there were fewer locals around, only those who had volunteered to work overtime. He was pleased to be back working and free from his shackles of the guardhouse. Nothing much had changed dockside, it was still just as chaotic. He had started to take more notice of the comings and goings of trucks and personnel since getting back to work, checking who was where and when at any particular time. The mystery man had told him that he would be driving the truck from one of the dock areas in Singapore. There were several, but he guessed whatever it was that he was supposed to load on to his truck would come from the Empire Dock where he now stood. This was the main dock area and the largest in Singapore with a navigable huge stone quayside approaching 6000 ft in length. He was also mindful of any special surveillance of areas or buildings. He realised he could move throughout the dock areas with impunity both on foot and in his truck, though there were still areas out of bounds to unauthorised personnel. The Mack's large unmistakeable bull nose which he drove had DOCKS stencilled in black across a white board attached to the radiator to provide further credence to its driver, its identity and its belonging. He was a well known individual and one of only a few white men who could speak the Malayan language. He could liaise with the locals without bringing any attention to himself. They were always willing to share any information they had, but up to now, nothing unusual had been unloaded or was being stored to their knowledge.

Since his release, he had been able to mix work with his training and preparation. He felt the first tingle of nerves as he realised this day was a huge event in his life. He had been too busy during his working day to think about it. He had awoken at 06.00 hours to do his daily workout before arriving at his workplace on the docks. This was not the best preparation, having to work an eight hour shift before one of the biggest wrestling contests of his life. This would be step one, in a total of three to the Far East Championships. Nerves and apprehension was not a bad thing for him, these helped him focus his mind.

He had not heard from Suzi since their brief encounter in Johor. He had asked Kazar to ensure that she got a ringside viewing for all three of his upcoming contests. He wanted her there, she would provide that extra stimulus should he need it. He didn't even know the girl that well, but he wanted to know more about her. She was obviously being paid by the mystery man, but had no idea what for, or what her role was. There was time to establish all these things later, he thought.

His physical preparation had gone exceedingly well and he was in great shape since his contest with Salvador. It had provided a perfect preparation platform for his forthcoming championship decider. Coming second this evening was not an option. He would win at any cost, he thought, but his challenger probably also thought the same.

It was the mystery man he saw first. He had an unmistakeable persona which he presented to his outside world. His entourage was also impressive in numbers, as they hung on his every word and catered for his every need. He had a central ringside seat at the Great World Arena, and was protected by his henchmen from anyone getting close to him. He noticed that no one was allowed to even walk in front of him. He was viewing him from one of the main vantage points close to the dressing rooms. He was waiting just before they announced his contest and before he would begin his slow entrance to the ring. He was impressed that the man had come to witness his contest, but could not help thinking there was an ulterior motive to him being there. He was now speaking to a gentleman in a lounge suit; he had broken through the cordon around the mystery man. His face was familiar, but he was not sure where he had seen him previously. Then the sudden realisation of who the man was hit him like a bolt from out of the blue.

'Holy shit,' he heard himself say. The man in conversation was the officer who he had seen momentarily at the Johor Palace. He was sure of it. It wasn't until he had seen both men together that he had made the connection. Worse still, it was the Colonel, the very man who accompanied Major Reece and visited him after he was attacked by the six guards.

'What the hell is he doing here, more importantly, what the hell was he doing at the palace?' He was talking quietly to himself as he took in the images before him. 'He must be involved in the operation, he has to be? He was there when the mystery man first broached the subject of making some serious money. If he was not involved, there would be no way the mystery man would raise such a delicate subject.' His mind was spinning. Kazar was also there now speaking to the Colonel like an old friend with his arm resting on his shoulder. You can only do that if you know someone well enough, he thought.

He could hear the announcement which would bring him forward to the ring, but he was transfixed to the spot. The crowd at The Great World arena erupted at the mention of Kid Callon, his contest was about to begin. They would welcome their rising star as one of their own. He would have great support this evening, he knew it. They were in awe of their star, someone they had seen from the very beginning of his wrestling career. They would wonder how someone so young could boss and dominate men ten years or more his senior. He was still only 21 years of age. He had chosen Hassan as his ringside second, he was an accomplished wrestler himself, but he was also a master of the sponge and the first aid bag.

'Come on, Kid, they have just called you.' Hassan could see his wrestler's mind was preoccupied as he prodded him to go forward. His mind operated in slow motion as he tried to evaluate the scene unfolding before him. This was exactly what he didn't need at such an important crossroads in his career. He tried to blot out what the Colonel's involvement could be. Hassan was wondering if Kid Callon had got stage fright, it happened to the best of them.

'Kid, come on, are you okay?' He didn't reply, but walked forward looking intently at the small group still talking together at the side of the ring.

He stopped momentarily to ask a question. 'Hassan, the smartly dressed man at the ringside with his men around him, who is he?' He pointed him out so that there was no misunderstanding which man he meant. The noise in the hall was deafening, and Hassan spoke directly into his ear with a cupped hand. He pulled away and mouthed to his second, 'are you sure?' Hassan nodded and mouthed back,

'I'm sure.'

The wrestling announcer was talking up the competition as tension in The Great World Arena was building towards the start of the contest. His mind was still trying to take in what he had just witnessed ringside. He also had his worst suspicions confirmed; he knew who the mystery man was.

The Colonel looked so different in civvies but now he was nowhere to be seen. He was scanning the ringside seats, looking for Suzi. Kazar had told him that she would be there. He needed her there now, more than anything. Her presence not only calmed him, but energised him too. He needed something to take away the images he had just seen.

He found her; she was there, her face standing out in the crowd, looking elegant and sophisticated. She was amongst the entourage of the mystery man, several rows back. His spirits lifted as they exchanged eye contact. Her smile was demure and inviting as she craned her neck to emphasise her position and her presence. She could sense that he was searching for her as the arena lights were dimmed to reveal the start of the commentary to the contest. The arena was cooled to some extent by the air conditioning units, though the units laboured somewhat in their attempt to maintain a fresh and comfortable temperature around the hall. Suzi was cooling her face with a brightly decorated ivory handled fan. High cheek bones highlighted her beauty beneath tissue-like translucent skin as delicate as finest porcelain from China. She was wearing ruby red lipstick enhancing the shape of her lips and mouth against brilliant white teeth, all this beauty supported by a background of beautifully coiffed black hair pushed back from her face and standing high on her forehead. Her soft coloured silk blouse was open and inviting with two top buttons unfastened. Flanked on both sides by two heavily built men, he wondered if they were there for a purpose, or was it just by chance she was sat there.

The entrance of Red Rivers to the ring re-tuned his concentration. The man never glanced at him. He simply went through his warm up routine, he didn't want to be intimidated by someone so talented, but mainly, so young. Kid Callon had had a distinguished career up to now and knew he would not be beaten this day. He was unbeaten in all of his contests so far. It was almost two years now since he had first stepped into this very ring, a ring which up to now had made his very own. He'd seen many battles won and lost here, but fortunately for him, in the many contests he'd fought, he had always come away victorious. Kid Callon was not going to let that crown slip now. Red Rivers knew he had a battle on his hands. The hour had arrived. It was 20.45 as the two men approached each other, hardly hearing the bell over the noise from the Arena.

Chapter 30

As he and his friends entered the foyer of the Raffles Hotel, the mood was reaching fever pitch. This venue was one of his favourites, especially after a successful evening on the wrestling circuit. It was almost midnight, but the hotel always provided a warm welcome for one of their prestigious sporting hero's. Kazar had once again organised this celebration. He knew somehow that his young wrestler would be unfazed by the enormity of his challenges ahead.

'One down, two to go!' Kazar was proposing a toast to the potential Light Heavyweight Wrestling Champion of the Far East.

'Let's not get ahead of ourselves, Kaz. That was one hell of a contest out there tonight. Rivers had me worried several times. I thought I was going to have to kill him. He just kept coming back at me.' He savoured the champagne bubbles as they danced on his tongue before slipping slowly down his throat and was looking for a top-up; his night still had some distance to run. The promoter had organised a room in the hotel expecting his wrestler's victorious outcome and inviting his friends along. Also there was Suzi. He wanted his young wrestler to enjoy and make the most of his triumphant evening in the ring, knowing that the challenges from now on would get tougher, not just in the ring, but more lucratively, outside it.

'Red Rivers was a tough opponent, yes, but I felt you were always in control, Kid?'

He was annoyed by his promoter's casual remark.

'Red Rivers was underestimated, Kaz, you underestimated him. I'd never seen him wrestle before. You have! I was one second away from defeat tonight. If Rivers had been able to apply one more ounce of pressure on that last move, then I would have gone. We would be drinking a consolation drink in one of the cheap bars on Orchard

Road.' He stamped his champagne flute on the table. The champagne had brought awareness as to how close he had come to defeat tonight. Though he had taken the first submission, Red Rivers had come back strongly to even up the match. He had never been put into a full nelson before. Red Rivers had craftily lured him into this back breaking move. Once the hold was applied, he only had a split second, he had to submit or suffer sever spinal injury. Alternatively he faced excruciating back problems. He couldn't afford to do that, but it had weakened him and had preventing him finishing off his opponent in his usual manner. He wanted Red Rivers out of the ring by knockout, but this was not to be. It took nine rounds to finally overcome his opponent, taking him further than any of his previous contenders. The days he spent recovering from his beating were a grim reminder of how much had been taken out of his body. His fights with the mask helped him, for sure, but the level and skill of his wrestling opponent tonight was leagues better. Red Rivers was not prepared to give up his challenge too lightly, but he did look broken as he accepted defeat from him.

'But you came back, Kid, you beat him, you need challenges like this. It re-focuses you. Every contest is not a done deal; you have to work for it. This is the Championship of the Far East; none of your contests are going to be a pushover.' Kazar was re-filling his glass as he smiled at his young wrestler. He was holding his back with the flat of his hand, flexing and stretching it, hoping that no lasting damage had been done. He would never again fall for that move, a move which nearly crippled him.

'Drink up, Kid, enjoy the moment.' Kaz was about to walk away when he grabbed his arm and pulled him back.

'Where's our, mystery friend, I thought he'd be here tonight?' Kaz, wasn't ready for this discussion, and knew there was more to his questioning. 'He was there, Kaz, you were speaking to him and his cronies too.'

Kazar stood to face him, waiting for the next question which he knew was coming.

'And who was the man in the suit you were talking to just before my contest began, you know, you had your hand on his shoulder. You must know who I mean?' He knew it was the Colonel, but he wanted to know how Kaz would handle it.

'Our mutual friend needed to get back to Johor; he had some business to attend to.'

'What, at 12 o'clock at night?'

'Yes, he works 24 hours a day, if necessary. He operates on only four hours sleep daily.'

'So who was the man?' He wondered if he was going to get a straight answer. Kaz had avoided the question up to now.

'He's an officer in the British Army.' Kaz had no reason to lie, because he knew he could not connect anything to the Colonel. He was unaware however, that he had seen the Colonel by chance in the Sultan's palace in Johor.

'What were you discussing with a British Officer? What could you two possibly have in common?'

'He just happened to be there.'

'Bullshit, don't give me that.' Callon was looking for some sign from his promoter, he knew he was lying. 'How do you know him, Kaz?'

'Oh, you know, I scratch his back every now and then and he scratches mine.'

'Does he have anything to do with your plan?'

'It's our plan, you are a part of it, remember.' Kazar was firm in his retort.

'I know nothing about it. I know I have to drive a truck, that's all. I don't even know if it's risky or dangerous.' He was getting confident in his questions; the champagne helped of course, but he wanted to know more details. This operation was beginning to play on his mind and he was in the *"need to know"* zone now. It almost cost him the contest this evening. You let your concentration waver for a second and you find yourself in a mess you cannot escape from, he thought. He felt this in real life too. He wasn't sure if he was in a mess, but he sure as hell knew he couldn't get out of it.

'Keep your voice down, Kid! And no, it's not dangerous, but yes, there are risks. For the kind of money we are speaking of, there has to be risks, you were told this from the very beginning.'

'Is the officer you spoke to involved in the plan then?' He wanted to know.

'No, he's not. Is that good enough for you now? Look, let's get the party moving, Kid, let's get some more drinks.'

He knew his line of questioning was going nowhere. He also knew he had been lied to on two occasions now. This has to be huge operation, he thought, and he was in it, right up to his armpits!

Chapter 31

As he entered his barracks, he was confronted by Steve. He was at the previous night's celebratory party, but left around one-o-clock in the morning to find some entertainment of his own choosing.

'Where did you get to last night, Kid, I expected you back here at least. The Major wants to see you in his office.'

He was nursing a hangover. He was not used to drinking champagne in quantity. He had stayed overnight at the Raffles Hotel with Suzi. Kazar had organised this for him. He had also told him to be careful, Suzi could face a backlash from her community if she was seen flaunting herself in public places with a non Muslim man. Two rooms had been booked to avoid any embarrassment on Suzi's part. They left separately after eating breakfast in his room. They spoke only briefly before saying their goodbyes, both knowing that this friendship could not continue or last. They had shared a night of intense passion, interrupted only by short bouts of sleep.

'He wants to see me? What's all that about, Steve, did he say what for?' He was rubbing his forehead and trying to stave off the retching which was suddenly working itself up through his windpipe to the back of his throat. The champagne combined with the famous Singapore sling was beginning to make its presence felt.

'No, there was no message, the Major's sidekick called in half an hour back, around 09.30. I told him you were out training. I would shoot over there if I was you. It seemed important, it's not every day the Major seeks your presence.'

He went to splash water over his face, he couldn't go to the Major's office looking like he did. He looked pale and dreadful, but there was nothing he could do about that in the time he had to sort himself out. He wondered if the Major had further news about his father. He changed into his khaki uniform and made his way to see the Major. He paused momentarily before setting foot on the step leading to his office, half expecting to be shouted down by some irate officer. He smiled and thought about the last time he got this far, but then quickly erased it from his mind.

He knocked on the door and the Corporal ushered him into the office.

'I understand Major Reece wants to see me, Corporal?' He stood close to the outside door trying to get as much air into his lungs as possible. He was hoping he wouldn't spew up on the Major's table.

'What's your name, soldier?'

'Callon, Derek Callon.'

After a few moments waiting and dispensing with all the pleasantries, he was standing across from Major Reece. It was less than a week since he'd been released from the guardhouse and he wondered what on earth it was the Major wanted to speak to him about.

The large man looked uncomfortable, something was clearly troubling him, he thought. He had known the Major for some time now, but had never seen him look like this. His face lacked any colour and he looked like he felt, sick. His initial thought were that he had bad news from the UK and that he was bringing himself to the point where he would tell him.

'I first want to congratulate you, soldier; you put up a good display last night. The RASC are very grateful of your achievements.'

'Were you there, sir?' he enquired.

'No, no I wasn't, I had other things to attend to. You know how it is. But good news travels fast around here, taking into consideration your recent behaviour, soldier, you have made quite a name for your self here and in Johor I understand?'

'Thank you, Sir, yes; I'm very proud of what I have achieved so far.' The Major scrutinised him. 'I mean from a wrestling point of view, Sir.'

'Yes, quite.' The Major was fidgeting with some envelopes from an open drawer. He took them out and then returned them almost immediately. Then he stood up and walked to the window behind his desk, before turning to face him.

'This is very awkward for me.' There was stunned silence; he wondered what the Major was going to say next.

'I know you've been approached?'

'Approached, Sir?'

'Yes, approached, to drive a truck? It's okay, Callon, I know all about it. Let's not make this difficult for each other.' He was feeling nauseous again, unsure if it was down to his hangover or not. Bile was beginning to enter his mouth, he had to swallow it; he had no other option. Sweat was peppering his brow and he felt seriously unwell. He could think of one response only.

'Sir, have I done something wrong?' He felt sure the Major was trying to hang something on him.

'No! no of course not. I need to explain a few things.' The Major sat down and ushered him to sit opposite him. He then proceeded to explain his part in the planned operation.

'We both have a great deal to gain from this operation, so we can't afford any mistakes.' He was flabbergasted that he knew about him and his intended role and that the Major was involved with whatever the plan was. The only thing he was sure about now was, it was unlawful and it was most definitely big!

Two senior officers, he thought. What the fuck is going on!

The Major continued, making the next point very clear indeed. 'The other thing we have to do is maintain strict security, is that understood?'

'Yes, of course, Sir.'

One other thing, soldier, we've not had this conversation.'

'Yes, clear, Sir, but I have no details. I'm still in the dark. Tell me, what is it I'm supposed to do?' Before the Major could answer, he continued. 'I know I've to drive a truck from one of the ports here in Singapore, and then take it into Johor. I haven't been told what the cargo will be or where it is.' He was beginning to come to terms with the discussion and he relaxed a little. He felt relieved in some way that the Major was involved.

'Let me say this first. You've been selected for this operation purely on your own merits. You have all the right credentials, plus we know we can trust and rely on you, soldier?'

'Yes, I understand, Sir.'

The Major continued.

'Listen carefully, Callon, this is what you need to do. The goods will arrive at the Empire Dock around the 1st or 2nd of August. They will go straight into the Bonded Warehouse section. You know this area don't you?'

'Yes, Sir.'

'We will arrange for you to gain access to the warehouse on the day of the operation. These facilities are closely monitored, guarded and locked. The plan will be conducted outside of normal working hours. The date has to be finalised, but it should be soon after the goods arrive. The date coincides with the wrestling Championship finals too, so there should be no conflict. Assuming you get to the finals, then our plan is to move just a few days afterwards. The goods in question are, let's say, sensitive, so they'll be securely stored. The Major waited until Callon had digested the information then continued. 'This is what you need to organise. You will need at least four men to help you load your truck, local men you can trust. Men who will keep their mouths shut. You will pay them from funds which I will provide, but make sure these men know nothing until the time is ready for us to move. We cannot afford the smallest leak here, Callon.'

I thought I was driving a bloody truck. Nobody mentioned loading it first? How the hell am I supposed to organise this?

'Sir, I've never done anything like this before...?'

The Major interjected.

'Neither have I, but one thing I know around this part of the world is that money talks.' The Major opened a drawer and pulled out the envelopes again. They each contained a wad of dollar notes. 'There are more than sufficient funds for the four men you need.' The Major passed the envelopes across the desk. 'Use it discretely and wisely. If you need more, you need to see me again. Use your language skills to get the men you want.'

'Sir, one more question, what will I be loading onto my Mack? You still haven't told me.'

The Major hesitated before answering,

'It's Chandu.'

What the fuck is Chandu?

'Chandu, Sir, what is Chandu?'

'It's Opium, black tar opium, also known as BTO.' The Major relaxed back in his chair and looked curiously across to his visitor and waited for a reaction. Callon had a look of despair and desperation on his face.

'What, drugs? I had no idea it was drugs, Sir, no idea at all?'

'Would it make a difference if you had known, Callon?'

I would be out of here like a bloody shot!

'I don't know anything about drugs, Sir…?'

The Major stopped him continuing.

'You don't need to know anything about drugs. We will ensure that you have a free passage in and out of the dock area without raising any alarms or concerns. Getting into the bonded warehouse will be organised in advance, or the door access will be open to you. We will see to all these arrangements. You organise yourself some hired help; then drive the truck into Malaysia after rendezvousing with the redcaps. They will provide your safe passage through the border from Singapore to Malaysia, that's it.' The Major was very matter of fact about his reply and trying desperately to undervalue the importance of what he had just said and what he expected of him. He could sense that his CO was not enjoying this discussion either.

That sound easy enough then! Fuck me!

'And what about the risks, Sir, are there any?'

'Look, Callon, the reason I'm telling you about this now, is so you can prepare yourself. You need to find the men you want, and we need to find the rota schedule for the customs personnel on the dock gates and at the border crossing. This takes time. The customs personnel are not under my command.' The Major looked directly at Callon. 'There are people involved in this operation that have shown concern about you too. I am telling you this to put your mind at ease. Look, we have a little over two weeks to prepare ourselves. Nothing will happen until after your last wrestling contest. We are aware of how much you want this Far East title. You're a very special individual, Callon, the likes of which we don't see around these parts.' He felt the praise was all part of the build up, he knew something else was coming.

'Between now and the date of the operation, I want you to plan your side. You will be expected to do only light work on the docks, but use your time wisely. Gather as much information as you can. You need to know those docks like the back of your hand.' A wry smile crossed the lips of the Major as though he had just offered him a huge monetary bonus, then continuing he said,

'The planning of this operation should help your preparations for the title too.'

You have to be bloody kidding me! How the hell do I concentrate with all this shit going on?

'You're excused now, Callon. When I have more details about dates etc, I will let you know. In the meantime, you keep your nose clean and keep quiet. No one has to breathe a word about this, are you clear?'

'Yes, sir, clear, but I'm unhappy about the cargo, Major, I had no idea it would be something like this. What happens if this goes belly up, what happens to me then?'

'Think positive, Callon, nothing is going to go wrong. A huge amount of money has already been paid to individuals to make sure this operation runs like clockwork. This operation has been months and months in the making, this is not something which could be organised in a few weeks.'

He left the Major's office, went back to his barracks and threw up. The rest of the room was deserted as he made his way to his bed, he needed to lie down and reflect on what he had to do. He realised that there was only one way back from this operation and that was to go through with it. Drugs, he bloody well hated them. Yet here he was, involved in a scandal that would probably send shockwaves throughout the Far East, if not beyond. This would be a drug heist to dwarf most drug heists, he realised the enormity of the operation.

The feeling of euphoria and success which he had enjoyed last night disappeared and seemed like a lifetime away. There was only one thing which allowed him to clear his thoughts and that was training. He needed to sleep first though, this was more important, he would train afterwards.

Chapter 32

Kazar picked his young wrestler up from his barracks and were now ringside at the first wrestling championship between the other two championship contenders, Jack 'Boulder' Harris and Miraj Kamrul. He would have to fight both these men and was looking to try and spot any weaknesses or strengths and to study their style. He was not surprised at the support this contest was receiving. Johor Bahru was alive with applause and anticipation. The clear favourite was Miraj Kamrul. This man had a reputation that went before him. This competition was building and he had been looking forward to this contest as much as his own against Red Rivers. It would be his first look at both these men and would allow an opportunist preview of what he could expect to face in the next two weekends. He also hoped he could mastermind a strategy that could see the demise of Kamrul in two weeks time.

As both men entered the ring, he wondered if these two men had also taken the opportunity to see him and Red Rivers wrestle. He could not remember seeing these men ringside, as both men were very distinctive in their appearance.

Both he and Kazar viewed their quarry. They concentrated first on Kamrul, studying his physique. This man was out of all physical proportion. He was older looking than he had imagined, he guessed he would be in his early thirties. Standing at only five foot tall, he possessed huge biceps and thighs. His thick arms were longer than you would expect for someone as small in stature as Kamrul. He had a huge barrel chest and a waistline to match. There was not a part on his body without hair, he wondered if this was a help or a hindrance. Harris was almost a foot taller and stoutly built. A large Texan hat was soon dispensed with and Harris revealed a balding pate. This made him look older than he probably was, but they both guessed similar in age to Kamrul, early thirties.

Kamrul was stealing most of the support over Harris, and he wondered what the support would be like when they wrestled together in the Great World arena. Many people in the crowd had seen him and wanted to shake his hand. This caught the attention of Kamrul in particular and confirmed that he did know who Kid Callon was after all. He motioned to him through the ropes with his hands to indicate he would squeeze the living daylights out of him. He instinctively left his seat with Kazar in pursuit trying to hold his young wrestler back. He jumped up onto the side of the ring to thunderous shouts from the crowd. A short battle of words ensued whilst Kamrul tried without success to get at his man. He moved along the outside of the ropes as Kamrul followed him, but he was prevented from this by his second and officials as they dragged the Indian wrestler back. He wanted his man in a rage when he wrestled him. He was surprised at how quickly this little man had taken the bait. Rage represents lack of discipline and technique and would be something he would be working on when they meet. He had jumped on the ringside purposely to judge Kamrul's temperament under fight conditions. He was certainly much pricklier than he could have wished for. He liked his opponents to get into a rage; this was playing into his hands.

The contest lasted three rounds with Kamrul coming away victorious. He had secured his second submission after Harris had put up a worthwhile performance. He had lasted as long as any of Kamrul's other opponents. Boulder Harris was a seasoned campaigner, but could not overcome the brute strength of his opponent on this occasion.

He and Kazar left the arena under no doubt that Kamrul was a formidable force and that it would take all his strength and knowhow to overcome this misshapen monster. The experience had given him some ideas and he would work on these leading up to when they meet on Saturday 2nd August. He was unafraid of what he had seen, but he would be taking nothing for granted.

After one contest each, he and Kamrul had come through victorious. Kamrul was still the favourite, but neither had been beaten. They were the only two contestants in the Far East who could boast of this feat. He however, had submissions against him, so this relegated him to underdog. He didn't mind this tag, in fact it was his preference going into a contest of this magnitude. He needed to dispose of Boulder Harris first of course, so this would be where most of his concentration would lie for the time being.

For the next phase of the competition scheduled for Saturday 26th July 1947, all four contestants would wrestle in the same venue. He would wrestle Boulder Harris first, starting at 20.00 hours, followed by Kamrul and Red Rivers, scheduled to start at 21.00 hours. The venue would be The Great World Arena, his preferred choice. No upsets were predicted, but he was intent on making his presence felt in more ways than one.

Chapter 33

The ten ton Mack shuddered to a halt as the huge diesel engine was shut down for the day. He lowered himself from the cab, his short sleeve shirt and khaki shorts displaying damp patches where sweat had permeated through the fabric. It had been another stifling hot day on the dock side. The air was still and muggy with hardly a breath of air to breathe. He had done his homework this week and was pleased at the outcome. He had spent a great deal of his time talking to the locals in their native tongue and dropping subtleties here and there whilst weighing up his options. He had identified at least seven individuals who he had known since he arrived in Singapore in early September '45. He had also been checking out the area where the bonded goods were warehoused and stored. This was a huge single story building made from breeze blocks and then rendered. There were many bays within the warehouse which could accommodate the black tar opium (BTO). Another plus point was that his truck could be driven into the warehouse. Two huge metal doors provided the height and width for his huge vehicle to enter. Loading of the consignment could all be done in secrecy, they would load the BTO out of normal working hours, but there were always a few people milling around after hours who could cause some problems if they were seen.

He observed the customs men on the gates leading to the dock entrance. He came onto these docks almost every day, but had taken little notice previously of the way they went about their business. He noticed with more interest the checks which they carried out with regards to paperwork. Nothing was allowed in or out of the docks without first checking that the documentation and paperwork were in order. The customs men would do a cursory check on the vehicles to make sure that the paperwork matched what was on the truck. Every now and then, a more intense search of a vehicle would be carried out, either randomly, or through suspicion of theft from the dockside area. Details of all vehicles were noted and written down. The customs men could vouch for every vehicle in or leaving the dock area. Under no circumstances were vehicles simply waved through. He wondered what would be organised for him when he approached the gate with no documents, no paperwork, nothing. Would he be simply allowed through with a wave of the hand, given there was always a minimum of two persons from the customs checking vehicles. They were always dressed in smart uniform with white collar and black tie, gold braiding on their caps and epaulettes. Whilst this area was not his concern according to the Major, he made himself aware of just what he could be facing.

The light duty of work on the docks had also allowed him to prepare well for his second championship wrestling contest. He had split his sessions of training up so that he could do a heavy workout in the morning before arriving at the docks. This would be his main session, followed by a large breakfast. He would work on the docks mainly supervising the local help as he continued to improve his dialogue of the Malay language. Further light training was followed by an equally light lunch taken in the canteen area on the docks. He would eat with the locals as they discussed his rise to stardom on the wrestling circuit. Many of the locals were amongst his band of supporters. These discussions were also useful to gain intelligence about the dock area. The men were always forthcoming about what was happening with respect to what was arriving and what was leaving.

His final training session was early evening when the sun had lost most of its fierce intensity. He used this time to improve and maintain his stamina with long runs as the sun was setting. He knew his training was going well, but he was having difficulties sleeping and he felt this was taking some of his energy. His sleep was interrupted by strange and weird dreams mainly relating to the drugs operation. He would awake from these nightmares, dripping with sweat. The outcome was always the same; he would have to fight his way out of trouble. He hoped that this was not an omen for the real thing. This would keep him awake for what seemed like hours as he consoled himself that it was only a dream. His thoughts would then take him home, back to England where he would be a wealthy man and have more than enough money to spend.

Amounts he could only dream about at this stage. He would continue his wrestling career where he left off here in Singapore, hopefully as the Light Heavyweight Champion of the Far East. The sport of wrestling was also well supported back in the UK, but his presence back there would not be anytime soon.

Chapter 34

'I just need to see her, Kaz, please bring her here to see me.' It had been over a week since he had seen Suzi, and whilst he recognised that they had no future together, he still wanted to see this Malayan beauty.

'It's bad luck to bring her in here, Kid, wait until after your contest.' Kaz was adamant that he should wait, but knew better than to argue at this stage with his prize fighter.

The tension was mounting as the wrestling championship neared its start point. The Great World Arena was packed to capacity. The spectators were expecting to see a wrestling contest unequalled in these parts. Immediately after his bout with Boulder Harris, Kamrul and Red Rivers would start their contest. Kid Callon was definitely not going to miss seeing his arch rival in action again. The more background he could gather on this little big man, the better.

As soon as Suzi walked into his dressing room, he knew there was a problem. They held each other for a few moments before speaking. He was resplendent in his long black silk dressing gown looking majestic and composed. His dark hair brushed back from a suntanned forehead without a blemish or mark. Within thirty minutes, he would be wrestling as if his life depended on it. He wanted this Championship more than anything.

'What is it, Suzi, why such a sad face?' She could not answer him as she buried her head into his chest. 'Tell me, what is it?' She was shaking her head in protest at his questioning. She didn't want to tell him that she'd been sacked from her position at the palace. Her infidelity was used as the cause for her dismissal. Staying overnight in a public place was considered sufficient to warrant this, irrespective of any wrong doing.

'It's okay, Ki, I can sort this out, I just need a little time.' It was almost time for his warm up, but her sadness concerned him. He called Kazar back into his changing room whilst Suzi took her seat in the main auditorium.

'What's wrong with Suzi, Kaz, she seems so unhappy? Do you know anything about why she's like this?' He was beginning to do his stretches and practise some of his holds. Hassan had been on standby to assist him for this reason, but for now he could not concentrate. He stopped his warm-up after Kaz refused to reply to his question.

'Kaz, you know what it is don't you, tell me for heavens sake, I need to know?'

'Not now, this is a bad time for you to hear any of this shit. You need to think about the contest, look, I promise you, I will tell you after your bout with Boulder Harris.'

'Just answer me one question, does this thing you call shit, have anything to do with our mystery friend?'

Kazar turned away from him with his head bowed, and spoke in a very soft voice and answered, 'Yes.'

'That's all I need for now, tell me, is he in the audience?'

His reply was the same as the previous one.

'Yes.' There was a pause then he continued to speak with his head bowed as though embarrassed to be standing there. 'He is ringside, and he wants to meet in my office after the competition is over. We have some things we need to discuss.'

He was grinding his teeth when he replied, 'I have some questions of my own, Kaz. I just hope the bastard gives me the answers.'

'Get ready, Kid, come on, forget about this for now, you have a big night ahead of you.'

Boulder Harris was going to be on the receiving end of the anger which was welling up in his head. He didn't know what was upsetting Suzi, but he felt whatever it was, it was connected to him, and he didn't like it one bit.

The backslapping continued until he was back in the confines of his Great World dressing room. It had taken Kid Callon only five rounds to see off Boulder Harris. The big man was not able to match the speed and agility of his young aggressor. He possessed good strength and a speed belying his outward appearance, but now found he was out of the competition; played two, lost two.

The 'Coup de Grâce' was when he, with help from the ropes, despatched his man out of the ring using the big man's momentum as a guided missile, falling into the entourage of the mystery man. Boulder Harris missed his intended target by inches, but the man was sprayed with blood and snot from a gaping cut on the bridge of Boulder's nose made seconds before he took off and landed. Even though the ringside seats were some 10 feet from the ringside, he managed to eject him the full distance to reach the first row of seats. It was one of the mystery man's entourage who bore the full brunt of this vicious and premeditated attack. Boulder was knocked out flat from the fall and had to be admitted to hospital along with the man who was sat ringside next to his boss. Sadly Jack Boulder Harris was too badly injured and would be unable to wrestle for the third slot. His intended target, the mystery man was unhurt, but he was sure that he had dented his pride. He glared at the mystery man as Boulder was being counted out. The two men exchanged glances momentarily, before the mystery man diverted his stare elsewhere. He realised from that moment, that he would not be giving this man any further wrestling tuition.

He was milking the applause when there was a commotion behind him. Shouts and applause were turning to jeers and jibes. He turned to see Kamrul standing on the outside of the ring. The only separation between them was 12 feet and the ropes. Kamrul was goading him to come towards him waving his long hairy arm, but he stood his ground, victorious in his moment of glory. Kamrul was already in his wrestling trunks ready to start his contest with Red Rivers. He wondered if Kamrul was playing games like he had the week previous. Was he trying to rile him into doing something stupid, he wondered? Kamrul continued to wave him forward shouting obscenities, in a language he did not recognise. He was using the bottom rope to stand on whilst holding the top rope. He was using the ropes as a springboard and jumping up and down like some crazy ape. The crowd could sense fireworks were about to start.

Just stay there little big man if you dare.

He feigned as if to run at Kamrul, but never moved from his position. Callon was now only eight feet away from Kamrul.

Don't move now, stay there you little short arse.

Officials were trying to get Kamrul to stand down, but he ignored everybody and waved then away. His eyes were glaring and fixed on his quarry, Kid Callon.

If you don't move this time, you are going somewhere where you're not expecting my little hairy friend.

He feigned again, inching closer, he was now only five feet from Kamrul. He stood his ground unmoved. Kamrul was now in the zone, the zone where Kid Callon wanted him and could do some serious damage.

Stay there Kamrul, you can bounce up and down as much as you want, I have plenty of target to hit.

Just for good measure, he feigned a move again but kept the same distance between them. He was checking for Kamrul's reflexes, but the man seemed unfazed by the antics. Kamrul stood fixed in his position on the ropes.

Callon bent his knees ever so slowly and ever so slightly, Kamrul did not even notice this small movement, he was preoccupied with his own hysterics.

Gotcha, you little hairy monster!

Within a split second, he was airborne and horizontal and pile driving a scissor kick with as much venom as he could muster into Kamrul's hairy chest. The arena went berserk with this audacious attack. Kamrul was flung backwards, falling from the edge of the ring to the ground, square across his shoulders. He lay on his back, unmoving for a good 20 seconds, he was stunned and he was hurt. He realised that under normal wrestling rules, Kamrul would have been counted out. No one on God's earth had been able to achieve that before, even if the circumstances were not under controlled fight conditions. It was one nil to Kid Callon, but he knew that his work next week would be a tough ride. The little big man was going to be a handful, but he had a plan now at least.

He raised his arms in triumph to the applauding crowd. He had technically knocked out both of his contenders in one night. He wondered how much this jarring of Kamrul's body would affect his contest with Red Rivers. He should capitalise on what he had just accomplished. Kamrul would be groggy, possibly even concussed. Kamrul was due to be wrestling in twenty minutes, but it would take him longer than that to recover from such a hard fall.

Kamrul was led back to his dressing room, both shaken and stirred.

Word had spread to the dressing room of Red Rivers that Kamrul was hurt. It would only be a matter of time before he would know if Red Rivers could capitalise on what he had presented him with. Whatever the outcome, he was not going to miss it. He quickly showered and sat ringside. He wanted to sit next to Suzi, but two heavies from the mystery man's entourage prevented him. They were not going to move for anyone and decided he was not prepared to push his insistence further. He'd done all the fighting he needed to do for one night. It was already 21.00 hours and there was no sign of either wrestler. A small announcement was hurriedly read out that the contest would begin at 21.30. This was met with loud jeers and catcalls. This crowd was now hungry for more action and they wanted it now. Kid Callon had certainly narrowed the odds between Red Rivers and Kamrul. A smile appeared across his lips as he realised the enormity of what he had done. There was nothing anyone could do about it either. It was Kamrul who created the confrontation, not him, he was the one doing the intimidating, and he had just paid a high price for it, probably with the Light Heavyweight Championship of the Far East.

Chapter 35

'She stays, Kaz, or I am out of here. Unless you tell me what the hell is going on, then count me out.' He was furious at what Kazar had just told him. They were in his Great World office after the conclusion of all the wrestling contests.

'Count you out of what?' Kazar wanted to know if he meant wrestling, or the drugs operation.

'You know exactly what I'm talking about and it's not the bloody wrestling championship.' He was prodding his finger at his promoter's chest and Kazar was not impressed by his antics.

'Just a minute, these things are both connected.' His reply was short and to the point and he pushed his wrestlers hand away as he spoke.

'And how in hell's name have you worked that one out?' He turned to Suzi and asked if she minded stepping outside for two minutes. 'Don't even think of playing that trick on me, Kaz, for there is no connection whatsoever between my wrestling and this operation.'

If Kaz says there's a connection, then I'm going to punch his bloody lights out!

'Oh yes there is, Kid, the connection is me. You cannot have one without the other. You should know this much, we've been planning this operation since early last year, and only now are the pieces beginning to fit together. In about ten days, we run with this operation and you're going to play a pivotal role in its execution. Before that of course, you fight Kamrul for the title.' He had never seen Kazar so determined about anything before. Kazar was always chasing money, he had seen that from day one when they met, but the stakes were obviously higher now and Kazar was not going to take any chances of not getting his fair share of the spoils.

'And how long do you think I've been working towards this title?'

there was real emotion in his voice, an emotion he had not experienced before. 'Does this count for nothing?' He turned away from Kazar with a look of complete disgust on his face.

'Let me see what I can do to get Suzi re-instated. I don't like this any more than you do, but you have to understand local cultures, Kid. These people don't take kindly to their women going with…,' he interrupted.

'Going with me? Is that what you were going to say? I wouldn't bloody mind, but it was you who set the whole thing up, what were you thinking about.' He paused for a moment, then realised what was happening. 'You, you set this up, Kaz, didn't you? You bloody well set me up too, you sneaky bastard, what was it, was she getting too close or too familiar?'

I could take you out now Kaz, you spineless bastard!

'It was both, Kid, too close and too familiar. Suzi was not supposed to fall in love with you. She was put there to assist our operation and help our mystery friend to recruit you, nothing more. In the confines of the palace, what went on between you two was considered acceptable. You were the perfect choice for this role, Kid and we wanted you. Yes, we used Suzi to achieve our objective, but now it has to end. This relationship is over and is not up for discussion.' Kaz studied his wrestler before continuing. 'Suzi also knew the consequences of her actions. She could have left the hotel with me, but no, she stayed. It was her choice.'

'You booked a fucking room for her, of course she stayed!'

'No, Kid, you're wrong. I knew about the room, but I didn't book it!'

'Who the hell did then?'

'Take a guess, Kid, who do you think? She was being tested, don't you get it?'

He hated the almost perfect English spoken by Kazar and his explanation of events. Both he and Suzi had been set up, and she had paid the price, losing her dignity and her job.

I despise you, mystery man, whoever the fuck you are. How could you do this to people? All that matters in your life is money, you have no feelings. Money means power and power means everything to you.

'It's over, Kid, forget her; let her go,' Kazar said. 'You really don't have a choice; you know what you want, and you also know what you have to do?'

'You have me over a barrel,' he said softly. 'I can't move one way or the other. You cunning bastards, you have me just where you want me.'

'Remember, Kid, the Light Heavyweight Championship of the Far East is beckoning. This should be your only concern.' Kazar paused, 'for now of course.'

'Please forgive me, Suzi,' he said, staring at Kazar with a look of hatred and disgust on his face, 'please forgive me!'

I want to walk away from this, Suzi, honest I do… I never wanted this outcome for you. This was never my intention!

He turned around very slowly 180 degrees, and turned back to Kaz, his eyes were glassy and moist as he tried to take on board what was happening. He was shaking his head, accepting that he had been duped and could do nothing about it.

Walk away, Callon, turn round and walk away. What's at stake here anyway, my Championship title and thousands and thousands of dollars? Fuck! This is not even a close contest!

'Get her re-instated, Kaz, do that for me will you. And make sure she gets home safe, please?'

Now who's a spineless bastard, Callon, you don't even have the stomach to face her now…It's better this way, I think…Oh fuck, I hate myself.

'Leave it with me, Kid, I will sort this out for her, and look, I'm sorry, it wasn't supposed to end like this.'

He could hear the sobs from Suzi and cries of despair as Kazar escorted her outside of the building and organised for her to be taken home.

I hate myself for this, Suzi, I have no means to change this situation. I am so sorry. I hope you can find it in yourself to forgive me one day.

'Let's toast, Kid Callon on an amazing display of all-in wrestling tonight.' The mystery man had brought several bottles of his finest pink champagne to the meeting in Kazar's office, but to start with, only one bottle would be opened. Everybody played by his rules, irrespective of the moment or the time of day. It was already 23.30 hours and the last thing that he wanted, was another meeting.

'You made Kamrul work tonight, Kid. I liked how you made him work for his place in the final.' The mystery man was trying to lift the despair which had fallen over the meeting. He also knew there was tension in the room and was cautious not to inflame the situation further. The mystery man could see that he was edgy and not his usual self. He knew the reasons why, it was through his instructions that Suzi was sacked. As far as he was concerned, she had gone beyond the call of duty. She had no right to do what she did. She'd stepped outside of her remit and she had paid the price. 'She belongs to me,' he said quietly to himself, and nothing was going to change that. 'If I cannot have her, then no one can.'

He replied to the mystery man with anger in his voice. 'Kamrul deserved exactly what he got tonight.'

'Yes, perhaps, but you could have a problem for next week.'

'Why, what problem is that?' There was suddenly alarm in his reply.

'Kamrul is injured if my understanding is correct?'

'Did he get injured wrestling Red Rivers?'

'No, you injured him, and he thinks he has a right to delay the final, he may have wrestled tonight with concussion, he complained of having dizzy spells and seeing double. It looks like he has a cracked rib as well. Currently he's at the hospital having checks.'

'Kaz, is this correct, can he do this?' Suddenly his interest was heightened.

'I need to check with the wrestling authorities, but yes, he can do this. If he's injured, what can we do? You can't wrestle his shadow next week.'

'How long would the delay be?' He was looking for answers. 'This puts my preparation way out of sync. I'm at the top of my game now, Kaz, I don't want a delay.' There was pleading in his eyes for a solution.

'There are some things we can't plan or control and this is one.' said Kazar. 'Let me talk to the authorities on Monday and see what their decision is. If Kamul is injured, then his people have to apply for a new date anyway. I know this for sure, but they have to prove his injuries conclusively. Kamrul needs to have a doctor's examination, explaining what the problem is. If it's concussion, we could have a delay of a week, maybe two, not more than that.' Kazar turned to the mystery man. 'You think he has a broken rib, yes?'

The mystery man nodded his head very slowly.

'In which case, we could have a delay of at least a month,' said Kazar.

'Oh fuck,' he said, with a grimace and look of despair on his face. He was now beginning to regret his scissor kick, he wanted to hurt his man, that was without doubt, but he had not intended an outcome like this.

Kamrul had beaten Red Rivers with two submissions, but it was clear he was not his usual self.

'If Kamrul has beaten Red Rivers suffering from concussion and a broken rib, then this man is some wrestler,' said the mystery man, 'and it speaks volumes in terms of the man's toughness.'

The kick and fall, resulting from his acrobatics had allowed Red Rivers to take an extra round from Kamrul. He had succumbed eventually in round four, but he had gone further than most. He wondered what a fully fit Kamrul would present and how many rounds he would last out.'

The mystery man wanted to lighten things up before the meeting got underway and asked him to demonstrate a few of the moves he had shown him previously. There were two other people in the meeting besides; it was the Chief of Customs for Malaysia and Richard, his opposite number for the Singapore customs. The mystery man raised his hands to administer an arm lock on Callon thinking he could take him by surprise. Without moving his feet, he grabbed his arm just above the wrist and squeezed. He squeezed really hard whilst looking directly into his eyes. There was no expression on his face as he intensified his grip and his stare. He was in no mood for fun and games, especially now.

I could squeeze the fucking daylights out of you, after what you have just done to Suzi.

'Okay, Kid, you have made your point, let go…let go, Kid.' He was hurting and grimacing now as Kazar came to his rescue and brought a sense of calm to the proceedings. The group made their way to the table.

'I think you have some questions, Kid, would you like to start the proceedings?' asked the mystery man as they gathered in strategic places around the table. He found himself at the far side of the table on his own, whilst the other four members sat opposite. The mystery man was rubbing his wrists, trying to get the blood flowing again.

'Yes, I want to know who'll be responsible for my exit from the dockside.' His expression remained sombre. Richard answered back, 'That be me, Kid, already I spoke to my people who on duty.' His English was only just good enough to understand.

He spoke back in Malayan, he asked Richard to repeat his answer in Malay. He wanted to make absolutely sure that there were no misunderstandings in what was been said. The answer came back clear about his responsibility. The meeting continued in Malayan. They were all surprised at his fluency in this difficult language. He managed to navigate himself around it with few problems, hesitating only when the word he was searching for would not come and stopping occasionally for specific word understanding.

'If you've already spoken to your people, it suggests we have a definite date when this will happen?' His question was directed back at Richard.

'Yes, it will be Wednesday 6th August according to my understanding.'

The mystery man confirmed the date, but said he needed some further information from his contacts. He assumed that he meant the Major and the Colonel. He already felt sick to his stomach about how things were panning out. He desperately wanted to wrestle for the Championship before he attempted this half-brained drug heist. If this heist goes wrong, then so does his chance at the title. He had to make sure that his priorities were kept in that order, wrestle first, then, and only then, would he consider his own role in a plan which lacked certainty and which he could not escape from.

He knew that if he did not act now or soon, then his chances for the title would dissolve away. There would be nothing anyone could do about his diversionary tactics. He was racking his brain to think of a tactical delay. Could he feign injury or illness he wondered? He would give this subject more thought, but he needed to act fast.

'And how do I identify the goods to load?'

The mystery man had all the answers. 'You will be given a specific bay number where the goods are stored. You need to load your vehicle in such a way that all the goods fit into your truck. I don't want even one stray pallet left. There should be no trace left of what you load, is that clear? And don't worry; you will have no problem to identify the goods. The cargo looks like nothing else stored on the docks.'

The mystery man shuffled in his chair, then said, 'What about your help to load the truck? Have you established who the men in your team will be?'

'I'm aware of what I need to do, I have several options,' he said firmly.

'Remember, loading will all be done by hand, so make sure you have dependable and strong help. You should complete this loading within two hours. The longer you are on the dock, the more chance you have of been discovered.'

Then Callon was told that on leaving the Empire Docks, he would be escorted to the Singapore customs by four Red Caps on motorcycles. The motorcade would consist of two riders out front and two riders bringing up the rear. This level of security and planning surprised him; he had no idea that such a risky operation would have this kind of assistance.

'Do the Military Police (Red Caps) know what the escorted consignment is?'

The mystery man interjected before the other members could say anything. 'No, no, they don't know, and it's not necessary for them to know.'

You lying bastard, of course they know. They will know what the risks are, just like me.

He could sense that he was lying, but as usual, he couldn't prove it.

'What happens when I reach the Singapore customs checkpoint, do the outriders travel with me?'

Richard spoke again in his native Malayan tongue.

'You will be waved through, just like at the docks. If necessary, I will be in attendance to provide extra insurance that nothing is held up. This part of the plan is heavily manned and I need to make sure that all personnel who have knowledge of your truck are briefed beforehand.'

'What about papers, you know, documents, will I be carrying anything?' The mystery man jumped in again, sounding impatient now. For once though, his ice cool exterior appeared to be melting.

'No, there will be no paperwork, it would not be advisable.' The four men smiled briefly after this comment. 'You should be waved through at every stopping point. No one will ask to see your documents, so don't worry.'

'Should be waved through?' he retorted; with a grim smile.

'*Will be.*' said the mystery man. 'Don't play with words. When you reach the Malaysian customs, my Chief Customs Officer here at my side, will make sure that you are ferried through promptly and efficiently, again without any questions asked or documents to provide.'

Whilst the mystery man was ending his sentence, the Chief Customs man for Malaysia was nodding his confirmation of what had been said.

'Will I still have the motorcycle escort?'

'Yes, of course.' This will be with you up to the point of dropping the goods in Johor.'

'Where exactly in Johor?' he asked.

'The motorcade will lead you to the final destination.'

The bastards are not going to tell me where the goods will be dropped in advance. I guess this is part of their risk assessment plan. If everything goes tits up, then they are not implicated in any way. I know some of the details, but not everything. Very smart on their part, thought Callon, but recognising there was nothing for him to fall back onto, only his own bayonet.

'Who's organising the Red Caps? Remember my reputation with these guys isn't brilliant?'

'Your Commanding Officer will arrange this; everyone has a role to play.'

Yes I'm sure they have, but everyone has cover except me. I will be the one holding the hand grenade with no pin!

After several more exchanges of questioning and detailed planning, the meeting was finally wound up.

'Let's conclude for now, gentlemen. There will be further meetings of course, but I thought it important that everyone knows each other and knows what their respective roles are.'

There was a brief shaking of hands. As the mystery man stood up, he could not help noticing that his suit still bore the remnants of Jack 'Boulder' Harris's blood and snot. It was smeared down the front of his trousers. It was some consolation at least, but he had hoped for a direct hit rather than just a little collateral damage.

'Let's meet again once more before Wednesday the 6th August to put the final pieces together of our operation. Kazar, you need to make sure the Major makes this meeting. I would suggest we convene in Johor, so let me know if there are any problems from your end.'

Before Kazar could answer him, the mystery man, still rubbing his wrist, was out of the door, showing a clean pair of heels. The bottles of pink champagne unopened, were placed carefully by Kazar into one of his cupboards as the other two men left his office. 'These will come in handy, we could have a few things to celebrate over the next few weeks,' said Kazar, looking at his forlorn wrestler.

'Come on, Kid, let me take you for a beer, I think we could both use one.' Kazar was looking for his keys to lock up his office; his work was done for the day. The mood in the office had been muted and the evening thus far was ending on a low note. This should have been a night of wild celebration, he thought, but instead, it was tense with sullen faces all round, this after securing his place in the final of the Light Heavyweight Championship of the Far East.

He was weighing up his options, sick at the thought of his Championship fight being delayed. He could almost touch the title now, it was that close. One more contest, that's all it was. So near, yet so far away. The drug heist was also weighing heavily on his mind. It was already very late, but he was determined to celebrate his win nonetheless. Kazar led him to his chauffeur driven car parked alongside the wrestling arena. They pulled away from outside the Great World Amusement park and through the gates supporting the huge Great World sign perched high above. They slid out on to Kim Seng Road and headed for the clubs in downtown Singapore. Both he and Kazar were too engrossed in conversation to notice a sleek black motor vehicle following them as they made their way into the city.

Chapter 36

They pulled up outside the Union Jack Club just opposite from the Raffles Hotel, it was just after midnight. A huge Union Jack flag was fluttering ever so gently in the midnight air above the grand entrance. They ordered a beer each and sat opposites at a small round table.

'Tell me about this drug operation, Kaz. Should I be worried about pulling this off successfully? It all seems so simple, but...'

'But what, Kid? Most of the details have been explained tonight. You heard the customs men, these people are the most important officials in their respective countries and they will make your passage across the causeway trouble free. You have to trust the integrity of these men; they have a lot of authority.'

'Yes, but do they have the balls to carry this out?' he said looking straight at Kazar's glare. 'I've been on the border crossing many times from Singapore to Malaysia, and it is always teeming with customs men and officials.'

'The men we spoke to tonight, they control the crossings. Remember, it's in their interest to see the safe passage of our cargo; they will also be paid well for their services. They don't want any problems.'

'I want you to promise me something, Kaz. If this does go wrong, you will not simply abandon me.'

He felt uneasy about the whole affair in spite of Kaz's reassurance. He was unhappy about his role and what he was expected to do. He had been lured into this mess involuntarily, he thought. Someone dangling such a huge amount of money was certainly going to turn heads, and it certainly turned his. The full realisation of the situation however, was that he could not escape from it.

'Nothing will go wrong, Kid, you're worrying too much about it, relax a little now and enjoy your success of tonight.' Kaz was finishing his beer as he added, 'I'll take you back to your barracks, it's getting really late, and you need your beauty sleep.'

'No, no thanks, I need some fresh air, I'll walk back to the camp. I need time to think.'

'No way, you come with me. I don't trust you out there at this time on your own. Look at what happened last time you were feeling this down.'

'I'll be okay, you go on ahead. I'm much calmer now. Thanks for the offer anyway and thanks for the beer.' He started to get up from his chair. 'I want you to promise me one other thing, Kaz. It's, Suzi, can you arrange for her to be at the final against Kamrul, whenever the contest is scheduled for?'

'I'm not sure that's a good idea, Kid, why don't you drop this whole thing here, let her get on with her life, and you get on with yours.'

'Kaz, I just need her to be there. I need to see her in the crowd...I, I don't even need to speak to her. I just want her to be there. She inspires me, surely you can understand that?'

'Okay, let's see what I can do, but I'm not promising.'

'Just do it, do it for me, please?' He left him at the table to finish his drink. He stood in the doorway of the club momentarily, took a large intake of breath and set off walking in the direction of his barracks.

It was a lovely warm evening with just a hint of a breeze, and perfect he thought for walking and thinking. He needed to hatch a plan which would delay the drug heist scheduled for the 6th August. He needed a delay of at least a month if his contest with Kamrul is postponed on the 2nd August. Worst case scenario, it could be another month before he got his chance at Kamrul, especially if he had a bust rib. 'How on earth can I delay the drug heist that long?' he said quietly to himself. 'Oh fuck! what a mess.'

Chapter 37

'What do you mean you haven't seen him, Steve?'

'I mean I haven't seen him. No one here has seen him since Saturday night. He didn't sleep in his bunk and didn't show up yesterday. The lads here just assumed he was with you.'

Kazar was beside himself with fear and was berating himself for not getting him back to his barracks early Sunday morning. Where could he be thought Kazar, it was now 36 hours since anyone had seen him? Maybe he had tried to get back in contact with Suzi? He knew how distraught he was. It was a distinct possibility, but a doubtful one, he thought. He could never find his way to the palace. No taxi would take him there; they would think he was some kind of nutcase. Something must have happened to him for sure, it had to be that, but what? There was too much at stake for him to just disappear. All the arrangements for the drug heist had been planned meticulously, maybe he's got cold feet about that, he thought. There was an enormous responsibility on his young shoulders and perhaps no one has taken this into consideration. The Kid was still only 21 and within reach of the Far East Wrestling Championship title. Maybe we've scrambled his brain so much with the drug heist as well, that he has just gone walkabout? Why was he so determined to walk to his barracks from The Union Jack Club? It was only a two mile walk, and he could cover that in 25 minutes or jog it in ten. Kazar was dreading his next telephone call.

Kazar had called Major Reece before speaking to the Colonel and agreed that they would meet at the Colonel's office.

'He's been missing almost 40 hours, Sir. I have no idea where he could be. He was very upset about the girl.' Kazar was edgy and breathing hard. 'It was the last thing we spoke about when I left him at the Union Jack Club.' The Colonel let Kazar continue without interrupting, he simply looked across to Major Reece and shook his head. 'There's also a delay for the Championship title fight too; the Kid was very upset about this. I was calling here today to tell him about the length of the delay, only to find he has not been seen for nearly two days. You can imagine how I feel about that, Colonel. I should have insisted on bringing back to the barracks.'

'What, you left him at the Union Jack Club? Did he say where he was going?' There was quiet annoyance in his query.

'He wanted to walk back to the barracks, Colonel, said he wanted to clear his head. He'd made his mind up, and when Callon's in that mood, he's not one to argue with.'

'No, quite,' said the Colonel. After a short pause, he continued. 'Well, if we don't find him soon, this buggers up all the plans.' He frowned and rubbed his forehead, knowing somehow his carefully planned operation was in jeopardy. He knew it could be weeks before he could get all the men involved and assembled for the operation on the same night again. This was his worst logistical nightmare, but the operation was still ten days away, so no need to panic yet. August 6th was still a safe bet for the heist plan to be rolled out.

The Colonel tried to consider what implications a delay in the drug operation would present. If the plan could not be carried out on the agreed date, what would happen to the drug consignment after that? It could be moved without any prior warning or notice and could simply be dumped out at sea; millions of potential dollars simply ending up on the ocean floor. The only benefactors would be the bloody fish! The Colonel was seething inside. This operation was the culmination of planning and recruiting which had been months and months in the making. It had to proceed on August 6th as planned, whatever happened. The only thing missing now was the application and the driver!

'I'm more concerned for the man's safety just now, sir; it's not in his nature to go missing. I've known the Kid for almost two years now, and he's never done anything like this before.' Kazar was showing great concern.

'There's always a first time for everything, Mr Kazar.' The Colonel turned his attention to the Major, 'what do you suggest we do from here, where the hell do we start looking?'

Kazar spoke before the Major could answer. 'I think the hospitals should be our first call.'

'Why the bloody hospitals? For God's sake man, think positive. What about the docks, maybe he turned up for work as usual this morning?' The Colonel continued, 'maybe he spent the night with a hooker and made his way to the docks from there, has anyone checked?'

Both men were shaking their heads.

'Here we are worrying our socks off and he could have been banging away all weekend for all we know. Okay, Major, said the Colonel, You check the docks before we go chasing shadows. I'm sure there's a logical explanation to this.' He felt better thinking that his man could be at work. He didn't want to contemplate the alternatives at this stage. He wanted this operation over more than anyone. The unknown and the risks involved were beginning to make him tense and irritable; he knew however, that in the meantime, he had to stay calm. He didn't want to make the call to the palace, but he knew he'd have to if Callon was not at his work on the docks.

The telephone rang in the Colonel's office. He knew who it was without having to second guess.

'Yes, tell me, Major, has our man turned up?'

'Negative, Sir, no one has seen him down at the docks. His Mack is exactly where he parked it last Friday evening.' The Colonel was now very concerned, more about his own predicament than the one that Callon could have possibly got himself into. He knew this was the worst possible outcome. If he has gone AWOL, then his own judgement of character was in question. He had never been wrong previously about his reading of a soldier, but this was as close to the wind he had ever sailed. Millions of dollars were at stake here, and his missing man was the person holding all the aces. He decided he would not make the call just yet. He wanted to wait a little longer on the basis that his lost soldier would walk into camp as large as life and as though nothing had happened. Every minute passing without the ace in the pack though was purgatory, and this showed on the Colonel's face.

'What next, Major? I need some bloody answers about this soldier and I need them damn well quick!'

Major Reece could hear the tension in the Colonel's voice on the telephone and could only imagine the agony across his face.

'I've already checked at the British military hospital, Sir, and there have been no admissions out of the ordinary in the past 48 hours.'

'He can't have vanished into thin air, Major. Find the bloody man for God's sake!'

The phone went down without any concern for the party on the receiving end. The Colonel paced across his office pondering and wondering when, or if, he should make the call. He stood with his hand on the receiver, lifted it from the cradle, then returned it before he walked across to his window and peered out into the glare of the mid-day sunshine.

'Where are you, Callon, where the fuck, are you?'

Chapter 38

When Sister Mary from Tan Tock Seng hospital contacted the Major informing him of an unidentified man admitted early on Sunday morning into her ward, Kazar and the Major rushed over to the hospital to see for themselves if indeed this unidentified person was in fact their missing man.

'When was this man admitted to your hospital, Sister?' The Major and Kazar were standing in the sanitized surroundings of a small foyer. The Sister had called around the various military bases to try and establish the identity of her unknown patient. Kazar was translating, the Sister could speak some English, but it was very difficult for the Major to understand.

'He was brought here by at least four men very early on Sunday morning. They carried him here and dropped him at the front door. They rang our night bell and our watchman who was close by, then saw the men running away.'

'We have a soldier missing, Sister, could we take a look at him? It's very important for us to know if this soldier is ours.' Kazar and the Major were equally anxious to know the state of the soldier in her ward.

'Is your patient hurt or injured, Sister?' Kazar was holding his breath and crossing his fingers. He didn't want to go through another rebuilding period with his young wrestler.

'He was unconscious when we found him, stripped of all his clothing and hence, no means of identification. By mid morning yesterday, he was in a state of acute delirium. He was shouting out and appeared to be fighting someone. We had a real mystery on our hands, he was shouting out in our own Malay language. We could not understand how a European looking man could speak our language.'

Kazar and the Major looked at each other and knew they had Kid

Callon back. They had no idea what state he was in, but at least they had him back.

The Major asked Kazar, 'Who would do this…and why? Does this sort of thing happen regularly here?'

'Very rarely, Major.' said Kazar, 'Singapore is normally a very safe place.'

'Did your watchman recognise the men, Sister, I mean, were they local men?'

'He only said they were not European.'

'How is he now, Sister?' asked Kazar.

'He is still quite ill, but his situation has been stabilised. It was lucky that the men brought him here when they did. Without urgent medical attention, he could easily have died.'

Both men had a look of resignation on their faces as the Sister continued.

'His most serious injuries are to his head and face. Fortunately there are no broken bones and there appears to be no brain injury. This man took quite a beating, but he's a very strong individual, Sir. He has a strong heart as well as a very strong body; without this, he could have perished.'

The Major was still curious, 'Ask the Sister to let us see him so we can assess the damage for ourselves.'

The Sister led them to a small private room. She knocked out of courtesy to her patient, knowing she would receive no reply, and held the door open for Kazar who was directly behind her. With the briefest of looks, Kazar acknowledged that it was their man. A short nod of the head to the Sister was sufficient.

'Just five minutes, gentlemen, this patient is still very ill.' The Sister left but kept the door open. She was insistent that five minutes was all they would get on this visit.

It was Kazar who laid a gentle hand on his shoulder. He didn't respond, but lay impassively with his eyes closed and breathing quite heavily. His head was heavily bandaged and his eyes remained closed, but were already black. His nose was cut on the bridge and swollen. His body was covered by blankets up to his chin; Kazar pulled the sheet back, to reveal bruises across his abdomen and arms. His shoulders were grazed as though he had been dragged across ground without protection from clothing.

'He's in a mess, Major, there's no quick fix from what I can see. I don't know what to think just now. This is a shocking beating, worse than the one he sustained in your guardhouse.'

The Major looked at his soldier and felt the first pangs of guilt. Up to that moment, he had not cared for the wellbeing of this young man. He only cared if his man would be okay to drive the truck on August 6th. The young man lying before him was braver than he would ever be. The six foot four inch frame of Major Reece was bowed in recognition of what this young man had just endured and all he could think about was his share of the spoils. He was ashamed of his own actions and turned to wait outside, trying hard not to show any outward signs of emotion.

'We will arrange for the patient to be transferred to the British Military Hospital today, Sister.' Kazar had not been able to speak to Callon, unsure if he was in a deep sleep or still unconscious, but at least the Military Hospital would be able to ascertain any serious or permanent damage. 'I cannot thank you enough, Sister for all your help and wonderful care. I presume it will be safe to move the patient?' asked Kazar.

'Yes, he's been awake and speaking to us, but very briefly. He knows he's in hospital but he cannot remember anything about how he got here. It will take time for his memory to recover exactly what happened. It may be his brain will shut out the incident totally and he'll never remember.'

'I called as soon as I knew where he was.' The Colonel was at his desk not relishing the phone call he was now having to make.

'But he's been missing nearly two days, you said?' The mystery man was holding back his anger. 'What do we do now, Colonel? I hope you have a contingency plan.'

'There is no contingency plan and you know it.' The Colonel was expecting this kind of reaction, after all the mystery man had the most to lose in this operation. 'We have to postpone the plan. We've no alternative. The man is still in hospital, and I have no idea when he will be released. From what I understand, he has had a fair old beating about the head, and will not be okay for August 6th. We are going to have to postpone.' The Colonel held the phone away from his ear expecting a tirade of abuse.

'No, no,' shouted the mystery man, down the phone. 'We cannot postpone the plan, have you any idea how long it's taken me to organise this damn operation?' He knew it could not go ahead, but he wanted to emphasise his reluctance at the postponement to the Colonel. 'Is there no way we can get this man back on his feet in time?'

The Colonel felt disgust at the question and wanted to slam the phone down. 'Up until five pm today, he has spoken only a few words to the hospital staff. He hasn't fully recovered consciousness yet. Does this answer your question?'

There was a short pause before he spoke again. 'So what do you suggest we do now Colonel, have you any bright ideas?' The tone was clipped and uncaring.

'We have to wait,'

'Wait, for how long?'

'I don't know. I have no information on the man's condition yet. Maybe we have to approach this from a different angle. We need to check when the key people involved could be in place again. This way we avoid creating any suspicion.' He paused before saying, 'I'll get back to you as soon as I hear anything.'

'Do that, as soon as you can, I'm concerned that these goods could disappear from under our noses. That would be a disaster, Colonel. You have to make sure that this does not happen. I have invested too much money and time to see these goods dumped out to sea.' The phone went down without any further pleasantries.

He was awakened by the clash of plates and cutlery coming together, and became aware he had some kind of saline drip attached to his left arm. With his peripheral vision, he could also see the edges of the head dressing, poking out just above his eye line. He wasn't sure how he felt. There was still a numbness throughout his body and assumed that some strong medication had been administered. He was aware that he had been moved, but was unaware where to. The ward was oblong shaped, with ten beds, five down each side. They were all occupied. He was in one of the very end beds.

He was trying to remember how he came to be in hospital, but his recollections were very vague. He remembered his victory over Boulder Harris and his scissor kick on Kamrul, and leaving him sprawled across the ringside seats. He could now remember leaving Kaz at the Union

Jack Club and walking back to camp. There was a car, a black car…but then nothing?

Suddenly he remembered his wrestling commitments. Shit! he thought, I need to get out of here, I need to train. There was panic in his mind. He made an attempt to get out of bed but was forced back by a sharp pain at the front of his head. His vision was blurred caused by his sudden movement, and he felt relief at getting his head back on the pillow.

A pretty, petite nurse was making her way down to his bed. She had seen his feeble attempt to get out of bed.

'What are you trying to do?' The nurse spoke English quite well.

'I need to get out of here; I have some important things to deal with.'

'I'm sorry, but you have to stay in bed.'

'Where am I, nurse?' he asked.

'You're in the British Military Hospital, Mr Callon.'

'What day is it?'

'It's Tuesday, you've been here since yesterday.' The nurse was tucking sheets back in as she was speaking to her patient. 'You need to take your rest, you are very seriously ill. Please, Mr Callon, no more talking.'

'What's the date?'

'It's the 29th of July.'

'How did I get here? you said it was Tuesday, nurse, is that right?'

'Yes.' You came here via Tan Tock Seng Hospital. It was they who stabilised you. You'd been there since early Sunday morning.' She was trying to help him to fill any gaps in his memory.

He put his hand to his forehead, it was swathed in bandages and it was sore.

'Tuesday, you say, Tuesday?' He was trying frantically to understand how many days he'd lost. 'Has anyone been to visit me, nurse?'

'No, not here, but two men arranged for you to be transferred here. One was an officer, that's all I know.' The nurse moved away before saying, 'try to get some rest, you've taken quite a beating to the head.'

His mind was playing tricks, trying to understand the significance of Tuesday. Something was happening today, but what was it? He kept having flashbacks, there was a car? Another sudden shock travelled through his body.

'But I need to fight Kamrul first…oh my God. Shit, shit, shit! The operation, it must be tomorrow. No, it's next week,' he said quietly under his breath. All this information was too much to take, he needed to sleep; he felt exhausted and closed his eyes.

In the middle of the afternoon he was awakened by something, unsure if it was a noise. He still had his eyes closed when he felt the gentle hand on his shoulder. It was Kazar.

'Hi, Kid. Welcome back to the real world. You've been out of it for a few days. It's nice to see you with your eyes open, even though you're not such a pretty sight. You look like shit, Kid.'

'What happened to me, Kaz, how did I end up in here?'

'We don't know for sure, we were hoping you could remember something, anything? Whoever did this, didn't want you found in a hurry. You were stripped naked when they found you with serious head injuries.'

'It's all very vague, I remember there was a car, that's all. How long do I have to stay in here, have they said anything?' Kaz was shaking his head as he was speaking.

'It's too early to know anything yet; it'll take time to mend that broken head of yours.'

'What about the Championship?'

'It's postponed. Don't you remember? You gave Kamrul a good kicking. He has concussion, plus you gave him a cracked rib. The contest will be in a month's time. He should be fully fit by then, but I'm not sure about you, Kid, you've taken a real old beating.'

'Yeah, I'd forgotten about the delay. There's lots of gaps in my mind which I can't fill, I'm very confused. What about the other job?' he said quietly. He was anxious to know what was happening with that.

'Don't let's talk about that now, only to say that, that has also been postponed. Don't ask me until when, because I don't know. It will depend on you getting out of here.' Kazar was making a move to leave. 'Listen, Kid, I'll be back to see you. You get some rest now.' He turned to leave when Callon asked him,

'Could this be the work of Kamrul? Would he do such a thing?'

'Anything's possible. Let me ask you this, how bad do you want this title?'

'It means everything to me, you know that.'

'And how bad do you think Kamrul wants the title? No, let me put it this way, what lengths would you go to, to ensure you got the title.'

'I wouldn't want to smash his bloody head in for God's sake.'

'Remember what you did to him. You hurt this guy. Not just physically, but mentally as well.'

'Okay, Kaz, I think I get your point, but one thing's for sure, if this was his handy work and he thinks he now has the upper hand, he can think again. This has just made me a whole lot more determined to win that belt.'

Kazar realised that his young wrestler had taken a severe mauling in the attack. He was all mixed up with dates and weeks and he would need time and space to unscramble his brain, but he could only admire his determination. This was a very positive sign for Kazar.

Chapter 39

'You're a very lucky young man, no permanent damage The doctor has given you a clean bill of health. You can go back to your barracks, you are discharged.' Kazar was helping him get his things together. There wasn't that much anyway, after all he had been stripped naked before being dumped on the steps of the hospital.

'That's great news, Kaz. I need to get back to my training, when do we start?' He was anxious to get out of the hospital; it had numbed all his senses. He had reached screaming pitch and was ready to get back to business as usual, ready to face all his challenges now, provided they were in the correct order. He had spent just under two weeks in hospital with little in the way of exercise, he had managed to do some daily press-ups out of the sight of the nurses, but that was all.

'Not so fast, Kid, you'll need a couple of days, then start slowly and build.' He knew Kaz was speaking sense, but he was irritable with lying around doing nothing.

The rearranged scheduled date for the Far East Championship was now Saturday August 30th at his favourite venue, the Great World Arena, so he had just three weeks to get himself match fit and regain his strength and stamina. His ordeal had nearly cost him his chance at the title, but due to his super strength and fitness, he had without doubt endured what a lesser man would have succumbed to.

Chapter 40

He was back training for his championship title, Kazar was watching his young wrestler with renewed interest from the ringside at the Great World Arena. He was looking to see if he could witness any residual traces of his beating. Hassan was putting him through his training schedule. The beating had slowed him down somewhat, but it had not destroyed his resolve. What had happened to him had only strengthened his forthright approach. After several rounds of gentle warm-up, he spoke to Kazar.

'I was followed, Kaz, after I left you at the club. I walked briskly and headed for the army barracks, I just needed space and time to think.' He was trying to piece together what had happened on the night he was stripped naked and left for dead on the steps of the hospital.

'There was a car fifty yards back crawling behind me. As I turned corners, so did the car. I couldn't see the occupants or how many there were. They kept a discreet distance. The streets were pretty deserted at that time, so the car was very conspicuous.' Kaz was studying his wrestler as he spoke about his ordeal.

'There was a lot of noise coming from one of the bars I was passing, so I decided to call in and check the car out from the safety of the bar room window. The car passed by slowly, but I could only see a driver. Within a few seconds four Asian guys came in and just scanned the room. They were not there to buy drinks, I was sure of that.' He shifted in his seat before continuing. 'They were looking for me, Kaz. I decided to make a quick exit as they were looking around the place. A couple of them went to check the toilet area. I made a beeline for the driver. He had stopped the car just ten yards past the bar. I dragged him out of the car before giving him a side-winder across the face. I think I broke his arm too. He was holding onto the steering wheel for dear life. I thumped hard down on his arm before he let go. I heard a crack as I yanked him out. You should've seen his face. He was not expecting me coming after him. It all happened so fast. I gave him a good slapping. I asked him who they were, but I had no time to get an answer. The other four guys were all over me in seconds. A couple of the guys were carrying weapons, truncheons I think, so I had no chance to overpower them. I didn't go down without a fight though. They would also be nursing some serious injuries.'

'Did any of them say anything as they attacked you?' Kaz was looking for clues as to who would carry out an attack like this.

'I just heard the driver scream. It gets a bit hazy after what I just described; a couple of blows on the head by the truncheon put paid to that. I'm sure though, that these were Kamrul's men. He's from India right?'

'Yes, why?'

'These men had an Indian caste or look to them, they were not locals. The hospital night watchman had said they were not European. It had to be his men, Kaz; Kamrul was not going to risk this title challenge without first making the odds a little more even. I hurt that guy when I scissor kicked him.'

'We've just to put this behind us now, and go forward. Fortunately you've no lasting damage, or broken bones. You've recovered well from that beating.'

He sat stony faced as he listened to Kazar. 'I won't be putting this behind me. Kamrul will pay for this. I don't care how strong this guy is supposed to be, he will pay for this big time, I will personally make sure of that.'

'What about the men who attacked you, could you recognise any of them?'

'I'm not sure, their faces just flashed in front of mine, I didn't have a chance to take a picture, that's for sure.'

He had wanted a delay, not in the wrestling sense, more because he was not relishing his part in the drug heist. Of course the delay which came about was not what he had in mind, but it had served its purpose. He was looking for a less painful way of staving off the inevitable. Now he could wrestle for the championship first, before he drove the truck with the illicit cargo on board. He could be more certain about the wrestling contest than the drug heist. The wrestling was down to him, the drug heist was at the behest of others.

He had done his morning training routine before making his way to the docks, and he was now almost back to full fitness. Spending a week plus lying on his back had done nothing for his preparation, but he was feeling good about his progress. He had taken things quite easy over the weekend by his standards and felt he could step up another gear. He was amazed at the speed of his own recovery. Once again he had come back from the brink of a very serious injury. He hoped he would never have to endure that journey again.

As he walked towards the Bonded Warehouse, there were more people around than he had seen previously. He decided to walk the full length of the building before spotting one of the peons he knew disappear within. He followed him through a side door on the pretence of making small talk. But he also wanted to view this special cargo which had been delivered under strict secrecy.

'You need special permission to be in here.' said a voice which seemed to come at him from nowhere. The instruction was spoken to him in English. It was one of the customs men checking on his recently arrived merchandise. He decided to answer back in Malayan thinking this would somehow lend greater authority to him being there.

'I work here, what's your problem?' His fluent reply in Malay made no impression on the guard and he received a caustic reply back.

'The problem is you're not supposed to be in here. Authorised personnel only, so please leave this area now.' He was scouring the various locations without trying to appear over suspicious, to see if anything remotely resembled what he had come in to look for. He had no idea of course what form the chandu or BTO would look like. He was going to delay his exit as long as possible.

'So, what's so special about this place?' he asked, as he started to walk away form the customs officer and further into the building.

'Sir, I must ask you to leave, immediately.' He was going to play this the hard way. He needed to try and eyeball the goods. He wanted to see exactly what it was he was supposed to move. He saw the man who he had spotted before and went in his general direction. He couldn't remember his name, though he had seen him at some of his contests.

'Hello, my friend.' He said enthusiastically, 'how are you doing? Have you been down to the wrestling arena lately?' He didn't know what else to say. Before he could answer, the customs man was on his shoulder,

'Sir, I must ask you to leave, now!'

The friend interjected. 'This man, boss; do you know who it is?'

'No,' said the customs man thinking he was perhaps an army officer.

'It's, Kid Callon, boss, the wrestler.' The custom man's face softened, he shook his hand and somehow was granted immediate immunity by the customs officer, who suddenly became very accommodating.

'Nice to meet you, Kid! Look, two minutes, and then please, leave. It's my job to protect these premises.' The customs man walked away as he replied.

'Yes, sure, officer,' He was alone with his friend now.

'What's with all the security around here?'

'It's because of this,' and as they walked along together for another 20 yards his new friend pointed to piles of pallets neatly stored in one of the huge bays. On the pallets were thousands of pot bellied little jars. There was no special security around the pallets, just neatly stacked in rows, patiently awaiting their next destination. He was quizzing his friend as if he knew nothing about what the jars contained.

'What the hell is this?' He asked inquisitively.

'It's known as chandu, boss. They also call it Black Tar Opium (BTO). They smoke this shit here, many people are hooked on this stuff. It sends them a little crazy but it also helps their pain.' The man continued looking around to make sure he was not being overheard. 'I've seen old men, crippled with pain, unable to stand or walk. They smoke this shit, then dance as if nothing is wrong with them. The problem is, this euphoria only lasts a very short time, boss, then they return to their original state, a little worse than before.' He was fascinated by this explanation as his friend carried on. 'The people become depressive and addicted, boss. There are many addicts here in Singapore boss, many.'

'So what's happening to this?'

'I think they're going to dump it, it's illegal here now, boss.'

'So what's with all the security?'

'In the wrong hands, this is worth a great deal of money, boss.' The man was gushing with information. They both walked over closer to where it was stored. He wanted to know more about this prized stash. He lifted one corner of a pallet to gauge its weight and guessed two men would be able to lift two pallets together without too much difficulty. Working flat out, he was doing the maths in his head. It would take at least four men, two hours to load his Mack. He picked one of the pot jars from its special storage unit and looked inside. He instinctively smelt the jar not knowing what to expect. True to its name, it looked and had the consistency of tar. His friend ushered him to replace it immediately.

'Please, boss, "no", this is big trouble for everyone in here. Every pot has to be accounted for. That's why they don't want anyone just walking around here. That small jar is worth a few thousand dollars.'

He wanted to sound surprised, 'Really, it's worth so much?'

'Yes, boss, please put it back.'

'When's it going to be dumped, do you know?'

'No, nobody knows when, but my guess is it will be some time soon, boss.'

'Last lot that was here was stolen.'

He felt the arrow pierce his heart. He was shocked to hear that remark. This meant that greater care would be made to prevent that happening a second time. Security would be very tight indeed, he thought.

'Stolen, when?'

'Eighteen months ago, boss.'

'Did they catch the people who stole it?'

'You never get to find out, boss, but I don't think so. I think it's kind of embarrassing to the authorities here, that tons of this stuff was stolen, right from under their noses. A few people got sacked, that's all I know.'

'Did they steal a large amount?'

'Same boss, same?' as he pointed to the whole consignment. 'Security was bad then, it's much better today.' He felt those words claw at him.

'Thanks, friend. Look, I need to get out of here; I don't want that customs guard chasing me. I'll see you around, take care.'

'Yes, boss, sure.'

He was making his way to the exit. At least he now knew what his quarry looked like and where it was stored. The mystery man was correct, it is an unmistakeable cargo.

He couldn't help thinking however, how finely balanced this heist would be between failure and success. Some of the things he had just heard from that local peon disturbed him, especially the increased security. His stomach turned as he thought about the job ahead of him. He was just glad that he would be wrestling before he attempted one of the biggest drug heists, probably this century.

He also had something else to worry about now. The peon had exposed his name to the customs guard. If he couldn't remember his name, he would sure as hell remember he was a famous wrestler.

'Shit, shit,' he said, out loud, wondering what the consequences would be for his stupid curiosity He realised he had just made his first big mistake.

Chapter 41

'Do you have the new schedule yet, Major?' The Colonel was demanding to get this operation over and done with. It was beginning to prey on his mind since the original deadline collapsed.

The Major was very upbeat about the new date as he leaned back in his office chair.

'It looks like we are good to go on Monday 15th September, Sir.' But aware this date would still not be good enough for the Colonel.

'Is that the best you can do for God's sake, it's almost three weeks away? You have no idea what grief this delay has caused me.' Major Reece had noticed the slight shaking of the Colonel's right hand as he simply ticked the date in his diary. No other mark was registered on the page. The tension of this heist was beginning to affect everyone involved.

'Yes, this date provides us with exactly the same personnel on the ground that we were going with originally. It's far safer to do it this way, Colonel. Introducing new people now would jeopardise all our plans. Bringing new people on board would also risk breaching our security.'

'It's just the BTO; I'm worried that we can keep it dockside for this period. The bloody politics surrounding this cargo is unbelievable. Everybody wants it dumping way out to sea, as soon as possible.' The Colonel stood and paced the Major's office floor, deep in thought. 'There are people in the establishment who want these goods unserviceable pronto. The longer it stays where it is, the greater the risk of it going missing,' said the Colonel lifting one eyebrow. 'We have to pay government officials to apply diversionary tactics on this cargo, but in the end, they cannot draw attention to themselves. They too need to be careful.' The Colonel sat down and waited for the Major's reply.

'I don't see any alternatives at the moment, Colonel.'

'What about, Callon, our driver, is he doing okay?'

'Yes, Sir.' Thankfully back to full fitness.'

'Thankfully,' said the Colonel. 'This man has damaged my bloody health! If it wasn't for his foolhardy behaviour, all this would be over now…and we would be somewhat richer for our troubles. Let's hope the silly bugger doesn't get injured when he fights that Indian guy. I understand he will be quite an opponent?'

The Major ignored the slur on injury to Callon and then asked,

'When do you want to meet next? I realise it should be close to 15th September, but I just want to make sure we all know what we are supposed to do, last minute stuff, Colonel, and all that?'

'It should be in Johor, let's schedule it for the weekend before, either Saturday the 13th or Sunday 14th September.' The Colonel stood again, this time preparing to leave.

'Sunday would be best, Colonel. Everything will still be very fresh in everyone's mind. What do you think, Sir?'

'Yes, okay, I'll speak to my man, you speak to your people, Major, and arrange accordingly. It should be early evening, I propose 18.00 hours. If it's any different, I will let you know. I won't be at the meeting, but I will be close by. For security reasons, you understand.'

The Major understood perfectly, he was protecting his own back!

And by the way, Callon, he *will* need to be there, he has to know every small detail from start to finish…except his drop off address of course!'

The Colonel turned and left without waiting for any further pleasantries.

Chapter 42

Kazar was supervising Callon's training schedule. He knew he was rusty, not having wrestled in competition for some weeks now. But there was also no point to risk injury before the championship final. He also had in the back of his mind the drug heist. He could not afford any further slip ups, irrespective of whose fault it would be. He was concerned enough, because Kid Callon's challenge against Kamrul was not a foregone conclusion. This man not only beat his challengers, he hurt them too. He wondered if Callon's immaturity would play a part against this seasoned campaigner Kamrul. It hadn't up to now of course. Callon was one of the most composed and comprehensive wrestlers on the circuit, but Kamrul, he was a different opponent. His wrestling skills fell way below what Callon could produce, but it was Kamrul's brute strength which concerned him most. He also thought about the recent beating which Callon endured at the hands of four men. Was it Kamrul who had ordered the attack, or was it just a case of being in the wrong place at the wrong time? Another injury on Callon would be a disaster now. He would have two weeks time to recover after wrestling Kamrul. Monday 15th September was the day scheduled for the heist and the date which Callon could not remove from his thoughts.

'This is it, Kid, the last push before the big one on Saturday.'

'Any news from the Kamrul camp, have you heard how he's progressing?'

'Reports suggest he's in good nick, back to full fitness. His threats about what he's going to do to you are well documented. He wants to wring your neck, but his main intention is to hurt you; he's going to make you pay for doing what you did to him. That's what I heard.'

Kazar was trying to gain his wrestler's reaction to his stark but threatening feedback from his opponent's camp.

'Have you informed their camp what I intend to do to him, Kaz?'

'Yes, of course I have. They also know about our suspicions and the cause of your injuries. They know the blame lies with them and Kamrul's team. They deny it, but that's what I'd expect from them anyway.'

'He needs to be fully fit, Kaz, because I will expose any small chink in his armoury. I also intend to get even. I'm not going to let that hairy predator have the last word.'

Kazar knew his man would be bursting to get even with Kamrul, but he also knew that he was still a very dangerous opponent. To win his last contest suffering a broken rib and concussion was without doubt a measure of the man's pain threshold and capabilities.

'Any new thoughts on my strategy, Kaz? I mean to beat him, not just give him a good contest?'

'Think about it, Kamrul has not been able to wrestle for the past four weeks and neither have you. This will be more in your favour, than in Kamrul's. His only weapon is his strength; his stamina has never been tested, and his technique overall is questionable. His contests last only three rounds on average. This could be your biggest advantage providing you can take him beyond three rounds.' Kazar was trying to play his opponent down; he needed to instil confidence to his wrestler.

'But how can I counter his strength?' he said, looking for some divine inspiration. 'His strength comes from his long arms, we both know that, and we can't take them away from him.'

'Kamrul has never fought you; I think we have more information on him than he has on you. He knows about your acrobatics,' said Kazar, making reference to his flying scissor kick. 'Other contestants have just become easy prey to his tactics, with your superior wrestling skills, you should be able to break some of his holds, where others before have failed.'

He thought about Kaz's reply.

'Yes, maybe Kamrul will underestimate my strength?'

'I doubt that, your reputation around the wrestling circuit hasn't gone totally unnoticed. He knows what you're capable of, don't worry about that, however, I know you could have some surprises for him?'

Kazar was pleased how his young wrestler was approaching this most important contest. Normally he decided a strategy having looked at his opponent close up and never asked for advice. His strategy was developed usually within a few seconds; either watching his opponents walk or gait, or how he offers himself into the ring. It was sometimes all he needed to see. For Kamrul though, it was different. He had studied him at close range and not detected any obvious weaknesses, except his temperament. His approach this time would have to be more measured and calculated.

'A fully fit Kamrul is a real handful, let's not delude ourselves. He can crush the life out of his opponents; no one has gone more than three rounds with this man, except Red Rivers.'

'Are you trying to make me feel better, because I can tell you, it's not working.' He studied for a moment. 'It has to be his stamina, Kaz; this has to be his weakness. If he has not gone more than three rounds, then he's never been tested beyond this. If I can stop him from squeezing the life out of me, then maybe this is my route. Take him beyond his 15 minute limit of wrestling and watch his strength disappear.'

'I'm not sure how you can accomplish this, you can't avoid him getting hold of you for four or five rounds; this isn't a boxing match. Maybe it can work for maybe one or two rounds, but we have to be more constructive than this. You also have to entertain your supporters, remember, you cannot continue to back away from him like some frightened child.'

Kazar realised that more thought and planning was needed for this contest. This would be the most important contest of his young wrestler's career.

He settled down to do some repetitive bench press routines. He would need to maximise his strength and be at his peak when he met Kamrul. He had less than a week to establish his formula for success. He contemplated his opening gambit and wondered if Kamrul would fall for his play acting again. If he did, then he would win!

Chapter 43

'I know it's caused untold problems,' said the mystery man, banging the table. He was speaking from his plush palace office to the senior customs man of Singapore and his own customs man. 'No one wanted a delay, but the reality is, we have no alternative but to accept it. Everyone is on edge including me.' He was annoyed at his Singaporean guest's reaction. 'We have to work together to sort this out, Richard.'

The head of Malaysia Customs was trying to keep his distance from any resulting conflict. As far as he was concerned, his side of the border was sorted out and he wanted to make that clear to the meeting.

'I've made the necessary arrangements from my side; my men accepted the change of date. After all, the problem is not with me on the Malaysia frontier, it will be getting through the Singapore customs which will be the trickiest part.'

Richard looked across at his opposite number. He knew he was under the microscope as he tried in vain to remain composed as he spoke.

'Yes, my people are getting nervous, surely you can understand that? My people are there to prevent such occurrences as this from happening. To suddenly reverse this thought process is difficult for them to take.'

'That's why we pay you and your people a lot of money. Eliminate your concerns, get rid of the nervous people.' The mystery man looked intently at Richard hoping he understood his instruction. 'If you have any doubts about this operation from your side, you better say it now. Too much money and energy has gone into this plan already, we cannot allow anything or anybody to influence or get in the way of this operation now, not at this late stage. This has to work, Richard. We have to make a success of this. You have to guarantee the goods leave Singapore without any difficulties?'

'I just wanted to bring these concerns to your attention,' said Richard. 'Delays of this magnitude play on people's minds. My people are getting nervous, that's understandable, I don't have to explain more, surely? The BTO is under close scrutiny by a lot of people, people from within my own department. They know the longer these goods remain on the ground; the risk of these goods falling into the wrong hands escalates dramatically. I'm walking a very fine line at the moment, on the one hand protecting the goods, and at the same time arranging for their illegal removal!'

'We all know about the risks, Richard, and the rewards, but the delay could not have been foreseen, our driver was attacked by people from your side of the water.' This last comment stung Richard, and he had no reply.

'You have to be at the border crossing when this consignment arrives?' said the Malaysian custom man, directing his question at Richard. 'If there are any problems, this needs to be countered and sorted out by you. No one else can do this. Yes?'

'I've said I'll be there, don't worry.' Small beads of sweat appeared on Richard's forehead, his reply was less than convincing. The Mystery man knew at that moment, that it was not the Singapore customs men who were nervous and afraid of this operation, it was the man sat opposite him. He could see why the Colonel had voiced his concerns some time back and was annoyed at his own misjudgement of the situation. It was Richard who had called this meeting, but all it had done was plant doubt in the minds of the people crucial to the operation's success. Richard at this moment was more of a liability than a help. The mystery man just hoped he could hold his nerve up to September 15th.

Chapter 44

It was the very first thing he thought about as he opened his eyes, from a sleep which at best was fragmented by bouts of self doubt. He had allowed himself an extra hour in his bunk; he knew he would need every ounce of stamina to overcome his arch rival Kamrul this very evening.

'The title and the belt could be mine by the end of today,' he said quietly to himself as he rose to his feet and pulled on his training gear. He would warm up with a light jog around the camp. He was feeling good about himself physically, he had recovered remarkably from his beating and had no visible after effects other than some slight grazing still, across the bridge of his nose. He was continuing to show his concern about the man he had never faced before though; he felt edgy and annoyed that his strategy to beat this man was still unclear in his mind. Both men had seen each other wrestle, but the main question was, who would come away victorious? It would be the man who could nullify the other's individual skills.

The barracks were unusually quiet for a Saturday as he looked around for someone to pass the time of day. He exited his quarters and immediately settled into a gentle jog. His route would take him round towards the perimeter of the parade ground, being careful not to stand on its surface. He turned a corner and was immediately brought to an abrupt halt as a carnival type atmosphere erupted around him. There were cheers, banners, flags and bunting tied to huts and posts wishing their man from the British army 436 RASC the very best in his quest for the Light Heavyweight Championship of the Far East. A feat never achieved by a white man. His friends and colleagues were shaking his hand as he passed by them wishing him the best. Most of the unit had turned out to show support and would be in the arena tonight when the Championship would be decided. He had not felt the camp's full support up until that moment, had only ever witnessed small pockets of fans from the camp wishing him well. Apart from a few close friends, he thought he had reached his pinnacle of success, unnoticed by many of his colleagues. He was taken aback with all the well wishers and was uplifted by their generous response. He could hear himself saying quietly under his breath as he jogged around the perimeter of the parade ground,

'I hope I don't let them down tonight!'

Chapter 45

As he entered the Great World Arena, there was an air of expectation from the lively crowd. Some of the early revellers were already shouting their allegiance to him. He hoped he would live up to this expectation as 21.00 hours approached for his contest to begin. This would be the most important sporting occasion that Singapore had staged since it was rescued from the clutches of the Japanese in September 1945. Almost two years on, he felt moved by the occasion, however, the next hour until his contest would seem like days.

Neither man had set eyes on each other since their last meeting, when the Indian wrestler found himself on the wrong side of the ring and out for the count. Tonight would be a different ball game though; there would be no fooling around or taking chances by either man. This was deadly serious business. He knew he would have to produce only his best. Anything less and he would be runner up, possibly seriously injured. Kamrul had made his intent very clear to his opponent. There would be no rematch in this contest, there would only be this one chance. Bearing in mind what he had done to Kamrul a month ago, with that accurate and deadly scissor kick, there would be no let up from his opponent to square the deal. He knew he had lit a raging fire under Kamrul and he would be ready for anything coming his way. He also had some squaring of his own to settle. That brutal attack on him leaving the Union Jack club was unforgiving and he wanted Kamrul to pay. One more hit on his head could have finished his wrestling career that night, possibly his life.

'How do you feel now, Kid?' Hassan wanted to know if he was in good spirits as he massaged his muscular back and arms.

'Nervous, but that massage has relaxed me. I think this is a good sign though, it keeps my mind focused.'

'Just remember your strategy, Kid.'

'I'm still working on that, Hassan; this is a work in progress for me.'

Kazar was also there urging his star wrestler on and encouraging him. 'You can do this, you know you can. Technically, you're the best wrestler without doubt, in this part of the world. Stay with what you know. Don't be tricked into going down Kamrul's route of brute force. You can beat this man using your skill alone.'

He listened intently to Kazar's good, sound advice. He had seen more contests than anyone on this small island and he valued his precious words of encouragement.

Kazar hesitated to speak again as Hassan finished his full body massage on Callon.

'Try to rile your man early on, get him upset, and get him annoyed. Hurt him if you can? even if you have to bend the rules a little.' He looked up from his massage table, winked and said,

'I intend to do just that, Kaz.' There was an air of mischievousness on his face as he stood up from the table.

'What time did she say she would be here, Kaz?'

'She should be here by now.' Kazar had been to the arena to look for Suzi, but found no trace of her in the hall. 'She promised me she'd come, Kid, I've no reason to doubt her.'

This was not what he wanted on his mind 30 minutes before the biggest contest of his life. He tried to put it out of his head and focus on his contest. Hassan was trying to relax him too, massaging his shoulders further as he stood upright glaring out to the arena, seeing banners and flags for both wrestlers. The atmosphere was beginning to reach cauldron pitch as chants for both men were heard. He felt the majority in the arena were for him. A huge contingent of army colleagues were also making their presence felt and their noise heard. One of their colleagues reaching this improbable height so young and so soon was an amazing feat in itself.

'Keep me posted? I want to know the minute she arrives, Kaz.'

He was trying to get himself into the zone. He stood motionless, his eyes were glaring and intense and a look of hatred crossed his face as he thought about his opponent. He needed to hate Kamrul in order to beat him. He thought about the attack on him by Kamrul's men; that was not meant to just hurt, that was meant to stop him for good.

This could only mean one thing, Kamrul was more worried about him than he could imagine.

'Are you ready, Kid?' said Hassan. 'They will be announcing you in a few minutes.' He was now dancing on his toes like a boxer, his long silk dressing gown fluttering with the movement, disguising his superbly toned and developed torso.

Kazar came towards him from the direction of the arena.

'Suzi's here, Kid, seated on the opposite side of the ring to where we are now, two rows back from the front.' He made no visible sign except a small nod of his head to acknowledge the news. His focus was now absolute. Kazar had never seen his wrestler with so much determination on his face. Everything in his vision, both direct and peripheral appeared to be blocked out.

The announcer was making his way to the ringside. The arena erupted in anticipation of seeing their man take to the ring. He was about to be welcomed into the main arena. As underdog, he would be announced before his Indian adversary.

The microphone burst into life welcoming the crowd to this historic event. The announcer spoke clearly and slowly advising the spectators of the journey Kid Callon had travelled to reach this moment. On the mention of his name, he started his walk to the ringside amid rapturous applause. He found it impossible to smile, his concentration was so intense. As he entered the ring amidst the adulation, he lifted his stonewall look and paraded to each corner of the ring with his arms aloft. He spotted Suzi and waved directly at her and mouthed, 'thank you.' as he worked his way around the ring. He couldn't fail to notice the mystery man. He was there with his protective shield around him. He wondered if he was there genuinely to watch him wrestle, or there just to keep an eye on him from an injury perspective; as though his presence would prevent anything happening to him. His colleagues from the army base were well charged up for the contest and shouting loud support for their man. He acknowledged the fans and retired to his corner, where Hassan was waiting. He administered further deep massage strokes to his wrestler's shoulders; he could feel them tightening up as he worked his fingers into the muscle.

'Relax, Kid, you're becoming tense, stay calm.'

As he settled himself into his corner and traded a few words with

Hassan, the announcer continued with his introductions. The buzz was with him, the adrenalin rush was coursing his body; he felt invincible. This is what he had been waiting for, for so long. He was flexing his legs, holding the top ropes as he squatted on his knees. Kamrul was making his way into the ring. Above the cheers, he could also hear the jeers from some of the onlookers. He caught his first glimpse of Kamrul as he waddled his way towards the ring. He had six of his people surrounding him as he made his way forward. He was sure that he recognised at least two of the faces from the night he received that vicious beating. He suddenly saw flash backs to the moment he was set upon with sticks or truncheons by the gang. Faces of the men flashed past him fleetingly in his head. He was sure it was them, it had to be, he thought. Kamrul was wearing a full length, silk gold robe fastened by a black silk tie across the waist. Standing at only five feet tall, this sight created quite a spectacle. Kamrul was trying to eyeball his opponent from his disadvantaged position of the ring side. As he stepped into the ring, he never released his stare from his opponent. He would not however, be intimidated by such tactics, instead, he casually unrobed and walked across to Kamrul's corner and offered his hand in a gesture of friendship. Two of his team were in the ring with him, and they stood in protective mode at Kamrul's side. He looked at both men unsmiling, before setting his welcoming gaze on Kamrul.

Go on Kamrul, I dare you, take my hand.

'May the best man win, Kamrul?'

The Indian wrestler was taken by surprise at this offer of friendship. He glanced down at his opponents hand, hesitated slightly and offered his hand back knowing that he was well protected by his team.

He took hold of Kamrul's hand, continuing to stare at his opponent and squeezed hard without showing any outward sign of pressure. To the onlooker, it was a gentlemanly act of good will.

Let's see how tough you really are, Kamrul, get ready to receive a huge dollop of your own fucking medicine.

He had a grip of iron which he knew Kamrul could not respond to, he had the initiative in the hold and squeezed harder and then smiled.

What are you going to do, little big man. You need to do something quickly before I crush the bones in your bloody hand.

He watched as Kamrul's facial features changed from passive to painful. He knew Kamrul would retaliate with his free hand. He had no other option as the bones in his right hand were beginning to grind together. Kamrul was beginning to react to the pressure and moving from side to side. His two protectors looked at each other wondering what was happening.

Try to hit me Kamrul. This is your only weapon of defence.

He didn't have long to wait, Kamrul thrust his left fist towards him in desperation, but he parried it immediately, anticipating the attack. In a single movement which appeared to be self protective, he threw the left heel of his hand underneath Kamrul's open jaw, bringing his teeth together with such force that he had no time to move his tongue away. He was immediately sprayed with blood which was now oozing from Kamrul's open mouth. He let go of Kamrul's hand; he cradled his chin in serious pain. All this happened so quickly and caught the referee off guard. Kamrul's two protectors came forward to attack him. He anticipated their actions too, and hit one square in the face with the flat of his hand sending him sprawling through the ropes backwards to the floor of the arena. He kicked the other man in the crutch and left him helpless and writhing in agony on the floor. The full capacity crowd were on their feet shouting wildly, wondering what was happening. The wrestling competition had just become an out of control boxing match.

The referee and the seconds from both corners came quickly between the two camps to try and bring order to the proceedings. More of Kamrul's protectors were trying to get into the ring to attack Kid Callon, but they were held back as more officials from the ringside jumped in to assist the referee. After a few minutes, a degree of calm came over the arena as both wrestlers settled on their stools in their respective corners.

'What happened, did you attack Kamrul?' said the referee. 'I need to sort this mess out before we go any further with this competition.'

'No, I didn't attack him, Kamrul tried to punch me while I was shaking his hand,' replied Callon. 'You saw what happened, I was defending myself. The other two misfits with him, they were going to attack me too. They clearly wanted to hurt me before the beginning of my contest.' The referee went to the judges sitting ringside, explaining Callon's version of events and could see that one of them was shaking his head and hunching his shoulders. They clearly hadn't seen what had created the chaos.

Kazar was now in the ring facing his wrestler also trying to understand what had just happened.

'Are you hurt, Kid? What the hell happened there?'

'No, I'm not hurt; no one laid a finger on me, Kaz. Let's just say I evened things up a little out there. Those two guys with Kamrul, they were part of the gang that attacked me. I remember them; they followed me into the bar.'

'They're discussing disqualification, Kid, this is serious, and this could be disastrous for you.'

'I was defending myself, Kaz, for fuck's sake, speak to the referee, the judges, whatever, but don't let them disqualify me!'

'When I said try to upset the man before you wrestle, I had no idea you were planning something like this?'

'I didn't plan it, Kaz. The sight of those two guys in the ring with Kamrul made me see red. I was incensed with rage; I couldn't stop myself. I intended giving Kamrul's hand a little squeeze, but I didn't plan this outcome.' He looked into Kaz's eyes and said, 'I'm not disappointed with the outcome though.'

Kazar turned with a wry smile on his face thinking, only Kid Callon could pull off a stunt like that and get away with it. He made his way to where the judges were sitting.

Kamrul was still unable to speak as his corner tried desperately to stem the flow of blood. He was shaking his right hand trying to rid it of the pain and cradling it across his left arm.

The referee was in Kamrul's corner now, getting his version of events. As he was doing so, he was checking his head, holding it upwards with both hands and glaring into his eyes.

'Are you okay, Kamrul, are you okay?' Kamrul pulled some wadding from his mouth which had been stuffed in there by his corner staff. He snorted, spraying the pristine white shirt of the referee unintentionally and splattering blood down his gold wrestling robe. He then tried to leave his corner of the ring and launch himself at Kid Callon. The referee and his second intervened and held him back.

'Calm down, Kamrul, I'm trying to sort this out,' said the referee.

He had a clear view of Kamrul across the ring and could see his discomfort.

That really hurts, doesn't it, Kamrul. Well it will hurt a lot more before tonight's contest is over. That's just for starters.

Kamrul continued to cradle his mouth with his left hand. He was opening and closing his jaw, clearly in pain. Kid Callon knew exactly where his focus lay now. It would be several minutes before Kamrul would be patched up as he allowed himself a minute of home time to think about his family back in the UK. This contest was for them. He hadn't been fair to them and he knew this to his discredit. He would repay them though, by bringing back to the UK this Championship Crown which he wanted now, more than ever. He thought about his father, and his sound advice;

'Get the first blow in,' he would say. In achieving this, half the battle would be over. He knew half the battle was not won, but he had achieved his first objective, to rile his opponent and secondly, to hurt him. He had achieved both. As far as he was concerned, he had won the first round with consummate ease and without making a hold or breaking sweat.

Kazar was making his way to his corner.

'We have the all clear to continue, Kid; I had to do some plea bargaining back there, so no more funny business. The main thing is, this contest continues. Kamrul needs a little time to organise himself; in the meantime, relax. As Kazar was about to leave the ring he turned back to his wrestler and said, 'great job, Kid, good luck for the rest of the contest.'

'Thanks Kaz, don't uncork the champagne just yet, but do keep it on ice.'

Chapter 46

After the unscheduled delay, the announcer declared that the contest for the Light Heavyweight Championship of the Far East would begin. Many people in the crowd were becoming anxious and wanted the contest started. The referee, bloodstained from Kamrul, indicated for the two men to wrestle after a loud bell was rung by the timekeeper. The little cocktail starter provided by Kid Callon had whetted the appetite of the crowd, who were now ready for the battle to commence;

He was coming forward towards his quarry and smiling, he could see in Kamrul's eyes that he was jumping with rage. He had hate written right across his face. He swung his long hairy arms in front of his large barrel chest. As Callon had discovered to his advantage several years previous, a man in rage loses his focus, his technique and his skill go out of the window. The only thing on his opponent's mind was retribution and revenge. He was mindful of course, that what Kamrul lacked in technique and skill, was more than made up for by his colossal strength. This main weapon of his for the time being was dented but, on the whole, remained undamaged.

Kamrul was anxious to get a firm hold of his man and show him first hand his strength potential. Immediately he went for a loose arm but was too slow to catch it. Kid Callon, unafraid of his wounded opponent went for a headlock and was successful in his first attempt. He tweaked the jaw with a hard jolt from the back of his wrist to make sure Kamrul was still hurting in this area. He dropped on to his knees with his man still in headlock and at high speed. The crowd enjoyed this move as a huge roar erupted against cheers and encouragement. A long arm crushed into the side of his face and forced his head backwards. He lost the headlock grip and immediately felt the uncompromising strength of Kamrul. He was now on his back and fighting off with all his strength and speed, one of Kamrul's death grips. He was quick and grabbed Kamrul's jaw and pulled it towards him. He could feel the electric shock this movement had on the Indian's body as he fought to stay on his back. Kamrul released enough for him to move away and get on his feet. In a fleeting movement, he pushed himself off from the top rope and just shoulder charged into Kamrul as he was getting up. It was like running into a brick wall. Kamrul had anticipated the charge and held his short, stocky body at just the right angle to absorb the charge. Callon bounced off and landed on his backside, surprised by the unmoving slab of his opponent. Kamrul was back on him immediately. He needed to slow the Kid down, his speed, skill and swift movement was something he had not encountered before. He grabbed Callon's foot and lifted his leg from the ground. With his ankle firmly tucked under his arm, Kamrul fell backwards into a sitting position against the ankle ligaments, straining and stretching them to their limit. He could not reach safety as the Indian had dragged him into the centre of the ring. He was still on his back, but he was out of arm's reach of Kamrul and had to endure this agony for precious seconds longer than he wanted to. With tremendous effort, using his abdominal strength and the leg which was held as a fulcrum, he sprung upwards and forward into a standing position. Stood on only one leg and now facing Kamrul, he hit him with a flat arm across the side of his face and jaw. He could not believe his luck, Kamrul had left his face unprotected and exposed by that move. The impact nearly shattered his jaw as he released his hold. He tried to apply a shoulder press as Kamrul squirmed on the canvas on his back. Kamrul had time and enough strength to resist the submission attempt and put his hand through the rope. The referee started to count as Kamrul checked his jaw again for any further damage. He stayed down on one knee moving his jaw from side to side. After a count of eight, he straightened his short body and studied his opponent momentarily. He realised that he had the full package with the young wrestler facing him and looking as mean as hell. In his wrestling career, he had never been on the canvas for a count of eight before and he wondered what was coming next. The bell rang for the close of round one.

As both men took on water in the corner, the crowd buzzed and knew that Kamrul's opponent was a different class to what he had faced before. No one came away from the first round against Kamrul either level or slightly in front. He had always managed to nail his opponent in some hold or another as he slowly squeezed the breath from their bodies. The bell rang as the referee called both men to wrestle.

Round 2

From the outset, Kid Callon attacked, he was less intimidated by Kamrul's strength, mainly because of his own strength defence. Both men offered their hands to each other and locked fingers in the centre of the ring. With each man's hand held high, he was able to observe close up his opponent's arm length and strength. Kamrul's arms belonged to a man some 18 inches taller and were incredibly strong. Kid Callon called on all of his strength reserves to fend off being moved backward onto the ropes. Kamrul released his right hand and had clear reach advantage and was able to grab and turn his man in one movement, around the neck. Kamrul was holding him by the throat; he extended a thumb and thrust it into his neck, restricting his windpipe and cutting off his air supply. He immediately reacted to this violation. The referee tried to intervene but Kamrul was able to push him out of the way using his opponent as a battering ram. Gasping for air as the pressure on the hold was maintained; Kid Callon was turning purple and moving frantically to try and free himself from this iron grip. His eyes were starting to pop, as he desperately tried to neutralise the hand squeezing his windpipe. The referee was shouting at Kamrul and slapping his back as he wheeled around avoiding face contact with the referee.

'Release, Kamrul, release, or I will disqualify you. Release, Kamrul, release!' The crowd was shouting their misgivings as some of the ringside seat members came to the ring and banged their fists on the canvas. It made no difference, he continued with his hold.

He could feel his strength ebbing away as he fought for air. In desperation, he swung his free hand into Kamrul's substantial gut but to no effect. He swung again, this time hitting the aggressor directly with his fist into his solar plexus. All grips were released immediately as he went to the canvas gasping for air and holding his throat. The vice like grip around his throat had damaged his windpipe and he was struggling to get air into his lungs. The referee was holding Kamrul back in his corner and berating him for his illegal hold.

'One more stunt like that, Kamrul and you'll be back in the changing room.' Kamrul was dismissive of the referee never once looking at him. 'Do you understand, Kamrul, I'm not going to tolerate those moves here.' He looked towards the judges still holding Kamrul with the heel of his hand. He continued to swing his arms in ape-like fashion, in anticipation of getting hold of his man to press home his advantage.

'Judges, please register an official warning to, Kamrul.' A short announcement was made over the tannoy system to this effect as Kid Callon continued to cough trying to regain his composure and his breath. The referee turned his attention to Kid Callon who was still smarting from the hold. The referee inspected his neck and could see the pressure marks left by Kamrul's thumb and fingers.

'Are you okay, Kid?' asked the referee, looking directly into his eyes to register any effects from the hold. It had been held for over 30 seconds before the release came.

'I'm okay, referee, but the bastard nearly choked me, keep your eye on him. I need water,' he said, as he straightened himself up, took a swig from his corner and prepared to wrestle. The referee had stopped the clock and asked for it restarted before bringing the two men together.

He was fully alert again, away from his corner in a flash, he was hurt but not down by any means. He moved quickly around his large opponent feigning to attack then withdrawing. He did this several times just out of arms reach as Kamrul pirouetted in slow motion in the centre of the ring, waiting for the intended attack. Kamrul did not have long to wait, Kid Callon, launched an outstretched leg and swung it with such force against Kamrul's heels that it upended him. Kamrul was on his backside in a flash. Before he could respond, he dropped on him with all his weight, displacing the air from the little big man's chest. He was then quickly on his feet before Kamrul could grab him.

You are going to pay for your little antics my friend, big time.

As Kamrul rolled over onto his stomach to attempt to get up, Kid Callon was on him again.

You are too fat and too slow, Kamrul.

He landed cowboy style on the middle of Kamrul's back with a leg either side of him. He reached down quickly and grabbed Kamrul under the chin with both hands and pulled back unmercifully into a face lock as his head and shoulders left the canvas. Kamrul was trying to grab anything that belonged to his aggressor as his long tentacles swung aimlessly behind him, finding nothing. As he pulled upwards with both hands, he pressed his thumbs into the joint where the jawbones articulate. Kamrul screamed as the pain intensified, the referee was on his knees and in the face of Kamrul asking him if he wanted to submit but got no response. Kamrul was hurting, but not enough to capitulate at this moment in time. He was now flat on the canvas with Callon on his back.

Come on you bastard, submit!

He released his grip slightly, letting his opponent think his torture was over, only to apply the pressure again, upwards and backwards against his neck and his chin. The little man was really hurting but was able to turn his body enough using his long arms to dislodge his attacker and release his grip. Both men landed on their sides, but this time Kamrul stayed down. The referee counted the seconds down as Kamrul inspected his jaw area carefully with both hands again. Callon was sure it was broken already, but was amazed at the man's ability to withstand pain. Kamrul, on the count of eight in the second successive round rose to his feet. Callon wanted to use the ropes as momentum to body check him but thought twice about it, considering the outcome of the last attempt. The two men approached each other again but Kid Callon was moving more swiftly, he lashed out with his right foot before the men made contact in karate fashion and landed the heel of his boot directly on Kamrul's kneecap. He retreated as Kamrul instinctively bent down to rub it with both hands. With Kamrul in a crouched position, he again attacked the jaw by giving him a side swipe across the face. His movements were too quick for Kamrul to counter, and whilst deciding which part of his body to defend, he exploded with a scissor kick at Kamrul's huge body. He only caught a glancing blow and he landed awkwardly on his back and elbow. Kamrul, seizing his opportunity, dropped his full weight on him and picked him up bodily from behind and wrapped his long arms around his opponent's midriff. He then squeezed for all he was worth. Once again, he found he was in a grip of iron with his arms helpless and encased beside him. He only had his legs to defend himself as he felt his torso being crushed. Kamrul now had him off his feet and was pacing around the ring with his quarry at his mercy. He waited until Kamrul's legs were parted enough and landed a back-heel kick right on the money, between Kamrul's legs! The hold was immediately broken as if a small explosion between the two men had occurred. He cared little whether that move was legal or not, but it worked and he was not rebuked by the referee. The bell sounded to end round two with honours even for the time being.

The crowd once again knew they were witnessing a very even contest at this stage, even though their styles were very different. The carnival atmosphere continued in the arena as chants for Kid Callon overshadowed those for Kamrul.

He observed the little big man as he trudged to his corner. He sat down with a heavy thud as his huge backside spilt over the side of his corner stool, he was breathing heavily. His Corner administered water into the wrestler's open mouth before he realised this was half way for Kamrul. He had never gone more than four rounds previously and these would have been short rounds, brought about by a submission before time was called. In an effort to make Kamrul more aware of him, he stood through the short break and stared at his opponent. Kamrul never looked up, but he knew his actions in the corner were under the gaze of Kid Callon.

Round 3

The referee stood in the centre of the ring and waved the two men together after the bell sounded for round three. Callon was again on his toes darting into Kamrul then feigning an attack, before retreating without any contact being made. He wanted a cheap shot at Kamrul's jaw, he knew he had to tweak this at least once in every round. He stopped his antics and held his hand out to his opponent again, as if wanting to shake it. He knew he wouldn't fall for that again, but as he approached Kamrul, he thrust himself swiftly downwards onto the floor and had one of his legs tucked under his arm. Because of his short stocky frame, Kamrul was difficult to get to ground. As he applied the hold, Kamrul had no option but to topple over onto the canvas. Just for good measure, he thumped his opponent's kneecap with the heel of his hand very hard, the same one he had kicked earlier. He winced, so he repeated the dose. Kamrul was now on the floor and on his back. Callon took the leg still in hold and wrapped it around his own neck. With all the strength he could muster, he straightened up and had the full weight of Kamrul suspended by his own knee. Kamrul was hurting and screaming. He was being swung round and round by Callon, to disorientate him. He let go, and the little big man fell to the canvas in a heap head first. Before he could get up, his kneecap was targeted again, this time with the heel of his boot. His thoughts were to target several areas on his opponent's body. He could not defend all of them, not at the same time anyway. He pounced again before Kamrul could stand up and performed a headlock on the ground, putting extra strain on his opponent's jaw. With his long rangy arms, Kamrul defended himself by swiping him in the face with his forearm. It worked as the grip was loosened. Callon was able to stand up and prepare himself for the next assault before Kamrul could get to his feet. He hurled himself into the ropes to maximise his momentum then crushed into Kamrul. He was hoping to catch him off guard, but only found himself enveloped by long open arms. The momentum in his run was not sufficient enough to unseat the little big man. Fortunately, he was able to free his right arm before his opponent applied any pressure. Kamrul squeezed his man in a bear hug, taking advantage of his long arms. With his free hand Callon tried to shove Kamrul's jaw up through his teeth, but he was equal to the challenge and was unmoved by the attempt. Callon began to feel the extent of his adversary's strength as air was being pressed from his body.

Please God, give me strength. Hold on, hold on Kid, and don't submit, no, no.

Callon put his free hand under Kamrul's chin again, but this time grabbed the pressure point above the throat and squeezed the nerve. This immediately cut off Kamrul's air supply. The airway remained open because Callon was not squeezing the windpipe, so the move was legal. He felt Kamrul's body go slightly limp and sensed the pressure point was working as the force upon him increased.

Oh thank you, God!

Kamrul could not escape the move as he tried valiantly to push his head back out of the way. The referee was close at hand to witness no wrongdoing. Millimetres either side of the nerve, and it would have no effect at all. Kamrul dropped to his knees and Callon sensed his chance. He rolled the little big man over onto his back whilst he was still supine, and grabbed both feet. He somersaulted over Kamrul, still holding his feet. Both men were now on their back, but Kamrul's shoulders were pinned to the floor for a count of three in an excruciating and inescapable hold. The bell was sounded to confirm the pinfall.

Kid Callon released his grip, amid bedlam in the hall. He has just achieved what no other wrestler in the Far East has been able to do; get a submission over Kamrul. His army of colleagues were all at the ringside cheering their young warrior on. That was a dramatic and flamboyant move and brought the cauldron in the arena to boiling point. He was punching the air to all four corners of the ring. He waved to Suzi in the crowd, she was gushing with pride at his achievement. Kamrul eventually rose to his feet with the help of his second and wondered how and what had happened to him. His father had shown him that pressure point move many years back. He had never used it in anger, until that moment. He looked to the heavens and wondered where that spark of inspiration had come from. He thought somehow, his father was looking after him. Without that move, he himself would have been staring down at his own submission as his spine was been crushed bit by bit by one of Kamrul's death grips.

Both men had been wrestling flat out for almost 15 minutes. The submission came at the end of the third round. Kamrul looked exhausted as he sat dismayed and staring into the gloom and blackness from his corner into the roof space above him. He knew he needed to keep his focus and his control of the contest, after all, the job up to now was only half completed.

Round 4

He was now on fire as the referee indicated 'wrestle' to both men, immediately after the bell had sounded. He rushed at Kamrul taking the initiative away from him, but not allowing those powerful arms to get a hold. He was moving so fast now that Kamrul was finding it difficult to keep him in his front vision. Kamrul's large body was turning slowly and laboriously in the centre of the ring. Once he was out of position, Callon hit Kamrul from the side and swiftly locked his own arm round that of Kamrul into a half nelson, straining the head and neck of his opponent. He then curled his leg around Kamrul's and tripped him to the floor still in hold. The two men had not grappled much on the floor previously as Callon had avoided this as much as possible. Having Kamrul on the canvas now was a different proposition; the little man was sweating profusely and breathing hard. The man was very tired; his strength was beginning to desert him. He was still a potential threat however, and he wondered if he was falling into some kind of a trap. Kamrul suddenly flexed his shoulder and broke the half nelson hold. The surge of power took him completely off guard. He was able to grab him and force him backward over his own leg. He knew he was immediately in trouble as he tried in vain to reach and exert pressure on one of Kamrul's vulnerable places. He pulled Callon towards him so that his arched back was over his knee.

Fuck, fuck, no, don't submit. God help me!!!...please!

Kamrul was able to lift his knee. Because of the angle of his head, Callon could just see Kamrul's smiling face as he increased the pressure. He was helpless, he could not move up, down, left or right. It was only a matter of time; no man could stand this for too long. Ironically, the kneecap he had been targeting on Kamrul was now pressed hard into the centre of his spine.

Please, God, help me out of this...no, don't submit, you can take this!

It was too painful to breathe now as Kamrul applied more pressure.

Submit now you stupid bloody fool. If this goes on, you will not be able to carry on and he will break your spine!

Callon shouted in despair and with intense urgency. 'Submit, Referee, submit!'

The referee slapped Kamrul on the shoulder, 'Release, Kamrul, release now, Kamrul!'

The bell rang to confirm the submission. Kamrul held the hold longer than he should have, piling the agony on his opponent. The Great World Arena had almost been silenced. No one had seen this coming after Kid Callon's domination of the contest so far. He lay flat on the canvas trying to get relief from the pressure on his spine. He knew he had been succoured this time. Hassan, having had little to do up to now, kept his man on the canvas and administered some deep manipulation on his lower back. The seconds for the start of the next round were running and he was still prone on the canvas. Kazar, his wrestling promoter was in the corner urging his young wrestler to stand up.

'Come on, Kid, come on, do this for your family.' The words of Kazar had a certain resonance to them, but his body wouldn't react.

Kamrul was in his corner shouting obscenities at him as he stayed on the canvas receiving treatment. Kamrul now stood the whole of the short interval, as though he had been injected with new life.

Within one minute of taking the lead in this contest, it was suddenly, honours even. Kid Callon was distraught. He had relaxed his own guard and paid the penalty.

'Ten seconds, Kid, that's all.' the referee was giving some urgency to him but he was still on the floor. Hassan was trying desperately to help his man up. The fifth round was due to start any second. Callon managed to crouch on his haunches, just as the bell for the start of the next round was rung.

Round 5

I'm in deep shit now. Come on Callon; get it together before this bloody ape wipes the floor with you. You can do this, come on. This is just a blip on your part. You had the man, come on get going. It's all square now, you can beat this pain.

Kamrul was on his man in a moment with the referee helpless to intervene. The time between rounds was up, and he had to defend himself. Kamrul suddenly had a renewed energy and vigour and was coming in for the kill. He grabbed a limp arm from Callon, stood him up and threw him against the ropes. He knew what was coming, but could do little about it. He slammed into Kamrul's solid body and bounced backwards flat on his backside. This caused further jarring to his already injured spine.

The Indian was now playing with his quarry; he knew he had his man just where he wanted him, shouting profanities and teasing him. Kamrul was parading around the outside of the ring arms raised aloft in a victory march whipping the spectators up and gesticulating back to those shouting against him. He applied further holds which he was just able to react to, but his strength was almost depleted now as he tried to fight the searing pain in the middle of his back.

Don't let him do this to you, Callon. You can't get beat, not tonight, please God, not tonight!

Kamrul was going for the total destruction of his man and was going to hurt him bad now. He picked the same arm he had been working on and weakening; there was little resistance from his opponent as he tried valiantly to protect his spine. He was thrown into the corner stanchion this time with tremendous force. There was very little cushioning of the impact and he sank to his knees holding his back. The pain seared through his bones as he curled foetus style in the corner. His back problem was mind numbing and getting worse as he tried in vain to provide some small comfort for himself.

You've got to do something, you're going down fast. Pride, Callon, come on, where is your pride? God help me…please!

It was brute force now, no technique required from Kamrul. He grabbed the same arm as previous. This was too easy, as he slammed his opponent with great force into the stanchion of his own corner this time. He was hurt bad now, and almost helpless to react. His whole body ached and he was bleeding from a head wound caused by a previous hold after being flung into the corner. He looked out helplessly towards the crowd who were willing their man to get up.

The referee had started his count;

One – Kazar and Hassan were shouting furiously at him to get up. 'Come on, Kid. Hold on, there's only 30 seconds left in this round.'

Two– *Don't let this happen, please God, said Callon to himself!*

Three – Kamrul was standing poised and ready to pounce, only feet behind the referee and swinging his long arms,

Four – *It's over. You gave it your best shot!*

Five – He could hear his army colleagues urging him to get up but felt helpless to react.

Six – *Just try to get up, move your self, maybe it's not over.* He moved his position slightly and managed to get up onto one knee. Kamrul was trying to push the referee out of the way. He wanted one last shot at his injured quarry. Kamrul knew he was home and dry.

Seven – *Get up for God's sake. He can't hurt you any more than you are hurt already.* It was like an electric shock to his body when he looked out to the many spectators urging him on. He suddenly had a vision before him, a vision which he hated, but one which only he could change. He raised a second knee and knelt, looking into her eyes. He had his back to Kamrul and the referee. He could almost smell the breath of his attacker on his neck as he waited for the kill.

Eight– Suzi was crying with a look of deep despair on her face. She was holding her face in cupped hands, hardly bearing to watch the man she had known only briefly, but so intimately. His pummelled body was still aching, but Callon made his final desperate move.

Nine – Kamrul was sensing victory now, one second to the title only. Kid Callon half stood as the referee backed away to allow the hairy predator towards his man for the last time. Kid Callon allowed Kamrul to take his arm again and thrust him into the ropes for one last slam against his rock solid torso. All of Kamrul's defences were relaxed, he had his man and he was going to teach him a lesson. Kamrul swung him into the ropes at speed; rebounding him into his own body. At the very last moment though, before impact with Kamrul, he changed his course of direction to pass him. At the same time he raised his right arm and caught him directly under the chin smashing his jaw, and crushing his windpipe. His head hit the canvas as he was catapulted backwards by the force. Kid Callon knew Kamrul was out for the count. The only way he would be getting up from that fall was on a hospital stretcher.

Chapter 47

Kid Callon had achieved what looked impossible. He had beaten all comers and taken the Light Heavyweight Wrestling Championship of the Far East. The whole arena was up on its feet, cheering the new Champion, the first white man to ever hold this title.

Kamrul was now being treated in the centre of the ring. Medical men and officials surrounded him looking anxious. The man had come within a second of standing where he was standing now.

Kamrul's broken body was taken from the ring directly to the hospital. Ironically, it would be the same hospital where Kid Callon had been left, beaten and naked just one month previously. He somehow felt justice had been both repaid and restored?

Kazar had organised a room for celebration at the best hotel in the world, Raffles.

'You did great tonight, Kid,' said Kazar, pouring a champagne for his number one wrestler.

'I thought I'd blown it, I can't begin to tell you the strength that little man possessed, it was truly awesome.' He took a moment to look around the room. These people were all there for him. His army colleagues, some never been in such luxurious surroundings, were in great spirits. They had lifted their man shoulder high around the ring after receiving his prestigious championship belt. He continued to wear the belt over his smart tailored trousers and white cotton shirt as his friends gathered.

'What a contest, Kid.' said Steve, 'Our money was on you tonight, but we thought we'd lost it in round five!'

'Yeah! me too, but you guys helped me through it, I could hear your support, I knew you were with me, it's what helped me through. I'm just thankful you guys were there and that you can celebrate with me tonight.'

'We wouldn't have missed it.' Steve was starting to get philosophical on his friend. 'No one believed you could pull this off, Kid, including me. Remember, I tried to talk you out of it, we all thought you were bloody mad at the time, now look at you!'

He was finishing his champagne when he felt the presence of someone to his right hand side.

'Excuse me, Sir.' It was a bell boy, looking magnificent in his white attire, tailored especially for the hotel's staff. 'There's a lady downstairs would like to speak to you.'

'Did she leave a name?' he asked, although he knew already who it was. Suzi had left the arena by the time things had calmed down. It was total chaos after the knockout and the presentations. He had searched for her, but couldn't see her anywhere in the hall.

'No, sir, she left no name.'

'Where downstairs?'

'If you would like to follow me, Sir, I will take you to her.' The bell boy turned and he followed obediently two steps behind.

Suzi was standing in the main foyer looking nervous and anxious.

'Thank you so much for coming tonight,' he said, and went to kiss her gently on the cheek. She pulled away and looked over his shoulder. Callon instinctively turned 180 degrees only to see the mystery man standing with several of his entourage by the exit.

'What is this, Suzi? What the hell is going on?' She'd been crying and went to dry her tear stained cheek with a white embroidered handkerchief.

'I've come to say goodbye, Ki. I was so proud of you tonight. You deserved your victory.' She hesitated before composing herself. 'We only knew each other a short time, but I was falling in love with you. This is not allowed for me.'

'What do you mean not allowed, what are you saying, Suzi?' He was trying to stay calm.

'I belong to someone else.' The words cut through his defence like a knife through butter.

'You belong to someone else, what do you mean, you're married?'

'No, but I know you are, Ki. Look, I've caused enough trouble already, I just came to say goodbye, that's all.'

'Who then, who do you belong to?' He turned round again and pointed to the mystery man. 'What, you belong to him?' He said it loud enough for everyone in the foyer to hear.

Suzi didn't confirm or deny the question, there was no need. He was going to confront the mystery man when Suzi pulled him back.

'Don't, Ki, or he will hurt you too, in other ways. You will make it worse for me also, please don't. I just want to say goodbye.' There was such love and passion on her face and in her words, he could hardly speak, his eyes, filling with tears. He traced her steps back to the Mystery man and out of his life forever. He held the vision as long as he could, hardly breathing; unmoving, until she walked out of sight.

'She never looked back,' he said, He wondered what the outcome of tonight's contest would have been, had he not seen Suzi for that fleeting glance in such distress. He was on the brink of submission, where life and energy was seeping from his body, wanting to save her from further misery. It was this vision that had urged him to continue, to go on and win and to lift that magnificent trophy belt. He would never get the chance to thank her now. 'Fuck,' he said, 'she never looked back!'

Chapter 48

It had been a roller coaster ride since lifting the wrestling trophy, but he had been back at his day job since the beginning of the week. He had been granted a week off to recover from his injuries and to pursue several company marketing arrangements organised by Kazar.

Kazar was taking every opportunity to make the most of his new found status as well. The Championship had propelled him and his wrestling career on to another level as the prime promoter in the Far East, and he was basking in both the glory and in the rewards. Both men had gained financially through their wrestling exploits. Kazar had recognised immediately the potential and raw talent of the young man, now Champion of the Far East, as he had sauntered almost nonchalantly into his life all those months back. They had travelled the road of fame together and conquered everything put in their way.

Major Reece had organised letters and photographs to be sent to his family back in the UK informing them of his new found success. He was grateful for the help offered by the Major. There would be a few surprises back in England when they received the news of his new sporting achievements.

Other things occupied his mind now though, he was restless and anxious about his next starring role, only defeat this time, could have far greater consequences. There would be far more at stake than simple reputations. It was three days before the drug heist was going to be carried out. From his side, he wanted to make sure all details were as before. He wandered towards the confines of the bonded warehouse. He chose his moment when he knew it would be quiet. Everything stops for lunch in Singapore, especially dockside. He tried the door where he knew the BTO goods were stored closest to, but it was locked.

'Shit! he said to himself as he turned to look for alternatives. He headed for the main front gate of the warehouse building. It had two huge metal doors for heavy vehicle access. There was a normal single personnel door too. He tried this small door expecting it to be locked, but surprisingly it opened inwards as he pressed the handle down. He ignored the sign which read 'Keep out, authorised personnel only,' and made his way to the bay in question. Everything was just as he had remembered it. Deep down, he was hoping that the consignment would have been dumped. This plan was not something he really wanted to get involved with, but he was in it up to his neck now. There was no one there to challenge him this time. He double checked the warehouse was empty of personnel. He could not risk being seen near these goods again, but he needed to make preparations. He set about counting the pallets quickly and taking rough measurements. He needed to know that this consignment would fit into his truck and what the best configuration was for loading. He would not have enough time on the day to work out these details. He left the scene, his heart thumping heavily in his chest, without being seen or raising concerns from anyone. He was surprised that there was no security in the building and that a door giving access to the multi million dollar haul, was left unlocked? He hoped the operation would run as smooth as this next Monday when the plan would take on a completely new dimension. It would be for real!

Chapter 49

It was the first time the full complement of known operational players involved in the drugs heist had been assembled in one place. The Colonel however was not at the meeting, but he was close by listening to the proceedings. Callon assumed the Major would be taking notes on his behalf. The Colonel would distance himself anyway from any operational detail. There would be no way he, nor his rank, could be associated with such a daring and audacious theft of government property. He did however, wonder what the Colonels 'cut' of the cake would be, on the assumption that it was successful; it would be very significant, he was sure of that.

The details of the operation were meticulously studied and now the clock was ticking. It was just over 24 hours before the execution of the plan. The Major confirmed that the black tar opium (BTO) was still in place at the Empire Dock's bonded warehouse. He gave the meeting, the details of the exact location where it would be. Callon mentioned in the meeting that he had seen the BTO for himself and that security at the time of his visit was non-existent.

'You bloody fool,' said the mystery man, 'what if someone had seen you wandering around?'

'No one did see me, and don't call me a bloody fool!' He stood up and glared at him across the table. Water and stationery were disturbed as his knee caught the underside of the table. He pushed it away from himself aggressively. He resented been called a fool, especially from him. 'I had a perfectly plausible reason for being there,' he lied.

Kazar ushered Callon to sit down. He gestured with his hand to stay calm.

'This is not the time,' he said, 'for impatience and squabbling, so gentleman, please, let's now continue and concentrate on the plan.'

'I cannot emphasise enough, how damaging this operation will be to the Singapore Government.

The mystery man was making eye contact with each member. His eyes stopped at Richard, the Singapore Head of Customs.

'Is everyone clear about what they have to do?' He paused, as if waiting for some sign from the Singapore customs official, which did not come. 'I've already put myself at great risk,' he said solemnly with head bowed as he delivered his next sentence. 'Because of the delay to this operation, I've had to personally intervene, at great cost to myself, to prevent the goods from being destroyed. The BTO was scheduled to be dumped out to sea two weeks back. There is great consternation concerning these goods within the government of Singapore. The black market demand is very high for this product.'

The Major interjected, 'There can be no further delay to this operation, and do I make myself clear?' The Colonel had asked for this statement to be made. No one spoke but heads were nodding in agreement to the terse statement.

'Gentlemen.' said the mystery man. 'I wish each of you success in carrying out your own tasks successfully. We each know what we have to do. You all have your timings of where to be and when. Let's toast to our success.' The mystery man pressed a button under his table and chilled pink champagne with glasses were brought in to the room. Callon could not help thinking that the toast was somewhat premature, there was still a great deal which could go wrong with this plan!

Chapter 50

It had been an ordinary day up until now. He was looking to park his truck in its usual place on the Empire Docks. After waiting several minutes in his park position, he flashed his headlights three times facing away from the customs office at no one in particular. He had returned to the dock area from completing his various drop-off assignments around Singapore. It was Monday 15th September 17.00 hours, the day and the time for the drug heist to commence. Coming through the customs gate, he had been stopped as usual, with the same amount of scrutiny from the customs officers. He studied the two men on duty to see if there was any hint of recognition. There was none, they acted and performed their duties normally. The customs office looked calm and relaxed. He had expected men to be bouncing from the walls, like the insides of his stomach. For him, this was somewhat disconcerting, he was now instantly recognisable because of his wrestling success and the customs men did not even make eye contact!

'Maybe that's how the custom officers operate,' he said softly to himself. 'They have to remain ice cool under pressure!' It could be a different set of officers on duty, he thought, at 19.30 hours when he would drive his Mack towards the gates and out towards the Johor Straits causeway into Malaysia. His mind was beginning to play tricks, he was now in a situation, that he was not comfortable in. Trying to make any sense of what he was doing or where he was going, made him very nervous.

His arrival at the dockside coincided with the last dockworkers making their way home. Four strong, handpicked men however, would not be going home just yet. They would make their way to the back of his truck and secrete themselves inside the large tarpaulin canopy for a short time. The signal of three headlight flashes into the disappearing light would give the 'all clear' for the men to move. They would remain under the canopy until he gave another signal. As he lay down across his large bucket seat out of sight from anyone, he stared up at the sky which was beginning to darken. This would be a day which would be etched on his mind until the day he dies. He did not hear the four men getting themselves into position on his truck, but he knew they were there as it moved slightly on its suspension as they climbed aboard. He never heard their footsteps or from which direction they came. He heard the faint taps to let him know they were in place. He was sure that all the dockyard personnel were now off site, but he needed to be absolutely certain, he could not afford to take the risks of someone seeing him, so for now, he laid across his large bucket seat and waited in silence.

PART 4

Chapter 51

…Check back right mirror, okay, rider in place. Front riders both in vision and in place.

He took great comfort knowing that the outriders were travelling with him. Their presence suggested authority and provided a protective shield around him and his cargo, as it lumbered forward ever so slowly. The motorcade formed a kind of unwritten guarantee that the heist would succeed. He stopped himself from thinking about the fortune he had been promised for his part of the plan, this was providing the operation was a complete success. There were still obstacles to overcome though; the job was far from done. He thought about his precarious situation and tried to blank this from his thoughts, but found it impossible.

What if it does go wrong, he thought, what are the consequences for me? Would it be me receiving the severest punishment? Shit! He quickly extinguished the thought as he trundled forward into the bright lights.

He pushed his hair back from his brow with splayed fingers and sweaty palms trying to clear the negativity from his head. His hair was matted with perspiration and flat to his scalp. Throbbing from the heavy diesel engine was transferred up through the large steering wheel of the Mack into his wide shoulders as it powered itself to the border crossing; groaning against its multi million dollar load of Chandu, moving at a slow pace only now. The heavy engine roared above the stillness as the customs check point loomed ever closer. With 30 metres to go, a quick check of the watch suggested pin point timing. For what seemed like the hundredth time, he checked his mirrors again.

Check back left mirror, okay, rider in place. Check back right mirror, okay, rider in place. Front riders both in vision and in place.

'There's safety in numbers,' he whispered under his breath, 'I'm not alone in this audacious act.' The two motorcyclists at the front came together; they were talking animatedly to each other going just fast enough to control their balance. One of the riders had one of his hands off his machine and waving some kind of instructions. Only 20 metres to the border; the only thing that separated this operation from success or failure now was a simple barrier. He could make out the faces of the border control men as he entered the bubble of daylight conditions. He didn't recognise anyone on duty, he thought, but then realised; he should know at least one face.

'Where the fuck is, Richard?' he said out loud.

Check back left mirror, okay, rider in place. Check back right mirror......what the hell is happening! Front riders, gone!!

'You bastards, no, no, no, how could you do this. Fuck, fuck, fuck you!!

The huge Mack shuddered to a halt in front of the border checkpoint. Two armed customs officers approached the vehicle with extreme caution. The driver sat staring into space, numbed by what he had just witnessed, hoping that the ground would open up and swallow him.

The Aftermath;

Try to visualise the scene which unfolded at that checkpoint. In spite of the meticulous planning and organisation, my father was left abandoned, alone, and very frightened at that Singapore border control. He was dragged from his cab with an automatic weapon pressed under his chin with threats to his life if he resisted. He had no paperwork and no idea where the considerable consignment of Black Tar Opium was supposed to be delivered; except that it was to an unknown address in Malaysia.

He was interrogated at length by the Singapore customs and Police. He could do nothing but plead his ignorance. The authorities realised that other people were involved, but no other person or persons were apprehended. The Singapore border customs men had witnessed the incredible about turn of the military police motorcyclists as they reached the checkpoint. All four riders were seen to speed away within yards of entering the barrier checkpoint.

The final destination of the BTO was unknown to my father, this was the organisers safeguard. Not knowing the final destination, could not implicate the main players. It continues to remain a mystery, why the truck had the motorcycle escort in the first place. Whilst it provided some measure of comfort to my father, it drew attention to itself as it made its way across Singapore. In 1947, the traffic was light anyway? I can only assume that the motorcade formation was part of the 'warning' system to the customs men that the consignment had arrived.

My father died in 2008, and up to his death, he could not explain what made the military police do the U turn at the very last second. The rest is just pure conjecture on my part; there could be many explanations about what happened that day, but here are three possible ones;

1. The military police were expecting a sign or a signal which

indicated that a safe passage through the Singapore customs was ready. Assuming the signal never came as the motorcade slowed towards its destination, they themselves panicked at the very last moment and fled.

2.   The Head of the Singapore Customs, considered a weak link, did in fact lose his head at the last moment. He should have been on the crossing to oversee safe passage from Singapore into Malaysia. It was the same man who had authorisation and command over the customs men at the docks and at the bonded warehouse, where subsequent safe passage was granted without questions asked. Something in-between clearly went awry.

3.   Another less credible explanation could be, that one or more of the military police motorcycle riders took exception to my father's wrestling success. In addition, some colleagues of the guards did get badly hurt in the attack on him in the guardhouse. Perhaps their action was some kind of retribution for their colleagues. I think this option is the most unlikely one, because large sums of money had already been handed over to the military police motorcyclists.

In my father's defence, he did not name any other person involved in the operation during his interrogation and his subsequent trial. He had every opportunity to name names, but refused. He realised that he had been duped. He was not proud of his actions, but agreeing to drive the truck on a 'gentleman's' agreement, without prior knowledge of what the risks or what the consignment consisted of, was something he felt he could not get out of. He regretted his actions, of course, and took the full responsibility for the botched operation, and paid the price.

By contrast, no one involved in the plan offered any help or contacted my father whilst awaiting his trial. He was sent to trial in a civil Singapore court, not a military one and was sentenced to 18 months imprisonment. He served his sentence at the infamous Changi Prison. My father never said as much, but there was an unwritten code, that if you get caught at whatever stage of the operation, you kept your mouth shut, or else!

My father was convinced that a degree of leniency had been afforded to him during sentencing. The multi million dollar drug haul did not fit the sentence. Conjecture on my father's part, was that someone within the 'circle' with power, had intervened. Thus he received a much reduced sentence.

It's assumed the drugs were eventually dumped out to sea, thereby preventing in some small way further suffering from those addicts unable to break the habit. Whilst this presented a small crumb of comfort to my father languishing in prison, he felt this unsuccessful heist would not have been the final chapter in this sordid and despicable black market trade.

Background information

Black Tar Opium. (BTO or Chandu).

When researching this subject, I was shocked and amazed to find out the reality behind the opiate substance, chandu, also known as black tar opium (BTO). I had only my father's vague description to go on when researching this subject. I remember from years ago how he described it. 'It looked like tar, in small pot bellied jars,' he would recall. This brief description turned up a whole amount of information from the internet. It didn't take me long to discover the dark past of this highly addictive opiate drug. I wanted to know why such quantities of this illegal drug were stored in Singapore, furthermore, how it had become such a target for the black market.

From the very beginning of the Colony, the use and sale of opium was legal. Important revenue was derived, foremost from opium and spirits. Opium provided the Colonial Government with a steady income right up to the outbreak of WW2. The Opium Commission set up in 1907 later ruled that prohibition of opium trade/farming as unnecessary as it would only serve to reduce the revenue. As a direct result of this action, the sale of opium was to become a government monopoly. The authorised sale of opium by retail took place solely in prescribed government shops. This practice had the desired affect of controlling and confining consumption to specified premises and known registered drug users.

It was the policy of the monopoly also to bring about a gradual reduction in the consumption of opium by addicts. The following gives an indication however, as to how slow this reduction was taking place.

In 1927, sales of opium through the monopoly totalled 30,000 lb, by 1935; this was reduced to 19,000 lb. This practice was also responsible for encouraging smuggling. As early as 1924, a total of 11.5 tons of smuggled opium was captured in the Straits Settlement.

The smuggling of opium went on unabated up to the end of 1941 and saw a revival from 1946 – 1955. After that decade, the decline was evident.

An addict, having been examined by a medical officer and duly certified, was registered and then *permitted to purchase* an allowance of opium from a government shop. At the time of the Japanese invasion in 1942, there were over 16,500 known addicts on the Singapore registers. It is thought that this rose to 30,000 during the occupation period. In the Federation of Malaya the figure was probably four times this number.

During the occupation of Singapore between 1942 and 1945, the Japanese took advantage of the huge stocks of opium left behind by the British. These goods were used as a source of immediate revenue. They carried on sales in the government retail shops and allowed anyone who could pay for chandu/opium to smoke it. The campaign since 1925 to promote gradual reduction of opium consumption was thus largely nullified, as opium addiction was openly encouraged.

During the International Military Tribunal for the Far East it had found Japan guilty of the war crime of deliberately promoting drug use among its conquered population in order to demoralise them.

The Opium and Chandu Proclamation on 1 Feb 1946 called on those in possession of opium, chandu, pipes, lamps or utensils to surrender them. This prohibition however, could not stop the craving of those pre-war registered addicts and those who had acquired the habit during the Japanese occupation. Traffickers quickly saw a golden opportunity to make fortunes when the addicts went underground. Communications were re-established with sources of supply and the highly profitable smuggling of the drug was resurrected.

The illicit or illegal trafficking of opium was largely in the hands of a *few powerful syndicates* dealing in considerable consignments at a time. Much of the trafficking was done through shipping, fishing vessels and aircraft. Some of the illicit drug trafficking was carried out by road, but as this story is testament to the outcome, was less successful.

The report from which these findings are taken, points out the principal reasons for the success of many traffickers at that time;
1.   The inability of the Customs Department as the sole enforcement authority, with its limited resources, to meet the challenge of both illicit and domestic consumption.

2. The preoccupation of senior customs officers with problems of reconstruction after the war.

3. Corruption amongst subordinate staff.

During the pre-war years leading up to the capitulation of Singapore to the Japanese, Singapore had become the main centre for illicit trafficking in opium. It catered for the South Malayan area, Borneo territories, Christmas Island and Indonesia. The volume of traffic amounted to 6,000 pound per month. (2.7 metric tonnes).

Singapore, by direct contrast today, is very strict about drug trafficking. According to Amnesty International, Singapore carried out 54 drug related hangings in 1994. In 1995, another 52 people faced the gallows. The numbers today are smaller, however, it's thought that the numbers remain in the 'dozens of executions per annum' making it the heaviest per-capita user of the death penalty in the world. Singapore executions are carried out quietly and without publicity behind the walls of the rebuilt Changi prison. The Singapore Government of today makes no announcements of, or refuses to give information about, people or life on death row. Singapore is co-operative to give publicity to the death penalty in abstraction, believing its existence is a sufficient deterrent to drug trafficking.

The Mystery Man.

Who was he? Up to the point of researching this book, there was no doubt in my mind who the mystery man was. It was none other than Sir Ibrahim Iskander Al Masyhur ibni Abu Bakar; better known as 'The Sultan of Johor,' one of the richest men in the world.

Many references had been made about this man by my father to ignore this fact. It was in the Sultan's Palace that the plan to traffic the opium was first, 'rolled out.' Many of the details were thrashed out during his time spent there. So, why do I doubt my father's recollection? According to my many discussions, the Sultan of Johor was a huge fan of wrestling, and my father spoke openly about teaching him simple holds and moves. He enjoyed the company of my father and was very fond of him, however my story perhaps misrepresents this fact, but certain things were added from my side for additional emphasis.

The Sultan of Johor spent a lot of time out of Malaysia after the occupation ended, and all this is documented; however, the thing that concerned me most was his age. The Sultan was born on 17th September 1873, which in 1946/47 would have made him 73/74 years of age. I always had a 'younger' person etched into my thoughts, and it is for this reason only why I doubt myself.

The Sultan had sons, and it is recorded that his eldest son Tunku Ismail, born 28th October 1894, (putting him in his early 50's during 1946/47), took over the responsibility of state affairs when his father was away. He would be presented on his father's behalf at official functions. Tunku Ismail for instance, officiated the opening ceremony of United Malays National Organisation's (UMNO) first congress which was held at Istana Besar in May 1946 whilst his father Sultan Ibrahim, resided in London.

Was the Mystery man Tunku Ismail, the acting Sultan of Johor in his father's absence?

Several years ago, when discussing the background of the book, my father made it very clear that he didn't want to reveal the identity of the Sultan. He was convinced that no one would believe this fact anyway!

My father went to his grave knowing, that in his lifetime, he never informed publicly anything that would tarnish this man's reputation.

I mention it today, not to bring sensationalism to the story, but only to tell the truth about what happened all those years ago.

It's for you the reader, to decide if it was the Sultan of Johor, his son, or not?

The Colonel and the Major.

It perhaps should not surprise me that high ranking officers of the British army could in any way be involved in such an audacious and daring operation as described in the pages of this book, but this was the case nonetheless.

It's worth noting that British military officers were directly involved with overseeing the handling and storage of chandu directly after the Japanese surrender.

The Colonel would have been at the signing of the Surrender Treaty with the Japanese when Singapore on September 12th 1945 in the Municipal Buildings was handed back to the control of the British. The Sultan of Johor (Sir Ibrahim Iskander) was also present at this signing. It was probably at this meeting in early September 1945 that the two men met and forged their friendship and later to hatch their audacious plan.

The Major, was very helpful and sensitive towards my father. It was the Major who granted my father special privileges to wrestle. Without his consent, my father would never have been able to reach the sporting heights that he scaled. Perhaps there was a different hidden agenda forming when he allowed those privileges to be given The Major however, did receive a personal letter from my mother. It had been months since she had heard from my father, and it was the Major who made sure he wrote back and contacted his family. It was the same man who supported him at the court martial and asked for leniency in his sentence.

Captain Black.

The Captain was indeed a thorn in my father's side. For some reason, he took an instant dislike to him and tried to make his life as miserable as possible. It was an accident waiting to happen. His transfer back to the UK was put down to injuries caused whilst serving in Singapore. It's not clear or certain whether these injuries were caused by my father?

Without wanting to defend my father's actions towards the Captain, he did think that the note he received about his father's illness, was going to result in the worst possible outcome. He genuinely felt his father was going to die of meningitis.

The photograph albums.

My father left behind three photograph albums, mainly of his time spent in Singapore. I have been able to derive many of my examples through this invaluable collection of prints from that era. I can place his arrival in Singapore through the photographs. Some of the more remarkable pictures show the signing of the Japanese surrender to Lord Louis Mountbatten on the 12th September 1945 in the Municipal buildings. Other pictures of that historic day show General Seishiro Itagaki of the seventh Area Army with fellow officers, heads bowed as they descend the steps of the Municipal Building immediately after the surrender signing.

I remember seeing the pictures as a young boy, but not again until researching for this book. These albums have provided me with a rich insight into my father's life back in the mid to late 1940's. The pictures present a journey back in time of a very talented young man and not 'The Untamed White Savage' from which this book takes its title. In addition to capturing this historic surrender signing event on camera, it also captures everyday life on the army camp, the guardhouse and the Singapore docks where he worked.

Suzi.

Some unexplained and unidentified photographs of beautiful young ladies are contained in the same albums. Suzi, therefore, is she a figment of my imagination or was she real? I leave that up to you the reader to make up your own mind!

Derek (Kid) Callon.

It was Major Reece who organised my father's voyage back to the UK from Singapore. This journey did not go without its fair share of controversy. Soon after sailing, my father was in an altercation with a senior naval officer and consequently spent the rest of the journey in the ship's cells.

My mother was aware my father was back in the UK, but she had few details of when he would be released from his naval captors. He arrived back home in December 1948, unannounced and unexpected at the dead of night and as a stranger to his own family, with only a few shillings change in his pockets. He bore only the outward resemblance of the 18 year old young man who had left the shores of the UK almost four years previously. He was more mature and more worldly wise, after all, he had become the All-in Wrestling Champion of the Far East; but inwardly, he was a changed man and the large amounts of money he earned wrestling, was gone. It would be some time before he settled back into a life similar to the one he left behind four years previously.

He served only nine months of his 18 month prison sentence in Changi Jail, reduced for good behaviour. During his incarceration, he trained as a cobbler, mending and repairing shoes. He also fell foul to meningitis, the life threatening disease which took his sister. This illness brought my father to the brink of death in a matter of weeks, but his inner strength and fitness kept him alive and pulled him through. He recovered fully and regained his incredible physique and strength.

His relationship with his son, Thomas, who was almost four when he arrived home was slow to develop at first, but grew immensely as time progressed. His relationship with my mother was not without its problems either. He had scaled the heights in sporting terms and lived like a prince, only to return to his ordinary life as a husband and father, sharing a home with his own mother and father. He continued to wrestle when he came back to the UK, but was disillusioned by the sport and retired, still only 23 years of age. My mother and father were married for almost 60 years before his untimely and unexpected death in 2008. He is survived by his wife, Georgina, three sons, and one daughter. He also leaves behind 9 grandchildren and twelve great grandchildren.

Footnote

I have thought about my father every single day since his death, and writing about him has made me aware of how special and gifted a human being he was. My father was no angel and his story is not meant to depict him in this way. 'The Untamed White Savage.' is indicative of his early sporting performances, and a phrase afforded to him by his wrestling promoter. I was born after these events took place, but from a very early age, learning bit by bit from his past, I realised, there was a great tale to be told. It has regrettably, taken me until now to tell his remarkable story. My father never saw the realisation of his early life exploits and he never bragged about his personal achievements or wrongdoings, but admits to making mistakes and misjudgements throughout his youth, but then who doesn't? To achieve what he did at such a tender age, from a sporting perspective, still leaves me in awe.

I still marvel at his boxing exploits during his army training days, his amazing wrestling feats were nothing short of extraordinary. He was only 21 when he achieved his Championship title of the Far East. Sadly, the belt he wore, and was presented with on that victorious night, was stolen on his sea journey home to the UK. We only have the photographs bearing witness to his success now.

Another remarkable feat was his ability to speak and learn the complex Malay language so well. Here was a man, who, by his own admission, had a very poor education. He could read quite well, but writing never came naturally to him. His truancy from school was testament to his learning difficulties which were never identified.

In writing and researching this book, I feel in some small part to have travelled this journey with my father. I have felt every punch and suffered every painful wrestling hold, as I seek to describe to the best of my ability, his wondrous talent and successes. I choose to forgive his indiscretions, on the basis that he was a young man, lured by the promise of unbelievable wealth, but duped by men of enormous influence, greed and power. My only regret is that I could not finish the story before his death; his legacy however, will live on through these pages. I am fortunate enough to carry his name and am proud to call Derek (Kid) Callon, my father.

Just for the record, some dates and times, (excluding the Operation Market Garden and the signing of the surrender treaty in Singapore) are not exact.* I felt it more appropriate to bring the depth and feeling of the story to you as I unravelled the events through my descriptions.

Kid Callon is sadly missed by his family. Rest in peace, Dad!

In summing up; it was his father, when speaking to my mother shortly after he arrived home, who said,

'Your husband, lass, has seen too many faces!'

* In addition, Officers and wrestling personnel names have been changed

32) *The only photograph existing of my father wearing the prestigious belt after winning the Light Heavyweight Championship of the Far East. This photograph was sent home to my mother after winning the contest.*

NOTE! My father fought for the Heavyweight Championship of the Far East against a Greek Born Australian by the name of Con Balasis but this was a contest too far. He was defeated by a technical knock out in the fourth round. As an amateur, Balasis was the National Champion of the USA and the Light Heavyweight Champion of the World.

33) The fortress gates of Changi prison. During the Japanese occupation, this prison was used to detain prisoners of war. The jail was built to house around 800 prisoners, but the Japanese held in excess of 10,000 allied servicemen between 1942 and 1945. This prison was also home to my father for 9 months, but after the occupation.

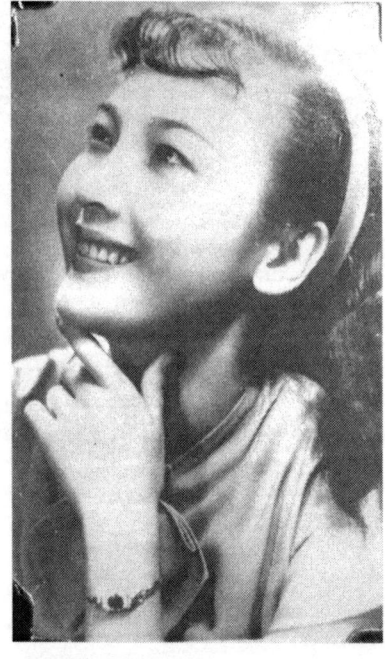

34) One of several unexplained photographs of pretty young ladies from the photograph albums. We will never know who they were or why their photographs were in there. Sadly, not even my father can answer these questions now.

35) My father on holiday and still cutting a formidable figure some 40 years after his early wrestling successes. He died with his complete family by his side in hospital on the 24th June 2008 aged 82.

Quote

It is the repetition of affirmations that leads to belief. And once that belief becomes a deep conviction, things begin to happen.

Muhammad Ali